"Get out of my house or I will kill you!"

She would never know whether it was the knife or the tone of voice that made the girl realize Olivia was serious. Thankfully she turned and raced through the broken patio door and disappeared into the darkness.

Olivia studied the blood-splattered floor, trembling, sweat pooling down her back, despite the cold air blowing in from the broken patio door.

Rosie's uncontrollable wailing pulled Olivia back to the present. She scooped her daughter up and raced back to the nursery. As she stepped inside, Bettie and Cassie launched themselves at her, tears and snot pouring down their heart-shaped faces.

"Mama, Mama, Mama," they cried in unison, climbing on her and over one another, their desire to be held and comforted so intense, they knocked her onto her butt.

She held them close and whispered into their ears, "It's okay. Y'all are safe. You're safe. Mommy's here. You're safe."

But that wasn't a promise she could keep. That's what that night proved.

PRAISE FOR
HOLLIE OVERTON

"What a compulsive read! A brilliant first novel that kept me transfixed and entertained until the very last page."
—*New York Times* bestselling author Tess Gerritsen

"Compelling.... Overton throws in enough twists, turns, and surprises to keep the reader wondering what on earth can happen next." —*Publishers Weekly*

"A suspenseful and satisfying psychological thriller by a writer who has hit her stride." —*Dallas Morning News*

"Overton spins a fast-moving, increasingly compelling tale."
—*Booklist*

"A gripping page-turner that will make you think about what it means to be free." —*Glamour* (South Africa)

By Hollie Overton

Baby Doll
The Walls
The Runaway
A Mother's Guide to the Apocalypse

A Mother's Guide to the Apocalypse

HOLLIE OVERTON

REDHOOK

This book is a work of fiction. Names, characters, places, and incidents are the product of the author's imagination or are used fictitiously. Any resemblance to actual events, locales, or persons, living or dead, is coincidental.

Copyright © 2025 by Hollie Overton
Excerpt from *The Ghosts of Beatrice Bird* copyright © 2023 by Louise Marley

Cover design by the Orbit art department
Cover images by Shutterstock
Cover copyright © 2025 by Hachette Book Group, Inc.
Author photograph by Heather Overton

Hachette Book Group supports the right to free expression and the value of copyright. The purpose of copyright is to encourage writers and artists to produce the creative works that enrich our culture.

The scanning, uploading, and distribution of this book without permission is a theft of the author's intellectual property. If you would like permission to use material from the book (other than for review purposes), please contact permissions@hbgusa.com. Thank you for your support of the author's rights.

Redhook
Hachette Book Group
1290 Avenue of the Americas
New York, NY 10104
hachettebookgroup.com

First Edition: August 2025

Redhook is an imprint of Orbit, a division of Hachette Book Group.
The Redhook name and logo are registered trademarks of Hachette Book Group, Inc.

The publisher is not responsible for websites (or their content) that are not owned by the publisher.

The Hachette Speakers Bureau provides a wide range of authors for speaking events. To find out more, go to hachettespeakersbureau.com or email HachetteSpeakers@hbgusa.com.

Redhook books may be purchased in bulk for business, educational, or promotional use. For information, please contact your local bookseller or the Hachette Book Group Special Markets Department at special.markets@hbgusa.com.

Library of Congress Cataloging-in-Publication Data
Names: Overton, Hollie, author.
Title: A mother's guide to the apocalypse / Hollie Overton.
Description: First edition. | New York : Redhook, 2025.
Identifiers: LCCN 2024060909 | ISBN 9780316482387 (trade paperback) |
    ISBN 9780316482363 (ebook)
Subjects: LCGFT: Thrillers (Fiction) | Novels.
Classification: LCC PS3615.V4745 M68 2025 | DDC 813/.6—dc23/eng/20241220
LC record available at https://lccn.loc.gov/2024060909

ISBNs: 9780316482387 (trade paperback), 9780316482363 (ebook)

Printed in the United States of America

LSC-C

Printing 1, 2025

To DB & my best bears, I love you more than the earth, the sun, the moon, and the stars.

prep·per

/ˈprepər/

NOUN, NORTH AMERICAN

A person who believes a catastrophic disaster or emergency will likely occur in the future and makes active preparations for it, typically by stockpiling food, ammunition, and other supplies.

Extinction is the rule. Survival is the exception.

—Carl Sagan

OLIVIA

It took longer than it should have for Olivia Clark to recognize that the world as she knew it was going to end—which seemed foolish, since all the signs were there.

The news ticker on the TVs hanging above the hip Beverly Hills bars that she frequented for work lunches, happy hours, and dinners.

On the *Today* show, which played in the background on the flatscreen TV while her husband, Sam, and their identical triplet daughters, Rosie, Bettie, and Cassie, ate breakfast.

On her cell phone in the late-night hours when she should have been sleeping but couldn't stop doom-scrolling.

California Faces Year-Round Fire Season.

27 Killed in San Antonio Riverwalk Shooting.

Government Shutdown Reaches Month Four.

17,000 Somali Die of Starvation.

Millions Left in Darkness for Days as New York's Power Grid Fails.

As alarming as it was, Sam, in his reassuring and annoyingly calm British manner, would remind her to focus on the positive.

"These headlines are designed to frighten you so that you click more, read more, fear more. But, Liv, they're not real life." He would wrap his arms around her and hold her tight. "*This* is real life."

Even with the challenges, Olivia recognized how wonderful her life was.

Real life was waking up to her alarm at six thirty like she'd been shot out of a cannon, pissed at all the people who insisted that once she became a mom, she would become a morning person.

Real life was slathering on enough concealer and foundation to cover the dark circles that had taken up residence under her eyes in the three years since she'd found out she was having triplets.

Real life was remaking three different breakfasts because Rosie didn't want yogurt, Bettie's eggs were too mushy, and Cassie's waffles weren't crispy enough.

Real life was wrestling three toddlers into Minnie Mouse dresses, taming three wild manes into ponytails, brushing three sets of teeth, putting on three sets of socks and shoes, and getting out the door for preschool drop-off without forgetting any of their three favorite stuffed animals.

Real life was slogging through forty-five minutes of traffic to her Studio City office, where she spent eight to ten hours reading scripts and meeting with producers, actors, and casting directors to find new and exciting ways to tell stories.

A MOTHER'S GUIDE TO THE APOCALYPSE 3

Real life was *finally* connecting with her husband after a hard day, only to lose her temper ten minutes later because he couldn't remember where the girls' pajamas were kept.

Real life was exhausting and messy and all-consuming, and Olivia loved it. She loved it so much that most days, she worried it would all fall apart.

With the help of her well-paid therapist, she attempted to keep her fears at bay, but it seemed like it was getting harder and harder. One night, after the girls went to bed, her younger brother, Lucas, dropped by to say hello and borrow money.

In typical Lucas fashion, he invited himself to dinner, joining her and Sam for takeout from their favorite Indian restaurant. As they dug into platters of tikka masala and saffron rice, Olivia recounted what she'd heard on NPR. "Y'all, it started as a story about wars and pandemics, and then they were saying we needed to give kindergartners bulletproof vests, and then there was another story about parasites in our water systems."

Sam groaned. "One of these days, I'm taking away all your devices, so you have to live in the moment."

Lucas, younger by four years and a self-proclaimed Luddite, agreed. "You've got a beautiful family, a job that people would kill for, and you're obsessing over things you have no power to change. You're such a fatalist, sis," he said as he refilled his glass of Cabernet.

Olivia resisted the urge to tell him to slow down—it

would only make him drink more—and laughed. "Word of the day *toilet paper*, baby bro?"

"If you spend your life waiting for the bad, it's gonna come for you eventually."

Her baby brother's words would prove prophetic.

Olivia thought she could outrun the bad. She'd done it all her life. After their mother OD'd when she was seventeen and Lucas was thirteen, Olivia worked two jobs for six months until she had enough to buy a car and drive cross-country from Conroe, Texas, to Los Angeles.

She rented a crappy one-bedroom apartment in Mar Vista for the two of them, and six months later, once she'd established residency, she enrolled at Santa Monica College. She took classes by day and served overpriced cocktails on the Sunset Strip by night, all while struggling to raise a teenage boy who wanted nothing to do with her.

Despite the odds, Olivia transferred to UCLA and graduated with a degree in film studies. Thanks to Bruce Miller, a fantastic film professor who took her under his wing and mentored her, Olivia landed a job as an assistant at one of the leading talent agencies. Six months into that job, she was poached by a top producer, and it was there that she met Mel, another assistant who became her best friend and producing partner. They found a script from a talented new female filmmaker and made it on a shoestring budget. A year later, that short won the Sundance Film Festival and was nominated for an Academy Award. By the time Olivia was thirty-three, she was one of the top film and TV producers in town. Meeting Sam and having her girls came later than she wanted, but she built a life that she loved.

She had to preserve it. Protect it.

But the acceleration of bad news kept coming.

US Airways Jet Explodes over Utah, Killing 190 Souls Onboard.

Rochester Snowstorm Leaves Thousands Dead, Hundreds More Buried Alive.

Voting Poll Raided by Freedom Fighters—Democracy on the Verge of Collapse.

One night after a particularly harrowing week, Olivia drove home from work through soul-crushing traffic, eager for cuddles from her three sweet babes.

Instead, she found chaos. The girls hated her homemade lasagna and demonstrated their displeasure by throwing it on the floor. While Sam was trying to clean it up, Bettie bit Rosie on the bum, and Rosie dropped her favorite penguin figurine, shattering it into a dozen pieces.

Sam and Olivia reacted like most jailers and turned on each other. After a harrowing bath and bedtime routine that lasted an hour but felt like ten, they wrestled the girls into bed and closed the door.

Olivia slipped on her sneakers and shouted, "I'm going for a run."

She was not a natural runner by any stretch of the

imagination, but thirty minutes of short sprints followed by five minutes of walking was enough to help her reset. Out of breath but feeling less off balance, she strolled through the predictably boring Woodland Hills subdivision. As she headed back toward home, she spotted a neighboring home with the garage door wide open. All the homes here had three-car garages, and most families, hers included, used the excess space for storage.

But this neighbor wasn't just stocking his garage with extra supplies. He was stocking up for something big. There were giant floor-to-ceiling shelves filled with toilet paper, paper towels, canned goods, and another wall of shelves all filled with gallon jugs of water.

On the opposite side of the garage hung a wall of what appeared to be weapons: knives lined up in size from small to hatchet. As she walked, she saw that he wasn't the only one who had gathered supplies. Olivia counted at least half a dozen homes that had similar setups.

When she returned home, order had been restored and Sam presented her with a cocktail. It made her laugh that this tough bloke from the north of England preferred Aperol spritzes to hard liquor, but she appreciated his lack of pretense. Sam was so unapologetically himself. She took a sip of her cocktail of choice, a margarita, and sighed with exhaustion and relief as she slipped off her sneakers. She curled up on the sofa and leaned into him, ignoring his teasing about how sweaty she was as she recounted what she'd seen. "It was crazy the amount of supplies they'd accumulated. It's like they were ready for the end of days," Olivia said.

Sam laughed. "Are you surprised? Don't you know doomsday preppers are having their moment?"

She laughed, too, but she didn't find it funny. The more she thought about those fully stocked garages, the more curious she became. When Sam drifted off to sleep that night, Olivia googled "disaster preparedness."

The amount of information coming at her made Olivia's head ache. She could almost hear Sam's teasing voice, "That stuff is bollocks, and you know it."

She quickly put down her phone and went to sleep. The next night, she pulled up the search again and realized the process wasn't that difficult. She was, by nature, a problem solver, so she did what she always did when something needed to be done: She made a list.

She wasn't consumed by it. Not yet. It was little different than all the social media influencers who preached the importance of self-care. If you were willing to sacrifice time daily for your skin-care regimen, why wouldn't you do the same for your well-being? At least that's how she explained it to Sam and Mel when the first Amazon packages began to arrive.

Water was crucial, perhaps one of the most important means of survival. Most people didn't realize how precious water was or how finite. Everyone acted like water was a limitless resource, even when the evidence showed otherwise. Other cities had already suffered from a lack of clean water, like Flint, Michigan, left to fend for itself after their water was poisoned with dangerous levels of lead. Literally, babies, children, women, and older people were drinking poisoned water, and no one cared.

A few years back, Olivia's assistant talked about how petrochemicals had poisoned the water in his hometown of Corpus Christi. Even though there were orders not to drink or bathe in it, most people ignored the warnings, content to shower in the toxic water. Those were examples in the States. Countless countries had never and would never have clean water. Everyone thought water shortages or toxic water couldn't happen here, but Olivia wasn't taking any chances. Water storage and purification became her first mission.

She'd always hated the taste of LA tap water, so she hired a water delivery service when they moved into their new home. Each month, a delivery driver would drop off five-gallon jugs. After a month, she tripled the order.

She purchased bottled water by the case when she went on her monthly Costco runs. Sam initially found it amusing, laughing each week when she made him haul the pallets in, until there was a giant wall of water assembled in the garage. She told him he wouldn't be laughing if the big earthquake struck and it took weeks or even months for water to be restored. She was about to launch into her

A MOTHER'S GUIDE TO THE APOCALYPSE 9

monologue about the Turkish earthquake and how little help they received, but Sam cut her off.

"I'd rather not think about it, luv," he said, an early sign of the disagreements that lay ahead.

Her research made it clear that bottled water wouldn't be a solid long-term solution, so she purchased bleaching tablets and storage containers for rainwater. She studied purification techniques on YouTube and wrote down the instructions for Sam and the girls in a large binder in case the internet was hacked, they went offline, or something happened to her.

She used Costco to build their food storage as well. Experts recommended enough canned goods for three months, but Olivia had a family of five, six if she counted Lucas, so six months seemed ideal.

She also relied on the dollar store to boost her grocery supply. There was one located next to the Starbucks where she got her daily oat milk latte (the world wasn't ending yet), and she would pop in and buy twenty dollars' worth of canned goods at a time.

Other times, she would buy half a dozen boxes of rice, pasta, cake and brownie mixes, sugar, salt, and flour. If the worst happened, they'd at least have dessert. It wasn't perfect, but if something happened, she could keep her family safe.

At least, that's what she thought before the great LA blackout changed everything.

Before they had the babies, Sam coached some of the country's best high school and college golfers, which meant quite a bit of travel. When Olivia went on bed rest during her pregnancy, he stopped traveling. She hadn't wanted him away when the girls were really little, but one of his top students had a big tournament in Palm Springs. They decided it was the right time for Sam to get back to work.

It was Olivia's first overnight alone with their daughters, which felt like a big deal. She asked Lucas if he wanted to come over and keep her company, but he said he wasn't sure since he had a catering gig in Pacific Palisades.

Sam couldn't hide his amusement. "No way Lucas shows. The last thing he wants to do is be your manny for the weekend."

Olivia couldn't deny that. Her brother was the fun uncle but couldn't be counted on to pick up milk, much less care for three demanding babies. Sam suggested that Olivia hire weekend help. "Don't be a martyr. Ask Serafina to stay over."

Olivia adored their nanny, but the poor woman worked fifty hours a week. Besides, it was two days. She told herself it would be fun.

Of course, she hadn't expected a historic heat wave in November. The temperature reached a record-breaking 105 degrees, nearly maxing out the state's power grid.

The heat was debilitating. By eight o'clock that morning, the air outside was suffocating, and she knew she'd have to get creative to keep the girls entertained. She loaded them in the car to go to IHOP for pancakes and bacon.

Inside the restaurant, Olivia embraced the stares, listening to people murmur, "They're triplets," or "Look at how identical they are," and she happily accepted the compliments over how well behaved her girls were.

It wasn't quite eleven o'clock and the temperature had climbed to almost a hundred degrees by the time they left the restaurant. The car-seat buckles were so hot that she had to run the air-conditioning and sit in the car and sing "Wheels on the Bus" for ten minutes before she could strap the girls in. When they returned home, Olivia unloaded everyone, cranked up the air-conditioning, and made blanket forts in the living room, where they played until nap time.

When they woke up, she distracted them from going outside with chocolate pudding and the bubble machine. By the time the sun began to set, it was still ninety-five degrees, but the girls didn't care. They exploded into the backyard in a toddler frenzy and shouted with joy as Olivia turned on the sprinklers.

Later, she heated up pizza and veggies, and the girls sat on a blanket in the grass in their damp swimsuits and devoured the food, their laughter filling the air. It was one of those memories that Olivia wanted to time-stamp, a moment she wished she could replay instead of the terrible events that followed.

As the sun set, Olivia ushered the girls upstairs and bathed them, put on lotion and pajamas. They read three books, and by the time she turned off the lights, the girls were already dozing off, as though they knew their mother needed an easy night.

An hour later, the rain began to fall. Slow at first, and then in heavy sheets that sounded like jackhammering outside the windows. She poured herself a glass of Cabernet and read two chapters of her favorite romance novel, then put herself to bed, knowing that if the girls were good today, tomorrow could be a disaster.

At three o'clock in the morning, Olivia jolted awake, startled by the overwhelming silence. She was so used to the ever-present white noise coming from the baby monitor that when she didn't hear it, she knew something was wrong. She reached for her phone but found she had forgotten to plug it in.

She could hear Sam's scolding voice: "Damnit, Liv, why is it so impossible to keep a phone charged?" She tried to turn on her bedside lamp, but that didn't work, either.

Shit! The power is out.

Olivia fumbled for her glasses, cursing under her breath when she realized she had no candles or flashlights on her home's second level. All that planning and preparing for the worst and here she was—literally in the fucking dark with three toddlers.

The girls were just as used to their sound machine as she

A MOTHER'S GUIDE TO THE APOCALYPSE   13

was, so it was no surprise when she heard the first baby cry. She could tell it was Cassie by the hiccuping sounds she made when upset—sounds that twisted at Olivia's insides, as though her baby were still connected to her. Unfortunately, Cassie would have to wait. The last thing Olivia wanted was to be fumbling around in the dark with three tiny people crawling over her.

She rushed into the kitchen and searched through the drawers for the matches. This was ridiculous. How did they not have a single matchbook or lighter in the house? She let out a relieved sigh when she located a lone matchbook in the back of the drawer. She lit half a dozen scented candles she found in the living room and placed them high enough so toddler hands couldn't reach them.

She wanted to go to the garage and look for flashlights, but the chorus of wails and cries for "Mama" was unbearable. She grabbed a box of Goldfish crackers and her iPad, relieved that it still had fifty percent battery life. She prayed that snacks and Daniel Tiger would calm them down and give her time to find more lighting sources.

The first thing she noticed when she rushed into their room was the suffocating stillness. All three babies stood in their cribs, sweat covering their hair, hands raised as they whimpered "Mama" and demanded to be picked up. She went one by one, taking them out and setting them on the carpet. Then she flopped down beside them, fumbling to open the crackers while starting their favorite show.

It took fifteen minutes to calm everyone down, but at last, there was a comfortable silence, and by silence, she meant the musical stylings of an animated tiger.

Her heart rate had settled into a normal rhythm when she heard the sound of glass breaking. *Goddamnit*, she thought. Why wasn't Sam here? She closed her eyes, remembering the technician from the security company asking if they wanted reinforced patio doors, because the ones they had were quite easy to break in the event of a robbery.

She'd weighed the cost and thought their overpriced alarm system was enough.

Wrong again, Olivia.

The only way to protect her children was to leave them alone in this room, and doing that would scare the living hell out of them. But there was no other choice. She slowly stood up.

"Stay right here and keep watching Daniel. Mama will be right back."

The screaming began instantly. Olivia ignored their desperate pleas as she hurried toward the door. Her daughters trailed after her, like three panicked ducklings, but she slammed the door before they could slip out. She was grateful for childproof door covers but wished the door was soundproof so she wouldn't have to hear their desperate wails.

Trying to tune them out, Olivia inched forward. It was still pitch-black, and she had no light to guide her. She stopped in the hall, eyes wide as she looked for a makeshift weapon.

She spotted the closet and prayed that Sam hadn't gotten rid of the golf clubs she'd purchased when they were first dating and she was still trying to impress him.

The squeak of the closet door was drowned out by the triplets wailing. Olivia almost cried from relief when she found one of the clubs and pulled it out. She held it tight and inched forward. Halfway to the living room, she spotted a man in her kitchen, a hoodie covering his head as he rifled through the drawers. She took a ragged breath and raised the club.

"Get out! Get out of my house!" Her voice came out part growl, part scream, as though something had possessed her. He turned.

Olivia froze. It wasn't a man at all. It was a young woman in her early twenties. Eyes wild and desperate, wearing a UCLA hoodie, she stared at Olivia, and then at the golf club clenched in Olivia's hand.

"What are you doing in my house?" Olivia shouted. "I have children. Small children. What the fuck are you doing here?"

Later, when she replayed the events, she hated that she had mentioned her daughters.

The intruder didn't blink. There was a giant butcher knife in her hand—one of Olivia's knives, the one she used to chop veggies. The one she always told the girls, "Never touch this or it could hurt you."

The girl gripped the handle so tightly, her knuckles were

white. "I can't find work. No one will hire me. I went to college. I studied and worked. I did what I was supposed to and I have nothing. I need...something," she said, an eerie flatness to her tone.

She moved toward Olivia, who raised the golf club as the girl came at her, a feral dog in attack mode.

"There's nothing out there! Nothing," the girl said again, as though the only way she could get Olivia to understand what she was experiencing was for Olivia to suffer.

The girl slammed into her with shocking force, the two of them landing hard on the white tile floor. Olivia's golf club flew across the room, yet somehow the girl held on to her knife. She lay on top of Olivia, eyes almost translucent with rage.

Olivia's breath came out in short spurts, her throat tight from screaming. This was her first time being in a fight, and she wondered how she was going to overpower this girl. As the young woman raised the knife, Olivia heard a scream.

She looked over to see Rosie standing a few feet away, dressed in her favorite pink puppy-dog pajamas, tears and snot pouring down her face.

"Mommy!" Rosie screamed. Olivia let out a guttural cry and flung the intruder off her as she kicked her in the stomach. The girl let out a pained cry, and at last her knife clattered to the floor.

Olivia picked it up and scooted backward, holding the

knife out in a defensive stance as she tried to keep Rosie away. Her attacker didn't care about Olivia's screaming child. She came for her again.

Olivia slashed at her. Once. Twice.

Blood dripped from the girl's hand. Olivia raised the knife again, the same disembodied sound coming from her: "Get out of my house or I will kill you!"

She would never know whether it was the knife or the tone of voice that made the girl realize Olivia was serious. Thankfully she turned and raced through the broken patio door and disappeared into the darkness.

Olivia studied the blood-splattered floor, trembling, sweat pooling down her back, despite the cold air blowing in from the broken patio door.

Rosie's uncontrollable wailing pulled Olivia back to the present. She scooped her daughter up and raced back to the nursery. As she stepped inside, Bettie and Cassie launched themselves at her, tears and snot pouring down their heart-shaped faces.

"Mama, Mama, Mama," they cried in unison, climbing on her and over one another, their desire to be held and comforted so intense, they knocked her onto her butt.

She held them close and whispered into their ears, "It's okay. Y'all are safe. You're safe. Mommy's here. You're safe."

But that wasn't a promise she could keep. That's what that night proved.

The break-in was the turning point: the moment she realized the world and the people in it could not be trusted.

The moment she acknowledged that people were going to grow more and more desperate and the systems meant to protect them would fail.

The moment she realized that water storage and food prepping weren't enough. And that no matter what came next, she had to be ready.

Of course, she had no clue what was coming for her.

No clue how much damage joining that damn prepper group and meeting Joey would cause her and her marriage.

There was no way she could know what would happen when Sam discovered how far she'd gone down the prepping rabbit hole, or how she would feel when her best friend betrayed her.

All of that was before the earthquake, floods, and fires.

Before the Collapse.

Before the countless decisions she could not take back.

Despite Olivia's desperation to hold on to what mattered most, six months later she was dead.

EIGHTEEN YEARS LATER

NEWCASTLE, ENGLAND

ROSIE

If there was one thing Rosie hated about being the old-est triplet (one and three minutes, thank you very much), it was being the responsible one. Rosie didn't like giving orders. She definitely didn't like spending her Friday night purging the attic of their father's belongings, but the new owners of the house were set to get the keys in less than a week.

She kicked a box in frustration. She had been her sisters' keeper their entire lives. Even at five years old, when they went to primary school for the first time, Rosie picked out their clothes and packed their lunches because their father was too emotional and overwhelmed with managing the house.

As they got older, Dad worked nonstop to build their food supply and keep the family safe from the extreme temperature changes. So it fell to Rosie to make sure their school field trip forms were signed, their uniforms were pressed, and they signed up to take their A-levels.

She was the one who put up the Christmas tree and decorations and bought all the presents. She didn't mind being the one they all relied on, but now that Dad needed them, they were all so bloody useless. Why couldn't they step up after Dad's diagnosis? Why did she have to manage it all?

Even now, she was the one responsible for the big decisions. There was simply no way they could afford the upkeep of their home and the adjacent greenhouse, in addition to Sam's care. Selling was the only option if they wanted to provide him with a comfortable retirement.

It had been over a month since she'd broken the news, inviting them to the local pub for a "sister talk." Sister talks had begun a decade ago when the girls were ten. After a neighbor kid was swept away during a storm, Dad said it was no longer safe to ride their bikes around the village. The girls decided they needed a strategy session to change his mind and said it was time for a "sister talk." Despite their best efforts, Dad held fast, but sister talks became a regular occurrence. If you scheduled a sister talk, that meant you had something urgent to discuss, and no one could refuse you, no matter what was going on.

When Rosie arrived at the Bay Horse Tavern for dinner, Bettie and Cassie were waiting, concern etched on their faces. Rosie got right to it. "We have to sell the house. We need the money for Dad's care."

Cassie was mid-bite of a chip. She slammed it down, splattering ketchup all over the table. "No bloody way.

A MOTHER'S GUIDE TO THE APOCALYPSE 23

We're not selling our home because of a far-off future some country doctor predicted."

Rosie looked over at Bettie, who chewed her lip nervously, revealing the small scar above it, a remnant from when Cassie dared her to ride through the village forest on her bike and a branch attacked her. "Bettie?" Rosie asked.

"I don't...I mean, Dad is sick, but he's fine. But of course, we'll need money one day," Bettie said.

"For fuck's sake," Rosie said with a groan. It shouldn't have surprised her that Bettie wouldn't have a strong opinion, since her entire persona was *Don't rock the boat.* This was ridiculous. Dad wasn't okay. Finding his car keys, his house keys, and his wallet had become a full-time job. Then there was the night he left his truck in town, engine still running, and returned home with no clue as to how he got there. But the onslaught of bad days wore on them all. A few weeks later, Dad grew confused as to why angry clients kept calling to complain. Rosie realized he was delivering groceries to one house, not the ten houses on his route. That was when she insisted Dad stop driving.

It got worse when Dad started to struggle to tell them apart. They were identical triplets, so people mixed them up all the time. Not Dad. He might call them by the wrong name when he was in a hurry, but never because he was confused. Now it happened frequently.

One morning, he came to breakfast, and in between

bites of toast, he went quiet, his sun-wrinkled face regarding them with confusion. "I don't understand. You all look alike . . . All three of you have . . . you have the same face."

Rosie didn't know what to say. Bettie burst into tears and ran out of the room. Cassie stayed calm, but Rosie could see the pain in her eyes. "We're identical triplets, Dad. Remember? Isn't that cool?"

Her words brought Dad back from wherever he disappeared to. He laughed.

"Of course. I'm amazed by my girls. I have been every day for twenty-one years."

Later that night, after Dad went to bed, Rosie brought up the care home again to her sisters, but Cassie resisted. "After all he's done for all of us, what kind of arseholes would we be to throw him in a home?"

It irritated her how dramatic Cassie was, but she didn't want to be the bad guy when it came to something this big. Still, they had to know it was coming.

"There's going to be a point when we can't deny it."

A week later, Sam went for a walk, and no one could find him. With a storm on the way, they called the police. It took another two hours to locate him, lying in agony in the middle of a nearby field. He'd tripped over his walking stick and sprained his ankle. Dehydrated and cranky, Sam had no understanding of why the girls were upset. "I got a bit lost. No need to kick up a fuss."

A MOTHER'S GUIDE TO THE APOCALYPSE   25

They were overdue for a fuss. This time, Rosie didn't call a sister talk or take a vote. "We're selling the house and moving Dad into a care home," she announced.

There were no arguments. Not from Bettie or Cassie.

Dad was another story.

Telling him was the hardest thing she'd ever done; her sisters had insisted they didn't have it in them. "It's not safe for you here alone when we're all at work and school," Rosie said gently.

She braced for outrage or anger, but to her surprise, Sam gave them a pained smile.

"My loves, the last thing I want is to be a burden. This will be good for all of us."

They hadn't realized they would have a version of that terrible conversation half a dozen times.

Some days, he battled them.

Other days, he wept or lashed out and called them names. They told themselves it wasn't him, it was the disease, but it didn't make it any easier. Rosie did her best to involve him in the packing process. She wanted him to understand and absorb the reality of leaving the only home he had known for almost two decades.

"Dad, we have to figure out what we can put into storage and what we can sell."

Sam agreed wholeheartedly when they told him they needed to purge the attic. "I'll get it done today," he promised as he shuffled outside to his beloved greenhouse.

Hours later, when he returned, covered in dirt and grime and satisfied as always by physical labor, Rosie would ask if he wanted help with the attic. "Oh no, I'm knackered. Remind me tomorrow."

Tomorrow came and went. The girls offered to do it themselves, but Sam would snap, "You're already locking me up like a convict. At least give me the privilege of handling my belongings myself."

So they waited, and now the clock was ticking. Next week, Rosie and Cassie were moving to a flat near Newcastle University where they would finish their courses.

Bettie was moving in with her partner, Max (God help her). Sam would relocate, not to a prison, but to Sunny Gardens, a lovely care facility.

Realizing that as usual, she would have to take charge, Rosie organized the purge. Bettie and Cassie had promised they'd be here, but she was all alone with a box of bin bags and a bottle of scotch.

She put on a vintage Taylor Swift CD on Granny's vintage CD player and got to work, trying not to feel overwhelmed by the piles of boxes. She focused on a stack near the back of the attic, a random assortment of old power cords for technology that no longer existed, and moth-eaten baby blankets hand-knitted by Granny.

Rosie grabbed one of the blankets and winced as a giant black binder tumbled out and landed on her foot. She cursed as she picked it up. Gold letters painted on the front of the binder read, FOR MY BABY GIRLS. She froze.

This binder belonged to her mother. She wasn't sure how she knew this. Rosie had never seen her mother's handwriting. In fact, she had very little to remember her mum by. She used to ask Dad why that was, and he would grow quiet, a grim, faraway look in his eyes.

"I took what I could carry. My most important cargo," he would say as he ruffled Rosie's hair.

She understood the sacrifices Dad made over the years since they left California. It wasn't that she didn't love him, but there was this deep ache inside her, a longing to know her mum.

Rosie took a deep breath and opened the binder. On the first page was a handwritten letter in the same elegant cursive as the cover.

To Rosie, Bettie, and Cassie, my precious girls.

I owe you an apology, though if you're reading this, it's likely too late. The truth is, I knew before you were born that our world was broken but I ignored it, because my desire to be a mom ... to be your mom ... clouded my judgment. I wanted to believe that my love was enough to keep y'all safe.

But that is not true. Half the country is underwater, the other half is burning. There's an irreparable fracture in our government that is about more than politics, and the ugliness it's unearthed terrifies me.

But the growing panic I feel is about what all of that means for your future. I have failed to prepare you for what's coming. What's worse is I am unprepared. My entire life I pursued a profession I loved, and though I still believe telling stories is a noble calling, it has made me useless. I have no applicable survival skills (neither does your father), and the people who can fend for themselves are the only ones who will survive.

Late at night, I lie awake, wishing I couldn't see what was coming. Wishing I didn't know how bad it would get. Some days I want to go to sleep and not wake up. I want to give up.

But then the sun rises, and I go to your room, and I open your door to see your bright, smiling faces. I hear each of you asking in your sweet, high-pitched bird voices for "Mama hugs" and "Mama kisses," and I know that I must keep going. For you. For my sweet babies. I want you to be ready. So I must be ready, too.

I am preparing our food, our water, and our supplies, and I'm training myself. None of this comes easy. There are people, including your father, who think I am overreacting. Maybe they're right and one day they will forgive me for my obsession. If I'm right, I hope I can forgive them for not listening.

I've considered the possibility that I might not be there for you one day, and enclosed in this notebook are survival tips you will need. (Your father jokingly calls it "A Mother's Guide to the Apocalypse.")

It is a guidebook. It's all the things I want you to know how to do when there is no Google or internet or anyone

A MOTHER'S GUIDE TO THE APOCALYPSE   29

who has this knowledge to pass along to you. I tried to be thorough, but I am sure there are things I have missed. Please know that I tried.

Lean on one another. Embrace one another's strengths, and remember I am always with you . . . forever and always.

Love,

Mama Bear

Rosie read and reread the letter, taking in every line. Her mum loved her so much. It was all there on the page.

She didn't realize that she was crying until she heard her sisters' panicked voices.

"Rosie, what is it? What's wrong?" Bettie asked.

She looked up to see Bettie and Cassie staring back at her, heads tilted in concern. Rosie rarely cried, but tears streamed down her face as she handed Bettie the binder. Cassie stood beside her, the two of them reading quickly, eyes widening in disbelief. Thy were so engrossed, they didn't notice as an old photograph fluttered to the ground.

Rosie bent down to pick it up. Staring back at her was a five-by-seven photo of her mother. Olivia stood on a red carpet, a banner behind her that read THE ACAD-EMY AWARDS, the words *Getty Images* superimposed on the image. Olivia's jet-black hair was shiny and long, her makeup flawless. She wore a slim-fitting black floor-length gown that showed off her figure.

Beside her was an equally stunning Black woman with

long blond braids, wearing a white satin tuxedo, the two of them grinning as though they owned the world.

Rosie knew from a school project that she did in year eight (much to Sam's dismay) that her mum had been nominated for an Academy Award for producing a short film, along with her partner, Melissa Warren. Rosie studied her mum's smile, and saw they shared a plump bottom lip and slightly smaller top lip and the same button nose. She wanted to absorb every detail. This was only the fourth photo of her mother Rosie had ever seen.

After the sisters had spent years hounding Granny for any information, she'd secretly presented them with three family photos, insisting they not show them to their father.

"The last thing we want is to upset him. He's so sensitive when it comes to your mum."

One of the photos was of Rosie and her sisters wrapped in red Christmas stockings on their first day home from the NICU. Her mum held two of them, her father one, their grins so wide with joy, it radiated from the photo.

The second picture was when they were a year old, the whole family wearing fuzzy matching Christmas jumpers, and the third during Easter, all five of them sporting bunny ears, looking ridiculously happy.

Rosie once asked Dad why they didn't have family photos. "I wish I could see what Mum looked like, and what our house looked like."

"We used to have hard copies of everything, and then

A MOTHER'S GUIDE TO THE APOCALYPSE   31

tablets and computers made it unnecessary. It was all right there in the palm of your hand. Until it wasn't. It was a reminder that some things are impermanent, and why this way is better."

Dad was always going on about how much better it was that there were limits on who could access technology. Global safety measures had been put in place to prevent what had happened during the Collapse from ever happening again. Even if the average working-class person could afford to use the internet or to buy those devices for their homes—and most couldn't—Sam was adamant that they would never own them. "We all learned the hard way that too much information is dangerous. Trust me, the simple life is the best life."

This photo Rosie now held seemed like a gift from her mother from the afterlife. Rosie turned it over and saw a note scribbled on the back.

Different handwriting. Sharp and sleek, like the woman in the picture.

Sammy, Sam, Sam, I tracked you down. Can you believe how young and beautiful Liv and I were? Every day I think about you and the girls, and I want to know how you're doing. I'm not sure this letter will find you, but I found your address and with the borders opening up, I'm taking a chance. Life here is different and hard, but Dom and I are alive and that makes us two of the lucky ones. I haven't given up on finding Olivia. Survivors are being discovered every day. What if she's out there somewhere? I know things were complicated when it all went down, but we both know how fragile life is and that what we all shared is special. My number is below. Please know that you and the girls are always in my thoughts, and I'll never give up on finding you or Liv. All my love, Mel.

Rosie stared, her gaze lingering on the date on the note. This was sent three years ago. Three years. She let out a gasp. Cassie put her hand on her shoulder.

"It's okay, Rosie. This is a lot to take in."

Bettie clicked her tongue, her trademark signal that she was annoyed. "We should all take a moment and process what we've learned."

Rosie wanted to scream. "Would you two shut up? You're missing the point." She held up the photo for them both to see. "It's Mum. She's not... I mean, she didn't..."

Rosie was never at a loss for words, but no words came out. She cleared her throat. "Don't you get it? Mum might still be alive."

For once, Rosie's sisters were stunned into silence, the revelation that life as they knew it would never be the same.

r/SoCalValleyPreppers

5,321 Members

GoJoe420

Welcome Newbies

We're glad you found us. A lotta preppers aren't happy about newcomers but that isn't how we roll. We're about learning from our neighbors and getting ready for the shit storm coming our way. So tell us why your here and how we can get you started. No shit talk or politiks allowed here. That ain't what we're about either! Don't be a dickhead or you'l be blocked.

VanNuysGuy405

Joey, you're the shit. Just got my bug out bag sorted and went to Home Depot to get supplies for my chicken coop. Gonna have my own eggs in no time. Thanks for having our backs.

SweetiePie24

I just graduated from University of Michigan and I've lived in Santa Monica for three months. But my parents lost their home in a flood last year. They weren't ready AT ALL. My friends think I'm nuts, but I'd rather be informed. Excited for all your tips.

Mamabear3

I'm Olivia and I live in Woodland Hills. Been lurking here ever since we had a robbery three weeks ago during the LA blackout. I'll be honest I've never been so scared. I have three toddler triplets. (yes my hands are full!) And I was so damn scared. When I think about what almost happened. Actually, I can't think about it unless I want to have another panic attack. But I'm scared and pissed and I have to do something. I'm not sure where to start since it all feels overwhelming but I figure anything helps.

VallE4Ever

Welcome Olivia! We're glad you're here. We'll get you hooked up & make sure you're safe so no one fucks with you..

GoJoe420

Hey Liv, I'm Joey in Canoga Park. Looks like were neighbors. Sorry it took that shit happening to bring you here but we're damn glad to have ya. Your in the right place. Check out the Beginer's Guide to prepping I shared and ask any questions. There are no dumb questions... unless your Van. Then nothin but dumb shit.

VanNuysGuy405

It's you're. But also fuck you Joe.

GoJoe420

You wish!

SweetiePie24

Don't let these two scare you off. Us ladies can prep with the best of 'em.

Mamabear3

Thanks y'all. I've got to pick up the kids from preschool, but I'll be back. (She says in her best Schwarzenegger voice)

VanNuysGuy405

A Terminator reference. I might be in love.

GoJoe420

Keep it in your pants, Van.

NEW PRIVATE CHAT

GoJoe420

Hey, I'm happy to help you get started. I recommend getting sorted with your water storage and then targeting food supply and going from there.

Mamabear3

That's it? Sounds simple.

GoJoe420

It's not, but I got you. I'll send a checklist. We'll mark things off one by one. Think you can do that?

Mamabear3

I can try!

GoJoe420

That's the prepper spirit.

CASSIE

Ten minutes had passed since Rosie discovered Mum's book, and she still hadn't moved. She sat there mumbling like an arsehole, "What if Mum isn't dead? What if she isn't dead?"

Cassie resisted the urge to shake her sister, knowing how Rosie was prone to lash out. She used to tease her sister that she resembled an adder, one of England's only venomous snakes. When they were in year six, Cassie asked the school librarian to print out a picture of the snake, and she taped it on the wall above Rosie's bed. The funny thing was it had taken Rosie a week to notice. When she did, she'd ripped it off the wall and chased Cassie around the house, shouting, "I'm going to bloody murder you."

Which only proved Cassie's point. Rosie's instinct was attack first, ask questions later. It wasn't as though Cassie didn't have questions about Mum, but acting like an overly emotional American (Dad's favorite insult) wouldn't help matters.

Of course, Bettie was acting equally ridiculous, sitting on the floor next to Rosie, patting her shoulder, and sniffling. *Always the drama queen*, Cassie thought. *Why can't you let drama unfold without inserting yourself?* she wanted to say.

"Mum can't be alive. She simply can't," Cassie said.

Rosie's head popped up like a marionette. "Oh really? How do you explain the letter we read, Cassandra?"

Cassie flinched. She wasn't sure what she hated more: the patronizing tone Rosie used, or that she'd used her full name. "I don't know. *Rosalind*. All I know is that a letter doesn't tell the whole story. If Dad lied about what happened, he had a good reason. He's probably protecting us."

Rosie scoffed and resumed staring at Mum's photo as though she might will her into existence.

Cassie knew that Dad wasn't a liar. She *knew* him. Talking about their mum pained him because he loved her so much. Mum died in the Los Angeles flood and mudslide. Two weeks later, the family moved back to Dad's hometown of Newcastle, to escape California's superstorms, fires, earthquakes, and political turmoil.

A few months after that, the big earthquake struck California, decimating the state and killing millions.

Eight months later, the US fractured, with seventeen states, including California, seceding from the Union and declaring their independence.

When Cassie and her sisters were little, Sam made this all seem connected, as if Mum's death equaled the world falling apart. But Rosie couldn't stop asking questions in that tireless manner of hers. She researched nonstop about the floods, looking into everything she could find about the victim remains that were discovered.

Cassie thought it was gross that her sister wanted details, but Rosie was an obsessed little weirdo. She kept a running list of questions in a spiral notebook she carried around like a tiny Agatha Christie. She begged the librarian to track down more information on the quakes. However, the borders between New Pacific and Britain were still heavily secured, and access to books or news about the previous decades was limited.

Unsurprisingly, Bettie got on board, and she and Rosie began a relentless campaign to get Dad to tell them more about Mum's death. The week of their thirteenth birthday, Dad gave in and called a family meeting. They waited for him in the conservatory.

Dad never drank, but that evening he poured a large scotch and settled onto Gran's floral sofa as winter rains pounded the windows.

"I know you want to know about your mum and how she died, so I'm going to tell you once, and then I do not want to discuss it again." He gazed back at them, his blue-gray eyes zeroing in on each of them, saving Rosie for last.

After their nodded assurances, he began. "The last time I saw your mum, she had a dinner in Hollywood with a director for her latest film. I was home with you three and had put you to bed when Liv called to say she was heading home. I said that I loved her and I would see her soon. She never made it. There was a flash flood in Laurel Canyon, and over a hundred and fifty people were swept away. A mudslide killed another fifty. I assumed she was there, but by that point the Collapse had begun. Things were moving so fast and I was scared. I wasn't sure I could keep you safe in LA, so I made the decision to bring you back here. To my home. To be near Granny so we could start over. And we did. I've worked so hard to give you three the best life."

That was the moment Dad began to cry. Dad never cried. He laughed. He teased. He mocked. He consoled. He did not cry.

Cassie rushed over to hug him while Rosie and Bettie sat in stunned silence. After he pulled himself together, Sam begged them to leave the past in the past. "Please, my loves, I can't discuss this. Not anymore. We have to move on. Can we please move on?"

The desperation in his voice made Cassie feel sick. Thankfully, Bettie agreed. "You're okay, Dad. It'll be okay."

Rosie's silence made it clear she wasn't satisfied. Dad could see that. "I promise to try and get more information about what happened."

Maybe he meant it, or maybe it was lip service. Cassie was convinced that Dad's emotional outburst was enough to make even Rosie back down, which was good. There was no reason to upset Dad after all he'd done. When he wasn't working, he spent time teaching them how to care for the house and the grounds or cook their own meals. When they were younger, he would sit and play dolls and build elaborate block castles, and play pretend anytime they asked. Sometimes he lost his temper and yelled, but he was never violent. He loved them with his whole heart.

Of course, it was no secret that Cassie was the closest to her father, but it wasn't part of any grand plan. She happened to like the same things he did, whether that was spending hours in the greenhouse planting new crops or riding with him when he made his food deliveries, the Beatles or the Rolling Stones blasting from the radio. Cassie just enjoyed their time together.

Not Rosie and Bettie. "It's a bloody bore," Bettie would say, preferring to play dress-up with Rosie.

But Cassie's entire world made sense when she was working side by side with Dad, watching the dirt and soil blossom into something tangible, watching the tomatoes or strawberries they planted and ate for supper or the roses and peonies that grew around their home. More than that, it was Cassie's time away from her sisters and all the comparisons. The plants never asked inane questions about whether she could feel her sisters' pain (no) or if they liked the same boys (*definitely* not).

This situation was different, though. She couldn't deny it. The idea that Mum hadn't died or that her death hadn't happened the way Dad said changed everything.

Cassie knew that if she defended their dad, it might kick off another round of the "just because you're the favorite doesn't mean you know everything about him" argument. But she also didn't want this to spiral into a bigger deal. And she could tell it was heading in that direction.

"I think we're all upset. Maybe we should—"

Rosie cut her off. "Dad never talked about Mum's funeral, and neither did Granny. I stopped asking questions, because it made him uncomfortable, but that was a mistake. I see that."

"Keep your voice down," Cassie insisted. "Or you'll wake Dad."

Rosie leapt to her feet and gently rested Mum's book on top of a nearby box as though it might shatter in pieces. "Maybe I should wake him."

"Don't you dare," Cassie said.

Rosie shook her head defiantly. "Fine. But the next good day Dad has, I'm asking some hard questions. We deserve answers before it's too late."

Cassie imagined Rosie shouting at their father, his eyes blinking at them in confusion. She stood toe-to-toe with her sister in a way she never had before. "Mum is gone, but Dad is here. There's no way I'm letting you upset him."

"You think being Dad's favorite matters now? Or that you're going to stop me?" Rosie asked, the challenge in her voice.

There it was. Adder Rosie appeared singing that same

jealous tune. Cassie looked over and saw Bettie sitting quietly, twisting her hands, and she couldn't help herself.

"Bettie, you don't get to sit there and not speak. Not this time. Grow a spine and tell us what you think," Cassie hissed.

Bettie glared at her. "Okay. Fine. Rosie's right. We deserve to know what really happened before Dad is too far gone."

The decision had been made. Sides had been chosen.

Rosie gestured to the piles of boxes still waiting to be sorted. "If we get to work, we can get this finished in a few hours," she said.

Cassie glared at her sisters. "You cunts seem to have it covered. I'll leave you to it."

She saw Bettie flinch. Her sister hated that word.

Cassie headed for the exit. "You're the cunt for walking away," Rosie called after her.

"Ro, shut it. Cassie, come back," Bettie pleaded.

Cassie ignored them both and headed down the stairs and around the corner to Dad's room. Every night before bed, she checked in to make sure Dad was okay, but tonight she felt a deeper sense of urgency.

She turned the knob and paused at the creak of the floorboards underneath her feet. Dad didn't stir, his snoring rattling the windows.

On the telly was a rerun of a 1990s show called *Friends*. She listened to Dad's heavy inhale and exhale mixed with the laugh track. She missed the days when she was young enough to crawl into bed and feel his strong arms wrap around her. Now he was thin, frail, and easily startled.

"You're good, Dad. I've got you," she whispered as she sank down onto the recliner in the corner of the room and blinked back tears. She wanted to shout at her sisters and remind them time was running out. What if they went digging into his past and found something terrible? Of course once Rosie set her mind to something, there was no stopping her. But this time, Cassie would have to fight back. She had to protect Dad at all costs.

BETTIE

If there was one thing Bettie hated, it was listening to her sisters argue. *Who took out the rubbish? Who stole whose blouse? Who ate the last Cadbury bar?* But this argument—this was on another level. If it were true and Dad lied about Mum's death, there was no coming back from that. It made her physically ill to think about. She couldn't even tell her boyfriend, Max, about it, and she told him everything.

Before this, Bettie found Rosie's constant battle for Dad's attention exhausting and pointless. Sure, Dad and Cassie were closer, but that didn't mean he loved them less. Rosie found landscaping and gardening as dull as Bettie did.

But once Granny died, Dad leaned on Cassie more and more, and Rosie responded by tightening her grip on her sisters. Her nagging to eat breakfast or bring a sweater bordered on obnoxious. She was trying to be a mother and a father, but nobody wanted or needed that.

Bettie also found it annoying that Cassie hadn't accepted Dad was sick. She kept making plans for the holidays as though he might still be cooking Sunday roast and cracking

Dad jokes, when in reality, they would be lucky if, in a year or two, he could still feed and bathe himself.

As the middle triplet, Bettie was exhausted at constantly being asked to pick a side. She was twenty-one, for Christ's sake. All she wanted to do was to enjoy her final year at uni and spend time with Max before they were forced to become adults. But Bettie couldn't pretend this wasn't happening. This was as adult as it got.

She and Rosie finished cleaning the attic in shocked silence, and around one a.m. Bettie went to bed, consumed with worries about Rosie's "next good day" proclamation.

She braced herself for a confrontation the following day, but Dad woke up coughing and sneezing. As he barked orders at them to make tea and toast with peanut butter, Cassie and Rosie moved around in stony silence. When Bettie tried to talk to them, they were so terse she decided they could both bugger off. She wasn't interested in brokering today's peace treaty.

The next day Dad's fever was over 102 degrees Fahrenheit and they all decided he should see a doctor. Bettie was supposed to have breakfast with Max but offered to cancel.

"Your sacrifice is noted, but I'll take Dad. I know his meds better than you two anyway," Cassie snapped.

Bettie rolled her eyes. This was Cassie's way of one-upping them, but she was right. She did know more about Dad's care.

Rosie seemed surprisingly grateful. "Thanks, Cass. We appreciate it."

A MOTHER'S GUIDE TO THE APOCALYPSE   47

Cassie wasn't the only one taken aback by Rosie's change in mood, but by then, Dad had shuffled out of his bedroom, dressed for the doctor.

"Are you ready to see Dr. Byer?" Cassie asked.

He grumbled. "Man is a wanker. Not even old enough to pull pints at the pub," he said as he pulled on his coat. As they headed to the door, he regarded Rosie and Bettie thoughtfully.

"Don't forget to walk Pepper."

The girls agreed, despite the fact that Pepper, their greyhound, died six years ago.

The minute the car pulled out of the driveway, Rosie tossed Bettie's coat at her. "Let's go."

Bettie blinked in confusion. "Go where?"

"I located Mum's friend Melissa in New Pacific and set up an international video call. Dr. McLaughlin has the technology to make it happen." Rosie took a breath, eyes sparkling with excitement. "Bets, we get to talk to Mum's best friend."

Bettie wasn't sure what scared her more: leaving Cassie out of something this big, or finding out that Rosie was right and Dad had lied to them about Mum.

"Ro, don't be daft. We can't do this without Cass. It's not right."

Bettie could see from Rosie's guilty expression that she agreed, but that wouldn't stop her. "Cassie's afraid of what we might learn. Which I get. I'm scared, too, but Bets, I've spent my whole life wanting..." Rosie paused. "This is my chance. Our chance."

"I'm supposed to meet Max for breakfast, and I think—"

Rosie let out an exasperated sigh. "Oh, for fuck's sake, fine, I'll go by myself."

Bettie already knew her sisters disliked her boyfriend. Or maybe they disliked the fact that he stood between the three of them. Whatever the case, Max was not anyone's favorite subject.

Rosie shrugged into her jacket and headed toward the door. Bettie waited, thinking about how hurt Cassie would be when she learned what they'd done. Bettie didn't have to go. She could let Rosie take the lead and manage the blowback from afar.

But then Bettie remembered the picture of her mum she still kept tucked under her pillow, and all the unanswered questions that remained. Those answers that were slipping away along with Dad's memory.

Damnit, I have to do this. Bettie grabbed her jacket and raced outside, waving for Rosie to wait. She climbed into Dad's old truck.

"I knew you'd make the right choice," Rosie said.

Bettie rolled her eyes. Rosie could never take the win.

Half an hour later, they arrived at a lovely flat two blocks from Newcastle University.

Dr. McLaughlin, Rosie's history lecturer, greeted them. "Rosalind, it's lovely to see you." She gave her a hug and reached out for Bettie's hand. "Bettie, it's wonderful to meet you as well." She paused. "The resemblance is striking. I simply can't believe it."

Bettie couldn't help herself. "Really? We've never heard that before," she said sweetly.

Dr. McLaughlin burst out laughing. "Apologies. I do abhor being a cliché. Please come in. I've already put the kettle on. A cuppa will settle your nerves."

Bettie appreciated the acknowledgment that they should be nervous as she studied Rosie's lecturer-turned-mentor. For the past three years, Dr. McLaughlin was all Rosie could talk about. The woman, in her late seventies, face wrinkled with lines and sunspots, was elegant in wide-legged pants and a vintage rainbow shacket. She projected an aura of motherly energy her sister desperately craved.

Dr. McLaughlin waved a manicured hand around. "Please take a look around."

The flat was tiny but orderly. There were books on everything from Woodstock to September 11, as well as an entire row of books devoted to pop music of the 1990s. On another shelf was a stack of books on conspiracy theories from the early 1990s to the 2000s.

On an antique credenza, relic iPhones, tablets, and giant desktop computers were displayed on risers, an ode to a time gone by. Dr. McLaughlin clocked Bettie's fascination as she poured the tea.

"Isn't it a marvel? To think we had the whole world at our fingertips, and it destroyed us."

Bettie thought about the wars that had broken out, the states and countries that fractured. The people who were forever divided by an unwillingness to listen or be heard and a technology that only made the divide worse.

"Our granny used to say these things made life easier. To communicate with people from all over the world. To share information. Do you ever miss it?" she asked.

Rosie looked surprised by the question, and Bettie wanted to smack her sister. Bettie didn't want to be a doctor like Rosie, but that didn't make her simple. She was a performer, which meant she was endlessly curious about the world around her.

Dr. McLaughlin tilted her head as she weighed the question. "It's true these things made our lives more efficient. Groceries, movies, TV, books, anything you wanted was readily available. Information, too, which had always required a level of effort to access, was available with the click of a button. But humans are wired to be challenged. When we aren't, we get bored, lazy, and in most cases cruel. We started to grow numb to the hardships of others because we were insulated from them. Do I miss being able to order supper with the press of a button? Certainly. Do I miss the tragedies that were allowed to occur because of this technology? Absolutely not."

"Why do you keep all of it?" Bettie wondered.

Rosie snorted. "Hello! She's a history lecturer."

Bettie glared back at her sister, but Dr. McLaughlin

offered up a gentle smile. "Yes, these things are a part of our history, but I keep them because they are a reminder of how little they mattered in the end. The technology most of us use is enough, and though leaving your cell phone at home used to feel like you'd lost an appendage, once we didn't have them, the world kept turning. We survived. We endured."

She glanced down at her watch. "It's almost ten. Shall we?"

Dr. McLaughlin gestured to the back of the flat and they followed her into her office. A massive white computer and monitor were set up on a desk in the corner, with books and papers piled alongside.

Not all technology was banned. You could own a cell phone, though it was costly and access to other countries—especially the States—was heavily restricted. If you wanted access to the international online network (ION) or what was once called the World Wide Web or the internet, you could apply for a government license, but that required a background check.

Once you were approved, you were issued a login. No more anonymous usernames or IP addresses. Everyone was tracked and monitored to make the system function. Someone like Dr. McLaughlin, who worked in academia, or her wife, Rita, who worked in British intelligence, had ION home access, but regular people like Bettie and her family did not. Some people argued it was classist, but Bettie thought her life was perfectly fine without all of that. She didn't miss what she'd never had.

Dr. McLaughlin sat down at the computer and typed quickly, a series of methodical keystrokes. "It's only in the last year that we've been able to connect regularly with New Pacific due to their lack of internet regulations. Now that they've signed the Access and Information Treaty, it's easier, but connecting in some of the more rural areas is still hard. Your mother's friend Melissa lives in a place called Idyllwild, a rather small village from the sound of it. She traveled to her local government office to access a video link, so we will have to see how good the connection is. Are you ready?"

Bettie looked over to find Rosie nervously gnawing at her nails, a stress response she hadn't seen in years. She took Rosie's hand in hers and squeezed. Rosie squeezed back.

The screen quickly changed, and an older grinning Black woman appeared.

Dr. McLaughlin smiled, her voice low. "I have a lecture, but take all the time you need. Just turn the lock when you leave."

She slipped out as the girls studied Melissa, sitting in a poorly lit office space, the drab gray background slightly blurry. Her once long braids were cropped short. She wore a sleeveless black Rolling Stones T-shirt and blotted at her neck with a colorful towel. She obviously looked older than the photo, but there was something else. A hardness in her expression. The same look Dad had, and so many other people who talked about those dark days. But Rosie didn't seem to notice. She took Mel in, her face lighting up, revealing her left dimple.

"Melissa, it's so nice to meet you."

"Oh no, please call me Mel. Or Auntie Mel works, too."

Auntie Mel. Bettie always wanted an aunt. Or an uncle. Any family really. She always longed for more people in their circle, a larger village to rely on.

"Auntie Mel sounds nice," Rosie said.

Mel leaned in as if she might be able to reach out and touch them, then shook her head, eyes brimming with tears.

"You girls look just like Liv. I mean, you always did, but it's uncanny. Beautiful like her."

"Thank you," Rosie and Bettie said in unison. Normally they hated when they spoke together, but this time they laughed.

So did Mel. "I used to be able to tell you apart in an instant, but you went and grew up on me. So who is who?"

Always the leader, Rosie spoke for the both of them. "I'm Rosie, and this is Bettie."

"Where's Cassie? And Sam?" Mel asked.

Bettie looked at Rosie knowingly.

Rosie shrugged. "Dad is a bit poorly, so Cassie took him to the doctor."

"Not serious, I hope."

Bettie sighed. "We think it's a cold, but Dad...He has dementia. It's not...He's not great."

"I'm real sorry to hear that," Mel said.

She took a ragged breath, and Bettie was surprised to see this stranger almost in tears. "Is it...I mean, how far has it progressed?" Mel asked.

"He's still got a lot of good days, but his moods change quite frequently. He's got a temper at times, and his short-term memory is not great. Neither is his long-term," Rosie said softly.

"I guess if the Collapse taught us anything, it's to be grateful for the days we have left. But I sure hate to hear that. Poor Sammy."

There was such genuine affection in Mel's voice that it surprised Bettie. So did the nickname. Bettie hadn't heard anyone call Dad *Sammy*, and Mel said it with such warmth. Her father had so few friends that she was eager to hear more. But Mel was already moving on.

"There's so much I want to discuss, but how have you been? Have you had a good life?" Mel asked. "Sorry, what an impossible question. Please excuse me. I ramble when I'm nervous."

Rosie laughed. "It's okay. It wasn't always easy. The weather events were hard on everyone, but Newcastle was prepared. Before things got bad, we had flood plans, and during the worst heat waves, the town had cooling stations and community pools. Dad learned to farm, so we had plenty of food when the shortages kicked off."

"Hold up, Sammy learned to farm? You're telling me the same man who didn't know what arugula was learned to grow his own food?"

Bettie burst out laughing. "Wait, Dad didn't know how to cook?"

"The man couldn't boil water. I swear it drove your mama crazy. She wouldn't send Sam to the grocery store because he would call her so many times to ask where things were."

"I guess people can change," Rosie said. "Dad loves to cook. He makes the best Sunday roast and mashed potatoes. Homemade chocolate chip cookies are his specialty."

"Sam Clark makes cookies? Now I've heard it all," Mel said with a chuckle.

How different was Dad? Bettie wondered. She wanted to know how they all knew one another and how close they were, but Melissa...Auntie Mel was full steam ahead. "So you moved back to Newcastle after all? I wrote Sam but wasn't sure my letters made it."

"Dad added extra rooms to Granny's flat, and a few years later we assumed the two homes behind ours after the current tenants abandoned theirs. Dad built a greenhouse and learned all kinds of planting and farming techniques so we could be self-sufficient," Rosie replied.

"We struggled, but Dad was never one to let us dwell," Bettie said.

"Sammy always liked to look on the bright side, but I'm

sure it helped keep your spirits up. We've all had to make changes and sacrifices for this new world," Mel said.

Bettie heard a sharpness in her voice, and she wanted to ask Mel what sacrifices she'd made, but she barely knew the woman.

"We're so happy we found you. We were hoping... We have questions about Mum's death," Rosie said. Bettie wondered how long it had taken her sister to get the courage to come out and ask that question.

Mel cleared her voice. "I don't... I mean we never knew for certain that Olivia died. Your mom disappeared."

Rosie cleared her throat. When she spoke, her voice was husky. "Dad said that Mum drowned in the Laurel Canyon flood."

She let out an angry sigh. "I'm sorry... She did go missing during that time, but that's not... I mean, maybe that's what happened. We didn't know. There was talk that your mom could have left..."

"She left us?" Bettie asked, her voice sharp. Granny always made it seem like Mum was a hundred percent devoted. *Could she have walked out on us? Is that why Dad lied?*

"Oh, honey, there was talk, but it didn't come from me," Mel said. "None of us wanted to believe it was possible."

"Then who did?"

Mel grew quiet. The answer hung in the air. *Sam. It was Sam.*

"Why would he think that?"

"It's complicated," Mel said.

"Do you think she's dead?" Rosie whispered.

"If she wasn't, I have to believe that she would have tried to find you, but I also know that communications were impossible back then. A lot of climate survivors were separated from their families, and Sam took off to England so quickly."

"So Mum might have tried to find us, but we were already gone?" Rosie asked. Her voice shook. She took a deep breath to steady herself as Mel considered her question.

"Maybe. After you all left, the earthquake hit, and shit got real. My son and I were in one of the climate camps for a few months before we made it out of the city. We were all so used to email and cell phones that once they were gone, it was impossible to communicate."

They were all silent, the air sucked out of the room as questions swirled around them. *Why would Dad lie? What really happened to Mum?*

At last, Mel found her voice. "What about your uncle Lucas? Have you spoken to him?"

Bettie and Rosie looked at each other, then back at the screen. Rosie's words came out in a whisper. "We have an uncle?"

Mel looked shocked. "Jesus, Sam didn't tell you anything, did he?"

Bettie didn't appreciate Mel's harsh tone, and she must have seen their expression, because her face softened.

"Lucas was your mom's little brother. They were best

friends though he drove her crazy. But Sam and Lucas never got along."

Bettie wanted to know more about that, but Rosie interrupted. "Where is Lucas? Would he know where Mum is?" Rosie asked.

"I have no idea. I've searched for him, but he disappeared as well. An old friend in the city thought she saw Liv in one of the climate camps once, but when she went back, the woman was gone."

Could it have been Mum? And if it was, why didn't she look for us?

Rosie reached into her bag. "Do you know anything about this?"

She held up Mum's guidebook. Recognition flashed in Mel's eyes. "I do. I have so much I want to tell you. So much I want to share with you. Why don't you come here? Come and see me."

"You want us to come to New Pacific?" Bettie asked incredulously.

"Special visas are being issued for Americans who want to return home, and there are lots of resources now for finding people who went missing during the Collapse. It could be a chance to know the truth one way or another."

Bettie had a sudden longing to see both where her mother was from and her own birthplace. Not to mention California was where movies and TV were made. It was where New Broadway formed. Bettie sang at school and for various events around the village, but no one in her family really cared about her performing. Her father was dismissive in his own way, reminding her that survival skills were what mattered these days. He wasn't opposed to her performing for fun, but "you want to find ways to improve society. It's up to all of us to keep this place alive," he would say.

She wondered what it would be like to live in a place where other people were creative and thriving. It was ridiculous to consider. Leaving here seemed impossible. She had her final term, her boyfriend, Max, whom she couldn't imagine being apart from, and of course there was Dad. He despised California. Their entire lives, he'd drilled into them how lucky they were to call Newcastle home. To be safe and loved and protected in this village was all he wanted. To go back and leave him behind would be the ultimate betrayal.

"Where would we stay?" Rosie asked.

Bettie's head whipped around to look at Rosie. Clearly her sister's loyalty lay elsewhere.

"Stay with me, at my home in Idyllwild. Then we can head down to LA and see if there's any new discoveries about your mom," Mel said.

"We can't leave. Not with Dad's health and the move," Bettie said.

Rosie cut her off. "Auntie Mel, we need to discuss this, but we'll get back to you soon."

Auntie Mel. The words rolled off Rosie's tongue

effortlessly. Rosie didn't know this woman and all of a sudden she was calling her *auntie*? Everything was moving too fast.

"The offer is open. Seriously, anytime. Liv was my best friend, and my life has never been the same since I lost her. If there's a chance we can find out what happened to her, I'm here to help. Plus, I would love to see Sam again."

Dad would never go there. Ever. "I don't think Dad is—" Bettie began gently, but Rosie cut her off again.

"We'll be in touch," she said.

Bettie was stunned to see that Rosie had disconnected the call. "Okay, I think we should take our time and not rush into…"

"I'm going to New Pacific with or without you and Cassie. This isn't up for debate," Rosie said.

She stood up, shoved Mum's binder back in her backpack, and headed for the door.

Bettie sat in the quiet room, the only sound the low hum of the computer. She understood that no matter how much she argued or begged and pleaded, and no matter who it hurt, Rosie was going to go, and Bettie would have to pick a side. The question was: Whose side would she choose?

SAM

Bloody hell. Sam heard shouting and jolted up in bed, drenched in sweat, his head aching. According to the wanker doctor at the local clinic, he was simply full of cold. But Sam felt like his head might explode. He wanted to go back to bed, but from the sounds of the battle being waged outside his room, that wouldn't happen anytime soon.

Sam glanced at the clock, one of those hideous plastic things with large numbers that old people used. He snorted, having almost forgotten he was considered an old person.

"Don't be such a cunt," one of the girls said, but he was having trouble placing which girl it was. His head felt heavier than usual. More words broke through, angry and indignant.

"I need to know the truth."

Sam had no context for the argument, but the girls never needed a reason to fight. Even as eleven-month-old babies, they kicked, pinched, and bit one another mercilessly, leaving marks on arms and backs, and bums. He thought that would be the worst of it, but their teenage years proved him wrong.

There was less physical violence, but the cruelty ratcheted up. The three hurled brutal insults at one another about who was fatter, dumber, and more useless, which never failed to shock him and his mum, God rest her soul. Sam intervened when it went too far, but he did his best not to overstep. He wanted them to find their way.

He heard them saying "Dad" repeatedly. He wanted to believe it was because they needed him or they were worried about him, but something in the inflection made him think otherwise. Whether it was his broken, tired brain that made their words unclear, he wasn't sure. Everything was a challenge these days. Locating his glasses, remembering names, basic life tasks. He could remember moments. Memories flickered in and out like an old-school television, complete with rabbit ears.

Sam and the girls speeding down the village streets as carefree as could be.

Driving with Liv in his green Jeep on their third date when they drove to Malibu and got a flat tire on the PCH.

His mum making cheese toasties, *Top of the Pops* blaring on the telly.

All pieces of a life, but none of it connected to anything. He was losing himself, but the most challenging part was losing his daughters and, soon enough, his home.

It pissed him off that no one asked what he wanted. No one cared enough to ask. Sometimes he felt so angry, he wanted to tear the bloody house apart, but that would only prove their point that he wasn't capable of living alone. It was all so infuriating.

Sometimes he envied his mum. She had said good night and drifted off to sleep forever.

"You're a selfish bitch. Always have been."

That was Cassie, he could tell, her voice growing louder.

"At least I'm not an idiot. Your hero worship makes it impossible for you to think Dad could lie to us."

Rosie thought he was a liar? Why would she think that? They'd been fussing over him so much lately and now they sounded... angry. What had he done?

He switched on the light, found his slippers, and slid his feet into them. He stood, his knees and feet aching. He wasn't that old, but a lifetime of teaching and gardening had taken its toll.

"Getting old isn't for the faint of heart," his mum used to say, and as with most things, she was right.

Sam headed down the hall and found all three girls in the kitchen, a face-off unfolding between Rosie and Cassie.

Bettie sat on the counter, curled up like a cat, a silent, patient observer.

"Jesus Christ, what is going on?"

They didn't hear him. They were still going round and round. Sam put his fingers together and whistled. The three of them jumped in unison.

"Dad, what are you doing out of bed?" Cassie asked.

"You tell me. Are you lassies trying to break the sound barrier?" he said.

Cassie gave him a sympathetic look, the equivalent of a pat on the head. "We'll keep it down. You should go back to bed."

Anger bubbled up. "I'm not the village idiot. What's all the shouting about?"

"It's nothing—" Cassie began.

Rosie cut her off. "It's about Mum."

Bettie froze.

Cassie flinched.

Sam saw Liv, a snapshot in his mind: seven months pregnant, about to pop, the two of them trapped in an elevator at the doctor's office as they waited to be rescued. He could hear Liv's laughter, like a favorite song on repeat.

"Only us. This would only happen to us," she said.

Then she looked down at her belly. "It's too soon to meet you three, so settle your butts down in there."

He shook away the memory. He wouldn't think about Liv. He couldn't.

"Why are you talking about her now?" Sam snapped.

Rosie pointed toward a large folder on the counter.

It was Sam's turn to freeze.

Olivia's manifesto. *A Mother's Guide to the Apocalypse*, he called it jokingly.

At the time, he understood that the break-in stole her sense of control. Prepping was her way of taking it back. But it became about so much more than that.

He blinked as he recalled the bitter rows they had. Olivia thought Sam wasn't taking her seriously about how bad things were going to get.

"We can't live in fear. We have to keep going," he'd told her.

He wanted to experience the joy their girls brought to their lives. Not prepare for doomsday. Liv had always been so rational, and it had all changed. He understood how terrifying it was, but they caught the girl. The young woman had been arrested, but then Liv refused to press charges. She wanted to get the girl help, but the system wasn't designed to help anyone. They were all on their own. Which was what Liv kept saying every time she placed a new order for fucking toilet paper.

Sam tried to be patient, but the constant list making and ordering of supplies began to drive him mad. The way she seemed to turn their garage into a bunker and their yard into a prepper kitchen almost overnight.

One day on the way to the girls' preschool for their annual Halloween parade, Liv asked Sam to take a class with her. "They teach you how to search for food and find water sources," she said.

Sam laughed. He genuinely thought she was kidding.

"It's not funny," she snapped.

He let out a frustrated grunt. "I've got thirty lessons a week. I'm home four afternoons a week with the girls while you're at work. I'm not spending my days off cosplaying Robinson fucking Crusoe."

There was a flash of fury in her eyes. "You're not taking this seriously. It's because you don't read or watch the news. You're not paying attention."

She was right about that. He realized it later, but at the

time he had clients who paid top dollar for his services. He didn't have time to trek to the wilderness of Calabasas with a bunch of REI rejects who wanted to learn how to eat edible berries.

"Dad, are you listening?" Rosie said sharply, bringing him back to the present.

It was Olivia, but there wasn't one of her. There were three.

"Dad, we're talking to you," Rosie said.

"For Christ's sake, Rosie, would you stop harassing him?" Cassie shouted back.

It wasn't Liv. It was his girls. All three of them eyeing him with that worried gaze he'd grown to hate.

Sam sank into one of the dining table chairs and dabbed at the sweat that had formed at the back of his neck. Memories of those final weeks with Liv made him uncomfortable. No, they made him want to run away again.

"Where did you find the book?" Sam asked, struggling to keep his voice neutral. He'd always been a yeller, but he'd been able to control it. These days his anger seemed to come faster and with less control.

"We talked to Melissa." Bettie's voice was gentle as she set a picture down in front of him along with a cup of milky sweet tea.

He stared at the image, wanting to rip it in half.

No. He wanted to set it on fire.

Fucking Melissa. He'd hoped that he would never hear

A MOTHER'S GUIDE TO THE APOCALYPSE   67

her name or see her face again. He almost swiped the tea away, mug and all, but stopped himself. He couldn't scare Bettie. Not his sweet girl.

What had Mel said about him? He couldn't read the girls' expressions, but if they knew the truth, wouldn't they come out and say it? Or was that why they were staring? Because what he'd done was so unforgivable?

"Mel said that Mum went missing, and no one knows what happened to her. You told us that she died. Which is it?"

His eyes lingered on Rosie's challenging glare, Bettie's hopeful gaze, and Cassie's worried frown.

"All these years, you never talked about Mum, and we respected that. I respected it. But I want to know what happened to her. Please tell us the truth," Rosie pleaded.

Sam closed his eyes so tight, he could see the whites of his eyelids. He regretted holding on to Liv's folder, but in the early days after they arrived back in England, it had given him a plan. A way forward.

"I don't know. She was gone . . . She left. How was I supposed to tell you that your own mum left?" Sam said. "It was easier that way."

"Easier for who?" Rosie asked bitterly.

Bettie moved over and put her arm around her sister's shoulders. He couldn't have felt more guilty if he were on the witness stand.

Panic gripped him. He had no words. Only tears. It

happened all the time. He was like a weepy lass in a bad indie film. Sam's tears seemed to anger Rosie, but she didn't yell. Hers was a quiet, simmering anger.

"Mel promised to help us figure out what happened to Mum. I'm going to New Pacific to see her," Rosie said.

"No, no, no," Sam muttered. The place that had broken his heart and ruined his marriage.

"You can't stop me. I'm applying for a visa and I'm going," Rosie said softly.

"I'm going, too, Dad," Bettie echoed, which shouldn't have surprised him. Where Rosie went, Bettie followed.

"They're fucking idiots. Let them go. We'll be fine here," Cassie said.

Damnit, he loved Cassie's unwavering loyalty, but he didn't deserve it. He thought about how Cassie would stay behind and help him move to the care home. There would be countless sleepless nights in a new bed while he wondered what was happening to Rosie and Bettie, who'd be an ocean away where Mel could fill their heads with lies. No, he couldn't let that happen.

"We stick together. If Rosie and Bettie are going, we all go," Sam said emphatically.

"That's impossible. You're not..." Cassie began.

"What? I'm not dead. Not yet anyway," he said sharply. "We all go. End of story."

He expected a battle of some kind from Cassie at least, but it seemed him agreeing sealed the deal. This was the last thing Sam wanted, but if he didn't go, if he let Mel poison them against him, he might lose his girls forever.

As Sam walked away, the girls launched into a conversation about the logistics of the trip, their voices swirling around him.

He loved them so much it hurt...

A memory of Olivia flooded back, the two of them standing on the porch of their home, her face streaked with tears as she pleaded with him. "Sam, do not do this to me. To us."

He'd turned away from her, no thoughts of their love story or his children, his entire body consumed by pure anger. It seemed so foolish, but he'd seen the signs and told her what was happening. She denied it. She told him he was wrong, but that kiss proved everything.

Liv tried to apologize, but he shoved her and walked away. She got back up. He was sure of it. Wasn't he? He was sure of the other things he'd done afterward. More than a kiss. So much more.

And then he remembered Liv slipping into bed beside him that night, her naked body pressing into his as she whispered, "Let's reset."

It was what they always said when things got hard and they needed a reminder that what they had together was worth fighting for.

But resetting wasn't easy when you'd made the biggest mistake of your life. When you'd done things that you could never take back. That was why he'd hoped this day would never come. But here it was. It was why Sam had to go with them. He could fake it. Pretend that he didn't hate Mel. Pretend that she hadn't destroyed him. He would see her one last time and tell her to keep her mouth shut before she ruined everything.

MAMA'S GUIDE TO HYDRATION

Let's get right to it. Hunger hurts, but dehydration kills. I hate being dramatic, but y'all need to know what you're up against. <u>Water is your salvation.</u> If you have regular water intake, you can survive up to two or three months without food. Crazy, right? But without water, you'll be lucky to survive for three days.

Water used to be so plentiful, we'd rinse our dishes <u>after</u> they were clean, and dump out or leave water bottles half full after we paid good money for them.

But water shortages are coming, which means that you're going to have to conserve what you have and be prepared to search for your own water.

Finding Water

Streams, ponds, rivers, creeks, and lakes are all great sources of water. Try to find running water if you can since it's generally safer than ponds and standing water.

When locating water, gravity is your friend. Water flows downhill, so places like valleys or ravines are a safe bet. Walking downhill is a simple way to test this.

ALWAYS trust your ears! If you hear running water, get running.

Once you find a water source, try to go as far upstream as you can. The farther upstream you go, the purer the water is since there's less of a chance for animals to pee, poop, or die in it or for other decaying matter to contaminate it. (Gross, but it is what it is!)

Remember, water can look sparkling and fresh, but it can still have gnarly microorganisms in it, so purifying is your friend!

You should also trust the local animals of your area. If you're able to track them, they can lead you to a water source.

Purifying Water

Most water is drinkable. Unless it's contaminated by chemicals or sewage, or is standing water, you can drink it as long as you treat it first. But because water is drinkable doesn't mean it's safe to drink. The last thing y'all want is diarrhea, giardiasis, or dysentery, so take your time to treat your water.

Boiling is the surest way to kill bacteria, parasites, viruses—all the little buggers that'll make you die by defecation—and it's also the easiest method.

Simply boil your water in a clean, heatproof container (preferably something stainless steel) for about ten minutes. Some people say you only need to boil water for one to five minutes. Those people usually get diarrhea.

A MOTHER'S GUIDE TO THE APOCALYPSE   73

The extra time won't kill y'all and it might save you a date with a parasite.

After the water boils, let it sit for twenty to thirty minutes before consuming it.

If you can't boil it, use purification tablets. I recommend chlorine dioxide tablets since they don't have much of a taste. Iodine tablets also work well so long as you're not pregnant. These little gems dissolve in your water and will kill virtually all harmful microorganisms.

These tablets will keep you healthy and your water pure. Most tablets come with the manufacturer's instructions, but they all work relatively the same.

Dissolve one to two tablets per liter of water, shake your container vigorously to dissolve, and wait for at least twenty minutes as the tablets purge your water of micro ne'er-do-wells. Your water may not taste like Fiji (my personal favorite back when we were dumb enough to pay two bucks for a single bottle of water), but it will be safe to drink.

One last thing: If you're looking to use water for bathing or non-consumption purposes, you can also use bleach to purify it. Make sure it's household bleach. Usually, it'll say 5.25% sodium hypochlorite on the packaging. Eight drops of bleach will purify one gallon of water. The bleach needs to be household bleach, not the laundry or bleach wipes type.

Personally, I'd prefer y'all not to use bleach to purify your water, but I'm writing this because I may not be there to keep you safe.

Storing Water

Now that you've located and purified your water, you need to store it. If it's possible, you should store enough water for three to five days. You're going to want to store your water in food-grade plastic or stainless-steel containers. A general rule of thumb for how much water a person needs is about a gallon a day. Try to keep your water in a cool, dark place, and don't let it sit for longer than six months.

Conserving Water

It physically hurts to think of y'all in a situation so dire that you need to conserve water for your survival, but this guide is all about keeping it real!

If you're desperate and need to ration water, the bare minimum an average size adult needs to survive is 350 mL. That's the minimum, which means you're going to feel shitty and it'll sap your energy, but it should keep you alive.

If you can't measure your water, drink only enough that you pee a little bit. It'll be gross and concentrated, but clear urine is a sign you're drinking too much. When you're rationing, you need all the water to absorb into your organs.

Also, make sure you have just enough water to stave off mental degradation (you need to keep the crazy at bay).

Another way to conserve water is to avoid eating. Digestion dehydrates you surprisingly fast. If you must eat, try to consume carbs and proteins. Fats require something like nine times the amount of water to digest because they're water-insoluble.

When rationing water, the devil is in the details. Breathing through your nose instead of your mouth decreases the surface area of your body that needs to rehydrate. Staying in the shade and lessening your physical activity will keep you from overheating and sweating. If you need to search an area for water, wake up early and walk around while it's cool.

One last thing... DON'T DRINK YOUR PEE!!!

I don't care how many "survival experts" or crazy people tell you that it's a viable option in the wild, y'all it is NOT. Your pee is waste. It's filled with nothing but stuff that's not supposed to be inside of you. If there's one last lesson I want to leave you with it's this—don't trust the piss drinkers.

Love,
Mama Bear

ROSIE

Rosie was going to find her mum. Not that she planned on saying that out loud, especially not to her sisters. They would have said she had lost the plot, and could she blame them? It was all a bit mad, but Rosie couldn't explain it. She knew deep down her mum was alive, and she had no choice but to keep going, no matter what her sisters thought.

That was, if the bloody bureaucracy didn't kill her first. For three days, Rosie skipped her classes, lying to her lecturers that she was ill while spending hours filling out forms at her local council office. Each day she watched the clerk hand over more documents to scan, sign, and return, including her American birth certificate, her British passport, as well as proof that she was a university student and enrolled in classes for her final term.

Once Rosie completed her application, she had to walk her sisters and Dad through the same process, which she imagined would be a nightmare, but thankfully once Dad agreed to go, everyone had gotten on the same page.

The trouble this time wasn't her family, but the red tape. New Pacific had the world's most stringent immigration policies. Thanks to the political conflicts they'd endured after the climate collapse and the fracture of the so-called United States, the government regulations were incredibly strict. Rosie thought it would be easier for her since she was born in America, but apparently, the New Pacific government had to make sure she wasn't a spy, or an enemy of the state, or something equally ridiculous. Once their paperwork was completed, Rosie joked to the clerk that she was surprised they hadn't asked for a blood sample. The dour-faced woman stared back at her with disapproval.

"Health checks are required once you land. If your visa is approved, you'll be given the medical instructions once you arrive in New Pacific."

There would be a blood test? Rosie couldn't hide her surprise, but it didn't matter. The clerk's disgust was obvious. "I simply cannot fathom anything being important enough to go *there*."

She wasn't surprised by the woman's disdain for America. Her father often expressed similar sentiments.

Not that it would have mattered either way. Rosie didn't care if her birthplace was riddled with crime or corruption. In fact, a part of her wanted to see a different world than their own, which was so safe and boring. There was no adventure here or chance that something unexpected might occur. All these years, she'd accepted the mundane nature of her life if it meant getting into medical school and pursuing her passion. But so far not a single school that

A MOTHER'S GUIDE TO THE APOCALYPSE   79

she'd applied to had accepted her. Dr. McLaughlin tried to comfort her: "Chin up, my love. It's still early days." But Rosie was starting to wonder if maybe medicine wasn't her destiny.

She could hear Cassie's derisive snort anytime she mentioned anything related to finding her purpose in life, but maybe that was what this was: a sign that she was destined to do something different entirely. Maybe her purpose was finding Mum to find out who she was meant to be.

Rosie was surprised to find the clerk staring at her, waiting for her to explain why she wanted to go to New Pacific.

She shrugged. "I guess finding out if my mother is really dead after nearly twenty years seems reason enough to go."

The woman's harsh features softened. She stamped Rosie's last documents. "You're all set, my love. You should have a response in seven to ten days. Travel safe."

Seven to ten days? Rosie wanted to scream, but she forced herself to focus on what she could control—her to-do list. She convinced her lecturers to let her take her midterms early, and while she generally found her coursework easy, this accelerated timeline meant that for once, Rosie had to study.

Her other task was much easier, which was convincing the buyers of their family home to extend the closing date so they had an additional month before they were forced to move. There was so much organizing to make this all work, but Rosie knew it would be worth it.

The only bright spots in her life as she waited for their visas were her daily video chats with Auntie Mel. After their first call, Dr. McLaughlin kindly offered Rosie the use of her videoconferencing system, and she'd taken full advantage of it. She knew that Bettie and Cassie found it odd how close she'd grown to Mel, but this woman knew her mother better than anyone besides Dad. Mel loved to talk about her and Olivia's wild LA days. "Your mom and I once crashed a Grammy party and found ourselves drinking with the Rolling Stones until five in the morning. Mick even gave your mom his number."

Rosie couldn't help herself. "That's Dad's favorite band."

Mel laughed. "Oh yes, your mom and Sam hadn't met yet, but your father was quite jealous when he found out. Mick Jagger was his idol."

Mel's stories helped Rosie build a picture of the woman who seemed like a blank space for so long.

"Were you surprised when Mum said she fell pregnant with us?" Rosie asked one rainy morning after class. They'd agreed to have a quick chat, but the call was almost an hour and still going strong.

"I have never been more surprised than I was that day your mom told me she was having triplets. We had a lunch scheduled at the Beverly Hills Hotel with this hotshot producer, and your mom asked me to meet her there half an hour earlier. She said it was urgent. Instantly, I thought maybe we lost our funding, or an actor dropped out of our latest film, but then your mother showed up and she's beaming. She looked fucking radiant, excuse my language. So I ask her what's going on and she said I should order a drink. I was always down to day-drink, but this producer was a bit uptight. Still your mom insisted, but she refused to join me, which should have tipped me off. Anyway, I order a vodka martini because why not, and after the waiter sets it down, your mom hands me an ultrasound photo."

Rosie leaned forward. "Did you freak out?"

Mel snorted. "I remember squealing so loudly the maître d' glared at me. I raised my glass and shouted, 'My best friend is knocked up! She's going to be a mom!' And when I looked back at your mom, she gestured for me to take a closer look. I picked up the ultrasound and saw BABY A, BABY B, AND BABY C written on it. I remember staring at it. 'Is this...Are you...Holy shit, you're having triplets?' And then she told me you were *identical*. That's one in two hundred million odds. Olivia began to laugh and so did I. Before long, we were laughing so hard we were both crying. Tears streaming down our faces. The producer found us laughing our asses off, thinking we'd both lost our minds."

Rosie had to swallow her anger at Dad for never telling her this story or any stories about their mum or their lives together, however brief. Sometimes she wanted to stop Mel and ask more questions. She wanted to know how blue her mum's eyes were or what she was wearing that day at lunch. She wanted to know about the baby shower and their birth and a million other things. But she was British, after all, so she let Mel talk, grateful that she had the inside scoop. Not that she didn't want her sisters to hear any of this. Once they were in California, she would have to share Mel, and that would be fine. But for now, she loved having Mel and her stories all to herself.

Unfortunately time dragged on with no visas in sight. By day eight, Rosie had completed her last exam for her Human Anatomy and Physiology course and decided that she would call the council office and beg them for an update.

To her surprise, as soon as she returned home she found four letters, each with the official UK government seal, waiting in the postbox. Rosie could hardly contain her excitement. She raced into the house ready to tell everyone, but quickly remembered that Cassie and Dad were at the garden center and Bettie had her dance performance midterm. Rosie was done being patient and she opened the letters, relieved to see that all of her sisters' visas had been approved. She almost left Dad's letter unread, but wanted to make sure they were sorted. And then she saw it—DENIED stamped in bright-red ink.

She scanned the letter. There was no reason listed for the denial. Nothing at all. Rosie hurried over to the phone and dialed the number on the letter, but the bloody office was closed for the day. She took a deep breath, left the house, and went straight to Dr. McLaughlin, who was puzzled by the lack of information.

A MOTHER'S GUIDE TO THE APOCALYPSE   83

"That's so strange," her wife, Rita, agreed.

Rita worked in British intelligence, though both she and Dr. McLaughlin were vague on the details. "It's boring desk work," Rita said.

But Dr. McLaughlin had on occasion mentioned that Rita was away on a work trip, and she never stopped worrying until she returned home, so Rosie assumed she did more than read spreadsheets. At least she hoped that was the case, and that Rita might be able to offer her assistance.

"What do you think it means that only Dad was rejected?" Rosie asked.

"Usually if they deny a visa, there's a reason listed. Give me a day or two and I'll make some calls," Rita promised.

Dr. McLaughlin patted her gently on the arm. "Don't worry. Nothing's final yet, and now that my Rita is on the case, you'll get answers whether you like them or not."

Rosie returned home and decided she would keep the passport nonsense to herself until it was sorted, but in her rush to leave, she left Cassie's and Bettie's visas on the counter. She quickly explained that there was an issue with Dad's but it was being handled.

"Are you sure? Maybe this is one of your signs that this trip is a mistake," Cassie said snidely.

"It's a clerical error. I'm sure of it," she said.

Two days passed. By noon on the third day, Rosie thought she might lose it. She was heading to a study session in the library when Dr. McLaughlin found her. "There's news about Sam's visa. Rita said if you want to come by later, she'll be at the flat."

Rosie didn't bother going to her study session, choosing to return to Dr. McLaughlin's home. Rita let her in. She was a serious woman and looked more so today.

"I reached out to a friend of friend in LA who worked in the New Pacific government. After the earthquake, the city went offline, and a great deal of data was lost. Police records, mortgage and housing documents seemingly vanished. But over the past few years, as the networks were rebuilt, they've been able to restore the majority of them, and they're coordinating with foreign governments to make sure we aren't allowing criminals back in their country."

"I don't understand. What does this have to do with my father?"

"Rosie, the reason your father's visa was denied is that the police want to question him…" Rita paused, as though saying the next words were too difficult.

"About what?" Rosie asked, trying to keep up.

There was a long pause. "About your mother's disappearance."

The force of Rita's words made Rosie lean back. "They think he…that he did something to Mum?"

"I don't know."

"Dad would never hurt anyone. It's not possible," she said flatly.

"I'm sure that's true. I'm just telling you what I learned."

Rosie sank back into her chair in disbelief. Rita continued, "New Pacific offered to approve the visa if your father would answer a few questions. Is that something you think he would do? Though I would be wary of doing so without legal counsel."

Rosie knew enough about the history of policing in America to know that Rita was right, but saying no could mean all of this came to a grinding halt, or worse—that she'd have to go alone. "Would it be okay if I left a message for Mel?" she asked.

"Of course. Let me know if I need to make a call and set everything up," Rita said.

Rosie smiled gratefully and, once Rita left, typed an email telling Mel she needed to speak urgently.

The next day, Rosie was back at Dr. McLaughlin's, in front of her computer, filling Mel in on what was happening.

Mel looked stricken as she listened. "I can't believe it..." She shook her head in disbelief. "It's...I mean, under the circumstances I would understand if you didn't want to come."

"No, I do. More than anything. Dad has nothing to hide. Right?" Rosie asked. She could hear the uncertainty in her voice and it made her ashamed, but it wasn't going to stop her.

"Of course not," Mel said. Mel knew Sam and Mum better than anyone, and she sounded certain.

"Then maybe we should come and get it all straightened out. I would need to find a lawyer first," Rosie said.

"I can handle that if you're sure Sam is up for it."

Was she? She had no clue what Dad was capable of. Not anymore. Rosie couldn't stop the tears welling in her eyes.

"It's all going to be okay. We're going to figure all of this out together," Mel said confidently.

"Thank you." Rosie paused. "Mel, can we keep this interview between the two of us until we get there? The family is already stressed about the travel. I don't want to add to it."

Mel raised her eyebrows, clearly surprised by Rosie's request, but she didn't push. "Whatever you think is best. I have to get back home, but I'll see you soon."

Rosie logged off and sank back in her seat. She hoped she wouldn't regret this decision. She hoped her sisters wouldn't hate her for deceiving them, but this was too important. Operation New Pacific was a go.

CASSIE

All Cassie wanted was to continue living her ordinary, uneventful life, studying, working in the greenhouse, going to the local pub for fish-and-chips with her sisters, and watching her favorite films with Dad. When she learned that Dad's visa had been denied, Cassie could barely conceal her excitement. Maybe they could forget about all of it.

But Rosie refused to give up. "I'll fix this. You'll see," she said.

Her words sounded like a threat. "What if you can't fix it?" she asked.

"Then I'll go alone. I mean it, Cassie."

Bettie sighed. "You're not going to America alone."

Cassie fought the urge to bark *traitor* at Bettie. In truth, she envied Rosie's fearlessness. All their lives, they'd functioned as a team. Now that they were almost finished with university, Rosie seemed eager to break free from the triplet bond. Cassie got the feeling that if Rosie left for California, she might be okay with staying there, and that thought made her desperately afraid. Who was she without her sisters? Without Dad? She was about to find out.

Three days later, Rosie returned home, dancing like a bloody fool, a giant grin on her face as she waved a piece of paper in the air. "Operation New Pacific is a go! Pack your bags, ladies and gent."

"Ro, what happened? How did you get it sorted?" Bettie asked.

Rosie shrugged. "Not important. Not anymore. Let's focus on getting ready for the trip."

Things moved at hyper speed after that. Cassie had to finish her own midterms, and then there was the issue of packing. Mel said temperatures in New Pacific reached over a hundred degrees Fahrenheit or thirty-seven degrees Celsius, slightly cooler in the evening.

Cassie hated the heat, and she decided she would wear as little as possible until Mel said with a gentle warning, "Bring a cover-up or two. There are still men here who think that because things went sideways in this country for a while, their dicks are meant to be worshipped, and they don't care if you disagree."

Mel must have seen the girls' looks of worry, because she quickly added with a laugh, "Don't worry. I've shot my share of dicks off, but let's not go inviting trouble."

After they hung up, Cassie turned to Rosie. "She's joking, don't you think? About the dicks? She has to be joking."

Rosie shrugged. "It's hard to tell, but if she's not, we're in good hands."

A MOTHER'S GUIDE TO THE APOCALYPSE   89

Cassie stifled a scream. They didn't even know Mel. "How can you be so calm about all this?"

Rosie looked at Cassie as though she were mental. "Because I've waited my whole life for answers about Mum. This is meant to be."

Cassie fervently disagreed, but it was useless to keep arguing. The following two days were a whirlwind. She spent hours organizing Dad's care, making sure he had enough medications for the next two weeks as well as all the paperwork the country required to transport it.

Her final task was to put together a calendar rotation for her botany classmates to care for the greenhouse, which almost did her in. She wanted everyone who was going to help out to know how important this place was: her oasis where she had spent hours, side by side with Dad, growing their food, watching her babies—which was what she called her flowers—blossom and bloom. The greenhouse was where she came when her sisters found their own passions: Rosie with debate during their school years and later her premed courses, Bettie on the stage and with Max. The greenhouse was where she would go. She had to hope that the people she'd tasked to care for it would show it the same love she had.

She tried to explain this to Bettie and Rosie, but they simply rolled their eyes. "They're plants, Cass. They'll survive for two weeks without you."

She hoped that was true. The alternative sounded unbearable.

Finally, the morning of their departure arrived. Cassie woke to find it pissing down rain. Foul weather to suit her mood, she thought. Her stomach churned and she knew coffee was a bad idea, but she drank it anyway. She found herself snapping at Bettie, who was entirely too cheerful for five o'clock in the morning, singing show tunes at the top of her lungs.

Dad was quiet but pleasant, having made peace with the trip and doing his best to help Cassie do the same. "Remember, I specialize in attitude adjustments. The tickle monster is here to destroy your bad mood," he said in the goofy voice he used when they were little as he raised his hands in mock attack.

She rolled her eyes. "Cut it out," she said sharply.

Bettie leaned over and whispered, "You can be an arsehole this whole trip, or you can remember that this could be the last trip the four of us take together and make the most of it. Your choice."

Damnit, Bettie was good. Cassie owed it to Dad to make the most of it.

At six o'clock, Max arrived to take the family to the airport, bounding out of the car with that restless energy of his. Cassie liked Max the way that you like your neighbor's overly excitable golden retriever: happy to see him but grateful he isn't yours. She could never understand what Bettie saw in him. He was average height, with average looks and an obsession with film and telly that bordered on obnoxious. Though it was an ungodly hour, Max pulled onto the motorway and launched into a mind-numbingly boring monologue on the significance of American cinema in the 1970s before eventually coming up for air. "And, Bets, you must absolutely try and see the old Hollywood sign and the Walk of Fame if they're allowing tours."

Cassie sighed. "Max, we aren't on a bloody sightseeing tour. We're..."

But she was silenced by Bettie's glare. "Go on, Max," Bettie said, and he resumed the list of places they simply had to see.

By the time Max pulled into Newcastle Airport, Cassie had already contemplated jumping out the car window if she had to hear one more filmmaking reference. She made a quick escape, with Rosie and Dad following close behind.

She had to stifle a laugh when Dad said a little too loud, "That lad could talk a glass eye to sleep."

Bettie and Max's goodbye was so embarrassingly over the top that Dad sighed deeply. "She's not going to war, son. Just across the pond. We'll be back in two weeks."

As Max pulled away, face beet-red, Cassie noticed how distraught Bettie seemed. "What is it?" she asked.

Bettie shrugged. "Max and I haven't been apart for more than a day or two in the last six years. We have no idea what to expect on this trip, so can you ease up, Cass? Please?"

Cassie was still acting like an arsehole, and she couldn't help herself. She glanced over at Dad to see how he was feeling, and he practically shouted, "If you don't stop watching me like I'm under government surveillance, I might lose my mind."

Rosie couldn't stop herself. "We're too late for that one."

A smile flashed across his face. Rosie snorted and Bettie giggled, and it broke the ice. At last, everyone exhaled. The nerves were there, but there was no turning back.

Thankfully, it was a short flight from Newcastle to London. After a brief layover, they boarded the flight to New Pacific and settled in for the six-hour journey. Dad said it used to take almost eleven hours, but thankfully the new jets were designed to travel much faster and more efficiently.

Per his doctors' instructions, Cassie gave Dad a prescription sleeping tablet. As they took off, the plane jerked and jolted. Rosie said, "Fuck it," and took one, too.

Bettie declined, said she didn't feel well, and instantly fell asleep.

Cassie didn't want to sleep. While she wasn't thrilled with this trip, she wanted to take it all in. She had no clue when she might travel again, and she wasn't going to waste the experience. She opened her spiral notebook, looked around, and began to write. She jotted notes down about the well-dressed businessmen and -women, the university students with their college sweatshirts and trainers. She was surprised by how few children were on the flight, but it made sense. The New Pacific government was not even a decade old, and while things were more stable, the high temperatures and even higher crime rates made it low on the list of places people wanted to travel.

Cassie thought how easy it must have been before the Collapse. Dad said there were no restrictions on how often you could fly, where you could go, or how long you could stay. He said when he was younger, people traveled everywhere.

Cassie understood wanderlust, and she could see it in her sisters, but everything she wanted she had in Newcastle. Once this pointless trip was over, she couldn't wait to return home.

Despite her best attempts to stay awake, the exhaustion of the last two weeks caught up to Cassie, and she drifted off.

"We are beginning our descent into beautiful Palm Springs, New Pacific."

Cassie jolted awake, wiping a sliver of drool from her mouth.

The captain continued. "Local temperature has cooled to a hundred and twelve degrees with forty percent humidity. We hope that you enjoy your time in our country."

Rosie and Bettie were awake, staring out the window as the California coastline came into view, the shimmering blue of the ocean stretching out for miles.

Seconds later, the blue was transformed into a sea of brown as ocean turned to desert. As the plane dipped lower and lower, Cassie saw hundreds of swimming pools that looked like tiny blue jewels all lined up in a row. She looked over at Dad, who appeared on the verge of tears.

"Dad...are you...What's wrong?" she asked, reaching for his hands, the rough calluses familiar and comforting.

"I didn't think I'd see this place again...It's been so long." He hesitated. "Your mum and I used to come here on holiday. First holiday ever, we came here."

Cassie and her sisters leaned in closer, surprised by Dad's sudden mention of Mum. They waited and he continued. "Drove three hours in hellish traffic, and when we got here it was over a hundred degrees and no air-conditioning in our hotel. Then there was a fire alarm at two in the morning and they evacuated us all. The next night at dinner, I had an allergic reaction to my seafood pasta and had to go to urgent care for a shot of Benadryl. It was a disaster of a weekend, but Liv never got upset or flustered. She had me laughing even when my face was the size of a balloon. I knew then I'd marry her and spend my life with her."

There was a haunted look in his eyes, a tremor in his voice that made Cassie wish they hadn't come.

As the plane made a gentle landing, everyone applauded and Cassie let out a relieved sigh. They were here. Only fourteen more days and she could forget this place ever existed.

A few minutes later, Sam and the girls gathered their stuff and stood up, waiting for the plane doors to open. An

American woman, her voice as loud as her floral blouse, gasped. "Oh my goodness, are y'all triplets?"

It seemed like everyone was staring. In Newcastle, the fascination with how alike they looked had faded years ago. Not to mention the English were not known for commenting aloud on people's appearance. They preferred to gossip in private. Cassie couldn't remember the last time someone had asked them this question, but Bettie was always ready and eager to talk to a stranger.

"We are. Identical triplets," Bettie said proudly. "Quite rare."

The woman pushed forward to get a better look. "I can't believe it. You're all so pretty. Like matching bookends."

Cassie groaned, resisting the urge to correct the lady and remind her bookends were generally sold in pairs of two, while regretting her outfit choice. They were each clad in jean shorts and white T-shirts with trainers. There were times in their lives when they made it a point not to look alike, changing their hair color or wearing distinctly different outfits (not that it made that much of a difference), but today was not that day.

The woman asked what felt like a thousand questions, forcing Sam into the conversation as he discussed how rare their birth was, and how lucky he was.

"Your mama must be so proud," she said.

Cassie and her sisters froze. Sam wore a somber expression on his face but played along. "She most certainly is."

Mercifully, the plane doors opened and passengers began to file out. Cassie hoped any attention would end once they got off the plane, but that did not happen.

Everyone noticed them.

The pilot said as they left the airplane, "Look out, it's triple trouble."

In the line for the bathroom, three teenage girls asked the same questions as the woman on the plane. The exact same questions.

Next, the baggage claim clerks wanted to say hi to the "clones," which Cassie found insulting. She had never experienced anything like this, and neither had her sisters.

"I feel like we're at the zoo, but we're the animals," Bettie whispered.

Sam chuckled. "This was how your mum and I felt when you were babies. Couldn't walk three feet without getting stopped."

"Must have driven you mad," Rosie said as they slowly made their way toward the giant sign that read IMMIGRATION AND CUSTOMS.

"Sometimes when we were in a hurry or you girls were in a bad mood, it bothered me. But mostly I felt proud. Our girls made people happy. What could be wrong with that?"

Cassie smiled, relieved that Dad was still in a good mood of his own. She hoped it would last, but she worried that the more tired, hot, and hungry he got, the less likely it was.

A MOTHER'S GUIDE TO THE APOCALYPSE   97

As the four of them headed toward the luggage claim, Cassie took in how different things were from back home. It wasn't simply the military-like security guards stationed all over, dressed in black and carrying giant automatic weapons. It was the dullness of their surroundings. Mel had told them light colors were best for the desert temperatures, but she had expected something tropical, not dreary shades of white and gray.

Everyone's voices were loud, but there was also a sense of unease, mistrustful gazes on their faces, and the hurried way everyone moved as though trouble were coming.

The biggest shock, though, was the technology on display. There were robots everywhere; they'd been designed to look vaguely human, but the effect was mostly disturbing. They were doing a variety of tasks: cleaning, scanning passports. There was even a robot woman standing by providing directions. Dad shook his head in disgust. "These damn things nearly destroyed us all, and the Yanks can't let it go."

This had been Dad and Granny's favorite topic, the downfall of America. They would talk nonstop about how foreign governments, including Britain, cracked down on artificial intelligence, but America considered themselves above it all and went all-in.

"This country always acted like the smartest kid in the room. They wanted to innovate, and they innovated themselves right into the scrap heap. Using all that AI energy, which increased the speed of climate change. And then the AI allowed hackers to infiltrate the voting systems, which caused chaos in their elections and led to the second insurrection, which was the beginning of the end of the 'United States.' Such rubbish."

Despite Dad's distaste for technology, Cassie could understand the appeal of robots doing certain tasks. If she were in charge, she imagined it would be nice not to have to deal with her employees' moods and inane questions, but it made her sad to think of all the people who lost their livelihoods and eventually their lives because leaders relied on these machines. Because they forgot the humans were crucial to preserving humanity.

"Pay attention, dumb-dumb," Rosie teased Cassie as she pointed to one of the few actual humans staffing the medical station.

All New Pacific visitors were required to undergo a medical scan; the results determined if you were able to stay. If you were found to have a serious illness, you were sent back to your homeland. "God forbid tourists get free health care," Dad said. Cassie knew it was silly to hope they'd find something, but a part of her still hoped they could get back on a plane and return home.

Cassie, Dad, and Rosie breezed through the medical scanners, but Bettie took ages. Cassie was starting to worry, but when Bettie emerged, she offered a false smile. "Sorry for the holdup," she said.

A MOTHER'S GUIDE TO THE APOCALYPSE 99

"Are you okay? What was that all about?" Rosie asked.

Bettie shrugged. "They had questions about my heart condition. I explained that it's not an issue, but they're quite thorough."

Cassie had almost forgotten about Bettie's heart troubles, it was all so long ago. When they were born at twenty-nine weeks, doctors detected a hole in Bettie's heart that needed immediate surgery to patch it. Thankfully, the procedure went smoothly, and from then on she had no other issues.

"You're sure you're okay?" Cassie asked.

"I'm here, aren't I?" Bettie snapped, but Cassie could see that Bettie's hands were trembling and her complexion was pale. She almost called her out. It would be easy enough. Despite Bettie's stellar acting skills onstage, she was by far the worst liar of the three of them.

But by now they'd reached passport inspection, the last stop before they officially arrived in New Pacific. There were dozens more robots standing in front of an automated gate. The last thing Cassie wanted to do was hold up the line of people. She would have to wait until later to grill Bettie.

She stepped up to the first robot. "Welcome to New Pacific, Cassandra Clark. Please scan your documents."

Cassie startled, trying not to feel unsettled by the fact that this machine knew her name. Dad talked a lot about facial recognition software and how dangerous it had been for governments and bad actors to have that information.

The longer she was here, the more she missed the analog world of Newcastle and ached to go home. A part of her wanted to turn right back around and book the next flight back to the UK. Instead she passed through the gate and waited as Rosie and Bettie went through a similar process. All three of them stood on the other side of the gate waiting for Dad. As he scanned his passport, bright-red lights began to flash and an alarm sounded. Guards seemed to appear from everywhere, all of them surrounding Sam with guns drawn. "Are you a citizen of what was formerly known as the United States?" a red-faced guard barked.

Sam looked stricken. The guard shouted again. "I asked you a question."

"I left two decades ago. I was born in England, and our family returned home before the Collapse."

The guard's eyes narrowed. "I think you meant to say *the redemption of this country.*"

Cassie winced. She remembered that some Americans didn't love the term *Collapse*. Many considered the event a rebirth.

"Come with us," the guard barked.

"Come with you? Where? I don't understand," Sam said.

Cassie could see the confusion and fear on his face, and she wanted to burst through the gate and drag him to the other side. Her heart was racing. "What do you mean he has to go with you? Why are you taking him?" she shouted, not caring who heard her.

"Please, what is this all about?" Sam pleaded.

"You're wanted for questioning in a missing persons investigation. For the disappearance of your wife, Olivia Clark."

Rosie gasped. "You can't do this. He's got an interview in two days. It's all been arranged with his lawyer," Rosie said.

Cassie whirled around, her face a mixture of rage and betrayal. "You *knew* about this? You knew and you let Dad come here?"

Bettie started to cry. It seemed as though the whole airport was watching their nightmare unfold. Sam looked pale and fragile, but he gave the girls a stern look. "Don't worry, my loves. This is all a big misunderstanding. I'll see you soon."

Cassie shook her head. "Dad, don't say a word until you speak to a lawyer. Please."

Today had been a good day. One of Dad's best, but there was no way to know how long it would last. What if he lost his temper like he so often did? What would the guards do then? As they led him toward an unmarked door, he glanced back with his trademark *we've got this* look.

Then he was gone.

"You have to move on," the official barked.

The girls startled in unison, like deer being shooed away. They headed through the security gates toward baggage claim. Rosie cleared her throat, trying to find her voice. "We need to find Mel. She'll help us. It'll all be okay."

Cassie heard the uncertainty. She had been angry with Rosie before, but this was something different. Right now, she hated her. Cassie grabbed Rosie's arm and squeezed. She needed her sister to hear her. To really listen this time.

"You better hope Mel is the savior you think she is, because if something happens to Dad, I will never forgive you."

ROSIE

There's always a solution. That was Dad's mantra. No matter what went wrong, he had a fix. A massive snowstorm wipes out power for two months? No problem. Dad just jerry-rigged a generator, which was able to keep all their food frozen. He built a campfire in the garden, where he grilled kebabs and roasted marshmallows. That winter was brutally cold, but Rosie only remembered how much fun they all had.

Then there was the time in year seven when Rosie got in trouble for fighting with Peter Gilroy, the snotty boy who relentlessly bullied Bettie, knowing she wouldn't fight back. Instead of getting mad, Dad organized a meeting with the boy's parents to discuss it. Later that night he returned home. "That boy's parents are both arseholes. If he messes with any of you girls again, you have my permission to knock him upside the head."

Which was what she kept trying to tell Cassie and Bettie as they hurried toward the airport exit in search of Mel. They would find a solution. Of course Rosie understood that her sisters were upset that she misled them about Dad's interview. She was upset, too. She didn't have *get Dad arrested* on her New Pacific to-do list.

She tried to say as much, but Cassie held up her hand and hissed, "No one wants to hear your pathetic excuses. Shut up."

Rosie looked to Bettie for help, but her sister gave her a disapproving nod. Rosie could handle Cassie's rage, but Bettie's quiet fury was disconcerting. She was trying to find the right words to make them understand, but the instant they stepped out of the terminal, a wall of heat slammed into them. All three girls staggered backward in shock.

"What in the hell?" Cassie asked.

The air was so hot and heavy, it literally stole your breath.

"I don't think human beings are meant to survive at this temperature," Bettie said, frantically waving her hand in front of her face as if it might cool her. Which it did not. It seemed like nothing would. For a brief moment, Rosie wanted to strip off her clothes to keep cool, but then she worried that the heat might physically blister her skin.

Rosie knew from the classes she had taken on evolution that over the years human beings adapted to extreme climates, their bodies developing physiological mechanisms to survive. There were countless examples, ranging from Siberian explorers gaining weight to adapt to the cold to residents of Malaysia, whose bodies had evolved to better regulate heat through sweat patterns. But for three girls from the north of England, this kind of heat was unprecedented.

Everyone around them seemed unbothered, though no

one stayed in place too long. She also noticed more guards stationed at each of the terminal doors, dressed in the same sheer ivory clothing, their black automatic weapons a stark contrast with the light fabrics.

The heat left her feeling dizzy and unsettled. She scanned the parking lot for Mel. Between the heat and her sisters' death glares, Rosie wasn't sure she was going to survive.

"Girls, hello! I'm here. Woo-hoo."

Rosie turned to see a woman at the end of the terminal waving at them. With her short gray braids and flowing white dress, Mel was impossible not to notice. She had a giant purple paisley satchel hung over one shoulder and moved toward them with purpose.

Rosie was surprised at how striking Mel was, but that wasn't all she noticed. Mel didn't have legs...or at the very least she didn't have her original legs. The ones she had now were a metallic silver, glinting in the bright sun. On her robot feet she wore two purple shoes the exact color of her handbag. She moved with ease and seemed to attract almost as much attention as the three of them. It wasn't her legs as much as her sheer presence. Rosie imagined that was how people had treated British royalty before the monarchy fell. An undeniable force that made everyone pay attention to her.

She reached them and gestured to her legs with a wry grin. "Didn't mean to surprise you. It's a hard thing to bring up in casual conversation. Like, *Hey, nice to meet you. Guess what? I have no legs.*"

"How did...I mean, what happened?" Rosie asked, genuinely curious.

"Mother Nature is one nasty bitch. Parting gift from the last big quake. Took everything, even my legs. But we're the lucky ones. We got out alive. A lotta folks didn't."

Rosie had seen images of the Great Quake in books and on TV programs documenting the Collapse, and reminded herself there hadn't been a quake in years. She hoped it stayed that way.

"Thankfully, it hasn't slowed me down," Mel said. She reached into her bag and handed Rosie and each of her sisters a small electronic fan and a pill case. "This heat is a real bitch. These are hydration tablets. You'll need to take them three times a day. They're designed to make you metabolize water quicker, which you'll need to survive these temps. The fans have a water setting."

She pressed a button, and cold water misted Rosie in the face. After a brief shock at the cold spray, Rosie found that the water felt great. She wasn't sure she would ever turn hers off.

Mel, meantime, was staring at them in disbelief. "I can't get over how grown-up you girls are. You were so little the last time I saw you."

"Okay, I'm sorry, but can we table the trip down memory lane until we figure out what the hell is going on with Dad?" Cassie's cursing startled Mel. Bettie put her hand on Cassie's shoulder, but she shook it off.

"What's wrong with Sam?" Mel asked, her smile instantly fading.

"They detained him. Said they had questions about Mum," Rosie said, her voice shakier than she wanted it to be.

Cassie took a breath, fighting back her tears. "Auntie Mel," she said mockingly, "you need to fix this. Right fucking now."

"I swear to Christ this was dealt with," Mel said.

Cassie's eyes flashed. "I still can't believe you and Rosie plotted to get Dad here, knowing this could happen. Knowing that he isn't well. What's wrong with you?"

"You need to show my mother a little respect or we're going to have a big fucking problem."

Startled by the deep baritone voice, Rosie and her sisters spun around to see a man towering over them. He wasn't much older than them, maybe mid-twenties, but he was massive, at least six foot five, hair cropped short. Despite the heat, he wore all black, which made him stand out in the sea of neutrals. Mel took in his expression of disapproval and wagged a finger at him.

"Don't listen to Dominic. My son wants everyone to think he's a tough guy, but he's a mushy-gushy teddy bear."

He rolled his eyes so hard, Rosie thought they might fall out of his head. There was something dangerous and unsettling about him. Mel had mentioned her son, but Rosie had been so consumed with learning about her mum, she hadn't asked any questions about him.

Add another checkmark to the regret column, she thought.

"Mama, this isn't right. I told you—" he began, as though they weren't there.

"Don't start, Dom. I understand why Cassie is upset. Rosie suggested that we keep Sam's interview quiet, and I went along with it because I wanted to see you girls. But let's keep it real. Your father didn't help the cause by disappearing right after Liv went missing. I imagine they want to get it all figured out. So do I."

Rosie flinched, feeling slightly betrayed by Mel calling her out and annoyed at her for making it seem like Dad might be guilty of wrongdoing. If Mel thought she was going to win over Cassie by tossing Rosie or Dad under the bus, she was wrong. Cassie might be the most stubborn of the sisters, but she was also loyal to the end. Mel would have to do more than that to get in her good graces. So would Rosie, for that matter.

"We don't have time for the blame game. I'm going inside to get this figured out. Dom, take the girls to the RV and we'll meet you there," Mel ordered.

Dominic looked like he wanted to protest, but Mel shot him a look so withering, he went silent. Cassie, on the other hand, wasn't having it, arms crossed in protest. "I'm not leaving here without Dad," Cassie said.

"Darling girl, of course not. My friend Victor is one of the best lawyers in the country. I'll get him on the phone and we'll bust your daddy out of here. Don't worry. We'll be on the road in no time. We need to get back home before it gets too late and the vultures descend."

Maybe it was the heat or the exhaustion or the stress of

Sam's detainment, but Rosie had questions. What kind of vultures lived in Palm Springs? Or were they figurative, and if so, what did that mean? There was no time to ask. Mel was already heading inside.

Dominic snapped his fingers to get their attention. "Come on, let's go," he barked as he reached for Rosie's and Bettie's suitcases.

Cassie grabbed hers before he could take it. "I can carry my own luggage."

"Suit yourself. It's a twenty-minute walk in hundred-and-twelve-degree heat."

The regret on Cassie's face was instant. If Rosie wasn't so exhausted, she might have laughed, but she was already in enough trouble with her sister.

As Dominic began walking, Rosie gasped, spotting the handgun he had holstered. Bettie and Cassie saw it, too. All three of them stopped and locked eyes, a simultaneous and silent *What the fuck?* Dad called it their triplet language, the way they communicated things without ever uttering a word.

"Are the Brits hard of hearing? I said let's move," Dominic snapped.

"Not until you tell us why you have a gun?" Cassie asked.

"Because people do bad things here, and this ensures I can stop them from trying to do those bad things to us," he said, speaking slowly as though they were small children.

"Bad things?" Bettie squeaked. "What kind of bad things?"

"Jesus, I told Mom you needed to know what this place was like before you came here, but she didn't listen. Now you're here, so I need you to pay attention. This is not a safe place. Not only that, but the three of you are bound to attract the kind of attention no one wants."

"What does that mean?" Cassie said.

"It means you need to move your asses before some degenerates decide they want to take one or all of you and make you their wives... or worse."

Rosie wasn't sure what was worse, but she sure as hell wasn't going to find out. She started walking. As Dominic picked up all the bags, even Cassie didn't protest as they trailed him. Dominic kept his voice low, his instructions short and clipped.

"Don't make eye contact with anyone. Don't stop and talk to anyone. If they ask for money or food, or if they have a child with them, ignore them. If someone asks where you live or where you're staying, say nothing. If they push the issue, I'll step in, but we don't want them to push the issue."

Rosie wondered why Mel hadn't mentioned any of this, but it didn't matter now. They were here. She reached out for Bettie's hand and was relieved when she squeezed it. Rosie didn't dare grab Cassie's hand, but Bettie did, the three of them walking side by side.

Now she could feel it. All eyes on them. She wasn't sure if it was the triplet factor or something more sinister. All she knew was that she had gotten her sisters into this, and she would do whatever she had to do to protect them. Whatever it took.

SAM

His girls would come for him. Sam was sure of that. The question was, *When?* He wasn't sure how much time had passed since the guards led him through a maze of drab fluorescent hallways and deposited him in this hot, airless room. There was no air-conditioning. No fans, no moving air of any kind. Every breath was a struggle, as though his lungs were a wet rag someone was squeezing.

Sam knew that if he didn't eat something and take his meds soon, his blood pressure would skyrocket. They had to know that, didn't they? Unless they didn't care?

He'd asked the guard who brought him here how long he would be here, but the man had said nothing, just shoved Sam into the boxlike room and slammed the door. They'd given him nothing.

No water.

No phone.

No details about his detainment.

He shifted in his seat, relieved, when at last the metal door swung open. Sam watched as a different beefy guard in a tan uniform entered. "I'm Officer Stanley from the

New Pacific Security Council," he said, giving Sam a dismissive glance.

The kid...everyone seemed like a kid these days, but this kid couldn't have been older than twenty-five. He was not a looker, that was for sure, with squinty eyes and puffed-up cheeks. Sam never remembered names anymore, didn't bother asking since he couldn't retain them. Instead, he used nicknames to keep people sorted. This was now Officer Blowfish.

"What is the New Pacific Security Council, and what am I doing here?" Sam asked, trying to summon a sense of authority in his voice.

The officer glared at him and launched into a scripted answer. "Before New Pacific's rebirth, there were hundreds of thousands of people who disappeared. While we assume some died of natural causes, many were victims of violent crimes. The president of New Pacific has made it a priority that we capture and prosecute any criminals in our midst."

He stared at Sam with disgust, as though he could tell he was rotten without him speaking. Sweat trickled down Sam's face, but he forced himself not to wipe it or look away to avoid looking guilty.

"You know there's no statute of limitations on murder, Mr. Clark. That's why we're here."

Murder? They thought he was a murderer.

"That's not...Olivia...Liv wasn't murdered."

"Oh really? Then would you care to tell us where she is?"

A MOTHER'S GUIDE TO THE APOCALYPSE   113

Sam blinked furiously. So much about those frantic final days in California was a blank. But the big life stuff he could recall with startling clarity. From that first instant when Liv ran into the bedroom, a pregnancy test in hand, screaming, "We did it. We made a baby"; to the two of them sitting in the doctor's office, hearing the ultrasound technician telling them there were not one, not two, but three babies; to hearing his girls' cries.

"I think I need a lawyer," Sam said softly. Officer Blowfish laughed.

"That's not how this works here."

Sam swallowed hard. How did it work?

"What the fuck happened to your wife?"

Sam didn't know. If he could go back in time, he would have paid closer attention, but Liv's desire to prepare for any emergency had seemed completely rational at first.

Sure, more and more Amazon packages began to arrive, but they were practical items. Flashlights and batteries. Matches and fire blankets. They'd just bought their home, and Liv had all sorts of facts and figures about the items required to keep them safe. She had always been the more practical of the two of them, so who was he to argue? He dutifully organized her purchases in the garage, with labels so they could find the things they needed.

Then one day he came home from a golf tournament in Palmdale to find thirty five-gallon water bottles stacked outside the garage. There was so much water, he could no longer fit his SUV in the garage. When he asked Liv about it, she got snippy, eyes flashing with annoyance, voice turned shrill.

"Samuel..." She also used his full name, which he hated even more. "Samuel, street parking is in abundance here, but one day water won't be. I won't let our babies suffer."

"Oh, because I was hoping they'd really suffer," he said, trying to make a joke. It did not go over well.

"I'm sorry, Sam, but one of us has to be a grown-up," Liv said.

She'd never once insulted him, but now every time he turned around she was making him feel useless. And then Joey came along, and the deliveries and her obsession continued.

When twelve gallons of oats arrived, Sam said nothing, choosing to keep the peace by making space in the already overflowing garage. He wanted to maintain the life they had, the trips to the park and family dinners, the wine and game nights with friends, the movie premieres and week-end getaways to Santa Barbara. Challenging Liv on any-thing, but especially anything that might affect the girls, only caused more fights. He told himself it was for the greater good not to rock the boat. In the end, it capsized anyway.

But he couldn't tell Officer Blowfish that. What did this man-child know about the pressures they felt back then to protect their families? He couldn't possibly understand how much Sam suffered watching his wife transform right before his eyes.

"Mr. Clark, I'm not going to ask again." Officer Blowfish was snapping his fingers in his face now. "You took your kids across the world knowing that your wife was missing, but you never even filed a missing persons report. Why was that?"

It wasn't an easy answer. Certainly not one that made Sam look good. They'd had a fight. Sam was angry, but so was Liv. What he'd done was unforgivable. He knew that. It was a marvel, he used to think, how you could love someone so much and still want to hurt them. To shut them up. To punish them the way they'd punished you. He wanted to do all that the day Olivia disappeared. But he hadn't. He'd let her go. He'd let her walk out of the house. Hadn't he?

As his brain played tricks on him, making him forget, making his words and world hazy, he knew how it all looked, and while he didn't know how this country had changed, he had a sense that the criminal justice system hadn't improved in the passing years.

After that night, Liv never returned.

Sam waited three days.

Three frightful, agonizing days.

Three days of toddlers begging for Mummy. Asking for Mummy. Wondering where Mummy had gone and why she wasn't coming back.

"We want hugs and kisses," they begged.

Sam fought with Lucas, Liv's little brother, who immediately began hurtling accusations at him. "This is your fault. You two have been arguing for months. There's gotta be a reason she left." Later Lucas said, "I know the reason. I know what you did."

He said he knew that Sam had a temper. Which was true. Sam had always been a hothead. He'd gotten into big fights with Liv over Joey and the damn prepping, but he would never hurt her.

Still, Lucas couldn't let it go. "I don't think the girls are safe with you. I think the cops should know what's going on here."

Sam lost it. He told Lucas to get the fuck out of his house, almost tossed him out, which hadn't helped the accusation that he had a temper. But if Liv wasn't there, if she wasn't coming home, then he sure wasn't going to let her low-life pot-smoking wannabe-musician brother threaten to take his children. Or threaten him at all.

After another week of searching for Liv, asking Mel and all her friends if they'd seen or heard from her after the terrible flood in Laurel Canyon shattered the city, Sam made a decision. He put the house on the market, organized a realtor to coordinate the sale, and went online and bought four plane tickets to London Heathrow without telling anyone. Not his boss at the golf club or the clients whom he'd spent a decade coaching, not his closest friends, and certainly not

Mel. He simply gathered the passports Liv had organized for them during her prepping and left. Across an ocean, and a lifetime away from their old life.

Sam expected someone to look for them, a phone call or an email or something, but the political uprising began six weeks later, and then—as though Mother Nature had been waiting for a sign—the dramatic weather events escalated, one after another, destroying whole cities and towns. No one cared about a British bloke and his triplets when the world was collapsing.

"Goddamnit, I want answers," Officer Blowfish said, shouting and stamping about.

Sam opened his mouth, fragments of that final fight with Liv still unspooling in his mind. "I loved my wife." His voice cracked.

"Fantastic. We need more than your word."

Officer Blowfish was in his face now, asking about Liv again, spittle spraying Sam's cheeks. Sam shifted back, wondering how long it would be before this man's fist connected with his face.

He got a reprieve in the form of pounding on the door, a sound so loud and sudden he almost fell out of his chair. The door swung open and a blast of cool air rushed in. Sam gripped his seat to steady himself, soaking up the cool breeze.

A stern-looking woman in the same tan uniform as Blowfish pointed to Sam, her eyes flashing. "He's done. Cut him loose," she barked.

"What? We just got started," Blowfish said, his cheeks reddening.

"Not anymore. I said he's done."

"So this fucker just gets to walk? I thought someone from LA was coming for him."

"I did, too, but they said to cut him loose." The stern woman tapped Sam on the shoulder. "C'mon, Gramps, move it."

Stern Face snapped her fingers at Sam, and he wondered what it was about these people and their snapping. Perhaps manners had died along with their country?

He almost said that, but now that he was free, he wasn't going to push his luck.

Stern Face led him through the maze of hallways and toward an exit door. If it was possible, the heat was worse here. Sam remembered the babymoon he took with Liv to Palm Springs; it was hot then, but this was a different heat altogether.

As he emerged through the exit doors toward the back of what he assumed was the airport, Sam spotted a giant silver RV idling near the exit. "Your ride's there, Gramps," Stern Face said before she slipped back inside.

Before he'd made it a few feet, he saw Rosie and Bettie racing toward him. Tears fell as his girls wrapped their arms around him.

Rosie kept saying, "I'm sorry, Dad. I'm so sorry."

He didn't know why she was sorry. "It's all right, my loves. I'm as good as new."

After a moment he heard a voice that stopped him in his tracks. "Sammy, Sam, Sam, it's good to see your face."

He looked up to see Mel and froze. He knew she would be here, but he thought she would look different. Wrinkled and stooped over. Old like him. Instead here she stood, tall and proud, her face lined but still beautiful.

For a moment, rage washed over him as he thought about the things she had done, all the ways in which she had gotten between him and Liv, but then it was gone and Sam stepped away from his daughters and rushed into Mel's arms. "I missed you," he whispered.

He didn't think about the girls or the past or anything else, he just pulled Mel into his arms and kissed her as if she were the only person who mattered.

r/SoCalValleyPreppers

7,500 Members

Mamabear3

Good Lord how does anyone do all this? I've been reading over all the prepping stuff and it's a full-time job. I already work sixty hours a week plus being a mom to my girls. When do you have time to do all this?

GoJoe420

Like my mama says "slow your roll." Prepping isn't something you're ever really done with. It's a way of life.

Valle4ever

Start small and keep going. It'll add up over time.

Mamabear3

I hear you. I just don't want to get caught flat footed. My girls are relying on me.

GoJoe420

you're already ahead of the game. And we're here to help u.

Mamabear3

Y'all are too kind. Gonna get my ass off here and check some more items off my list.

BETTIE

They were all stunned by the kiss. Everyone, it seemed, but Mel. She lingered in Sam's embrace for a moment, her eyes bright. "It's good to see you, Sammy. There's so much to catch up on, but we should get this show on the road."

Cassie stopped her. "So that's it? It's all sorted out?"

Mel paused. "They said they may want to speak to him again, but this time they'll do it through my attorney. It'll be fine."

Bettie was about to lose it. "So Dad isn't in the clear?"

"Not yet, but I'm working on it. My lawyer will call us later to discuss."

"See there, Bets, it's being handled," Rosie said.

Bettie wanted to believe that, but something about the lack of urgency in Mel made her uncomfortable. It didn't help that Bettie's head ached from the heat and the travel and the unknown of it all, not to mention the news she'd gotten at the airport. And what the hell was that kiss all about?

She watched as Dominic moved toward Dad. "Bet you don't remember me, Mr. Clark," he said.

Dad's brow furrowed, his answer clear: He had no clue who Dominic was.

"I'm Mel's son. Dominic."

"Dom? Little Dom. You're a bloody giant now."

"Heard that a few times. Got my father's height, or so I've been told."

Sam reached out to shake his hand. "Good to see you."

"It's good to see you, too. You must be thirsty. Let's get you something cold to drink."

"He needs food, too, or it'll mess with his blood sugar."

"You heard the boss," Dad said with a laugh.

"We've got plenty of snacks in the RV," Dominic said.

Bettie was surprised at how soft and gentle Dominic seemed now, completely different from the man who had greeted them.

"Got any lager? A cold lager would be lovely," Dad asked.

Bettie turned to look at Cassie, expecting an hour-long lecture about the dangers of mixing Dad's medications with booze, but Cassie was still focused on Dad's detainment.

"Dad, are you really okay? What did the police say? What were they asking you exactly?"

Before Dad could answer, Mel intervened. "Let's discuss all of that once we're safely back at the compound. We really do need to get moving."

She gestured toward the giant vehicle. As Bettie climbed in, Mel caught her gaze and lowered her voice in a conspiratorial manner. "I imagine that kiss was surprising. It's ancient history, but your father and I had a brief fling before he met your mom. I'm sure he's confused."

Dad and Mel had a fling? Why hadn't she mentioned this before? That was odd, wasn't it? More important, what else was she keeping secret? The pit in Bettie's stomach seemed to expand, but she was too tired to ask more questions. She headed toward the back and took a seat on the sofa bench. Her sisters fanned out and found other spots.

"Dom, put the pedal to the metal. I wanna be close to home before that damn sun sets," Mel called out as she settled in a front seat next to Sam and Cassie.

There was a silent exchange between mother and son, something Bettie was familiar with, the ways a family communicates wordlessly.

She was already on edge after Dominic's outburst outside the airport, and this did nothing to soothe her nerves. She shifted in her seat, still unable to wrap her head around when to tell her sisters her news. She couldn't imagine it going over well, but it wasn't right to be upset at Rosie for deceiving them and then do the same. She knew that once she told them the truth, everything would change, and she wasn't ready for it. Not with things already so uncertain.

The RV rumbled to a start as Dominic expertly navigated the giant vehicle out of the airport parking lot and onto the deserted highway. Mel and Dad had settled across from each other in the booth, beers open in front of them.

Rosie sat grinning foolishly while Cassie glared at her, shooting worried glances at Dad like she was his personal guard dog.

Bettie stared out the window, amazed at how the sun seemed so close that she could reach out and touch it. The sky was such a brilliant blue, it didn't seem quite real. But the beauty couldn't erase the uneasiness that had gripped her since they arrived. Dad kissing Mel like they were long-lost lovers. Rosie's inexcusable lie, and now her own news. She wasn't quite sure how she was going to handle any of it.

As they headed down the motorway, Bettie spotted what seemed like hundreds of people traveling in giant packs. They carried tents and backpacks as they slowly ambled down the dusty strip of road. Bettie studied them: all faces, shapes, and sizes. From small babies and their mums to elderly women. There weren't as many men, at least not young ones, and everyone wore looks of deep suffering.

"Who are all those people? Where are they going?" Rosie asked as the RV sped by them.

"Climate refugees," Mel said. "A lot of people opted not to settle in one place after the Collapse, especially not in the cities. They're a new generation of nomads."

"It seems dangerous walking in this heat," Bettie said, her eyes lingering on a mother, a tiny baby strapped to her chest.

"It is. Lots of 'em die out here due to the temperatures,

but it's not safe in the outlying areas so they keep moving. Unfortunately, these areas aren't as well policed since the real concentration of wealth and resources remains in the cities," Mel explained.

"And the exploitation of most of the people," Dominic said under his breath.

"Don't get him started. That is why we prefer the boonies. It's not fancy out here, but we mind our own business and do our best to keep one another safe," Mel said.

Bettie watched the refugees in horror as she blinked away tears wondering how that baby would survive the temperatures. She looked over to see Rosie watching her and looked away. She didn't need Rosie trying to make amends now. But of course that's exactly what Rosie wanted. She scooted next to Bettie and put her hand on hers. "I'm sorry about what I did, but it seemed like the only way."

This was classic Rosie. Apologize and then immediately ruin the apology by negating it with why you weren't actually sorry. "What you did was wrong. I need to hear you say that."

Rosie was quiet for a minute. She sighed. "You're right. I'm sorry. I owe Cass and Dad an apology, too."

Bettie couldn't believe it. Maybe hell was freezing over? Or maybe Rosie recognized the seriousness of the situation? "I know you think Mel is great, but we should be careful. We don't know her. Or her past with Dad or Mum. Which that kiss clearly demonstrated."

"I know. I do. But let's get settled, and then we'll figure out what's going on. We don't have to rush this."

Bettie stiffened. They were supposed to be back in the UK in two weeks. Of course there was a rush, especially for Bettie now that she'd gotten such life-changing news. She wondered if this was the moment to come clean. Rosie would take it the hardest, so she could start with her. Rip the Band-Aid off. "Rosie, there's something you should know…"

Bettie's words were drowned out by the violent screech of metal against metal as her entire body jolted forward. Bettie wasn't sure if the scream that came next came from her or one of her sisters.

She glanced behind her and saw a giant red pickup truck, half a dozen men in balaclavas sitting in the back.

Bettie gasped as Rosie, always her protector, reached for her. In the front of the RV, Cassie and Dad held on to each other.

Mel seemed unfazed as she stood, her balance remarkable as the truck slammed into them again. "Buckle up and hang on," she shouted.

"What's happening?" Dad asked.

Mel didn't answer, just inched her way toward the back of the RV.

Cassie pointed to Dad's seat belt. "Dad, you heard her. Buckle up."

He did as she asked. Seconds later they were struck again. Everyone fastened their seat belts except for Mel, who kept moving, silver legs clanging against the metal of the seats. She wobbled but stayed upright.

"Mama, you okay?" Dominic called out.

Bettie could see Dominic gripping the steering wheel as the RV picked up speed. It seemed dangerous for this giant vehicle to be traveling at such high speeds, but Dominic seemed equally unbothered.

"Right as rain, sugar," she said as she reached the back of the RV.

"What's happening?" Rosie shouted.

"Bunch of road pirates trying to take something that's not theirs. Don't worry. We've got it handled."

Bettie recalled Dominic's warning about the three of them being targets. Were they what these men wanted? To Bettie's shock, Mel pulled out a large pistol from a compartment in the rear of the RV.

She opened one of the small back windows. "Dom, honey, keep it steady."

With unwavering precision, Mel fired three expert shots, the truck's tires exploding upon impact. The driver desperately tried to maintain control, but the truck spun 360 degrees before it landed in a ditch.

Bettie looked over at her sisters, all of them equally dumbfounded. Sam shook his head in stunned disbelief. "Mel, you've lost your bloody mind."

But Bettie clocked a hint of approval...maybe even admiration.

Mel laughed as she calmly placed the gun back in the compartment and headed back toward her seat. "We've all had to adapt to our circumstances, Samuel."

Bettie's heart was racing, hand on her stomach, a gnawing sense of fear she could no longer escape.

This wasn't at all what she'd imagined when she came here, and she wanted to leave. Right this minute. She wanted to land at Newcastle Airport and rush to Max's flat. She wanted to knock on his door and watch him wrap his arms around her. She wanted him to make her favorite shepherd's pie and put on *The Sound of Music*, her favorite musical, and pretend this trip had never happened. But then she remembered the way he shook his head, his brown hair flopping over his eyes. "I don't think this is a good idea. Don't let Rosie bully you into going."

Rosie hadn't forced her to come. Bettie was a grown woman. She came here on her own. Besides, regret was pointless. They were here now. She wanted answers about Mum, and this was the only way to get them.

But all Bettie could think about was that truck hitting them. The power of it. The look of hatred in the driver's eyes. Why would he hate them? Bettie tried her deep breathing, the technique she'd learned after Granny died. Six, three, nine had been on her daily rotation, but she couldn't stop the hyperventilating that followed.

The tears came next. A steady flow until she was sobbing. Bettie had always been the most sensitive in the

A MOTHER'S GUIDE TO THE APOCALYPSE 129

family. The one who cried over sad movies. The one who cried at TV weddings and funerals. The one who couldn't go to Granny's funeral because she couldn't stop crying and didn't want to ruin the service. The one her sisters could make cry by simply looking at her. She hated it, hated that she couldn't seem to control her emotions. It was also what made her a good performer, but damnit, now she couldn't stop. Before long, both Cassie and Rosie were beside her.

"Bettie Spaghetti, it's going to be okay," Rosie whispered. Cassie stroked her hair. "We've got you, Bets. It's been a long day and you haven't eaten. You always get sad when you're hungry."

It was true, but now she was too nauseous to eat. She leaned into her sisters. She loved how they knew her better than anyone. No matter how hard he tried, even Max would never be as close to her. Which was why she felt so guilty keeping this secret. The thought of lying to her sisters only made her cry harder.

Cassie began singing first. Rosie joined in.

"Oh my Mama told me there'll be days like this."

Dad's favorite Van Morrison song. Bettie's favorite song. She let her sisters hold her and sing to her, and despite her best intentions, Bettie drifted off to sleep.

It wasn't until Rosie nudged her that Bettie stirred. "Wake up, Bets. You have to see this."

Bettie bolted upright. They were in a massive forest with dozens of trees covered in fairy lights. Bettie watched as

Dominic navigated the giant RV through what looked like trees. When the breeze blew, however, she could see that giant sheets of leaves had been sewn together to create a kind of camouflage. "We built our own little optical illusion. A way to keep out potential intruders. Or at least to give us time to prepare," Mel said.

Bettie wondered what kind of intruders she was talking about. More people like the ones they'd encountered on the road?

"We've been here almost fifteen years now, and things are mostly secure, but you can never be too careful. After the Collapse, people lost their minds, and the violence was..." Mel trailed off, her expression distant. "I prefer the quiet to the chaos of the cities. Who would have thought that when I bought this place for a weekend getaway, it would be our salvation. We're a small group. It's me and Dom, and an actor friend, Eduardo, and his husband, Mark. We're entirely self-sufficient, all of us living and working on the compound. I'll show you how it all works tomorrow."

Bettie didn't want a tour of Mel's compound. She wanted to know what the plan was to find information about their mother after all this time—not to mention figuring out what the authorities wanted with Dad. They'd let him go, so it couldn't be that serious, but something told her it wasn't over.

Dominic stopped and parked the RV beside two massive golf carts.

A MOTHER'S GUIDE TO THE APOCALYPSE   131

Mel stood up. "Dom will deliver everyone's bags later. Cassie, Rosie, and Sam, you can ride with Dom. Bettie, why don't you ride with me?"

Bettie looked over at Mel in surprise, and then at Rosie, who was eyeing her with a *say the word and I'll go with you* expression.

Bettie shook her head. She didn't need Rosie's protection. Mel had answers to questions they all wanted. Why wouldn't she go with her?

They all climbed out of the RV. Bettie watched as Dad gently lowered himself into the front seat of the golf cart, Rosie and Cassie taking seats in the back. They waved as they took off. Bettie climbed into the other golf cart beside Mel.

"Hold on, sugar. We're only about five minutes away."

Mel navigated the golf cart down a rocky path. Bettie hated silences. Her sisters used to joke that there was never a silence Bettie couldn't fill. But it was part of how she got attention. When you were a triplet, you had to do something to be heard.

Mel broke the silence. "How far along are you?"

Bettie froze. Mel couldn't know. It wasn't possible. Bettie had only discovered the news herself a few hours before, when the doctor screening her at the airport congratulated her. She had been confused until the woman pointed to the image on the X-ray scan. "This machine scans your whole body and tells us any medical issues you might be experiencing, and it can, of course, detect pregnancy. We possess advanced technology created right here in New Pacific. I can see that you're surprised, but don't worry. There are plenty of options for a young woman here if you'd like to speak to someone."

Bettie had been too stunned to do anything more than shake her head. "It's wonderful news. I should go and tell my family," she lied.

She hadn't felt like herself for weeks but figured it was due to the stress of her exams and traveling abroad. She'd never once considered she might be pregnant.

"I wish I could say it was a gift of mine. That I could tell, but I have a friend who works airport security. They track all international pregnancies. A practice I don't approve of, but it's a holdover from before the Collapse."

Mel was the last person she intended to tell her secret to, but she was relieved to be able to share her news with someone. "I still... I can't believe it."

"One helluva surprise, isn't it? I had the same shock. Hooked up with a director at the Toronto Film Festival, and nine months later I'm looking at Dominic's red smushed-up face, falling head over heels in love with my boy."

"It was planned?" she asked softly.

"Fuck no." It came out harsh, but Mel's smile softened her words. "Sorry. I wanted to be a mom eventually, but I had terrible luck with men. Anyway, I went to TIFF and met this hot new director. The man was drop-dead gorgeous and he knew it. It was meant to be a hookup, but next thing I know I'm throwing up my Cobb salad at Canter's and he's telling me he's engaged to be married to the star of his film. And before I can blink, the doctors are placing Dom on my chest. Best moment of my life. Do you want it?" Mel asked. Her words running together.

Bettie considered this. "I don't know. I love my boyfriend. We planned to move to London after graduation and work in the theater. But we can't do that, can we? Not with a baby."

"You can do anything you want, hon. Anything at all."

Tears welled in Bettie's eyes. For the first time since she'd gotten the news about her mum, she missed her, or the idea of her, in a way she hadn't before. She didn't know anything about being someone's mum.

"What if I mess it up?" she asked.

"It's hard as shit parenting a child, but if I can do it when the world is falling apart, you'll do fine."

Mel's voice was so reassuring, Bettie wanted to believe her.

By now she could see half a dozen wood cabins sitting side by side. It reminded her of where an American summer-camp movie might film. In the center of the compound was a gazebo and a firepit, which added to the storybook effect. Mel pulled the golf cart into a spot near the front of a row of cabins and switched off the motor.

"That first cabin is where you girls will bunk. Sam has his own cabin right next door. Dominic and I live in the main house, and Eduardo and Mark are in the back cabin. The others are empty, for guests, but we don't get many of those nowadays. Wash up and rest, and if you're feeling up for it, dinner is in an hour. I'll make sure to leave you extra vitamins and nutrients. It's more important now than ever that you look after yourself."

"Thank you," Bettie said, and wondered if she had misjudged Mel. She paused. "My sisters don't know... about the baby," she said.

"I won't say a word, but you'd be better off not telling anyone at all. A lot of things have gotten better since the Collapse, but babies are still a hot commodity these days."

Bettie blinked, her confusion apparent. "A commodity?"

"People are desperate. Looking to monetize everything. If it's not the people who can't have kids taking 'em, it's those damn pronatalists who can never have enough kids of their own. Better to be safe than sorry and keep your news to yourself."

A shiver ran down Bettie's spine. If someone wanted to sell her baby, they would have to steal it. But what would that mean for her?

Mel was already heading out, disappearing into her cabin. Bettie wanted to throw up, and it had nothing to do with the life growing inside her. She couldn't stay here. She had made up her mind. She would get through dinner and then she was going to book a ticket home and get as far away from this place as possible... with or without her sisters.

ROSIE

The buzzing sensation she felt reminded Rosie of the first time she'd gotten piss drunk on lager and whiskey shots for her twenty-first birthday, except today there was no hangover. It was the ultimate adrenaline rush. After the road shooting, Rosie could have climbed a mountain or run a marathon, she was so wired. It seemed strange that a near-death experience made her feel this way, but it did.

Not that she wasn't scared. She almost pissed herself when it all went down, but there was something about being that close to danger, something about the uncertainty of the moment, that reinvigorated her. She envied the confident way Mel wielded the gun; how unafraid her expression was when the attack began. No fear, no hesitation. That's how Rosie wanted to live her life. She could tell by Cassie's silence and Bettie's tearful breakdown that they did not feel the same, and she understood her reaction wasn't normal. Rosie didn't know what to make of it. Something about being here made her feel different. As though anything were possible.

She promised herself that she'd talk to her sisters after

they all got some rest. It didn't matter if they were at odds; she owed it to them to smooth things over. She was definitely worried about Bettie. Something wasn't right.

When she asked Mel if Bettie was okay, she smiled reassuringly. "She's tired. Said she needed a shower. We generally do dinner at five o'clock, but of course we're delayed. I told Sam that I could bring him a plate, but he said he wanted to join us. It's up to you if you want to do the same. There will be time to meet everyone tomorrow."

Rosie was surprised that Dad wasn't going straight to bed and more than a little concerned. Exhaustion made his symptoms worse, and nighttime amplified the sundowning symptoms. With everything that had already happened, the last thing they needed was Dad losing his temper.

But Rosie couldn't imagine it would go over well if she suggested he skip dinner. She wasn't sure if Dad knew she'd lied about the interview, but her sisters were mad enough that she decided not to rock the boat.

"I'll wash up and see you there," Rosie said.

"I look forward to it." Mel turned to go. Then she stopped, a troubled expression on her face.

"Rosie, I'm sorry about earlier. I should have been upfront about the challenges that come with living here. It's still a hard place. It was selfish of me to mislead you. I wanted to see all of you again, and I let that cloud my judgment."

Rosie appreciated Mel's honesty. "I would have come no matter what."

A MOTHER'S GUIDE TO THE APOCALYPSE   137

Which was true. She had questions, of course. About their kiss. About Mel's past with Dad. But like she told Bettie, that could wait.

Mel's smile grew wider. "I'm glad to hear that. Tomorrow, after we've all gotten some rest, we'll strategize about Sam and the interview, but for now let's eat. Everything's better with a full belly."

Mel reached out and gave Rosie a hug, and that feeling of warmth and security rushed over her. This was what she'd missed about not having a mum. Hugs. Physical comfort and reassurance.

That wasn't to say Granny and Dad didn't try, but they weren't huggers by nature. Their way of life was *Keep calm and carry on,* which always made Rosie feel like an outsider. She needed...more.

As Mel headed off, Rosie found her way into the cabin. There were two twin beds on the ground floor, decorated with simple rose-colored quilts. Bettie had laid claim to the bed in the corner, her nightclothes already neatly laid out on her pillow. There was no sign of Cassie except for her bag by the door.

There was a third bed in an upstairs loft, which Rosie decided to take so that Cassie and Bettie could complain about her in peace. She was about to climb the stairs when the door to the bathroom opened and Bettie emerged, fresh from the shower, dressed in lightweight white shorts and a white T-shirt, a towel wrapped around her hair.

"How are you feeling?" Rosie asked.

"Grand. Couldn't be happier to be here in this hellscape."

"Bets, can we talk?" Rosie began.

Bettie waved her off. "I'm really hungry, Rosie. We'll talk when I don't want to strangle you."

She slipped out before Rosie could say anything else. Rosie always hated Bettie's silent treatment, but she would eventually cave. She wasn't sure about Cassie.

God, her sisters were bloody exhausting. Or maybe the adrenaline was fading. Rosie had to keep moving or she worried she might collapse right into bed.

She climbed up to the loft and opened her suitcase to get her change of clothes. As she reached for a pair of clean shorts and a T-shirt, her eyes landed on her mother's notebook tucked neatly in the suitcase.

She sank down onto the bed and opened the book, touching the pages, her hands tracing over her mother's writing, grateful for the physical reminder of why they had come here. They were one step closer to getting answers, she reminded herself. Sleep could wait.

Twenty minutes later, dressed in her own shorts and T-shirt, hair still damp from the shower, Rosie walked across the property to the main cabin, twinkle lights guiding her way. She entered to hear Otis Redding's "I've Got Dreams" playing on a speaker. She loved this song. So did her father. Otis Redding was one of his favorite artists, and she had that familiar sense of warmth every time he played it while he cooked.

Mel was busy in the kitchen, filling large bowls with pasta and sauce. Dominic stood beside his mother, uncorking several bottles of wine.

A giant wooden table filled the space. Dad and Cassie sat at one end, quietly sifting through photos. At the other end, Bettie sat with two very handsome older gentlemen, her smile so bright it surprised Rosie.

Mel called out, "Rosie, move your butt. Dinner's ready."

Amused by Mel's enthusiasm, Rosie made her way over to the table and took a seat across from Bettie as Mel set down a basket of piping-hot bread.

"Dig in. I made that bread myself. One of the many skills I developed during one of our lockdowns that I thought would be useless, but let me tell you, it came in handy."

Dominic snorted. "Mom made enough bread to feed this town until the end of time."

Mel pointed to his belly. "Kept you nice and full. You better believe we'd have all gone hungry if I hadn't learned these things. Especially when animals became scarce." Mel looked at the sisters. "But I'm not gonna bore you with all that."

Rosie wasn't bored at all. She wanted to know everything about the place her parents once called home, but Mel was already moving on.

"Rosie, this is Mark, our resident witch doctor, formerly one of the top talent managers in Los Angeles."

"Back in my more useless days. Nowadays, I consider

myself more of a healer, but Mel loves to antagonize me with the whole witch-doctor bit."

"It's one of my few pleasures in life," she said with a laugh. "Besides, it's quite the transformation. He was a total shark back in the day. Made some brilliant deals that led to—"

"A few gems and a whole lotta stinkers. But those wheeling and dealing days are done. Now I'm content with the life we've built here." He smiled at Mel and turned to the man beside him. "My apologies. I'm sure he needs no introduction, but this is my husband, Eduardo Santiago."

Rosie let out a small gasp and realized why Bettie was grinning. This man was the star of some of her sister's favorite movies. No wonder he looked familiar.

"You should say I'm a recovering actor. Unlike my husband, I'm still completely useless."

Mel smacked him lightly on the arm. "Not true. Eduardo is a gifted gardener. All the vegetables that we're eating tonight, he grew himself."

Cassie's smile widened at that. "They look delicious. I'd love a tour of your garden at some point."

"I'd be happy to oblige," he said.

"But you have to know the impact you had. I've watched your films at least a hundred times," Bettie insisted. "*Never Walk Away* is my all-time favorite film. I know every line. It's so devastating. I loved it so much, I hosted a screening of it at my university."

A MOTHER'S GUIDE TO THE APOCALYPSE 141

Rosie wished she had a camera to capture Bettie's look of awe.

Eduardo was equally amused. He looked over at Mel. "Did you put her up to this?"

Mel shook her head. "Nope, but I'm not surprised that your talent endures, or that recognizing great talent runs in the family. When we were first making our way, your mom found a script she said Eduardo had to star in. Of course he was already a household name. His manager wouldn't take our calls."

She glared at Mark, who shrugged. "What can I say? Even geniuses get it wrong now and then."

"Olivia didn't care how many *no*s she got," Mel replied. "We had a lot of big names vying for the lead role, but she said it had to be him. *Eduardo is the one. We can't give up,* so she got on a plane to Atlanta where he was shooting a movie and drove to the middle of bumblefuck and stalked him until he came out of his trailer."

Eduardo was laughing. "She was a sight. Four months' pregnant with you lot, but she looked seven. She waddled over to the trailers and demanded to see me. I swear, the line producer wanted to call the cops. They were looking at her like, *Who the fuck does this lady think she is?* But I was enraptured watching Olivia outside my trailer, out of breath, holding her belly, a bound script in hand. She said, 'Mr. Santiago, this script is special. Whoever plays this role will have their pick of jobs. I know it. I can't tell you how, but I do. My question for you is, do you really want to say no and make the biggest mistake of your career?'

"I looked at her and said, 'If it's not a giant hit, I get to keep your kid.' I was teasing, of course, but she laughed. 'I'm having triplets. Take your pick.'"

Everyone was laughing now. Dad's eyes had lit up at the mention of Olivia.

Eduardo continued. "But I liked Liv, and I loved the script. In fact, I almost fired my manager for not bringing it to me."

Mark snorted. "You're so full of shit. I told him the premise and he passed."

"I'll agree to disagree. The good news was, I didn't have to take any of Olivia's babies. She was right. That movie was my biggest hit. Oscars, all the money in the world. And then a few years later, none of it mattered."

A sorrowful look flashed across Eduardo's face. "I loved making movies. It was a dream come true for a kid growing up in Cuba. But we all learned hard lessons after the Collapse. The real world was coming for us. We just didn't know it."

"Olivia did," Sam said flatly.

The laughter died. Silence fell. Mel and her friends exchanged guilty looks. Sam's comment brought them all back to the present. The reason they were here. The silence lingered until Mel cleared her throat and motioned for everyone to dig in. "Food's getting cold. Go on. Help yourselves. Dom, pour the damn wine."

"You know I need to get ready to go to LA," Dominic said, clearly annoyed.

"It can wait a few days."

"I've already planned it."

"It can wait a day or two. Right now we're entertaining our guests."

He sighed deeply but did as he was told. Rosie couldn't help being amused at the sight of this giant man being put in his place by his mother.

Across the table, Rosie watched as Dad happily accepted a second glass of Cabernet. She caught Bettie staring at him as well. They were both waiting for Cassie to scold their father—beer and now wine—but Cassie didn't say a word. She simply took a glass Dominic offered and downed it. Rosie couldn't help but think they were in an upside-down world. She took a sip of her own.

They all ate, though thankfully the silence was less tense. Sam looked over at Dom. "You still play football?" Sam asked.

Dom smiled. "No, sir. Not in years."

Sam smiled. "He was obsessed as a kid. Didn't go anywhere without a ball in his hands."

"No time for sports after the Collapse," Dominic said matter-of-factly. "No time for anything besides survival."

"I hear that. You were always a good kid."

Mel smiled proudly. "He's an even better man. After I got injured, he had to do everything until I could get off my ass, literally and figuratively. He keeps the homestead running, going back and forth to that awful city to stock up on supplies. I'm lucky to have him."

Dominic stared down at his pasta as though he hoped he might disappear into it. Mel took mercy on him and turned the conversation back to the girls. "You're almost done with university? What are your plans?"

There was no way for Mel to know how hard things would be when they returned. That with Dad in the care home, life as they knew it would be over. But this wasn't the time or place to share that.

"I'm waiting to hear about medical school," Rosie said. She kept it vague, not wanting anyone, even her sisters, to know about the rejections.

"That's impressive. A doctor in the family," Eduardo said.

"Did Bettie tell you that she's an actor?" Rosie asked.

"Really? How fantastic!" Eduardo said.

Bettie glared at her sister. "I'm studying drama at university and I've done a few plays, but that's all."

"My Bets will make a wonderful drama teacher," Sam said.

"Why not pursue a career as a performer? I've heard London still has a bustling stage and film scene," Eduardo said.

Sam scoffed. "She's too smart to go down that road."

This had been an argument between Bettie and Sam

A MOTHER'S GUIDE TO THE APOCALYPSE 145

for years. Rosie found it amusing, because as much as the world had changed, parental disappointment endured. She knew there was something deeper behind Dad's disapproval—resentment for their mum's career and whatever went on before they were born—but all of that went unsaid. She could see Bettie's unease and stepped in again.

"Cassie is studying horticulture. She received a grant from the university to continue her efforts in growing plants and food systems that have gone extinct," Rosie said helpfully.

Cassie shrugged, but it was impossible not to see the pride in her eyes. For a moment, both sisters seemed to forget how angry they were, which was a relief for Rosie. Her world didn't make sense when her sisters were mad at her.

"You've clearly done a great job raising these girls, Sam," Mel said.

Dad shrugged. "Can't take much credit," he said, shoving food into his mouth. He'd always been a fast eater, but as he got older, he lacked the awareness that it wasn't a contest. Sauce stained his graying beard and dripped onto his shirt. Rosie resisted the urge to grab a napkin and wipe it off, but of course Cassie couldn't. Sam swatted her hand away and kept eating.

"Of course you can. It must have been difficult leaving here without Liv. Moving so far away."

The comment sounded innocuous enough to Rosie, but her dad's eyes flashed. He slammed down his fork.

"What the fuck are you trying to say, Mel?"

Everyone went still again. Rosie glanced over and saw Dominic gritting his teeth.

"Nothing, Sam. It was a compliment. That's all."

"Are we all going to sit here and act like the shit that happened with Liv didn't happen? All of us are to blame. We saw her spiraling. We all saw it, and we didn't do a thing to stop it."

Mel glanced at the girls nervously. "Sam, now isn't the time."

"Oh really, when is the time? They're gonna find out about it all. Liv's crazy ideas ended up not being crazy at all. Her obsession with that whack job Joey..."

Mark and Eduardo looked at each other. "Should we go?" Eduardo asked.

Mel waved her hand for them to stay. "Joey was and still is a predator. He preyed on Liv's fears and her weakness, and he's still doing it only on a bigger scale. Now he's got a whole compound. They call themselves the Guardians and control half of LA."

"The Guardians?" Cassie asked.

Dominic snorted. "A tribute to an old movie called *Guardians of the Galaxy.*"

Cassie and Rosie stared back blankly. Bettie didn't bother hiding her annoyance at her sister's ignorance of cinema history. "It was a popular sci-fi movie back in the day."

"Yeah, Joey was a failed actor and big-time sci-fi geek.

A MOTHER'S GUIDE TO THE APOCALYPSE 147

Probably still is. Liked to think of himself as a savior of the world. Which is a joke. The only thing Joey and the Guardians guard is their wealth," Mel said.

"But how is he connected to Mum?" Rosie asked. She hated feeling behind the plot.

Sam shrugged, the fire in his gaze cooling to a simmer as quickly as it was ignited. He picked his fork back up and resumed eating. That was how most conversations went these days. He would get worked up, and then whatever thoughts or feelings had bubbled up would be gone, the rest of them still reeling from his outburst.

But Mel was on a roll. "Joey was a doomsday prepper. That's what they called people back in the day who thought the apocalypse was coming and started hoarding food and supplies. More often than not they were anti-government types, convinced that elected officials were gonna fuck shit up, which, newsflash, was true. When social media took off, preppers got these huge followings, made all kinds of money off exploiting people's fears. That's what happened with your mama. She joined a Reddit prepper group that Joey started, and he was all too happy to give her tips. It was an online friendship or something, but then . . ."

At this, Mel trailed off. Cassie hadn't said a word since Rosie walked in, but now she was curious. "This Joey person. Would he know about Mum? Did you ever speak to him?"

"I don't know what he knows. I met him once at this meeting your mama dragged me to. I found it all a bit unsettling, everyone so jazzed about the worst coming to pass. All I wanted to do was get out of there. Saw him again at your birthday and thought he was an idiot. Told Liv as much."

"Do you know where he lives? How we could find him?"

"He's got a compound in Silverlake. Fucker has a stranglehold on the pharmaceutical needs of this entire region so we have no choice but to do business with him, but Dom handles that. I can't... It's not good for me to get involved."

"He's still alive?" Rosie asked.

"Unfortunately. World would be a better place without him," Mel said. "No chance he'll be any help."

"If he knew Mum back then, maybe we should talk to him?" Cassie said.

"That's not happening," Dominic said, clearly annoyed.

"Why not?" Cassie insisted.

Rosie was annoyed, too. Why couldn't Cassie read the bloody room?

Mel forced a smile. "We don't need Joey. Okay?" Her words had a harsh quality.

Rosie saw a flicker of anger on Cassie's face. Cassie hated being told what to do. She was about to speak when Sam's voice broke through.

"She was fucking him, wasn't she?" Dad's voice was soft, but the tone set Rosie on edge. "Was Liv fucking him?" he asked again, his voice louder. "Tell me."

Mel was slow to answer, which was all it took for Sam to

lose it. He shoved his plate and glass off the table, sending sauce and wine flying. Everyone jumped up.

"Tell me the truth, Mel. Tell me. Did she fuck him?"

Then Sam began to cry. No, that wasn't right. He began to weep, loud despairing sobs. "I need to know."

"I have sedatives," Mark said.

Cassie shook her head. "He has pills. He needs to rest. It's been... it's been quite a day."

She put her arm around Sam. "Come on, Dad. Let's go to bed." The icy glare she gave Rosie made it clear forgiveness would not be coming tonight.

Bettie looked at the mess and back at Mel. "I'm sorry about this. I'm not feeling so good," she said.

Mel gave her arm a squeeze. Rosie saw something pass between them, but she had no idea what. "Go rest up, honey. I'll bring some club soda by later."

As Bettie hurried out, Rosie's head spun with questions. About Joey and the prepping and whether their father's accusation that their mother was cheating had any merit.

Mel must have seen the warring emotions on her face. She patted Rosie's hand. "Go on to bed. I know there's so much you want to know, and we'll get to it. I promise."

Rosie didn't want to leave, but she was so exhausted she could barely stand. She was halfway back to her cabin when she realized she'd forgotten her bag. She turned back around and was reaching for the door when she heard Dominic's angry voice.

"What kind of game are you playing here? When they find out what you're doing, you think they're going to want to stay?"

Mel's voice was angry and indignant. "Watch your tone, Dominic. They need this as much as I do."

"This obsession with them is as insane as Olivia's prepping. None of this is going to turn out the way you want. They're gonna hate you like she did."

Dominic burst through the door so quickly, Rosie didn't have time to pretend she wasn't listening. He stopped and glared at her. "I forgot my bag."

He leaned in close, his breath smelling faintly of wine. "You should all go home. As soon as possible, because nothing good is going to come from this trip. I can promise you that."

His words were gentle, which made it worse. Like a warning from a good friend who saw things you could not.

He was gone before Rosie could respond. She'd orchestrated all of this, and now it felt unwieldy and overwhelming. She was scared—and what was worse, she couldn't turn to her sisters, because they were mad at her and they had every right to be. Rosie stood there in the darkness as lights were switched off, the entire compound going to bed, and wondered what she was going to do now.

CASSIE

The industrial-size fans blew nonstop, but the temperature felt almost unbearable. Cassie groaned as she woke up to find her sheets stuck to her body. Rosie and Cassie were still fast asleep, but Cassie couldn't lie there any longer. She needed to move and think.

She climbed out of bed, careful not to wake her sisters, then slipped on a pair of shorts, a sports bra, and her favorite trainers. It wasn't quite dawn; sunlight was almost peeking through. The air was hot and thick.

Cassie started to run, making her way through the lush forest. She'd been running for only ten minutes when she spotted a massive garden at the edge of the forest, filled with strawberries, tomatoes, peppers, and eggplant. It was as close to home as she'd get here. She wasn't alone. Despite the early-morning hour, Eduardo and Dominic were digging and turning over the soil, both men dripping with sweat as though they'd been at this for hours.

"Hey there, you wanna give us a hand?" Eduardo called out when he spotted her.

"We're almost done," Dominic said, giving Cassie a dismissive look.

"And if she helps, we'll be done sooner," Eduardo said. He motioned to a basket nearby. "Grab a bucket and start picking."

Cassie eagerly joined the assembly line. After all that travel, it felt good to get her hands dirty. "These berries look great, but if you put down some aluminum foil here and here, you could increase the sunlight exposure and likely grow even bigger ones," Cassie said.

Eduardo smiled. "Beauty and brains, I see. Like I said, I'm a novice. We'll take any and all tips you can spare."

Dominic cut in. "I think we're good. Besides, she's leaving soon."

The anger in his tone caught Cassie off guard. Eduardo shook his head. "It's a little early, Dominic, to be mad-dogging anyone."

He gestured to his basket of vegetables that was nearly overflowing. "I'm going to take these up to the main house. If you don't mind bringing the rest when you're done." He gave Dominic a knowing stare. "Are you leaving in the morning?"

"Unless Mom changes her mind."

"Be safe. You know how much she worries."

"Yeah, yeah, I know. I'll go there and back like I always do," Dominic promised.

As Eduardo headed off, Cassie resumed picking strawberries, refusing to let Dominic intimidate her. She hated

A MOTHER'S GUIDE TO THE APOCALYPSE 153

men who thought their mere presence would make her submissive.

"When are you and your sisters going home?" he asked.

"Isn't that a question for your mom? She said she was going to help us look into what happened to our mum, and then she said she was going to help Dad with whatever mess he's gotten himself in. And so far all she's done is take us on a trip down memory lane. In case it's not clear, I can't wait to leave, but I do need to get closure. For my father and my sisters."

She slammed down her basket, not caring that it spilled over. Let him pick his own damn berries. She had a run to finish. She had gone only a few feet when Dominic called out, "There's nothing to find."

Cassie stopped and spun around. "What? What do you mean?"

"My mom doesn't know shit about where Olivia is or where to look. She wishes she did. She's spent decades searching. She wanted you girls and your dad to come back here."

"So what the fuck is this interview about? Who wants to talk to my dad?"

"I don't know. Neither does she. But if you and your sisters are expecting to find something real, you're out of luck."

Cassie's blood boiled. It was either keep running or fight Dominic. She wasn't sure she liked her chances with the latter, so she took off. No destination in mind. One foot in front of the other.

Half an hour later, Cassie was exhausted but ready to confront Mel about being a liar. But all that went out the window when she found Sam and Rosie all cozy on the sofa next to Mel, laughing as they looked through family photos. They all looked too comfortable, she thought—as though they could stay here forever.

"Where's Bettie?" Cassie asked as she grabbed a glass of water and downed it.

"She needed to lie down," Rosie said. "Not sure why. She slept until nine o'clock."

Mel waved her hand in dismissal. "The jet lag and heat will get you. Let the poor girl sleep."

Cassie shrugged. She didn't care if Bettie slept the whole day away. It was Mel she didn't trust. Not Rosie, though. She was clearly Mel's biggest fan. "Cass, come look at these photos. There are so many of Mum and Dad. They looked like movie stars," Rosie said excitedly.

"I lost so much in the quake, but not my photos," Mel said gratefully.

She held up a picture. "Sammy, remember this Halloween? Liv and the girls dressed up as Barbies, and you were Ken."

"Liv loved Halloween. Her costume parties were epic. Themed food and drinks. Everyone wanted an invite," he said fondly.

"Wasn't she a hottie?" Mel asked.

"She was," Sam said.

A MOTHER'S GUIDE TO THE APOCALYPSE 155

Cassie could hear the pain in his voice. But damn, it was true. Her mum had a smile so disarming, you couldn't look away. There was another photo of Mum dressed as Barbie, her arm slung around a handsome blond man in jeans, a white T-shirt, and a leather jacket with a cigarette in his mouth. They looked so similar, down to their matching left-cheek dimples.

"Who is this?" Cassie asked, picking up the picture to study it.

"That's your uncle Lucas," Mel said.

"He was something else that night," Sam said with a snort. "Got so piss drunk on tequila, he threw up in our rosebushes and then slept with your mum's assistant. In that order."

Rosie giggled. "What was he like?"

Mel and Sam spoke in unison. "A loser."

They laughed and looked at each other, such familiarity in their exchange that it made Cassie wonder how close they'd really been.

Sam shook his head. "Lotta heartache in your mum's family, but Lucas thought it gave him permission to be an arse."

It was clear her father was not a fan of her uncle, but they were wasting time discussing him. There were bigger issues to focus on. "Any news about Dad's interview?" Cassie asked.

Dad looked up from the photo album. "Aye, Cassie,

enough with the nagging. If I'm not worried, why should you be? Let's enjoy some time with old friends."

Cassie was shocked. Dad never scolded her. Ever. And now here he was taking Mel's side.

Mel shook her head. "It's okay. I spoke to Victor, and he said that no one seems to know what's going on. Literally they have no record of an interview being scheduled, which is good news. He did say there's a flag on Sam's passport, meaning you can't leave yet. But Victor is on it. He knows that you're staying here and how to contact us. I imagine if it were urgent, we'd have heard from the officials. We have to be patient and let Victor do his thing."

They were currently stuck in this horrid place with Mel, who had already lied to get them here, and she wanted them to be patient. No chance.

She imagined sharing what Dominic had told her with her sisters. Would Rosie care? Would Bettie take Rosie's side? Her sisters came here for answers. That's what Cassie wanted to give them.

The good news was that Cassie's run had given her time to think. The only other person who knew her mum before she disappeared was Joey, the prepper. Cassie had decided she was going to talk to him. But to do that she needed Dominic's help. Which of course she knew he would never give willingly. But thankfully, Sam had taught them well. She had a plan. Now all she had to do was wait for the right moment to *execute it.*

BETTIE

Despite Mel's insistence that they would talk about Mum, and Dad's interview, two days passed and all she did was tell stories and show them pictures. Bettie's plan to head home hadn't changed, but every time she planned to bring it up, she either had to throw up or needed to lie down. Bettie wasn't sure why her pregnancy symptoms had waited until now to present themselves, but she did not appreciate it. Not one bit.

She was worried that her sisters would notice, but Rosie was busy being besties with Mel, and Cassie kept disappearing on one of her ridiculous runs. Dad was quiet, but she could see him studying Mel, and she wondered what he was thinking. Still, no one said anything, all of them living in a weird kind of limbo.

By the middle of the third day with no mention of Dad's interview or the search for Mum, Bettie was going stir-crazy. She desperately needed to speak to Max and let him know she was okay. She hurried toward Mel's cabin to search for her but found Eduardo in her kitchen instead.

"Have you seen Mel and Rosie?" she asked.

"They went for a walk. Should be back soon." He carefully took a pan of muffins out of the oven. Bettie's stomach growled, and for the first time she felt hungry.

"Want one?" he asked.

"I think I'd like two," she said.

Eduardo laughed. "I love a girl who can eat."

He put two giant blueberry muffins on her plate and added a pat of butter. She'd never smelled anything so good. Or maybe that was the hormones talking.

This felt so surreal. Eating muffins in America that were baked by an actor she'd worshipped since she was a child. She thought back to all the times she'd forced Rosie and Cassie to watch his films. And all the times she'd spent memorizing his most famous lines. Now she was here with him.

For as long as Bettie could remember, singing and dancing and putting on shows made her happy. Growing up, she had built-in castmates, but as her sisters got older, they grew bored with playing pretend. Cassie wanted to be knee-deep in dirt and mud with Dad, and Rosie was busy obsessing over Mum or micromanaging the house. She hated that they didn't want to join her, but after her first production without them, Bettie realized it was a gift. Being onstage was the one place in her life where she could be Bettie Clark, not one of the Clark triplets.

But even that future seemed elusive now. Now she'd just be someone's mum. She hated how selfish that sounded, but it was true. She'd always wanted a bigger life outside

Newcastle. Her granny once said she was a lot like her mum in that way. "She had a wanderer's spirit. Big dreams that others didn't think were possible, but they were. She did it. You can, too."

Bettie wasn't sure she was that brave. Or maybe her bravery came from being part of a trio. That there was always strength in numbers.

Then there was Max. She wasn't clueless as to how her sisters felt about him. They got that bored, *rescue me* look every time he started talking, but they didn't say anything more because he was... boring. To them at least.

Bettie loved him, no doubt. She saw his passion for film and TV and books, and knew that he would make a wonderful father one day. She could already see him buying baby books and searching for teaching jobs in the arts so he could support them. He would be the guy who would build a crib by hand and put together all the toys, and make the Sunday roasts and her favorite puddings, and rub her feet anytime she asked. It was a future that sounded perfect in a few years—but how could she perform in a show in London, or do commercials or TV, with a baby? How could she figure out if she had talent if she was trying to raise a child? She tried to shake away all the doubts. She needed to tell Max before she started freaking out.

"Think we could go into town?" she asked Eduardo hopefully. It was the only way she could video-chat, but they had to coordinate with Dr. McLaughlin first.

Eduardo shook his head as he gestured outside. "There's a storm coming. You can smell it in the air. I'm not sure you noticed driving in, but the roads are a mess. Add in rain and wind, and it's a death trap. Not to mention it's getting late, and we don't want to be out at night."

"What happens at night?" Bettie wondered.

"Damn road pirates are out in full force."

"Are they the people who tried to run us off the road?" Bettie asked.

"Exactly. Those assholes move in packs robbing people and doing other things you don't even want to think about."

Indeed, Bettie did not want to think about that. "What about the police?" she asked.

"What police? After the Collapse, we were all basically left to fend for ourselves unless we want to pay for protection—which isn't happening. Those of us who have chosen to live out here have accepted that we're on our own."

"I thought from the way Mel talked about this place that there were more of you living here?" Bettie said.

"There were. We had about thirty people at one point. But a lot of folks disagreed with Mel's rules. She wanted a locked community. A safe space. The others wanted to be free to come and go. Others joined up with the Guardians when they got real power."

There was something in the way he spoke that made Bettie uneasy. Mel wanted to keep everyone here? Was that why she'd brought them here? It made her nervous, especially when she thought about Mel's excitement over the baby.

As if he could read her mind, Eduardo spoke, "Mel told me...about the..." He made a cradle rocking gesture.

Bettie flinched, surprised by Mel's betrayal.

"It's all very new," Bettie said tersely.

"Of course. Mum's the word. No pun intended. She wanted me to look out for you. Extra protein and care. We're a family here," Eduardo said kindly.

She wanted to believe that, but Bettie had her own family to worry about. She finished her muffin and smiled at Eduardo. "I think I'm going to go to bed early. We can talk about going to town in the morning?" she asked.

"Absolutely," Eduardo said cheerfully. "I'll be your chauffeur, milady."

She forced a laugh, but Bettie wasn't amused. She was off balance in a way pregnancy hormones couldn't explain away. She hurried back to her cabin, but there was no sign of Rosie or Cassie. She thought about checking in on Dad, but she was so exhausted. She lay back on the bed, promising herself she would close her eyes for only a moment. She needed to talk to her sisters and they needed to come up with a plan, because as far as Bettie could tell, coming here had nothing to do with finding her mum. But if that was the case, why the hell were they here?

r/SoCalValleyPreppers

7,000 Members

SHOUT OUT YOUR PREPPER SUCCESSES

Mamabear3

Thanks to everyone here I have water storage sorted. Figured I'd post a photo for those of you who were asking.

Tex2022

Damn, Mamabear3 has big money with that set-up. Must be nice.

Valle4Ever

Guess I know where I'm going when the big one comes!

Tex022

Prepping would be a helluva lot easier If I had that kind of money.

PRIVATE CHAT

GoJoe420

Hey don't let those shitheads get to u. They're jealous.

Mamabear3

I wasn't trying to show off. I didn't think...

GoJoe420

Nah, don't sweat it. I'll keep 'em in line. Your doing great.

Mamabear3

My husband might disagree.

GoJoe420

He won't when shit goes down and hes got clean water & a full belly. Keep doing your thing. Your one of us. I know it.

SAM

It was the middle of the night when Sam heard footsteps. He bolted upright, his breathing heavy. He scanned the pitch-black room, but there was nothing, not even a shadow. It was footsteps, wasn't it? He thought back to the police interview room and Officer Blowfish's angry red face. Was it him? Or one of the men from the motorway coming for them?

Sam heaved a sigh of relief at the silence that followed and laid his head back on the pillow, willing himself not to cry. They'd been here for several days, and it took all he had not to call Mel out or pretend he didn't hate her guts. Every picture she shared, every story she told, he wondered if she had forgotten. Because he hadn't.

Now he was waiting for some interview so that someone else could accuse him of hurting his wife or lying about what had happened. Why would he do that?

Sam wiped away the tears. *Goddamnit, I have to stop this. Tears aren't going to help anyone.* He got up, and moved over to his bag. He reached into the inside pocket and pulled out a pack of cigarettes and a matchbook. Last year when he got his diagnosis, the girls insisted he quit smoking. He hadn't fought them on it, though their demands made him feel more childish than the tears. He'd taken to asking Paul, the lad who tended the lawn, to buy him a pack of cigarettes every few weeks. Smoking calmed him and steadied his thoughts, which he needed now more than ever.

Sam moved over to the window and opened it, lit a match, and took a deep drag.

He didn't like it here. Not the unbearable heat or the faux cheer from Mel and her band of merry followers. He didn't remember Eduardo and Mark that well, but he didn't like them, either. He'd never been comfortable with Hollywood types, and the Collapse hadn't changed that. He had seen them watching him, judging him, and he had no idea why... other than it must be because they thought he hurt Liv. That's what everyone seemed to think. Wasn't it?

All Sam wanted to do was return home, enjoy a pint at the pub, and tinker in his greenhouse.

There it was. He heard it again. Footsteps?

He turned back around and gasped, shocked to see Olivia standing by the window. She looked as beautiful as the day they met, with her heart-shaped face, full lips, and green eyes boring into him. Unchanged by time, her skin as smooth and wrinkle-free as ever. "You got old," she said flatly.

Sam didn't know how to respond. He had gotten old, and

he hated it. He hated the wrinkles, and daily pains in his back and knees. He hated the worry about his girls' future when he died, a worry that weighed him down. He hated that his brain had malfunctioned and there were words he could never find and memories he could not recover.

"You shouldn't have come back," Olivia said, eyes flashing.

"I had to," he mumbled. "The girls insisted, and I couldn't tell them no."

"You were always so soft. All these years, Sam, you fought to keep them safe, and you brought them back here? To this place. To this woman?"

More tears welled in his eyes. How could he tell her that he tried, but the girls weren't babies anymore? They were strong-willed young women who did what they wanted. They were their own people, which was what they'd always wanted for their children. They didn't... He stopped. Who was Olivia to be giving him orders?

"What the fuck are you doing here, Liv?"

"I know about Mel," she whispered. "I've always known."

He jumped, the accusation a gunshot in the dark. He fumbled for the light switch, but Liv was gone.

He sank onto the bed and reached for the bottle of water Cassie left on the nightstand. He downed it in two gulps, then lay back down. He remembered the doctor saying it would get harder and harder to separate fact from fiction, but now that he was here, his brain felt fuzzier than ever.

Rest would help calm him, but the jet lag and Olivia's accusation left him wide awake. He kept thinking about Mel and why she'd brought them here.

What he needed was a walk. Fresh air always cleared his head, and though this air was like bloody soup, it was better than lying here.

Sam stood, grabbed his shoes, and stepped outside. As he walked, he remembered his encounter with Mel. He still couldn't believe it had been almost thirty years since they met.

At seventeen, Sam caught the attention of a scout and earned a full scholarship to play golf at UCLA. He planned on returning home to Newcastle or London if the right opportunity came calling. He considered working in the entertainment business but couldn't bear the thought of being trapped inside an office eight hours a day.

He hit the jackpot when a former coach recommended him for a full-time job teaching golf at the Riviera Country Club. LA wasn't a place he loved—too many phony people and unbearable traffic—but he did love the weather. He told himself and his mum that he would stay one year and then come home.

To his surprise, he liked the job more than he thought he would. His clients were almost exclusively industry types, all wheelers and dealers who had great Hollywood stories and better tips. He was averaging two to three hundred dollars per day.

The women were equally attentive, a surprising but well-appreciated perk. He hadn't been at the club for long when he met Mel. She signed up for golf lessons after another client recommended him as a consultant on a new film. Mel was three years older and already a force of nature in Hollywood.

"Show me what I need to know," she said with a challenge. Sam could see that she was equally interested in what he could do *off* the golf course. Their "relationship" lasted two months. The sex was great. The conversation was, too. Mel had the best stories about the industry and her upbringing in Brooklyn. She took him to all the best restaurants and parties and refused to let him pay.

The first time they went out, Mel insisted on paying. "It would take you four hours standing on the putting green to make what this meal cost. I've got it."

Some men might have felt emasculated by Mel, but she'd signed a deal with a major studio to produce movies and put a down payment on a house in Silverlake. She *could* afford it. Besides, he liked a woman confident enough to take charge. They were having fun until she changed the game. A month into dating, she asked him to move in with her. "I've got plenty of room. It'll be great," she said.

Sam had been blindsided. He was twenty-eight and loved his freedom. He liked her, but not enough to give up his place. "I can't...I mean, I don't think we're there yet," he said.

Mel was over thirty, and he could tell that she was desperate for the next step. "When will you be ready?" she asked. "Or am I supposed to wait around?"

He sighed. "I'm not sure this is going to work."

She tossed back her whiskey and gave him a terse smile. "I'm so over men who don't want to grow up. Have a nice life, Sam," she said.

To be honest, he didn't think about Mel after that. He kept teaching at the club and landed a part-time job coaching golf at an exclusive private high school. That first year passed, and then another year and another. He grew to enjoy his easy and uncomplicated life. He dated a lot but never met anyone worth giving up his freedom.

Until Olivia blew into his life.

Every fall, his club hosted a fundraiser for underprivileged inner-city kids. Sam considered it good karma and always donated a free lesson for the cause. Usually, it was with a sweet blue-haired lady whose husband bought the lesson hoping she would learn to love the game.

Instead it was Olivia looking for a hobby to help offset her workaholic tendencies. The minute he saw her, he felt like Tweety Bird when he gets hit upside the head and sees stars. It was embarrassing how off balance she made him feel. He tried to focus on the necessary instructions: how to hold the club and track the ball, all the basics he'd taught for almost a decade that in her presence seemed foreign.

He let out a sigh of relief when the lesson ended and he

hadn't humiliated himself. He went to shake Liv's hand, and she held it tightly.

"Is it weird that I don't want to let go?"

Sam shook his head. He didn't want to, either.

Olivia smiled. "Then it won't be weird when I do this."

She kissed him right in front of the pro shop where his co-workers and club members were watching. Sam worked hard to keep his private life private, but he kissed her back.

"Have dinner at my place tonight?" he said.

She agreed and then didn't leave for three days. When she went home, he packed a bag and came with her. For weeks, they alternated whose apartment they stayed at depending on who had the earlier morning.

They were as opposite as one could imagine, especially their upbringings. Sam had grown up with two parents who doted on him and encouraged him to follow his dreams, even if it meant moving halfway across the world. His only hardship had been losing his father to cancer, but even then, the illness had been mercifully brief.

Olivia, on the other hand, had been dealt a shite hand. Her mum was an addict who could never stay clean. Liv and her little brother, Lucas, lived with their grandmother while their mum cycled in and out of jail and rehab. When Liv was seventeen, the two women died a few months apart, leaving Liv to support her younger brother.

Sam could see the effect this had on her. Liv worried about everything, always panicking that the roof might cave in, always holding her breath, convinced the good times couldn't last. He did his best to remind her how lucky she was, but the kind of trauma she'd experienced wasn't easy to overcome.

Their relationship grew more serious than either of them expected. He hadn't given it much thought, but when Olivia asked if he wanted kids, he said yes. He wanted all of it with her.

"Good answer. I think it's time you meet my family. It's my brother, Lucas, and my best friend and business partner, Melissa, but they're the most important people in my life. I want them to like you."

Sam laughed. "Everyone likes me."

It might have been true, but it didn't ease his nerves. He was relieved when they set a date to meet up for happy hour. Olivia had meetings all day, so they drove separately. Sam arrived at the Studio City Tavern to find Olivia and Lucas already sipping cocktails and munching on mozzarella sticks. He watched them from across the room. She was laughing, clearly amused by her brother. Lucas had untapped energy, not dissimilar to an untrained golden retriever.

When Sam approached, Lucas puffed up and shook his hand. He peppered Sam with questions about where he was born, how long he'd lived in LA, what he did for work, and his intentions with his sister, which Liv found hysterical. "Seriously, Lucas, leave the man alone."

Lucas laughed and asked Olivia if he could borrow

A MOTHER'S GUIDE TO THE APOCALYPSE   173

a hundred bucks so he could hit up *ladies' night* at a Hollywood club. She handed over the money, no questions asked. Lucas shook Sam's hand again and said, "If my sis likes you, that's good enough for me, but Mel's gonna make you work for her approval."

Olivia laughed as Lucas headed out. "That's high praise coming from Lucas. He generally does not like my suitors."

Sam stared at Liv in mock horror. "You've had other suitors? Don't tell me I'm dating a ruined woman?"

"And now you're ruined, too." She kissed him passionately. They were still kissing when a voice broke through: "Jesus Christ, Liv, get a damn room."

Thankfully, Liv was watching Mel's face and not Sam's when they pulled apart and didn't see his mouth drop open. Olivia's best friend Mel was *the* Melissa he had hooked up with all those years ago. Based on Mel's surprised expression, she hadn't put the golf pro clues together, either, but Mel didn't skip a beat. "Nice to meet you, Sam. I've heard so much about you."

Over drinks and appetizers, he learned that shortly after they stopped seeing each other, Mel had gotten pregnant by a director she met at the Toronto International Film Festival, a man who was not interested in being a father, which meant she was now a solo parent to a two-year-old son, Dominic. She clearly loved him, and she seemed more grounded and mature than the woman he'd met years earlier. He could tell by how Olivia finished Mel's sentences that they were more sisters than friends. He knew he had to tell Liv about their past, but Sam wanted to find the right moment. The minute Liv went to the bathroom, Mel shut him down. "No woman wants to imagine her best friend fucking the man she's in love with."

Sam froze. Liv was in love with him? Had she said as much? He loved her, too, but it was so early in their relationship that he didn't want to scare her.

Mel saw the look on his face. "Come on, you have to see it. You're both goners. But this...us...might ruin what you're building. I know better than anyone that Liv is tough as nails, but she's also insecure. She's dated a string of losers, and either they've been out the door before things got serious or she trusted them and they fucked her over. You're the first guy to break down her walls. Don't ruin this by being honest over something that was nothing."

Sam was shite at lying, but Mel made a good case. He and Mel were never serious and Liv was it for him. Why would he risk it?

Three months later he proposed. Five months later they got married, and two years after that, Liv got pregnant with the girls.

Mel was always there. For bridesmaid duties. For Lamaze classes when Sam had to travel to out-of-town tournaments. For late-night feedings when Liv called her and said she wasn't sure they would survive the sleep deprivation that went with parenting triplet newborns.

A MOTHER'S GUIDE TO THE APOCALYPSE 175

She was a good friend to both of them. There was never any question... until the prepping began. At first, they both took it in stride, teasing Liv about building the bunker and sending funny memes about doomsday prepper freaks. But the more serious Liv became about preparing for some unknown event, the more worried they became. On the long drive home from the club, he would call Mel, not Liv. They'd talk about how they could convince Liv to see a therapist and stop the prepping.

When it became clear that wasn't going to work and Joey was all she could talk about, they talked more and more about things that had nothing to do with Liv. Their own pressures and fears. Things you talked to a spouse about. Or a lover.

If you'd asked Sam back then, he would have said Mel was his best friend, too. But something happened. Something he'd regretted. Something that burned down his life.

Sam turned and made his way toward Mel's cabin. A lone lantern sat by the front door, casting an orange glow on the house. Sam picked it up and made his way inside, his own footsteps creaking on the wooden floors as he reached Mel's bedroom.

The door was ajar, but he could see Mel lying in bed in her white nightgown. The floor creaked again and she woke instantly, blinking away sleep. She reached toward the nightstand drawer, and Sam was almost certain she was reaching for a weapon.

"Mel."

She sat up. "Sam? Are you okay?"

He moved toward her. She patted the bed, and he sat down. She gently stroked his cheek. "I missed you, Sammy Sam. I missed you so much."

She leaned in and kissed him. All the questions that were jumbled up in his head became clear. That night all those years ago before he lost Liv replayed in his mind like a movie. Not a movie. A horror film. A white heat formed in his belly and traveled through his body. In seconds, his hands were around Mel's throat.

"You ruined everything," Sam said through gritted teeth as Mel clawed at his face. He knew he should feel badly, but all he could think about was making her suffer the way she'd made him suffer. He wanted her to feel the pain he'd spent decades running from. As he squeezed and squeezed, he wondered if this was why he had to come here. Maybe this was how it was meant to end.

ROSIE

The explosion of sound rocked the tiny wood cabin, sending Rosie tumbling out of bed and onto her feet. "What was that?" Rosie said. "It sounded like a gunshot."

Cassie and Bettie popped out of bed in unison, everyone fighting to shake off their exhaustion. Rosie flipped on the beside lamp, and without another word they all raced next door to Sam's cabin.

Rosie arrived first and flung open the door. Her sisters bumped into her as they surveyed the room. Dad was gone. All that remained were his rumbled bed linens and the acrid smell of cigarette smoke. In the distance, they heard shouting.

It was coming from Mel's. No words were needed as they took off again. Rosie and her sisters burst inside, stumbling around in the dark, and made their way to the back of the house, where the shouting had grown louder.

They entered the room and froze. A dazed Sam sat on the bed, his face covered in long red scratches. Mel stood in front of him, her impressive frame shielding Sam from Dominic, who held a pistol in his hand.

"What are you doing?" screamed Bettie.

Rosie stepped forward. Cassie did the same, neither caring what happened next. Their only thoughts were about protecting Dad. Dom pointed the gun at them. "Don't. Not till we figure out what happened."

Sweat dripped down his brow. She could see how close his finger was to the trigger.

"Dominic, honey, for the last time, I told you it was a misunderstanding."

"Ma, how the fuck is this man's hands around your neck a misunderstanding?" Dominic said furiously.

The girls' eyes widened as they zeroed in on Sam, who was crying and rocking back and forth. Rosie's insides twisted as she took in the finger-shaped bruise forming on Mel's neck, where—if Dominic was telling the truth—her father's hands had dug into her flesh. This didn't compute. Sam had a bit of a temper, but he wasn't a violent person. In fact, he used to get upset with them if they stepped on an ant or tried to harm a ladybird.

"Tell them what you did," Sam said flatly. "Tell them how you destroyed our family."

"What's he talking about?" Cassie asked.

"I don't know. He's confused," Mel insisted. "He came in here and was upset and confused and it escalated."

"I think you're keeping something from us. Come on. We're not bloody idiots," Cassie demanded.

"It's complicated," Mel began.

"No shit," Cassie said.

"That's enough," Dominic shouted. "Ma, this obsession with these people has to stop. Aunt Olivia lost her mind, which was bad enough, but she's the one who gave up on her kids. Long before she left. I heard what she said about them..."

Dominic's gaze landed on Sam. "Stop it," Mel said forcefully.

Dominic wasn't listening. "I heard her say the girls were a mistake."

Dominic might as well have fired the gun directly into Rosie's heart. She was surprised that Sam appeared unaffected by Dom's words, now in a world of his own making.

Mel stood and disarmed Dominic as easily as if he were a toddler and she was taking away his favorite toy. "Dominic, that's enough."

Bettie moved over to Dad and gently touched his shoulder.

He looked up at her with confusion on his face. "Can we go home?"

"Soon, Dad. Very soon. But let's get you to bed."

As she led Sam out, Bettie looked at her sisters. "I'm done here, and so is Dad. That's final."

She could see Bettie's resolve and knew there would be no changing her mind. Rosie didn't want to give up. Cassie had the greenhouse to go home to. Bettie had Max. Rosie had nothing but this chance at uncovering the truth.

Maybe Bettie and Cassie could take Dad home and Rosie would stay behind with Mel. But she also needed to know why Dad, mild-mannered Dad, would do something so terrible to Mel.

Dominic and Mel were arguing now. "This doesn't change anything. You need to go to LA," Mel said.

"Now you want me to go? And leave you alone with that man, a man who tried to attack you?"

"I'm not alone. I have the girls and Mark and Eduardo. But you have to go."

Dominic let out a frustrated sigh. He was a grown man, but Mel ran the show. "You need to end this. Before someone gets hurt."

He left without a glance at Rosie or Cassie. "End what?" Rosie asked. When Mel didn't answer, she pressed on. "Why would Dad come to your room? Why would he do *that*?" she added as she gestured to the marks on Mel's neck.

"It's...a long story."

"You're lying," Cassie snapped.

Rosie's eyes widened. She couldn't believe Cassie would be so rude.

"Cassie..." But Cassie was done, too. She turned and walked away.

Rosie shot Mel a sympathetic look. "I'm sorry. I need to check on her."

She hurried after Cassie. "Wait up. Will you stop."

Cassie whirled around. "She's a liar, Rosie. I'm sorry if

you're too damn obsessed with finding Mum to see it, but she is. We have to end this."

Cassie resumed walking, heading past the cabin and toward the woods. "Cass, where are you going?"

"None of your damn business. Do not follow me, Ro. I mean it."

Rosie had never seen Cassie this upset, but she was right. Mel was hiding something. She wasn't sure if it was about Dad or Mum, but whatever it was, Rosie was determined to find out before anyone else got hurt.

MAMA'S GUIDE TO NOT STARVING

HOW TO FORAGE, HARVEST, AND LIVE OFF THE LAND

Writing this when food waste is so prevalent feels bizarre. Last week I threw away a bag of arugula, three bell peppers, and half a serving of leftover meat loaf that your father forgot to eat.

Of course, writing about how to survive the impending apocalypse in the cozy office of my dream house is equally bizarre. If you could travel back in time to when I was your age and see how much food, water, and, well... everything we threw away, you'd think it was an alternative reality. A reality I wish more than anything you will live in.

Growing up, I spent a lot of time with my meemaw (that's South Texan for grandma) because my mama was in and out of rehab. Meemaw was born at the tail end of the Great Depression, and God love her she lived her life as if she were still suffering through it. She reused and repurposed everything. The idea of wasting anything was unspeakable. But wasting food? Unforgivable.

She'd chide your uncle Lucas or me for not finishing every last bite on our plates and scoffed at the idea of going out to eat.

As much as I wish I could say I internalized her teachings, I didn't. We waste so much shit! But chances are if you're reading this, there's no more Costco.

No more farmers markets.

Definitely no more Whole Foods.

You are the one sourcing and preparing your food. It's all on you.

Food storage and preparation are now the difference between life and death. Which means you should never underestimate the fundamentals of food storage. Below are some basics that will stretch your food far enough to make me and Meemaw proud.

Food Preparation

When you get a new food item, the countdown toward expiration begins. For the most part, you can't stop food from going bad, but if you're smart about it, you can prolong the shelf life of your foods, sometimes by years. Food storage and preparation are all about keeping five things at bay:

1. Oxygen: It may be one of the life-giving compounds for humans, but from a food preservation standpoint, oxygen is the enemy. As its name

implies, oxygen oxidizes things. I won't bore you with the molecular complexities of oxidation since I don't know them (I'm a movie producer, sue me, lol). But I do know that oxidized food is rancid, will give you the runs, and may kill you (apologies in advance for how much bathroom talk is in this guide but it is what it is).

2. Moisture: Moisture causes rot and creates a friendly environment for unfriendly guests, namely mold, bacteria, and pests. Keeping things dry keeps them more shelf-stable.

3. Critters: This may be my Southern roots showing, but a critter is any animal with four or more legs that wants to eat your food. They're an immediate threat. As I write this, rodents are responsible for eating and destroying 22 percent of the world's food supply annually. This one will be difficult to prevent, because animals are tenacious as hell. Keeping a dog or cat around to fend off rodents will make your life much easier. Airtight containers keep bugs and insects out. And if your food and ingredients are stored in safe, secure places, you'll prevent bigger, unwanted pests like bears, mountain lions, and strange people from eating your shit.

4. Light: I'm not sure why sunlight is so hard on food. I read an article once that UV radiation can break down cell walls or something like that, but the

point is, unless you're keeping plants alive, keep your food in as dark a place as possible. Burying canned goods in the ground is a pretty solid strategy for prolonging their shelf life. More on that later.

5. Heat: Heat may be good for sterilizing water and cooking food, but it's also a great way to spoil meats, produce, and pretty much any canned good you have. Almost all instructions for canned goods and most ingredients say to store your pantry staples in a cool and dark environment.

Food Storage

Enter cold storage. Refrigerators and freezers are the best sources of cold storage, because they are temperature-controlled and get cold enough to slow or even kill microorganisms. If you don't have a fridge or freezer, root cellars, basements, and pantries are your next best bet.

If you have a freezer (God, I hope you all have a freezer), you can freeze soups, meats, dairy—pretty much anything—for up to six months. Remember to wrap your food tightly first. You may be able to get away with leaving your food in the freezer longer, but try not to. Freezer burn won't hurt you, but your food won't taste good.

You've got this. I know you do.

Love,
Mama Bear

CASSIE

Cassie stood in the shadows and surveyed the three parked cars in the makeshift garage that were in various stages of repair and refurbishing.

Next to them was a gleaming black Harley-Davidson motorbike. She'd spent the last few days orienting herself to her surroundings, something Dad had drilled into her and her sisters for as long as she could remember. She'd located the water storage facility, the greenhouse where Eduardo worked, and Dominic's garage.

She watched as Dominic angrily loaded up the saddlebags on his motorbike with bottles of water and bags of food in preparation for his trip.

Cassie dug into the pocket of her shorts and took out one of her father's contraband cigarettes. Dad thought he was so clever asking Paul to buy them for him, completely unaware that Paul was so terrified of Cassie that he told her everything her father said.

She knew that smoking was terrible, but Dad had lost so much of his independence, and smoking made him happy, so she decided why the hell not let him have this small pleasure. She hadn't told her sisters about it, or that she herself enjoyed a cigarette now and then. It helped steady her nerves, which she desperately needed right now for what would come next.

She lit the tip and waited. It didn't take long. The scent of tobacco wafted over to Dominic, who glanced out at the woods. "Who's out there?"

There was no fear in his voice. She was certain he had a weapon nearby, which was why she quickly stepped out of the shadows. "Just one of the unwanted fucking kids," she said in her best exaggerated American accent.

She thought she saw a flicker of remorse, but then it was gone. "I don't have time for this. I'm leaving."

"I know that. I'm coming with you."

He laughed. "Yeah, right."

"Your mum said that Joey knows my mum, and you do business with him. I need to talk to him, find out what he knows so that my family can put all this shite behind us."

"You want to talk to Joey? You don't even know who he is."

"Sure I do. Two-time petty criminal from the San Fernando Valley. Founder of the Guardians, a doomsday prepper group that started in the Valley and moved to Silverlake after the Collapse. Runs a criminal enterprise aka gang in modern-day New Pacific," Cassie said.

Dominic looked surprised. "How did you . . ."

Cassie reached into her pocket and pulled out a bootleg Apple cell phone that she'd purchased from Allan, one of her classmates at university. It was a relic, he said, but it worked. He'd rigged it to connect to an underground virtual network, allowing Cassie to make calls and search dark web databases as needed.

Cassie didn't know much or really care about technology, but there was no way she was coming here unprepared. Obviously, there were risks if she was caught with a banned device, but Allan had given her a protective case that scanners couldn't detect. "If Joey can give us clues about our mum, and we can figure out what happened once and for all, we can go home."

"Joey is a human shit stain. The kind of person who only has power when the power dynamic shifts, and that's because he has no moral code whatsoever. We do business with him because he cornered the market on medications. He's got drugs that my mom needs that the doctors can't get..."

He stopped himself, annoyed that he'd revealed too much. "Even if I didn't care whether you come along, which I do, Mom would have my ass. LA isn't a good place for anyone, especially—"

"Please don't say *girls*. I have had enough women's studies courses to last a lifetime and cannot handle any more misogyny," Cassie interrupted.

"Fine. It doesn't matter. You're not coming, and that's all there is to say about that."

Dominic reached for a hook on the wall where several

sets of keys were hanging. A confused look flashed across his face.

"Looking for these?" Cassie asked.

He turned around to see Cassie holding the keys to his motorcycle. "Take me or I'll drive myself," she said flatly.

Dominic laughed, which came out an amused bark. "You wouldn't know where to go."

She shrugged and pulled out a current New Pacific map that Dr. McLaughlin had printed for her before they left. Thanks to Dad's *always be prepared* motto.

"I'll figure it out," Cassie said with more conviction than she felt.

She'd read her mum's chapter on navigation and purchased a compass, but her track record for getting lost in their small village was well documented and lovingly mocked by her sisters. But she wasn't going to wait for Dad to get arrested while Mel brainwashed Rosie. Cassie shook the keys impatiently. "Clock's ticking."

Dominic let out an exasperated sigh. "This might be the stupidest thing anyone's done."

Cassie remained unbothered. She had two sisters. She was used to being insulted.

Dominic handed over a spare helmet. She struggled to buckle the strap. Annoyed, Dominic reached out to help. She almost shook him away, but her bravado didn't extend to cracking her skull if they crashed. His hands quickly adjusted the helmet, ensuring it was secure. "It's not too late to change your mind," he said softly, his hands touching her chin.

She looked up, refusing to let him see her uncertainty. "I want my father to live out whatever time he has left, whatever time we have left with him, at home. Our home, not here in this place where everyone is looking at him like he's..."

She trailed off. Like what? Like a liar? Or a killer?

Dominic gave in and climbed onto the bike. "Don't you want to tell your sisters that you're leaving?" he asked.

How daft does he think I am? "So you can leave me? Don't worry. I left them a note."

Cassie steeled herself as she climbed on the back of the bike. She knew Bettie would be hurt that Cassie hadn't told her face-to-face what she was doing. Rosie would be irate. Or maybe she would understand. Cassie had always been the one vying to be part of the group, and accepting when she wasn't. At the end of the day, this wasn't about the three of them. It was Dad's life, and if she was being honest, she wanted proof that he would never hurt their mum. Because he wouldn't.

As Dominic started the motorbike, and the engine roared to life, her arms tightened around his waist. She couldn't help the nervous flutter she felt in her stomach. She'd never done anything even slightly reckless. All her life, Cassie had been content to let Rosie call the shots, but she was done. She didn't know what she was going to find out in LA, but being in control felt bloody good.

r/SoCalValleyPreppers

8,200 Members

PRIVATE CHAT

GoJoe420
Hey, you good?

GoJoe420
Just checking in. I really hope you didn't let those idiot's comments get to you. The guys felt bad.

Mamabear3
Did they?

GoJoe420
Nah, but I wanted you to feel better.

Mamabear3
Sorry, I had a big week at work (it's award season) and I barely had any time for myself. But I'm good. Got my planter beds in this week. I told the girls we're going to grow our own strawberries and they're so excited.

GoJoe420

Hot damn. That's what Im talking about. U should try pota-
toes to.

Mamabear3

I'll add it to the list.
Can I ask you a question?

GoJoe420

Shoot.

Mamabear3

What got you into prepping?

GoJoe420

Real talk? I love my parents but they ain't worth shit when
it comes to looking after themselves. My mom was in a car
wreck a few years back and it messed her up real good.
She can walk but she's always in pain. My dad manages
a car wash, and cracks open a Budweiser when he walks
through the door then moves on to his good buddy Jack
Daniel. I work in construction, so I cover the bills, but it's
all on me to care for them if something happens. I started
getting into prepping and figured there were more regular
folk out there like me who might want to share tips. When
I started this group, there was 4 of us & now we got over
eight thousand members.

Mamabear3

I'm so grateful for your help. It's made me feel so much better building my supplies up. I know my husband thinks I'm silly doing all this, but he wasn't there when the break-in happened.

GoJoe420

Where was he?

Mamabear3

Traveling for work. Sam doesn't read the papers or watch the news. He lives in this blissful bubble. He's so relentlessly positive that sometimes it blinds him to how bad things actually are. Or how scared I am that we won't be able to protect the girls.

GoJoe420

That's how it is for a lotta folks. We're wrong and their ain't nothing we gotta prepare for, at least we're ready. What's the other option? Watching my mom & dad suffer? Watching your kiddos starve? No fucking thank u.

Mamabear3

Does anyone think your prepping is nuts?

GoJoe420

Um... everyone lol. I broke up with my girl over it.

Mamabear3

Really? I'm sorry to hear that.

GoJoe420

Me too. Emily and I went to high school together. Connected a few years back and BAM. Where the fuck u been all my life. She's a great girl. Real smart. A NICU nurse at Cedars-Sinai. Not sure what she saw in a bum like me but we were good together. We set a wedding date. But she hated the prepping. At first she was like okay, it's a little weird, but you do you. Then she told me she didn't want to hear about it anymore. Said it stressed her out & she saw enough stressful shit at work. I tried. I really did, but it was like she was asking me to hide who I was. Fucking wrecked me to call it quits, because she was the one, but you've gotta live your life on your terms.

Mamabear3

Yeah, I hear you. My family and friends act like I'm selling meth. The other day my brother Lucas said it was embar-rassing. Keeps telling me not to talk about it because people will think I'm nuts. Lucas loves telling me how wrong I am about everything except when he wants to borrow money.

Go4Joe420

When I hear that shit, I'm glad I'm an only child.

Mamabear3

I love him, but he drives me crazy sometimes.

GoJoe420

Family usually does, but it's all we've got in this world.

Mamabear3

It's true. We lost our Mama when Lucas was so young and it's been the two of us for so long. But it does get tiring looking after him as well as the girls.
Think you and Emily have a chance to get back together?

GoJoe420

Nah, last I heard she hooked up with some doctor. Probably planning her fancy new life as a Beverly Hills housewife. I'm not bitter but if she thinks all his money is gonna protect her from what's coming, she's a damn sheep.

Mamabear3

What do you think is coming?

GoJoe420

War. Famine. Technological collapse. Take your pick.

Mamabear3

You seem so calm about it all.

GoJoe420

I am calm, but only 'cuz I stay ready. I got food storage, home security & a plan for what would happen if shit got real bad. For years we've expected the government to take over, but I don't think they're gonna be able to handle what happens next.

Mamabear3

On that happy note, I've gotta run. The girls have swimming lessons.

GoJoe420

Stay safe out there, Mama. We'll talk soon.

BETTIE

Did you know about this? Did you know?" Bettie couldn't stop the shrillness in her voice as she shook Rosie awake. When she didn't immediately respond, Bettie pulled off the thin white sheet covering her. Rosie startled, blinking at Bettie in confusion. "Bets, what are you doing?"

"Did you know, Ro? Did you?" Bettie shouted. She thrust Cassie's handwritten note at her.

Rosie sat up, still drowsy with sleep, and read out loud.

One of us has to fix this mess, and it's not going to be you idiots. I'm going to LA with Dominic to talk to Joey and find out if he knows anything about Mum. I'll be in touch soon. Take care of Dad.

P.S. I love you both. Don't be mad.

"She went to LA?" Rosie said in disbelief.

Bettie understood the outrage. Cassie wasn't the impulsive type.

"You think I would have been okay with Cassie going to LA without us? Of course she didn't tell me," Rosie snapped. She let out a frustrated exhale. "Does Dad know?"

Bettie shook her head. "No, but we have to tell him."

"Yeah, sure, let's tell our father who attacked Mel last night that his favorite daughter has gone off to a city he despises with a man he doesn't know."

Bettie glared at Rosie. "I know lying is your new favorite thing, but Cassie is his daughter. We're not keeping this from him. And I don't know why he did what he did last night, but Mel is hiding something and I'm done ignoring that. Do you understand?"

Rosie looked surprised by Bettie's intensity, but they needed to get on the same page and quickly.

"Fine. You talk to Dad and I'll get dressed. We'll meet in Mel's cabin in fifteen minutes and find out where Cassie is and how to get her back."

Bettie headed to the door. Rosie grabbed Bettie's hand. "We're gonna get through this, Bets."

Bettie was totally and utterly annoyed by Rosie, but she'd said what Bettie needed to hear. She squeezed Rosie's hand back. Her sister's steady resolve always made her feel better.

A minute later, she was knocking softly on Dad's cabin door.

"Come in," he said.

Bettie pushed open the door, expecting to find Dad in bed, but he was dressed in his nice khaki slacks and a T-shirt, his hair combed neatly, sitting up in one of the desk chairs. He almost looked like his old self. "How's my favorite girl?" he asked.

"I'm okay. I'm worried. We all are."

Sam grimaced. "I'm sorry about last night. I don't...I can't explain why I did that. I'd never hurt anyone. You have to believe that."

She did. Didn't she?

"What happened with Mel? I know something did. You can tell us."

Sam shook his head. "I can't tell you, Bets. I can't."

Tears spilled down his cheeks, and Bettie resisted the urge to shout at him. She needed to know. Were they in danger? Had Mel done something to Mum? What was he hiding? She wanted to push him harder, to shout at him until he broke, but she wasn't cruel. He was sick and scared, and she needed to protect him the way Cassie would.

She decided then and there she'd get answers from Mel. For a moment, Bettie hesitated. Maybe she shouldn't tell him about Cassie. But then she imagined how hurt and betrayed he would feel when he found out they'd lied. She took a deep breath. She would tell him enough to keep him informed but not worried.

"You should know that Cassie went to LA with Dominic."

"She did what?" Sam asked, eyes wide with disbelief.

"It's okay. She'll be back soon. It's a quick trip to get supplies."

"What supplies? Why would she do that?" Bettie could see Dad getting agitated.

"I'm not sure, but Cass can take care of herself. You made sure of it."

"She'll be back soon? She said that?"

Bettie forced a smile. "Yes. Just a quick trip there and back." She hoped Cassie wasn't going to make a liar of her, too.

"Okay, that's good. She'll be good. My Cassie always is."

"Are you hungry? We can go get something to eat?"

He shook his head. "I was going to take a walk, but a nap sounds good."

"Of course," Bettie said. She wondered if he was afraid to see Mel, but she was almost relieved not to have them meet face-to-face. "I'll check in on you later."

She gave him a kiss on the cheek. He looked up at her. "You're a good lass, Bets. I'm a lucky man."

Bettie blinked away tears as she left. She wasn't going to be a weepy mess when she saw Mel.

Rosie and Bettie arrived at the main cabin at the same time, and they found Mel at the dining table eating toast and berries, her neck a deep shade of crimson, the hand-print bruises more shocking in the light of day. She seemed unbothered until she spotted both girls heading her way.

"What is it? What's wrong?"

"Where is Dominic?" Bettie asked.

"He went to LA for supplies," Mel said, shrugging.

"With our sister. He took Cass, and we need to know exactly where he is."

A MOTHER'S GUIDE TO THE APOCALYPSE 203

Confused, Mel pushed her plate away.

"I'm afraid you need to start over. Dominic took her?"

Rosie thrust the note at Mel, who let out a string of expletives.

"When I see that little shit, I'm going to..." She stopped as she took in their worried faces. "Trust me, Dom is more than capable of protecting your sister. He's armed, and he knows the city better than anyone. I wouldn't worry."

"Too late. We're already worried. Our sister is in a city you said you never set foot in because it's too dangerous. Mel, we don't care if Dominic has a bloody armed militia with him, we need to find Cass. Which means we need a car and a driver or a bloody map and we'll find them ourselves," Rosie said.

At last, Bettie thought, *Rosie is growing a backbone.*

Mel waved her hands helplessly. "I wish you could go, but you would need to apply for a travel pass to enter the city."

"Cassie didn't have one," Bettie said.

"Dominic does. The passes offer an extra level of security to the residents of LA, especially since there are still people within our borders who aren't happy we seceded. I never go there, so I don't have one."

"Then how do we get one?" Bettie insisted.

"You can apply at the post office, but they take three to five days to process, which is unnecessary because by then Cassie and Dom will be safe and sound."

Bettie stifled a scream. A travel pass? Why hadn't she done more research on this place? Why had she blindly trusted Rosie to handle it all? Oh right, because that's what she always did. Blindly trust people who let her down.

As Bettie seethed, Mel tried to reassure her. "I'll call Dom on the satellite phone. We'll talk to them soon."

Bettie expected Rosie to put up a fight and say, *Forget the damn permit, we'll go to LA without one, consequences be damned*, but Rosie relented. "If you're sure they'll be back soon, we'll wait. We still need to discuss what happened last night with Dad."

Bettie saw Mel's confidence waver, but her neutral expression returned. "I have no idea what possessed Sam to lash out. I don't want to blame his illness, but cognitive issues can cause behavioral changes, especially if someone already has a temper."

"How did you..."

"Your mother mentioned it once or twice. She said that Sam would yell and stomp around and then it would all be over."

Rosie glanced at Bettie knowingly. "He's lost it on his doctors before. They warned us mood changes were possible."

Bettie stared at her sister. Dad had always been a bit hot-tempered, but he was never violent. For a moment, Bettie wondered if Mel had special powers. Why was Rosie always so quick to agree with her? It was maddening. Bettie was done waiting around.

A MOTHER'S GUIDE TO THE APOCALYPSE 205

"I need to call Max. It's been three days since we spoke, and he'll be worried. Dr. McLaughlin said if I email her, she'll contact Max and get a video chat organized."

"Sounds good. I'll ring Ellen down at the store and ask her to email your professor to set up the call. Once you're confirmed, Eduardo can drive you into town."

Bettie hesitated. She had no idea where Cassie was. Could she really leave Rosie behind, too? She took a deep breath. Her other option was hoping Rosie came to her senses and saw that Mel was hiding something. Which didn't seem likely.

"That would be great," Bettie said.

An hour later, Eduardo appeared in Mel's cabin, dressed in linen pants and a fitted polo shirt, looking like he was off to a yacht party. He spotted Bettie staring at him, and he smiled. "Just because the world fell apart doesn't mean I have to do the same. Clothes still make the man."

To her surprise, Bettie laughed. He was as charming in real life as she'd hoped he would be. She waved goodbye to Rosie and Mel, who were looking through more photos, and checked in on Sam, who was sleeping. Eduardo led Bettie to a small sedan parked in the makeshift auto repair area. She climbed in beside him and buckled her seat belt.

"It's a short drive to the general store, so no need to worry. My vampire days are behind me."

Bettie looked down to find she was gripping the armrest so tightly she could see her veins. She let out a laugh, remembering his portrayal of Count Dracula in a remake of the classic film.

"Sorry, this trip has proven more stressful than I imagined."

"I understand. You're dealing with a lot, but don't worry. Mel's got it handled."

He said it so confidently, she wished she could believe him. Instead she leaned back in her seat and watched in silence as he navigated the car down the back roads.

"Once we're in town, be careful who you talk to. All pregnancies are tracked and recorded in a database, part of an unfortunate holdover in the law from our previous government, so there is a small chance you could be questioned."

"Questioned about what?"

"Health care. Eating habits. Where you plan to have the child? People ask lots of questions that are none of their business. But that's why I'm here. To encourage them to mind their business."

He patted his waistband, and Bettie looked over to find that Eduardo had a small handgun tucked into it. "Who knew all my weapons training would come in handy?"

He was referencing his James Bond days back when he was on billboards and everyone knew his name, but Bettie's head was swimming. She hated this bloody country and their weapons. She'd thought this place had changed, but there were so many guns, and rules, and things to worry about, it all didn't sound much different from the old days. Maybe, like people, places never really changed.

"I heard about what happened with Sam last night. My grandmother had dementia. It's a bastard of an illness."

"Yes, it is," Bettie said. But her father's illness was the last thing she wanted to discuss. "You and Mel go way back?" she asked.

"As far as I can remember. We met in our late twenties and hit it off instantly. Your mum and I were good friends, but Liv was always about her family, which made Mel a bit of an outsider. And as close as Mel and Liv were, they were also business partners, which can complicate things. Mel was more financially minded. Your mother was all about the art, which left them at odds. Didn't help when the business began to change. Less money for the producers. More oversight. Artificial intelligence and the lack of appreciation for the medium made it hard to make great films. Your mom was a fighter, though, and insisted on making a few films that unfortunately did not do well. The company lost money. Which might have been okay if it hadn't coincided with all her prepping. Then your mom and Mel had some big falling-out. I don't know the details, but I do know Mel never stopped regretting what happened."

Mel and Mum had a fight? Is that what Dad was upset about? Bettie had so many more questions, but they'd arrived in town. It was small and cozy, with quaint-looking shops lining the streets. But there was nothing quaint about the pickup trucks filled with men, women, and teenagers carrying guns as they shopped. Bettie looked at Eduardo with surprise. "Why does everyone have a weapon?" she asked.

"There's a lotta mistrust post-Collapse—for both the government and one another. *Love thy neighbor* is no longer a way of life. More like *Kill or be killed*. Which is why we should be as quick as we can."

Bettie nodded as Eduardo continued driving. In the distance, she spotted a large football field and hundreds of army-green tents lined up in a row. "What's that?"

"Climate camp. Lot of 'em shut down, but there's still half a dozen across the country. The ones out here in the middle of nowhere are mostly for the sick and elderly. The ones in the cities get more funding and are focused on kids and women."

He slowed to stop at a streetlight. Bettie could see the tired, sunburned faces of the aging men and women who lived there, shuffling about in ragged and faded clothing, eyes haunted by things they'd seen. "I thought things were better here. It's been so long since the Collapse," she said softly.

"They're certainly better, but nothing changes overnight. Mel and Dom, me and Mark, we were protected by our money and our ability to do whatever it took to survive, but not everyone was so lucky. Some people had to walk through the shit, and when they came out, there was just more shit. This may always be their way of life. It happened in the Depression. Why should post-Collapse be any different?"

It was a depressing question. Eduardo looked over at her. "You're not telling me your country is immune to suffering?"

Bettie had no answer. *Dad protected us so much from the outside world. Maybe too much,* Bettie thought. Seeing this kind of suffering made her deeply sad.

Thankfully, Eduardo pulled into the parking lot of the general store. It was a simply constructed building with an old-timey sign that read GENERAL STORE hanging in the front window.

"I thought we were going to city hall?" Bettie asked.

"This is it. We're in the boonies, kiddo. Everyone and everything does double duty. Town doc moonlights as the sheriff. City hall is also the general store. It's the way of the new world."

He gestured to the store. "Mel said you have your own email account?"

"I do," she said. Dr. McLaughlin had created an account for Bettie and her sisters to use.

"In that case, I'll stay here and take a little catnap. Mark's snoring is something else. The man's a real window rattler. If you need me, give a shout."

A wave of relief flooded Bettie. She hadn't been sure if

her plan would work with him watching over her. But now she could at least try and figure out a way to escape Mel and this place.

As Mel promised, she found Ellen inside, stocking waters in a small cooler. "Hi, I'm Bettie. Mel said that I could use your video-chat system?"

Bettie was self-conscious about her words. Was that what they called it? She must have been close enough, though, because Ellen gave a curt nod and escorted her to a back office, opened the computer, and logged Bettie in. She slipped out of the room with a "Come get me if you need me."

Bettie waited patiently for the computer to connect, letting out a relieved sigh when Dr. McLaughlin appeared on the screen.

"Bettie, it's good to see you," she said. "I wasn't able to reach Max, but I left him a message."

Bettie nodded, relieved to see someone she trusted. "I'm actually here because I need to talk to you. I'm... We're..." Bettie's voice shook, and tears filled her eyes.

"Are you okay?"

Bettie took a ragged breath, thinking about all they'd endured.

Dad's detainment and the threat of another interview.

Dad attacking Mel.

Cassie leaving for LA with Dominic.

The news of the baby.

A MOTHER'S GUIDE TO THE APOCALYPSE   211

"No, I'm not. We're not. Cassie went to LA to search for Mum and we don't have a permit to go to LA and search for her and I'm not sure where we would look..." Bettie began, her words pouring out.

"A permit? What permit?" Off camera, Bettie heard a sharp voice. Dr. McLaughlin waved off whoever was speaking, but the voice continued. "That's bollocks. You don't need a permit to travel throughout New Pacific. That's only required if you're going to the rebel states."

They didn't need a permit? Was it possible that Mel had lied about that, too? What else had she lied about? Dad's interview? Cassie and Dominic? Was her sister safe?

Dr. McLaughlin was calling her name. "Bettie! My wife, Rita, is here with me. She wants to speak to you."

A woman appeared, a gray bob framing her face; she wore tortoiseshell glasses, and concern was etched on her face. Rita was as unassuming as they came, which made sense for someone in British intelligence. "Hi, Bettie, I've heard a lot about you and your sisters. I'm not sure if you know but I work in the government. I'd like you to tell me everything that's occurred since your arrival, and we'll go from there."

Terror gripped Bettie. She wanted to cry.

No, she wanted to run. To hurry back to Mel's and tell Rosie what she knew and let her take charge, the way she always did. But Rosie wasn't here. This was Bettie's chance to be the leader. All those instructions her mum had left telling them what to do in the event that things fell apart. Well, here she was. *This* was her moment.

Bettie started from when they first arrived. When she was done, Rita looked troubled as she typed on a screen beside her. "I'm not sure what's going on. I can see that there's a flag in our system on all your passports, which says you can't travel, but there is no additional information. Which is quite odd."

"So Dad isn't wanted for questioning? Or anything related to my mum?"

"No. If he were wanted for questioning, the British consulate would have been contacted and they would have assigned him a solicitor."

"But he was detained when we arrived. It doesn't make sense."

"No, it doesn't. I don't know what game this woman is playing, or why she's lying to you, but she's definitely lying."

There was more typing in the background, and Rita frowned again. "It says here that Mel was hospitalized a few years back. In a mental health care facility. Apparently she attacked her own son."

Bettie's eyes widened. "Dominic?"

"She suffered a nervous breakdown and attacked him when he tried to get her help. She was hospitalized for three months. Of course, that was several years ago. It appears she's on medication and hasn't had any issues in the interim."

Until now? Bettie wondered. She leaned back. All her fears about Mel being a liar were now confirmed—and the woman was dangerous. Maybe she'd provoked Dad, and that was why he attacked her?

"What do we do now?" Bettie said, her voice barely a whisper.

"I have to make some calls and see how to clear up the hold on your passports. Once that's done, we can arrange for transport for you and your family back to the UK. I know you were hoping to find news about your mum, but from what I can tell, this woman has sent you there on some kind of wild goose chase."

A wave of crushing disappointment hit Bettie. All of this for nothing. She couldn't imagine how Rosie would feel, or what she might say, but at this point Bettie didn't care. She wanted to go home.

But not without Cassie. That was out of the question.

"We can't leave without Cass, but I've got no clue where she is or where to start. I don't..."

"Take a deep breath, Bettie. We'll find her. All you have to do is go back to Mel's and pretend that nothing is wrong until I can get all this sorted. Can you do that?"

Bettie grimaced. She wasn't the strong one. Not like her sisters. But she didn't have a choice.

"I'll do whatever I have to if it means keeping my family safe."

"Good girl," Rita said. "Keep your chin up. I have Mel's

address, and I'll send someone to get you. It won't be long before you're all back home and you can forget any of this happened."

Bettie ached for that moment. "Will you tell Max that I'm okay? That I love him and I'll see him soon."

"Of course," Dr. McLaughlin said. "We'll let him know."

"Thank you. Both of you," she said tearfully as she clicked off, grateful that she had found an ally.

Now all Bettie had to do was channel all her courage and acting training. She wasn't sure what game Mel was playing, but she had no choice but to play along.

r/SoCalValleyPreppers

8,522 members

PRIVATE CHAT

Mamabear3
Do you think it's possible to die from lack of sleep? I might be dying.

GoJoe420
What's keeping u up?

Mamabear3
Cassie decided there are werewolves in her room and I have to feed them at five o'clock every morning.

GoJoe420
If that's not the cutest thing I ever heard...

Mamabear3
Says the man <u>not</u> getting up at 5am to feed them.

GoJoe420
True. But it's gonna end soon and youll be missing it.

Mamabear3

You're probably right. I thought night feeds would kill me and now I look at pictures from those days and think, "It wasn't that bad." Do you want kids? Sometimes I worry I'm so selfish for bringing them into this messed up world.

GoJoe420

That's horseshit. We gotta live 4 today. Sure I want little ones of my own, a whole mess of them. And trust me, when I find a special lady, I ain't gonna let anything, not even my worries about the future stop me. So cut the shit, Liv. You're clearly a great mama or you wouldn't be prepping.

Mamabear3

I don't know. I lost it this morning when the girls were fighting because they didn't want to wear pajamas even though it was pajama day at school and then we were running late, & Bettie screamed the whole drive because I wouldn't stop for ice cream.

GoJoe420

My mama lost her shit on me every day for thirty five years and she's still the best damn woman I know. Kids don't remember any of that. They just remember the love.

Mamabear3
I hope you're right.

GoJoe420
I usually am. You & your man good?

Mamabear3
Good? I'm not sure. We used to have so much time for each other and now between work and the girls, it feels like we're business partners. I want us to get back to each other but where is the time?

GoJoe420
Gotta make the time. Ain't that different from prepping. Take control of it.

Mamabear3
You make it sound easy.

GoJoe420
Most things are. We just get in our own damn way.

Mamabear3
Yeah, I need to do better with him. He's a good man.

GoJoe420
And you're a good woman.

Mamabear3
That's true. Thanks for letting me vent.

GoJoe420
Anytime! Gonna send u that podcast the others were talking about. Got a lotta good tips on getting your bug out bag ready.

Mamabear3
Thanks Joey. Talk soon.

CASSIE

Three hours later, Dominic and Cassie were still driving. Neither of them had said a word. Cassie loved the sound of the wind roaring as they sped down the motorway, and the temperature was at least fifteen degrees cooler. She wasn't sure if it was getting away from Mel or the desert air, but she could breathe again.

What surprised her most as they drove was how desolate and apocalyptic everything looked. There must have been hundreds of vehicles abandoned on the side of the motorway, like a twister had picked up the contents of a car lot and dumped them in the middle of nowhere.

"What's all this?" Cassie asked through the microphone in her helmet as they whizzed past the cars.

"The cars were abandoned during the firestorms, and later, climate refugees used them as shelter and a place to leave supplies for family and friends as they were passing through. There's a whole network of people who travel among the countries of what used to be the United States. So you'll go from New Pacific to New Nevada, and you can stop off here and rest or gear up."

"I'm surprised no one steals them," Cassie said.

"There are patrols who oversee these roads who shoot to kill if you try."

The more Cassie learned about this place, the less she wanted to stay. Especially every time they hit a pothole, and she felt like she had survived another near-death experience.

"Why are these roads so shite?" she asked.

"New Pacific refused to fund road construction, since the earthquake aftershocks lasted for so long. Said it'd be a waste of money only for them to be destroyed again. But we haven't had any quakes in three years, and the fault lines have been dormant. Yet the money people still say it's a waste of resources, especially since fewer people drive now. Which is mostly because of the roads." He laughed again. "Make it make sense."

Cassie was praying she could return to England before she experienced an earthquake. She didn't realize she'd said that out loud until Dom started to speak.

"There was a time when you didn't think about it. When I was a kid, we had them all the time. Small ones though. A hard jolt here. A heavy shake there. I hate to say we got used to it, but like Seattle got used to rain, or New Yorkers to the smell of trash, we adapted. We'd all heard the 'big one' was coming for so long that we got comfortable. Not your mum, though. She kept talking about it. Driving my mom and Sam crazy."

A MOTHER'S GUIDE TO THE APOCALYPSE   221

Cassie's breath quickened as she thought of her mum's notebook and all the worries that had consumed her.

"Then Aunt Liv was gone and so were you and Sam, and it was me and Mom and it just seemed like bad things kept happening. Water conservation days and heat warnings, all sorts of climate stuff that I knew wasn't good, but I was a ten-year-old kid, playing sports and daydreaming about kissing a girl. I was all set to go to a soccer camp at UCLA. It's funny 'cuz you never know when your life will change. Mom and I were both sleeping when the big one hit. Not sure why so many quakes happen in the middle of the night, but it was like a bomb went off. One minute, we were upstairs in our beds, and the next, the ceiling exploded, and I was lying on concrete and covered in dust. A fucking 8.0 earthquake. Complete devastation in less than thirty seconds."

He grew quiet for a moment, focused on the potholes ahead.

"What happened to your mum? I mean, you don't have to tell me... I'm curious." She was more than a little curious, but tried to play it cool.

Dominic cleared his throat. "After the shaking stopped, I heard Mom screaming my name. It sounded like a wounded animal... this... this high-pitched, desperate, inhuman wail that still gives me nightmares. I'd sprained my wrist and broken a few ribs when I fell, but that sound... I had to get to her. I climbed through rubble and wires, knowing that she was hurt, but also afraid. I could smell smoke and gasoline and I understood there was a possibility that the house could go up in flames."

He paused again. "When I found Mom, I had to move piles of concrete and steel beams. Took almost half an hour. When I moved that last beam, I almost threw up. Her legs were crushed. I knew I couldn't move her. No way. So I..." He paused. "So I left her and ran to get help. It was chaos. So many houses on our block were gone. Nothing but rubble and dirt. It was the apocalypse, just like Aunt Liv warned."

Dominic put on his blinker and made a turn, and as the sun began to rise, Cassie could see the city in the distance. Her mum's home. The place where she'd been born. She felt Dominic tense up.

"What is it?" Cassie asked.

"We're being followed. I thought I lost them a few miles back, but they're definitely tailing us."

"Who is it?"

"I don't know, and I have no intention of finding out. Hold on."

A pit formed in Cassie's stomach as Dominic gunned the engine and the bike surged forward even faster. Cassie let out a gasp and gripped him tighter as he wove through the city streets. She kept her eyes focused on the road ahead. *It'll be okay. You'll be okay*, she said to herself, parroting one of Rosie's ridiculous mantras.

A MOTHER'S GUIDE TO THE APOCALYPSE 223

As the bike surged forward, a bullet exploded from a chamber, kicking up dirt as it narrowly missed them. "Sonofabitch, hold on," Dominic shouted.

He made a hairpin turn, the bike kicking up more dirt and rocks, and then made so many turns into small streets and alleyways that she had to close her eyes to stop the spinning. Dominic gunned the engine and before long they were roaring up a large canyon, their hunters suddenly gone.

"Can we slow down?" Cassie said breathlessly.

"Not till I'm sure we're in the clear," he said. "Hold on. It's gonna get bumpy."

Cassie wasn't sure how it was possible to get any bumpier, but she held on for dear life as they climbed higher and higher into the canyon. She wasn't sure if they drove another ten minutes or an hour, but at last he began to slow.

"We're okay. For now at least," he said, letting out a ragged breath. He reached an overlook, navigated the bike to the side of the road, and turned off the engine. Cassie took in the 360-degree view of the city, a skyline filled with skyscrapers on one side and burned-out half-built buildings on the other.

"Isn't much now, but this used to be a famous overlook where tourists came to take pictures. Now it's a view over a graveyard," Dominic said as he climbed off the bike and stretched his arms.

He pointed down below. "The city has been split into

sections. The West Side and what used to be Beverly Hills were destroyed by the quake, floods, and fires, but the climate is bearable so people still flock here. If you can afford to pay off the gangs, you can make it a home, but they're pretty ruthless. City officials tried to police it, but they gave up. They made the decision to focus on rebuilding Hollywood and downtown and let the other half of the city fend for itself."

"So who was following us? One of the gangs?"

"Maybe. Or a Guardian patrol. They're always scouting for new girls for their breeding program."

"Breeding?" Cassie said. "Please don't tell me that's..."

"It's exactly what you think it is. The Guardians want to repopulate the world. Rebuild what was lost. Back in the day, there was this whole pronatalist movement, all these dickhead Silicon Valley tech titans got worried about declining birth rates and they started spreading their nonsense to the masses so pretty soon dickheads like Joey were listening to podcasts telling 'em they needed to breed. When they realized they couldn't brainwash enough women to join the cause, they decided to take them and sell them for the highest price."

Cassie felt sick to her stomach. "Joey...he's the leader of the Guardians?"

"Yeah, the Collapse showed us all who were heroes and who were monsters."

"Which one are you?" Cassie asked softly.

A MOTHER'S GUIDE TO THE APOCALYPSE 225

Dominic shrugged. "Depends on the day. Or who you ask, I guess."

Cassie wondered if she should be afraid, but she wasn't. The adrenaline had given them both a sense of energy. Dominic opened the saddlebag and pulled out a blanket and a bottle of water. He laid the blanket down and gestured for her to sit and drink. Cassie didn't argue, drinking as she took in the view. This was her mother's city. Cassie's own home for the briefest time. For all her father's negative talk about this place, Cassie was glad to see it. To see where she'd come from. She closed her eyes, imagined her mum and dad taking her and her sisters on adventures around the city, imagined a life here, going to movie premieres with Mum and learning golf with Dad. All the memories they'd never experience.

A wave of regret washed over her. She wanted her sisters here. That was the problem with being a triplet. You could never have anything all your own. Even your memories were forever shared, and if they weren't you felt like you were cheating.

"You okay?" Dominic asked. "That was pretty intense back there."

Cassie focused her attention on Dominic. He had taken off his helmet, and she could see his face now, but it showed no emotion. Despite their close call with death, he was as dispassionate as he'd been back in Idyllwild.

"I'm...processing," she said.

He looked at her and shook his head. "You must think I'm the biggest asshole."

Cassie laughed. "Do *you* think you're an asshole?"

He sighed. "Probably. It's nothing personal."

"The way you've been acting toward me feels pretty personal."

"I know. You should hear the rest of the story about my mom to understand why I didn't want you here. If you're willing to listen."

Cassie leaned against the bike and gestured for him to continue.

"When I left after the quake, I saw our next-door neighbor who was a surgeon at Cedars-Sinai. That was the one bit of good luck we had. So many people were begging for help, but I got to him first. Back at what was left of our house, we dug through rubble to find a blanket and cut enough pieces to make a tourniquet to stop the bleeding. We settled Mom on a makeshift gurney using my surfboard, and we were able to get another neighbor's SUV to take her to the hospital. It was only ten minutes away, but so many buildings had been toppled, cars flattened like pancakes, it took an hour to get there. The doctor stopped the bleeding but I had to keep talking to Mom to keep her awake, make sure she didn't go into shock. I've never been in a war zone, but everyone who lived through that quake said that's what it was like. There were bloody bodies everywhere. Crushed limbs. Children crying. Fuck, grown men crying. So many

A MOTHER'S GUIDE TO THE APOCALYPSE 227

people got turned away from the hospital. So many never had a chance. I believe in hell for sure after what I saw that day. But there has to be a God as well, because we got Mom help. Got her emergency surgery. There was no way she should have lived but she did. Through surgery and the amputation of both of her legs. Through two infections and all the bullshit she had to go through to survive months in a hospital during one of the worst natural disasters in history. There was no more FEMA or government aid to rebuild or provide for citizens. They said fuck you. We can't finance all this. You're on your own now. We were on our own." He stopped and stared out at the endless city beneath them. Then took a deep breath as though he were about to make his final confession.

"But after everything was over, Mom never stopped obsessing over Sam and Liv and you girls. Said she had to right her wrongs."

"What does that mean?"

He shrugged. "She told me it wasn't my business, which almost made it worse. Sometimes it was like I wasn't there. Mom was so stuck in the past, she couldn't see her own son. I was still a kid, and it didn't matter what I thought. I did as I was told. As I got older, though, I had to figure things out. How to get our money out of the bank and how to feed us all. How to fight off the predators, both human and animal, all while Mom struggled physically and mentally." He paused, clearly uncertain about what else to reveal.

"Struggled with what? She seems pretty together."

He hesitated again. "She had a breakdown a few years back...all the shit we did and still have to do to keep safe. You do these things and you say you're okay. If you shoot someone and never see them fall, maybe they didn't die. If you shoot someone and you do see them fall, you know they were gonna kill you. That's the world we lived in. I think it all kind of caught up to her. She's better now, but I can't...let her get back there."

"You still left her today?"

"Didn't have a choice. She needs meds, and I can only get them in LA."

"But after what happened last night, aren't you worried about your mum and my dad being alone together?"

"Worried is my natural resting state, but she's not alone. Eduardo and Mark are there, and so are your sisters. Besides, when it comes to self-protection, Mom's fine. She let her guard down once with Sam. She won't do it again."

The idea that her father was dangerous went unsaid, but so did the notion that Mel would do something to Sam if he came after her again.

"I've never left my dad before today. Or my sisters."

Cassie was surprised by how much she enjoyed talking to someone who didn't know the Clark triplets. "I used to read books about how kids would go off and live their own lives in different cities and towns and countries. Sometimes they would only see their families on holidays, and I simply couldn't comprehend it. I wouldn't know what to do without my sisters, and that makes me..." She trailed off.

"Makes you what?" Dominic asked.

"Makes me feel pathetic. Like I can't be my own person."

"Fuck, I haven't been my own person ever. My mom calls all the shots. But maybe that's better than the alternative. Where you're forced to walk this world alone. Lotta people had to do that after the Collapse."

Cassie hadn't thought about that. "I wish I knew Mum. She's this distant figure. I can *almost* hear her voice. Or see her face. I can *almost* remember what she smelled like or how her arms felt when she would hold me, but then it's gone. I came here hoping that we'd strike out. Hoping...I don't know. Hoping I could avoid feeling the longing and pain that haunt my sisters."

Dominic looked at her. Really looked at her. "Your mom was amazing, you know. So smart. You could ask her how big the earth was or how many bones were in the human body or how many Super Bowls the Dallas Cowboys won and she knew. She was so funny, too. She loved making fun of your dad's stuffy British ways and could do the best British accent. And don't get me started on my mom. Whenever she got too big for her britches, Aunt Liv would say, 'Mel, settle down. Your shit stinks like the rest of ours.' And you know what? Mom would settle down. Just 'cuz Aunt Liv said it. And I know that more than anything she loved you. Everyone knew that."

Cassie was surprised by the tears in her eyes. This was what she needed. A reminder of how much Mum had loved her. A reminder of why she had come here.

Something shifted between them. She was glad Dominic was here. That she was here with him. And if she were being honest, she didn't want to leave. She didn't want to face Joey or the Guardians or the mistakes her mum made.

As if he were reading her mind, Dominic gestured to the city below.

"We should wait a bit longer before we head back down to be sure they're not waiting us out. I've got another blanket in the back if you want to lie down and rest for a bit."

Cassie was exhausted, but there was no way she could sleep. "I'm good," she said.

Dominic shrugged. He sat beside her and they stared down at the city stretched out before them. They weren't friends, but they were no longer enemies. At least for now.

MAMA'S GUIDE TO FINDING SHELTER

Urban Spaces

Growing up, all I wanted was a home. One of those fancy homes from the magazines or TV shows that I watched with bright cheery kitchens and cozy living rooms and a backyard with swings and a slide and an in-ground swimming pool. Instead, your uncle Lucas and I lived in roach-infested apartments and motels, moving every time Mama's checks bounced, which was usually once a month.

The fact that your dad and I bought the house of our dreams is one of my proudest moments. Of course, your uncle Lucas said it was ostentatious and unnecessary. I said he shouldn't use words he couldn't spell and that it wasn't his place to comment on how I spend <u>my</u> money.

But when someone broke into our home, I realized having a safe space to stay is one of the most important aspects of our lives.

Survival expert Donny Dust said it best: Free shelter is the best shelter. Any type of shelter that's already standing, secure, and ready to protect you from the elements is better than having to make one. You're not on *Million Dollar*

Listing (this was a reality show where multimillion-dollar homes were profiled for the masses to dream about purchasing when they'd never ever be able to) so keep an open mind for anything that will protect you from the elements and predators. Abandoned houses and buildings (preferably one story since they're more structurally sound) are the first urban shelters to come to mind, but bridges, bunkers, drains, and farms are all fair game. Once you find something that looks sufficient, go through a checklist.

Scout It Out

You could stumble upon the Taj Mahal and call it home, but it won't mean much if it's in a hazardous waste zone. The same could be said if it's in an area with known gangs or militias, which could become commonplace at some point.

Watch the building for signs of life. There could be wild animals or people you don't want to mess with.

Once you've established it's abandoned, find the easiest way to access the shelter. But be smart and look out for traps (the Hollywood producer in me thinks everywhere and everything is booby-trapped). And for the love of God, have an exit strategy. Getting out of a shelter is as important as getting in.

Come Prepared

Even if the perimeter is clear, you won't know what's inside the building until you actually go in. Make sure you're wearing closed-toe shoes in case there's broken glass, nails, or any other dangerous stuff on the floors. You'll want gloves in case you need to move something. Respirators, face masks, or bandannas are good to have in case there are chemical hazards or asbestos.

Flashlights are a must.

Bring a weapon for protection, preferably something that is blunt, durable, and gives you range to get the hell out of there if needed.

This seems obvious but NEVER GO ALONE. You're lucky. You've got one another. Stick together.

Set Up Shop

Now that y'all know this place is safe, you can start making it yours. The first step is to make it difficult for outsiders to enter. Board up and fortify any entry points and lock all doors and windows.

Pick the safest room, preferably near the exit, to stay in. It should be well insulated and have proper ventilation.

From there, see if there's any non-contaminated water to purify in the building's pipes, water heater, and toilet tank. You should also search your new shelter for tools and provisions. If you're in a house with a fireplace, make a fire.

Building Shelter in the Wild

I feel like a hack for writing this because any brush I had with the wilderness was when your father and I got bored with our central heating and air-conditioning and decided to "rough it." Which meant tents from REI and no Wi-Fi. Your father used to tease me for bringing charcuterie fixings, but he didn't have a leg to stand on because he always had to have his gluten-free bread and fancy Belgian beer.

I remember a few years before I started prepping hearing a podcast about climate change, and they said that we had to get comfortable with being uncomfortable. It shut me down. I didn't want to be uncomfortable, and I sure don't want that for you. But those who can get used to being uncomfortable will be the last people standing... and that, my darling girls, must be you!

There are many dangers that come with living in the wild, and exposure is one of the biggest. The human body's optimal core temperature is 98.6 degrees. Hypothermia occurs when your body drops below 95 degrees, which can take place in as little as ten to fifteen minutes if you're cold and wet enough.

On the flip side, hyperpyrexia (overheating) starts at 104 degrees. A person can have a heatstroke in ten to fifteen minutes, so finding shelter to keep you cool or warm depending on the season or location is critical.

Location, Location, Location

Build your shelter in a safe place. Floods, insects, and predators are what you should be on the lookout for. Never build on low ground or near a body of water as a flash flood will wipe out anything you've built.

A MOTHER'S GUIDE TO THE APOCALYPSE 235

Look for places that are free of rocks and, if possible, not too windy. Pick a spot that has a good amount of construction materials like fallen branches and dead trees so you can build your camp in one place. Also leaves. You're going to need a lot of leaves.

Note: You can always find a better spot for shelter, so seek out as many options as you can.

Let Nature Work for You

When building shelter, work smarter, not harder. Remember, the best shelter is a free one. Let nature work for you. Caves, fallen trees, rock overhangs, and boulder fields are excellent options, assuming they're safe.

Using natural shelters will conserve your resources, tools, time, and calories, allowing y'all to use these elsewhere for other important tasks like finding water, starting a fire, and foraging. This line of thinking also extends to construction materials. Use what nature has already supplied to build your shelter rather than sawing logs for hours and using up your rope. You're trying to escape the elements, not be on the cover of *Architectural Digest*.

Lastly, when it comes to shelter, bigger isn't better. Smaller shelters heat up quicker and are easier to make. Wherever you are, wherever you lay your head, I hope you're together and I hope you know that I'm always with you.

Love Always,
Mama Bear

ROSIE

The first glass of wine was Mel's idea. Rosie's sisters weren't big drinkers, but Rosie loved a pint at the pub with friends or a glass of crisp pinot grigio on a hot day, or a port with Sam in the conservatory on a cold, wet night.

Mel poured two large glasses of "the good stuff," a buttery chardonnay that made Rosie understand why California was once considered the mecca of wine. They had serious matters to discuss, but one glass of wine couldn't hurt, especially if it helped loosen Mel up.

It hadn't taken more than a few sips before Mel was sharing stories about Mum.

"One day your father had to be at a tournament in Pasadena, so your mom was on solo baby duty. She calls me and she's hysterical. I thought someone died, but no, one of you girls, I think it was Cass, had taken off their diaper and smeared poo all over the wall. Your mom had a sensitive tummy and she begged me to come over."

"Did you do it?" Rosie asked.

"You better believe it. I've got a stomach like an ox. Brought gloves and a mask and got to work on sanitizing your room. I swear your poor mama was green and looked like she'd been in battle."

Rosie laughed, but she wasn't naive. Somehow Mel always made herself the hero of stories about Olivia. "You two were so close. What did you think about her prepping?"

Her question took Mel by surprise, her mouth pursing as she considered it. "Looking back, I didn't understand that we weren't the same people in our thirties or forties as we were at twenty-two, or now in my sixties. Becoming a mom changed Olivia deeply. It changed our friendship, and it wasn't... I didn't handle it well."

She trailed off. Rosie sensed there was more to this story and knew the best way to get answers. "How about another bottle of wine?"

Mel grinned. "Now you're talking."

She popped open the bottle, but instead of resuming their conversation, Mel turned on the record player, a relic from a different time. Tina Turner's "What's Love Got to Do with It" began to play. Mel gestured for Rosie to join her on the makeshift dance floor.

They were still dancing and singing at the top of their lungs when the music stopped, both of them sweaty and out of breath, the record player making a terrible screeching sound.

"What's going on?" Bettie asked as she turned off the record player. Her gaze landed on the empty wine bottles. "Where is Dad, Ro?"

A MOTHER'S GUIDE TO THE APOCALYPSE 239

"I took him a sandwich for dinner, but he was sleeping. What is it? What's wrong?" Rosie had never seen her sister this agitated. No, it wasn't that. Bettie seemed afraid. Goose bumps danced up and down Rosie's arms. "Is it about Cass? Did something happen?"

"We need to talk," Bettie said. "In private."

"Is it about Cassie? Or Dad?" Rosie asked, trying not to panic. "Because if it is..."

"Jesus Christ, Rosie, Mel's a bloody liar. Is that what you want me to say?" Bettie's hand went up to her mouth. But it was too late.

"What are you going on about?" Rosie demanded.

"I'd like to know as well," Mel said calmly, which only made Bettie seem less in control.

"We should never have come here. Mel is a liar. All of this...it's all been lies. Dad doesn't have another interview scheduled, but for some reason none of us are allowed to leave this country, and no one knows why. And we *don't* need a bloody permit to travel to LA. It's all lies. Isn't that right, Mel?"

Rosie's gaze bored into Mel. "Is that true?" she demanded.

Mel shrugged. "I'm not the only one lying, am I, Bettie?"

"You bitch," Bettie spat out. Rosie flinched. As the peacemaker of the family, anger didn't come easily to Bettie, but Mel's words triggered something. "You think I care if you tell? I'll tell her myself. Rosie, I'm pregnant. I found out when we got here, and I was overwhelmed and trying to find the right time to tell you and Cass. Mel said she'd keep my secret, but I don't want her to anymore. It doesn't matter. Does it? What matters is our family, and this woman is fucking with it."

The amount of information combined with all the wine made Rosie dizzy. She glanced at Bettie's belly, unable to imagine that there was a baby in there. Her sister was going to be a mum. But that wasn't the point. Why was Bettie calling Mel a liar?

"Mel, what's going on here? What aren't you telling us?" Mel didn't say anything, the silence seemingly endless.

"Why are we here? Why all the games? What do you know about Mum?" Rosie asked, firing her questions off rapidly.

Mel didn't answer. "Bloody tell us already!" Rosie shouted.

Mel's shoulders sagged. "Nothing. I don't know anything about Olivia. I didn't..."

She took a deep breath. "All these years I dreamed of seeing you girls and Sam again. I wanted to see the women you've become...and I wanted to..."

"Punish me?" Dad's voice startled them all.

Her father looked more in control than he had in months, his gaze steady and intent.

"You did all this. The least you can do is be honest to the girls. Tell them."

"I made mistakes, Sammy. I know I did. That's why I wanted you to come—so I could make amends. And then you got here, and it's been so good being back together. I know it's crazy, but there's still something between us. Maybe there's a second chance here."

Rosie's mouth fell open in disbelief. Bettie stood frozen.

Sam scoffed. "You're out of your bloody mind."

He turned to Rosie and Bettie, a haunted look in his eyes. "I guess you can't outrun the truth. No matter how hard you try." He let out a heavy exhale. "I never talked about your mum because I was too ashamed. But now that you've brought us all this way, Melissa can tell you what really happened. Tell them how you ruined our lives and broke their mother's heart."

r/SoCalValleyPreppers

9,120 Members

__PRIVATE CHAT__

GoJoe420
I swear to Christ sometimes running this group is worse than fucking babysitting. Did you know Van asked if he could camp in my backyard? Can you imagine what my Mom & Dad would say?

Mamabear3
I thought you and Van were best friends.

GoJoe420
We are, but my parents think he's odd.

Mamabear3
Is that because he is? The man wears baby tees and wants to start a yurt rental company.

GoJoe420
Lol. Yeah, it's true that he's weird as fuck, but he's always had my back. I got busted a few years back for a DUI and he

A MOTHER'S GUIDE TO THE APOCALYPSE 243

drove me to work every day for three months. But I can't let him live on my land. Not yet.

Mamabear3

Then tell him that. Conflict resolution is all about communication. And trust me friendships are hard. Try working with your friends.

GoJoe420

Don't they say not to do that.

Mamabear3

They do. Too bad I didn't listen. No seriously, I love Mel. She's my best friend. We survived the disaster that was our twenties together, but lately she's driving me nuts. She's always gotta be right. Always has to have her way. Not to mention she hates it now that I have my own family. She doesn't say that, but I can tell it annoys her that I'm not her sad, single friend anymore.

GoJoe420

She doesn't have kids?

Mamabear3

A son. Had a fling years ago and he wasn't interested in being a dad. She hates being single, but acts like I should be single too. Or we should be a happy trio.

GoJoe420

Threesomes are fun. Or so I've heard 😊

Mamabear3

Hey, keep this PG. I've got kids sleeping in the next room.

GoJoe420

He, he, he...

Mamabear3

Mel is the best, but sometimes I want to make plans without her acting like I'm cheating on her. Wait...How did our conversation about Van turn into me bitching about Mel?

GoJoe420

You needed to get it off your chest.

Mamabear3

I guess. Now I feel like an asshole making it all about me. Where were we?

GoJoe420

Nah, I'm feeling better. You're right about Van. I think I'm gonna check out that land we talked about buying. Maybe I'll pull the trigger and he can camp there.

Mamabear3

That's really nice, Joe.

GoJoe420

What can I say? I'm a giver.

Mamabear3

Too true. Alright, I gotta sleep before I'm back on werewolf feeding duty. We'll talk later.

GoJoe420

I'm counting on it.

SAM

The silence lingered, but Sam didn't say a word. Melissa's eyes filled with tears, as though she were the victim here. *Still an asshole*, he thought.

"Olivia got everything she wanted. The handsome husband, the children in triplicate, the dream house, and..."

"And me... She took your leftovers. Isn't that what you said?"

"But I thought it was just a fling?" Rosie said.

"So did I. I didn't meet your mum until years later and that's when I found out that Mel was her best friend. She said Liv might not date me if she knew we'd had a fling. I knew that Liv was the real deal, the love of my life, so I didn't say a word. I trusted Mel." A bitter laugh escaped. "Biggest mistake of my life."

"Sammy, I didn't..."

He thought he would make her tell the story, but he needed to be the one to say it out loud. After all these years, it was time that he confessed.

"Mel and I were both worried about your mum, and the prepping, but instead of stopping her, Mel indulged her. She would let her talk about it nonstop, and encouraged her to lean on Joey and their damn prepping group. A week before Liv went missing, I came home from work and your mum wasn't there—but Mel was. When I asked where your mum had gone, she said to a prepper meeting, and she offered to babysit. I knew it wasn't Mel's fault that Liv went, but that didn't make me any less angry."

Sam took a heavy breath. "You girls were fast asleep, so when she suggested that we open a bottle of wine, I said yes. I wanted to escape. Needed to. It had been months since I'd slept in the same room with your mum. I told her it would be easier if she was closer to you girls when you woke up, but the truth was I hated seeing Liv's face buried in her phone while she ordered more supplies or texted Joey about what to buy for their bug-out bags." Sam's words came out in a rush.

Bettie reached out to try to calm him. "It's okay, Dad. You don't need to..."

"No, please. I have to do this. What happened next wasn't Mel's fault entirely. I'm an adult. I have to take responsibility for the role I played in all of it."

Sam closed his eyes, remembering that night. Mel's hand in his. It felt nice. Comforting. The silence that settled around them as the energy shifted. Then her hand on his leg. Moving farther up. *This is wrong*, he thought, but he didn't stop her when she leaned over and kissed him or when her hand moved to his lap. He should have stopped

A MOTHER'S GUIDE TO THE APOCALYPSE 249

it then. He should have told her no. The biggest mistake of his life was not stopping her.

"You act like you didn't want it? You did. We'd been flirting for months."

"That's bullshit," Sam said.

Mel laughed bitterly. "It's easy to rewrite history, but we both knew that Liv wasn't the same person. She was falling apart, and you and the girls needed someone who could love and care for you. I saw a future with us, Sam. We could have been good together," Mel said.

Sam hated the pathetic whimper in her voice. He glanced at Rosie and Bettie, who looked at Mel with undisguised pity. He looked away before he could see what they thought of him.

"I had a family. A wife I loved. I told you that. You promised not to say anything. And then..."

"I told Liv," Melissa said flatly. "I told her that she'd wrecked her marriage and someone who loved Sam should step in. That she should get out of the way and let me have him."

Her words were ugly and unhinged, but that was Mel for you. Over the years as she accumulated power in Hollywood, no one told Mel no. She assumed no one ever would.

"When I turned you down, it was too much for you, wasn't it? You had to make sure no one came out unscathed. You told Liv that we were in love and that I was going to leave her and the girls. You lied to her," he spat out.

He'd worked so hard to forget Liv's face when she came home that day. Her eyes swollen and red from crying, makeup smeared, a look of betrayal he could never forget. "You fucked Mel. You fucked her," Olivia whispered.

She'd come at him, crying, hitting him, and he let her. He deserved it. When she was done, he held her close and wept. Begged her for forgiveness. By the time they'd both stopped crying and raging, all that was left was silence. When he spoke, he gave her an out.

"I told your mum we could get a divorce. I said I understood if that's what she wanted. I didn't want to lose you girls, but I wasn't sure we could ever come back from what I'd done. If she could."

He wiped at the tears. "It had been months since we talked about what we wanted. I said all that mattered to me was her and the girls. If she was scared about the future, then we would find a way that we could feel safe together. She admitted Joey was starting to scare her. He had all these plans for a commune, and he joked about Liv and you girls living with him. Joining the Guardians."

Sam spat out the Guardians' name. "She said she wished we could start over, and I suggested moving back to England. We'd be far away from Mel and Joey. Were we running away from our problems? Maybe, but we both saw it as a possibility. She was still so angry, and she had a work dinner, but we agreed to talk that night. Only Liv never came home. She never came..."

Sam bit back a sob. Rosie went to hug him, but he held up his hand.

"I didn't talk to you girls about your mum because every time I thought about her, I remembered how I broke her heart. When she didn't come home that night, I kept thinking maybe she changed her mind, maybe she decided she was wrong about a second chance. Hearing her name, seeing her picture made me weak, and I couldn't afford to be weak. Not when my daughters needed me. But Liv was always with me. I took the guidebook she wrote and made it my bible. I learned everything I needed to know for us to survive and more. Because I couldn't save your mum, but I could save our girls."

Rosie didn't need to look at Bettie to know her sister was crying. Rosie couldn't stop her own tears. Sam sagged in his seat, his confession complete as he waited, expecting them to turn on him. Expecting them to hate him. Instead he felt their arms wrap him up. They held on so tight, he couldn't breathe.

"It's okay, Dad. We love you. We'll always love you."

Sam let out a strangled sob and hugged them back. He wasn't sure how long they sat there. When he looked up, he saw Mel watching. He didn't bother hiding his contempt.

"You ... you stupid cow, instead of letting the past be the past, you bring us back so you can try and wreck our lives all over again. Manipulating my girls. It's unforgivable."

"I loved you, Sammy. I still do. I should have never let you go."

"Did you hurt our mum?" Rosie asked.

Sam froze. *Is that possible? Jesus Christ, did Mel do something to Liv?* He'd never once considered it. She was a narcissist but not a murderer. *Right?*

"What? Of course not," Mel said, indignant. "You think it's been easy for me? Do you know what we've been through here? How much shit we've had to endure to survive? How much we've suffered? I thought if I could have you all back, it could be different. We could be happy."

He couldn't listen to Mel's shitty justifications anymore. Bettie blinked back her shock at Sam's confession. But it was Rosie's expression that broke him. She had always desperately wanted her mum back, and Mel had preyed on that desperation.

"It was all lies," she said softly, finally processing.

Sam reached for Rosie's hand. "I wish this trip had been different, but there's nothing Mel can tell us about Liv that we don't already know. Nothing at all."

At this, Rosie stood up. "You're right. We're done with her. Let's go."

That was Rosie. Once she'd gotten her head wrapped around something, she was laser focused.

Bettie shook her head. "Ro, we can't leave. Rita knows that we're here and that Cassie is missing, and she's working to get our passports sorted. We can't risk leaving and not have her find us."

Cassie still isn't back? Sam thought. Bloody hell. He'd

A MOTHER'S GUIDE TO THE APOCALYPSE 253

forgotten she'd left. Dominic had always been a good boy, but he wasn't a boy anymore, was he? So what did that mean? Were they stuck here? Was that what Mel wanted all along?

He felt dizzy, recalling a twisted Stephen King movie he'd watched where the lady broke the author's legs and held him hostage. Would Mel do that to him? Did it matter if she did? They couldn't leave without Cassie, but staying here was the ultimate punishment.

Why was this happening? The girls were silent, too. It stretched on until Eduardo, slightly out of breath, burst inside. "Mel, there's a guy here from the city. Said he's been sent to transport Sam and the girls back to LA."

"What guy?"

"A cop. Or so he says?" Eduardo said with a shrug.

Bettie's shoulders sagged with relief. "Rita promised she'd send someone. That must be who's here."

"We should get our stuff." Rosie moved toward the door.

Mel stood. "Hold up. Let's see who and what this man is about before y'all run off with him."

Sam considered telling Mel to stuff it. Who was she to tell them what to do? But she knew this place and the people in it better than he did.

A few minutes later, Eduardo returned in the golf cart with a tall unassuming man in a dark suit towering over him. Eduardo gestured for him to enter and then stood awkwardly behind him, as though he were the footman waiting for instructions. The man gave Mel a terse nod. "How are you all this evening?"

Mel gave a tight smile. "Doing fine. How can we help you?"

"I'm Deputy Taylor from the LA Security Council, and I'm here to take Sam, Rosie, Bettie, and Cassie Clark back to the airport, where they'll be transported back to the United Kingdom."

Sam noticed the man and Mel exchange a look, but he couldn't read it.

"Did Rita send you?" Bettie asked eagerly.

The man smiled. "She sure did. Said we'd get you straightened out."

"Great. We need a few minutes to pack our belongings, and talk to Rita about…"

"You're not going anywhere. Not with this fucker," Mel said.

Sam's eyes widened. Maybe they really were trapped here.

"You're not a fucking cop. Who are you?"

Rosie and Bettie startled at her tone and inched closer to Sam. "Just a guy following orders." He lifted up his jacket to reveal the glint of his gun.

"Bloody hell," Sam shouted. He stepped forward, not sure what he planned to do, but Eduardo already had his own gun out. Before the guy could turn around, he slammed it into the back of the deputy's head, and the man crumpled to the floor.

Sam gasped. The girls screamed in unison. Mel kicked at the man's crumpled body, and he didn't move. She knelt down and pulled at his collar to reveal the familiar tattoo with stars and the black and silver PROTECTOR OF THE UNIVERSE scrawled in ink.

"I could tell from Eduardo's expression something was wrong. Not to mention his hesitation when Bettie asked about Rita. Asshole isn't a cop from LA. He's a Guardian."

"The question is, Why is he here now? What do they want with Sam and the girls?" Eduardo asked.

"Do you know?" Rosie asked.

"Do you?" Bettie echoed.

Mel looked equally worried. "No, but it's not good."

For the first time since they had arrived, Mel looked rattled. She flipped through the man's wallet. "He doesn't have a Guardians badge on him, which means he's low-level. An errand boy."

"An errand boy still means his intentions were unpleasant. Mel, this is bad. They'll come for him if he doesn't come back."

"How did they know someone was coming for us?" Rosie asked.

Mel didn't answer for a moment, her eyes flickering back to Sam and the girls. "I don't know. We need to wait for Dominic. See what he thinks about all of this."

"There's no waiting. They can't stay here. They need to

go to LA and find Dom and Cassie, and we'll clean up this mess," Eduardo said.

Sam wondered what he meant by *clean up*, then realized he didn't want to know the answer.

Mel sighed and moved over to a desk in the corner. She pulled out a set of car keys, a satellite phone, and a small map and handed them to Rosie.

"Take the sedan at the end of the drive. This is my satellite phone. The first number is programmed to Dom's phone. If he doesn't answer, keep calling. He'll eventually call you back."

Sam felt a flicker of anger that Mel was burdening Rosie with this responsibility, but that was his ego talking. He wasn't capable of leading the charge. Not anymore. All that mattered was getting out of here.

Rosie and Bettie hurried toward the door. Before Sam could leave, Mel stopped him. "I am sorry, Sammy. Promise me you'll come back and we can talk it out?"

She was bloody daft if she thought he'd ever come back here. But he was happy to play along. "I promise."

She leaned over and kissed him. Sam resisted the urge to push her away, willing to indulge Mel for a few more minutes. For so long, Sam hadn't been sure who he hated more—Mel or himself. But admitting what he'd done and the damage that he'd caused felt good; now he could let go and forget about this stupid cunt once and for all.

r/SoCalValleyPreppers

10,000 Members

PRIVATE CHAT

GoJoe420
Been talking 2 the fellas & we're gonna do our first in-person meet up. You in?

GoJoe420
I guess that's a no?

GoJoe420
I'm a big boy. I won't be butt hurt if it's not what u want. B nice to put a face to a name. I'll shoot over the address of the bar. It's in Van Nuys next week so stop by if you can.

Mamabear3
Hey, I'm sorry. The girls are in their no sleep era and work has been killing me (never work with A-list actors or directors. Actually never work in Hollywood.)

GoJoe420
Copy that. So u think you can make it to our shindig?

Mamabear3

Sam has a tournament that week but I'll ask our nanny if she can stay for bedtime. Stay tuned.

PRIVATE CHAT

GoJoe420

Okay Mama, I didn't realize u were such hot shit in this town.

Mamabear3

Stop it. I'm not.

GoJoe420

That's not what the Google says. Bryan sent me the link. You won a fucking Oscar?

Mamabear420

It was for a short film.

GoJoe420

Do you or do you not have an Oscar in your house?

Mamabear420

I do.

GoJoe420

Then your hot shit.

Mamabear3

You're right. I really am.

GoJoe420

The fellas were pretty amped that someone as fancy as yourself showed up at a dive bar & drank them under the table.

Mamabear3

They would not have been impressed to see me puking up half a bottle of tequila into my neighbors hedges. I had to tell the girls Mama had a stomachache.

GoJoe420

Not that Mama is getting old & can't hold her liquor?

Mamabear3

Harsh, but true.

GoJoe420

Well, the fellas are big fans and stunned that someone as fancy as you wants to hang out with us bums.

Mamabear3

Y'all said prepping was for everyone.

GoJoe420

It is, but rich folks like yourself think their money will save 'em.

Mamabear3

It might for some people, but we're not that rich.

GoJoe420

Yeah right.

Mamabear3

Don't get me wrong we're comfortable, but not the "buy your way out of trouble" comfortable. We've got a massive mortgage and our nanny costs an arm and a leg and don't get me started about food and clothes for these tiny monsters. The stuff I'm learning from you and the group, that's our safety net.

GoJoe420

The student has become the master.

Mamabear3

I wish. I've got a lot to learn but it's been fun.

GoJoe420

Glad to hear it.

PRIVATE CHAT

Mamabear3

Did you see the news about Nebraska? The damn tornadoes killed almost five thousand people.

GoJoe420

Fucking tragic. There were whole towns wiped out. Is that why your up so late?

Mamabear3

No. Bettie had a stomachache so I had to hold her until she fell asleep. Then Sam and I got into another fight.

GoJoe420

About what?

Mamabear3

My obsession with the future. He's asked that I stop the prepping. Stop the groups and the researching and buying anything else.

GoJoe420

Are you going to?

Mamabear3

I don't know. There's still so much on my list.

GoJoe420

Want me to talk to him?

Mamabear3

That's a hard pass. Unless I want to wind up in divorce court.

GoJoe420

Why's that?

Not that it's any of my business.

Mamabear3

Sam thinks we're having an affair.

GoJoe420

Ha. What did u tell him?

Mamabear3

That he's acting like a macho asshole and it's the twenty first century and I can have male friends. But still...my marriage means everything to me. I love Sam. I love our family.

GoJoe420

I know. And I hate 2 see u upset.

Mamabear3

Maybe he's right. Maybe I need to take a beat. Find some balance. I just saw the time. I've got to get ready to head to set. It's gonna be a late one but we'll talk soon.

GoJoe420

Can't wait. Don't let those actors give you any shit and if they do, I'll find 'em and set 'em straight.

Mamabear3

Lol. Will do.

CASSIE

An hour later, Cassie and Dominic were back on the road, speeding down the canyon toward Hollywood. Dominic said that he had a few more errands to run before they made it to Joey's. Cassie was anxious, eager to talk to him and get back to her sisters, but she didn't argue. Now that she and Dom weren't at odds, she enjoyed seeing the city with him, guiding her.

As he drove, Cassie's breath caught when she spotted the infamous Hollywood sign, so lovingly preserved it didn't seem quite real. The roads had recently been paved a deep, dark granite color that made them appear as though they were freshly washed. Cassie couldn't stop her smile. "Bettie would love this."

"Don't look too closely or you'll see the prison labor they use to keep it this clean. They're good at sanitizing the truth."

As Dominic made his way down Hollywood Boulevard past what used to be the old Pantages Theatre, Cassie saw a row of well-maintained lofts and office buildings. What made them stand out were barbed-wire fences surrounding them, as well as signs reading THESE PROPERTIES ARE UNDER 24-HOUR SURVEILLANCE.

Cassie could see a drone flying above the buildings and armed guards stationed at every corner. The image was a stark contrast with the laughter and squeals of the schoolchildren who played on a nearby playground, water spraying them from a giant splash pad.

"What is that?" she asked Dominic.

"A climate refugee camp. A lot of folks from Arizona and Nevada—basically anyplace where the temperatures got too hot to live—came here. There are smaller camps, but this one is strictly for orphans. There are about twenty-five hundred babies, elementary school kids, and teenagers in that camp alone."

Cassie frowned. "But the earthquake was years ago. The climate scientists said things have stabilized now that so many people died and we stopped using fossil fuels and expensive tech. I don't get it. Why are there so many orphans?" she asked.

"A lot of the people who survived the fires, floods, and earthquakes were too sick to care for their kids. Or they had no resources to survive the aftermath of the collapse. Then you have the people who popped out a few kids 'cuz they thought they could sell 'em when the fertility rates cratered. I could tell you hundreds of stories about how a kid ends up there, but none of 'em are good."

"Who looks after them?" Cassie asked softly. It was hard losing her mum, but they'd always had Dad.

A MOTHER'S GUIDE TO THE APOCALYPSE 265

"They have staff who live on the property, and their living expenses are paid and they get a small stipend. It's not a glamorous job, but plenty of climate survivors wanted to give back. Makes me think we're not entirely doomed," he said.

Cassie wasn't sure about that. She couldn't help but think about how sad it would be to grow up behind bars like these. Obviously, her family wasn't immune to the unbearable heat waves and freezes that gripped the world, as well as the constant food shortages, but her memories consisted of running free in the woods behind the property with her sisters. Making campfires with Dad. Learning to cook and forage and make homemade bread with Granny. How lucky was she that she'd led that life instead of one like this?

As promised, Dominic parked his bike at a run-down housing complex and removed a large bag from the bike compartment. When he returned, he opened the bag to survey his haul.

Cassie spotted half a dozen envelopes stuffed with cash and was reminded of the Hollywood movies she'd seen. "Is this...I mean, do you sell drugs?" she asked carefully, not wanting to break their tentative truce.

He snorted as he put away the newest haul. "I'd make a lot more money if that was the case. It's much more boring than that. I find and refurbish old batteries. For various items. Computers. Phones. Cars. They're priced extremely high now so the government can suppress how we all communicate. This is one of the only ways that ordinary people can afford them. I help them out with this stuff. They offer protection if we need it. But I'm done for the day."

Cassie heard a buzzing sound and froze. Dominic cursed and reached into the compartment, pulling out a compact satellite phone. "It's Mom. If I pick this up, she'll give me hell and insist we come home."

"Then don't pick it up."

Conflicted, Dominic studied the phone and sighed again. He placed it back in the compartment. "Last stop is Joey's, but I want to be real with you."

He paused, that intense look returning. "I respect your mom who wanted to be ready, but back then most preppers were whack jobs. And Joey? He's the king of 'em. But I can't deny that he saw the future and monopolized it. Dude started out prepping, then when the city went offline and started a war with the other states, Joey capitalized on the disorganization and greed. He built a massive network of men and women who wanted to get their hands dirty. The Guardians control transportation and agriculture, and while that don't mean shit to us in the mountains, they also control pharmaceuticals, both legal and illegal. Which means the difference between Mom being slightly nutty and Mom going off the fucking rails."

"What about the local hospitals? They don't have medications?"

He rolled his eyes. "The Guardians control it all. It's like the drug cartels back in the day. If you have the supply, you can do whatever you want to control the demand."

"What else do I need to know?" Cassie asked.

"If Joey wants something, he takes it, especially if he sees a monetary value. That includes people. So I'll ask him about Aunt Liv, and you stay under the radar. Got it?"

"Got it," she said.

"If Joey fucks around, we leave. I'm not going to war with the Guardians and neither are you."

"Okay, okay, I've got it." Cassie didn't care who asked the questions. She just wanted answers.

As he drove deeper into Silverlake, Cassie took in the hundreds of lemon, orange, and olive trees, which created a mysterious *Secret Garden* effect. Bougainvillea bloomed effortlessly, as though it were showing off, and the scent of jasmine filled her nose. For the first time, she wished she'd thought to bring her film camera to take pictures. Her lecturers would go wild over the foliage, most of which they'd never seen and likely never would.

"This place is unreal," she said breathlessly.

"It's also one of the most dangerous neighborhoods in the whole damn city. A lot of people who come here never leave."

His words were chilling. He turned down a winding street and headed up one of the steepest hills Cassie had ever seen, but by now she knew he had it handled. He reached the top and parked the bike near the shade of a massive walnut tree. Cassie saw a wrought-iron gate with a metallic sign that read, THE GUARDIANS.

In the compartment of the bike, Dominic's phone buzzed again.

"Maybe you should answer it," Cassie said.

"And have Mom chew me a new one? No thanks! We'll call her when we're heading home... which won't be long. You hear me? This is a brief fact-finding mission. In and out."

"Loud and clear, Captain," Cassie said sarcastically as she saluted him. As they approached the gate, Dominic pressed a button, and it slowly opened. She followed him as he led her up a steeper hill, feeling out of breath before they reached the halfway mark.

Dominic looked back, unable to hide his grin. "Need me to carry you?" he asked, a sarcastic grin on his face.

Cassie glared back at him. At home she was all about physical labor, but the heat and the lack of food and sleep had her depleted. She ignored his mocking and continued forward.

Ten minutes later, she was almost wheezing as they reached the top of the hill. But it was worth the climb. The Guardians had erected dozens of tiny homes, tucked into a hill that zigzagged across the massive property. The landscaping was extraordinary. Hundreds of cacti and succulents bloomed as though they were showing off. Not to

A MOTHER'S GUIDE TO THE APOCALYPSE 269

mention the many California poppies, bright-orange flowers popping against all the green.

"It must take so much water to get all this to blossom," Cassie said. "You don't have water shortages anymore?"

Though there was plenty of water for now, they'd enacted conservation legislation to ensure there were never issues again.

"Not to the extent we once experienced, but it wouldn't matter if there were. Joey and the Guardians control this part of the town's water supply. They insist landscaping is instrumental to the rejuvenation process. That in order to create life out of nothing, you have to nurture it. They believe that as long as they are in charge, humans will endure."

The beauty of this place was undeniable. Of course, having clocked the Guardian flag flying high from each of the tiny homes, she understood that these people had no allegiance to any government but their own.

The screen door at the first house opened. A tiny dark-haired woman with pigtail braids and overalls emerged, a chunky baby strapped to her chest. She greeted Dominic with a wide smile, one that signified they were friends. "Dom, you're as handsome as ever."

His demeanor changed instantly, warm and open, and completely fake. Not that the Guardian could tell.

He smiled at her and ruffled the baby's curls. "Now, Esther, don't flirt too much or I'll have to fight Joey for you."

She laughed. "He could use a reminder of how good he's got it here."

"Always happy to help the cause. It's good to see you and this little lady . . . She keeps growing."

"This baby bird never stops eating, but it's a blessing that we'll take after all our sorrows."

Dominic nodded. "May there be many more blessings for us all." Esther appeared pleased by his response. "This is for you," he continued. He handed her two of the envelopes of cash he had gotten on his deliveries.

Her smile grew brighter. "Now, this is well timed. We just got a delivery. Follow me. We'll get you set up," she said. Then her gaze landed on Cassie. "Hold up, who's this?"

"My name is . . ."

Dominic shook his head. "She's here with me. We need ten minutes with Joey."

"He's on a scout but he should be back soon," she said. Cassie remembered Dominic's breeder comments; was this what he'd meant? She wondered if they should go. Get out of here. But then she would have come all this way for nothing. She could see Rosie's smug face and Bettie's disappointment. No, they were close. She could stick it out.

"She can wait here while you get your shipment. We won't be long."

Dominic gave Cassie a *remember what I said* look. She nodded back. *Message received.*

As Esther and Dominic disappeared inside the house, Cassie took in her surroundings. The landscaping reminded her of the photos in her textbooks that she'd read. A climate designed to nurture beautiful things. A place that watered and grew and grew until it destroyed itself. She wished she could pick all the flowers and transport them back to England, but nothing like this would ever grow in their cold, wet climate.

A few feet ahead, she spotted a set of steps that led to one of the poppy beds. She remembered Dominic's warning, but she wasn't spying. Why would they care if she studied their plants?

Cassie climbed the two steps and knelt down to get a better look. She really missed getting her hands dirty and wondered if Dad felt the same. He used to get so excited when they'd grow something new. Even more so when they were able to bring a plant or food back from the brink of extinction. For years during the drought, nothing grew. After two years, the rains returned, and they got to witness the miracle of life growing all around them again.

Cassie looked at the poppies and couldn't help herself. The second bloom practically leapt into her hand. She held it and was admiring the petal when she heard a click, the unmistakable sound of a shotgun being racked.

She looked up to find a sea of angry faces staring back at her. A young woman—no, she was a teenager, younger than Cassie—pointed the gun right at her.

Cassie had opened her mouth to tell the girl she was with Dominic when she heard him shout, "Hold on. Stop!"

The girl's face made it clear she had no intention of listening. Cassie looked back down at the flower petals in her hand, and then dropped them as if she were holding poison before looking back up. The last thing she saw was the butt of the gun coming at her face, and then nothing but darkness.

r/SoCalValleyPreppers

10,640 Members

PRIVATE CHAT

Mamabear3
It's all fucked. It's totally fucked.

GoJoe420
Gonna need a clarification. The world?? The traffic? The Lakers defense?

Mamabear3
We've got evil squirrels that are destroying everything we planted and there's pantry moths in the flour I just bought. Not to mention I read over all the stuff you and the guys sent over about navigation and there's no way I can learn all that because I can barely find my way to Trader Joe's without my GPS. And I haven't slept in a week because the girls all have earaches and Sam has to go to Dallas for a tournament.

GoJoe420
Damn, Mama take a breath.

Mamabear3

I'm...I feel so overwhelmed.

GoJoe420

Life will do that to ya. But prepping ain't meant to make you feel like your failing. It's meant to make you feel powerful.

Mamabear3

I haven't felt powerful in years.

GoJoe420

Bullshit. You're a badass boss and a badass mom, you're in a slump. Listen, get in your car & don't stop driving till you reach the water. Take a walk in the sand, breathe in the ocean air. Let nature's medicine remind you it'll b okay. And if that don't work, remember what Joey's mama always says.

Mamabear3

What's that?

GoJoe420

The world ain't got room for whiners, only winners.

Mamabear3

Wow...That's pretty deep.

GoJoe420

That's my Mama for ya. The Canoga Park philosopher! Or u can do what my dad does.

Mamabear3

What's that?

GoJoe420

Drink a fifth of whiskey & pass the fuck out.

Mamabear3

Don't tempt me.
Sigh... thanks Joe. It felt good to get this all off my chest.

PRIVATE CHAT

Mamabear3

I got my food storage set up and I think we're good for at least eleven months.

GoJoe420

Hot damn, Liv. That's fucking fantastic.

Mamabear3

It feels good. Even though Lucas came over & gave me shit about it.

GoJoe420

What did he say?

Mamabear3

That I'm pissing my money away.

GoJoe420

I guess he'd rather u give it to him?

Mamabear3

That's what I said. It didn't go over well. Anyway, I'm feeling good. Gonna work on our car emergency kit next.

GoJoe420

Music to my ears. Be sure & let me know if you got any questions.

Mamabear3

I always do. How's your mama feeling?

GoJoe420

Her hip is healing so now she has time to be on my ass about finding a wife. I told her all the good ones are taken.

Mamabear3

You'll find someone when the time is right.

GoJoe420
Can u tell her that?

Mamabear3
I'll be happy to. Tell her Olivia knows all and sees all.

GoJoe420
You bet your ass I will. Now get some rest.

PRIVATE CHAT

GoJoe420
We missed you at the meeting last week.

Mamabear3
I know. My dumbass brother got a DUI and I had to bail him out of jail. Then I found out he got evicted last month, and wanted to stay with us... which was not going to work unless I wanted to end up in prison for manslaughter so I had to help find him a new apartment. As you can imagine, Sam was thrilled.

GoJoe420
Someone needs to cut the apron strings on baby bro.

Mamabear3
Sam said that too. I know he needs to stand on his own, but he was so young when our Mama died, I feel bad. Now I'm worried he'll never function without me.

GoJoe420

What would happen if he had 2?

Mamabear3

I don't know. I think about that a lot. It'd be one thing if I could count on him but he rarely visits the girls anymore. I had to stop telling them he was coming over because they'd be so disappointed when he didn't show. He still owes me the six grand that I loaned him to buy the car, and now in addition to covering the deposit on his apartment, I'm footing his Uber bill until he gets his license back.

GoJoe420

I'll say it again, Mama. Ain't no way that baby bird is flying if you don't kick him outta the nest.

Mamabear3

You might be right.

GoJoe420

I am on this one. Seen plenty of fellas wiling 2 take a free ride if your giving it.

Mamabear3

You're making too much sense.
Oh shit, it's almost midnight and the girls have their Halloween parade at school in the morning. I have to go but I'll see you at the meeting next week?

A MOTHER'S GUIDE TO THE APOCALYPSE 279

GoJoe420

I'll be there and I'll bring that water purifier for you to try.

Mamabear3

You're an angel. Oh, we're having a third birthday party for the girls in two weeks. Would you want to come?

GoJoe420

Your sure u want to be seen with me? I thought our group was ur dirty little secret.

Mamabear3

"Go into the light, Carol Anne."

GoJoe420

Is that another one of ur movie references?

Mamabear3

Poltergeist? You haven't seen it? Come on, Joey. Add it to the list.

GoJoe420

Writing it down now.

Mamabear3

Good, I expect a detailed report at the meeting.

GoJoe420

Yes ma'am.

BETTIE

It was almost four o'clock in the afternoon by the time Rosie pulled out of Mel's compound and made it onto the motorway. The thought of driving terrified Bettie, and that was before she knew there would be a million potholes, abandoned cars, and more likely than not roaming bandits looking to rape and kill them. Add in driving on the opposite side of the road, and it was all too much.

Unsurprisingly, Rosie was as fearless in the driver's seat as she was holding court with all the other academics at university. From the back of the car, Sam's loud snores echoed in the tight space. Bettie didn't know how her father was able to sleep after everything that had happened, but she was relieved. By the time they'd reached the car, he looked like he'd aged a decade. For the first hour, he hadn't said anything, simply stared out the window as Rosie drove away before drifting off.

Now, as the sun began to set, Bettie hoped they weren't making a mistake. They had no idea where they were headed, or why the Guardians had come for them. Bettie wanted answers, which was why she kept calling the satellite phone.

"Hey, Bets, maybe give it a rest. We'll try them again in an hour or so," Rosie said.

Bettie sighed and set the phone down. "Think if Mel hadn't told Mum about what happened, things between her and Dad might be different?" she asked softly.

"Does it matter? Dad made mistakes. Sounds like Mum did, too. All I care about now is finding Cassie, so we can go home before anyone else comes for us."

Bettie hated to see her sister out of fight. "So that's it? You're giving up."

Rosie kept her eyes on the road, but Bettie could see the hurt. "She's been gone eighteen years, Bets. I just...It was bloody stupid to think I could find her. The sooner we go home, the better."

Rosie's eyes lingered on Bettie's stomach. Bettie should have known Rosie would be thinking about her and the baby. "Ro, I didn't know until we got here. I swear. They told me at the airport when they did the health scan. It's not...I mean, I didn't expect this."

Rosie shot a worried glance at Bettie. "You don't sound excited?"

"I want to be. I love Max, but being a mom isn't what I want. Maybe one day, but not now."

"But, Bettie, you know you'll be..."

Rosie hit a pothole so hard, the whole vehicle seemed to levitate before slamming back to the ground. Bettie gasped, her hand instinctively going to her belly.

A MOTHER'S GUIDE TO THE APOCALYPSE 283

Rosie's eyes widened. "You okay?"

Bettie took a deep breath. "I'm fine. Do you have any water?"

Rosie motioned to her bag on the floor. Bettie reached down into it and gasped so loudly, Sam startled in his sleep, then stilled.

Bettie looked at Rosie, her voice a low hiss. "You have a gun in your bag? A gun?"

"It's a pistol if we're going to get specific."

"Where did you get a pistol?" Bettie demanded.

"In one of the drawers at Mel's. She had them everywhere. Quite reckless if you ask me."

Bettie opened her mouth to speak but didn't know where to start.

Rosie took this as an opportunity to present her case. "It's a precaution. You remember what Mel said about this place. We can't rely on anyone else to protect us. We have to protect ourselves. That's what Dad taught us."

Exasperated, Bettie pushed the bag closed. "I hope you know what you're doing."

Rosie laughed. "I have no idea, Bets, but we have to be ready for whatever comes our way like Mum wanted us to."

Bettie resisted the urge to mention that Mum's planning and prepping hadn't worked out all that well, but she was so exhausted, she thought she might fall over. She reached for the satellite phone one last time and began to dial again. She couldn't worry about Rosie and the damn gun. *Focus on Cassie*, she told herself. All she cared about was getting her sister back. That was all that mattered.

r/SoCalValleyPreppers

11,000 Members

PRIVATE CHAT

GoJoe420
U alive over there?
We missed u at the last meeting. What's going on?

GoJoe420
Seriously Liv, you good?
Liv?

Mamabear3
Sorry for the radio silence. Sam found all the bug out bags I made for the girls and lost his shit.

GoJoe420
Why? They were dope!

Mamabear3
He didn't think so. He thought it was, "fucking psychotic." We had a huge fight and then he staged an intervention.

GoJoe420
With who?

Mamabear3
Lucas, Sam, and Melissa. The holy trinity.

GoJoe420
Sounds like a "them" problem.

Mamabear3
I wish. Now they're saying I need to go to therapy. It was a whole scene.

GoJoe420
I told ya it might happen.

Mamabear3
Yeah, but it feels really shitty when the people you love don't listen or respect what you want.

GoJoe420
I know. But you'll figure it out. For ur family's sake.

Mamabear3
You're right. Listen, I've got to get the girls ready for family pictures which should be fun since Sam and I aren't speaking right now, but I promise not to go radio silent again.

GoJoe420

You better not.

———————

Mamabear3

Are you okay? I'm really sorry.

GoJoe420

For what?

Mamabear3

The party... Lucas was such an asshole and please don't get me started on Sam.

GoJoe420

Nah, I get it. Men have always been jealous of my good looks.

Mamabear3

Seriously, it wasn't cool Lucas putting you on the spot.

GoJoe420

It didn't bug me. I like talking about prepping. Your little brother thinks he's smarter than he is. And Sam is fine. He's a good dude. He's worried I'm coming for his wife.

Mamabear3

That's ridiculous.

GoJoe420

It's human nature, but we're good. I appreciated the invite. The little ones are so damn cute.

Mamabear3

They loved the race track. They haven't stopped playing with it since they opened it.

GoJoe3

Uncle Joe knows what the kiddos like. I forgot to ask, did u hear about the break-ins happening around u?

Mamabear3

I'm trying not to think about it.

GoJoe420

No. That's not how we roll. We don't bury our heads. We get ready. We're all going 2 the gun range for our next meeting. Wanna join us? Or are you afraid of messing up your manicure?

Mamabear3

You're such a prick. You know that, don't you?

GoJoe420

😄 Oh yeah. Every woman I've dated would agree. What do u say? U in?

Mamabear3

Alright, but don't be embarrassed when I show you up.

GoJoe420

I'm still pissed u didn't tell me u knew how 2 shoot.

Mamabear3

I grew up in the country. Until my Daddy took off when I was eight, we went hunting every weekend. I joined Junior Army Officer Training Corp my freshmen year in high school but mom kept getting arrested and I couldn't get to training. Everyone where I come from knows how to shoot.

GoJoe420

You earned some real street cred with the fellas.

Mamabear3

They thought I was some uptight LA suit slumming it didn't they?

GoJoe420

Pretty much. Did u miss it?

Mamabear3

I was surprised. It felt good to shoot again.

GoJoe420

U need protection. U know that don't u?

Mamabear3

Sam would never allow it.

GoJoe420

What's Union Jack going 2 do if someone breaks in? Or the systems shut down & there's no one to call for help. U got lucky once. won't happen again.

Mamabear3

He's so against guns in the house. If the girls found them...

GoJoe420

That's what gun safes are for. Millions of people have 'em and they ain't had no issues. It's the irresponsible owners that give us a bad rap.

Mamabear3

I know.

GoJoe420

What would u have done if that chick who broke in had a gun & not a knife? Come on, Mama, you've gotta think bigger now.

Or not. I ain't gonna pressure u. I just want u to be...

Mamabear3

You're right. When are you going?

GoJoe420

This weekend. In Camarillo. My buddy Aaron has a booth at the gun show. We can drive down & find you something small & compact. Sound good?

Mamabear3

Let's do it.

CASSIE

Cassie stirred and instantly regretted it. She wondered if it were possible to detach her face from her physical person until the pain wore off. She let out a grunt and tentatively touched her cheek—a terrible decision that she regretted immediately.

"Careful, she got you right in the cheekbone. It's pretty swollen, but you're lucky. Nothing is broken."

Ah yes, so lucky. The luckiest girl alive.

"There's an ice pack on the nightstand," Dominic continued, his voice way too loud for her throbbing skull.

Cassie tried to blink away the pain. Her vision was blurry, but she could see Dominic sitting in a cozy leather chair in the corner, seemingly unbothered by their situation. The room itself was small and dark, curtains pulled tight, the decor bright and cheery with floral-patterned bedding and a vase of orange poppies on the nightstand.

Cassie winced again. Her hatred for poppies would last a lifetime. "I asked Esther for painkillers, but I imagine she's waiting till the big man returns before offering any shred of kindness," Dominic said.

Cassie groaned as she swung her feet out of bed. The smallest movement made her face ache. "What happened?"

"You touched their property. To quote Esther, you *'vandalized* their property and disrespected their space.'"

"A flower crumbled in my hand? How is that my fault?"

"They aren't interested in excuses. You're an outsider who came onto their property and touched their shit. Those poppies are what they use to make the opiates that keep this place running and their girls strung out. It's messing with their bottom line. When I said *don't touch anything,* I fucking meant it. Now you have a reminder of how serious they are."

"So we're their prisoners now?"

"Until Joey decides to honor us with his presence."

"You don't seem worried."

"You think I came here without a backup plan? Joey knows that I have friends of my own, the people who provide us with protection, but that doesn't mean he's not gonna be a prick about what went down. The man will want us to beg for forgiveness."

Cassie swallowed hard, not liking the sound of that. It was getting later and later, and she knew that her sisters would be panicked by now.

But Cassie's real concern was Dad. She couldn't believe she'd done this to him. She blinked away tears. This was her punishment for thinking she could be the family savior without consequences.

She picked up the ice pack, put it on her face, and gasped at the cold. Dominic sighed again. *This bloke's sighs could have their own symphony*, she thought.

Dominic stood, reached into his pocket and pulled out a gray handkerchief, and then walked over and wrapped the fabric around the ice pack.

"Okay?" he asked, gesturing to her face.

"Go ahead."

He gently held the cold cloth to her face. "Better?"

She gave a slight nod, the cold now bearable, providing momentarily relief, his touch surprisingly gentle.

"I'm sorry I didn't stop them in time. I tried. If it makes you feel any better, Mom will have my ass when she sees those bruises."

"It does make me feel quite a bit better," Cassie said.

Dominic laughed, a laugh that she hadn't heard before now, one that made the corners of his eyes crinkle.

Cassie giggled, and then winced at the pain coursing through her face. But it felt good to laugh. How long had it been since she last laughed? Since Rosie started scheming to come here? Cassie had been in such a dark place since Dad's diagnosis that she couldn't recall feeling happy. She kept laughing as tears began to fall from her eyes, but there was nothing funny about all of this. She had made such a mistake coming here.

Dominic pulled the ice pack away and reached out to touch her bruised brow at the same time Cassie did.

"We're going to be fine."

"Promise?"

He nodded. Neither one of them moved. They stood there in the quiet, darkness beginning to fall. A few hours ago she wasn't sure she liked him, and now...

He looked at her and she stared back and then she leaned forward and pressed her lips to his. It was gentle at first, but she wanted more.

Dominic swore under his breath but kissed her back. This time the pain from her battered face vanished as his hands pulled her closer to him.

This was the last thing Cassie should be doing. She knew that, but she wanted desperately to escape. To forget about Dad and her sisters and Mum, and be here with Dominic.

A snort of laughter broke the spell. She jerked away and Dominic stepped forward protectively as they turned to find Joey in the doorway grinning at them.

"Dominic, always the ladies' man. Wanna introduce me to your lady friend? She made quite the stir."

Cassie studied Joey. He wasn't tall, maybe five-six, but he was built, the type of frame bodybuilders preferred but hadn't been as common after the Collapse because no one had the time to train when survival was so pressing. He wore camouflage pants and a black T-shirt, the sleeves tight against his muscles, a dizzying number of tattoos covering his arms. They were indecipherable except for a giant tattoo on the center of his biceps. It was a navy flag and silver stars, the words PROTECTOR OF THE UNIVERSE written in silver ink.

He had long gray hair that was tied into a ponytail, which reminded her of Willie Nelson, the old country singer her father adored. He had the aura of a man who expected people to fear him, but Cassie wasn't intimidated. He reminded her of someone's grandpa playing at being a soldier.

Dominic opened his mouth to say something, but Cassie beat him to it. "I'm Cassandra Clark. You knew my mum...Olivia Clark."

The bravado faded, replaced by a flicker of surprise that she assumed came from hearing Olivia's name. Joey studied her as though he were cataloging their similarities. "I'll be damned. One of Liv's triplets, huh?"

Cassie hated how he said her mum's name with such ease and hated him more when he winked at Dom. "You go three for three, you get a special prize?"

Dominic clenched his fists. She imagined he'd love to go toe-to-toe with Joey, but Cassie didn't care about any of that. "I'm here because you knew my mum. I wanted to see if you might help me piece together what happened to her."

Joey snorted. "They got a whole government department for that shit. Sign a bunch of papers, pay a fee, and one day you'll get a letter in the mail that says, *We ain't found shit.*"

Dominic reached for Cassie's hand. "I told you this was pointless. Let's go."

Cassie shook free from him. She couldn't leave now. She studied Joey, willing him to give her the smallest crumb about her mum. Something that would appease Rosie so they could pack up and go home instead of Cassie being forced to admit that she'd done all this and gotten nothing but a battered face. She thought about begging, but then remembered what she'd learned in her psych class. You had to appeal to their egos.

"Mel was right. You *are* a shithead."

She grabbed Dominic's hand, taking strength from its warmth. He squeezed it as they headed toward the door.

"Mel's always been a bitch. Your mother found that out the hard way."

Cassie saw Dominic flinch, but he didn't take the bait, still gently steering her toward the door. She didn't stop him. Joey stepped forward and blocked the exit.

"Joey, don't fucking do this," Dominic said, his voice a low growl.

"I know where she is. Your mum," Joey said, exaggerating the word *mum*.

Cassie froze mid-step. Dominic let go of her hand and reached down to grip Cassie's shoulders. She could feel his breath hot on her neck. "This guy is full of shit. You can't trust him," he said, not bothering to whisper. "We should go now."

What if he isn't full of shit? "She's alive? My mum's alive?"

"C'mon, girly, let's take a walk. I'll tell you all about Liv and where to find her."

Everything about Joey screamed danger, but she followed him out the door and into the night. Dominic trailed her, but Joey put a hand up to stop him. "Just you. I don't need this fella glaring at me the whole time."

Dominic's hands clenched again. "Fuck that. I'm not leaving you alone with her."

Cassie almost laughed. His macho act reminded her of the old Clint Eastwood bootleg films her dad and Bettie watched. "Dominic, I can handle myself."

"Mel will fucking kill me if I leave you with him," Dominic said insistently. "I'd never forgive myself."

"Mel isn't here, and I don't need a bodyguard."

"Cassie . . ."

She leaned in close, so her mouth was right against his ear. "My dad raised three daughters during the Collapse. I can handle myself. I promise. If you hear me whistle, and you will hear it, come get me. But I won't need you. I'll be fine."

He hesitated but apparently had the good sense to know he wouldn't win this fight.

"Joey, none of your bullshit, okay? Cassie's not one of your girls," Dominic called after her.

Joey laughed as they headed up a steep trail. "Don't be silly. Cass here is family. I would never mistreat family."

Cass. It was her family nickname, but coming from Joey it sounded threatening. He also struck her as the kind of man who would sell his own family if it meant padding his pockets, but her decision was made.

Joey grinned a cartoonish smile. "I hope you're ready to hear the truth about your mama. 'Cuz I got a lotta shit to say."

Her whole body buzzed with the realization that she might learn the truth about Mum. This whole time Cassie had insisted to her sisters and even to herself that she didn't care. That her mum being gone hadn't mattered. But it did. It always had.

All these years, Cassie had judged Rosie for her obsession over Mum, for not simply moving on. She'd been so angry at Rosie for pushing them to come here, but it made sense now. She was sad that she hadn't realized it before, but now that she was here with Joey, she got it.

Cassie understood Rosie in a deeper way now, understood the ache and longing for what they'd lost. She knew Mel was full of shit, and maybe Joey was, too. But that wasn't going to stop her from going all-in to get the answers she wanted.

As Cassie headed away from Dominic, she could feel his gaze on her, but she resisted the urge to look back. After eighteen years, she was going to learn the truth about her mum.

r/SoCalValleyPreppers

11,950 Members

PRIVATE CHAT

Mamabear3
What the hell are you doing?

GoJoe420
Eating some tacos before I head back 2 work. Why?

Mamabear3
That's not what I'm asking. Bryan was talking about the land you bought and he said you ordered and I quote, "a motherfucking shit ton of weapons" and that you're gonna start making moves. What does that mean?

GoJoe420
It means we gotta start thinking bigger than sitting around a coffee shop shooting the shit. You see it. The fires, the floods, the protests. It's gonna be go-time very soon & all of us like minded folks need 2 stick together. We're gonna have plenty of room for u and the girls...

Mamabear3
And Sam?

GoJoe420
Of course. If he's onboard.

Mamabear3
We're a package deal, Joey.
Me, Sam, and the girls. They're my family.

GoJoe420
I know that, Liv. I was teasing.

Mamabear3
You swore you weren't one of those end of days nut jobs.

GoJoe420
I'm not. I'm a realist. And shit is getting real.
You're not mad right?

Mamabear3
I want to make sure I'm not hanging out with the Branch Davidian's or Jim Jones. I would really prefer that the girls and I not burn to death because of some white man's God complex.

GoJo420

For fuck's sake, Liv u know me. I'm not looking 2 be a messiah. I want to take care of me & my own.

Mamabear3

Right. Okay.

GoJoe420

We good?

Mamabear3

We're good.

CASSIE

For the first twenty minutes, Joey gave Cassie a home tour that felt endless. "Got this plot of land dirt-cheap since it'd been decimated by the fires and earthquakes, but we saw the potential. Had all the bones of a good homestead."

Cassie glanced around. "You're not worried about another earthquake knocking it all down again?"

Joey shrugged. "I play the odds. Maybe there'll be another—what do they call it?—'cataclysmic event' in my lifetime. Maybe not. But we were ready then, and we'll be ready now."

"Where is everyone?" Cassie asked, surprised by how few people she'd seen walking around.

"Suppertime. We all eat together. Keeps the family unit tight. I told 'em I had a VIP to entertain," he said with a chuckle. They'd reached the end of the compound. There was a small patio set up with a firepit and another small guesthouse tucked into the side of the hill. Joey gestured for her to follow him.

This space was too secluded and too far from Dominic if things took a bad turn. No way in hell would he hear her whistle. No one would hear her at all.

She considered her options. If she said no, Joey might refuse to tell her what he knew about Mum. She could keep searching, but the clock was ticking. Her father's interview loomed, and she needed to find closure so they could return home. She had no other choice.

"Leave the door open," she said. Joey shrugged and followed her inside, clearly confident that an open door meant nothing for someone like him.

The small cabin was decorated with dozens of photos of Los Angeles, before and after the earthquake that toppled it. It was a macabre sight. LA glistening in the night, and then the landscape forever changed, barren, with charred buildings stretched out as far as the eye could see.

"Pretty fucking cool, isn't it? I keep it as a constant reminder that there ain't nothing in this world that's permanent."

He gestured to another wall where half a dozen maps hung. "These are maps of all the property we control, and the inner workings of our goods and services business. The house upstairs is where my wives and children live."

When Cassie didn't comment or question him about his plural use of "wives," he laughed.

"I like it. You see this is how it should be. We get to experience life free from judgment and the incessant policing of our values."

For the past three years, Cassie had been through similar arguments with the privileged university wankers who were almost as annoying as Joey about how a civil society should operate. She realized that what it came down to was men believing the rules didn't matter to them.

She would have been smart to keep her mouth shut, but she couldn't help herself. "It's not new for men to have multiple wives. It's actually rather predictable. Honestly, Joey, I don't bloody care if you have a thousand wives, I want to know where my mum is."

He burst out laughing. "Hot damn, you've got your mama's fire. That's what I loved about her."

Cassie struggled not to grimace. The thought of this man having a relationship with her mum made her physically sick. "You loved my mum. Did she feel the same about you?"

He paused. "She did not. I think she liked me 'cuz I made her feel heard. We were so scared about the future that when you met someone with a similar vibe, it was like, *bam*, I need to know that person."

"How did you and Mum meet?"

"In an internet forum called Reddit. I started the group and man, I was fucking obsessed. I worked for a commercial construction company, so I spent my days building shit, but as soon as I'd get home, I'd crack open a Bud Light and dive in. We were all trading tips, making content as we called it back then, figuring out how to get ready for all of this. We started with about fifty people but before the systems went down there were about fifteen thousand. About five thousand are still Guardians."

"What happened to the rest?"

"Lot of 'em died. Some of 'em couldn't hang with the rules. Didn't see our vision. But that's cool. We've made our mark."

Cassie briefly wondered how many didn't get to leave, but she'd learned long ago not to ask questions she didn't want to know the answer to.

"And Mum?" she said.

"When Liv joined the group, we had an instant connection. She was like, 'I'm not a religious or political nut job, just a mom who wants a plan.' That's all I wanted, too, and I promised her we'd keep our political opinions to ourselves. Our group was about survival."

Cassie had always been good at reading people, and Joey was no different. "You didn't know who my mum was?"

Joey laughed. "You mean that she was hot shit? Not at the time. But I googled her. You know about the Google?" he asked.

Cassie rolled her eyes. "Yes, I have read a thing or two about it."

Joey laughed. "Right. Right. So I did what the kids called Google stalking and found out everything. I couldn't believe that this hot-ass movie producer who hung out with celebrities wanted to hang with me and my crew and talk prepping. I thought she'd be uptight but she was dope. Totally down to learn and dive in."

Cassie found it impossible that her mum, the glamorous

A MOTHER'S GUIDE TO THE APOCALYPSE   307

woman she'd seen pictures of, would want to spend time with this . . . absolute gobshite, but she kept that thought to herself. "Was it just one meeting?"

"At first, but we texted all the time. We'd send prepping tips or various news articles warning one another about some new crisis on the horizon. It was bleak, but we all decided we weren't going to live with our heads in the sand. It felt good knowing we weren't alone in the knowing. We still kept it light. We'd send each other funny memes about the end of the world."

Joey looked at Cassie with another amused smile. She found herself channeling Dominic's trademark sigh. "Yes, Joey, I know what a meme is," Cassie said.

"You're a smart girl, aren't you? Your mama was so damn smart. If we discussed the best types of water purifying systems, she would have links with the most affordable ones in our inbox in minutes. She had the vision before anyone else could see."

"Were you and Mum having an affair?"

Joey let out a guffaw. "I like it. Cut straight to the point. That's how I operate. Trust me, I woulda banged Liv in a heartbeat, but that wasn't in the cards. I kissed her once after a meeting. There had been a lotta bad stuff going on. All those fires that destroyed most of Phoenix and New Mexico and killed fifty thousand people. The New York City flood had already killed thousands and left Queens uninhabitable. Liv was distraught, talking about you girls, and how she still didn't feel ready for what was coming. Not to mention she was fighting with your daddy. She was crying and I was trying to comfort her and we kissed. Now I'm used to ladies being mad at Ol' Joe, but I liked Liv and never meant to fuck things up. She was going on and on, saying that your daddy knew I wanted more than friendship and that she hadn't seen it and she'd sworn he was wrong and now I'd made her out to be a fool."

Joey held up his hands like he was innocent of any crime. "I told her to forget it. We got caught up in a moment. Focus on the mission. We had plenty to do. To be honest, I felt sorry for her. Your daddy had his head so far up his ass. Cozy in his big ol' mansion with his air-conditioning and electronics and his wife making millions, and he thought it'd be like that forever. But money didn't matter when it all fell apart. I mean, it did, but what really counted was how self-sufficient you were. Sammy couldn't get on board with what Liv wanted. I'd have been frustrated, too. They fought a lot."

Cassie gritted her teeth. "You don't know anything about my father or what he's done to ensure our survival."

Joey grinned. She despised that grin, despised him. "Hey, I may not have been Sammy's biggest fan, but the man had cojones. Few days after that kiss, he shows up at my jobsite out in Reseda in his golf polo, and he's all guns a-blazing with his posh accent. 'I swear if you lay a hand on my wife, I'll bloody kill you.' Lemme tell you, the fellas at the job got a kick out of that one. I texted Liv to tell her, but that kiss was the last time I saw her. She disappeared a week later. Sam called me but I told him I ain't heard from her. Besides, I had enough shit to focus on after that. The quake killed my mom and pops, even my dog, but thankfully I was ready. Had my bug-out bag and all our gear ready to go. Spent a few years bouncing around the Valley, trying to help with the rebuild since we had all the money and goods and systems locked up, but the government wasn't interested in us 'cuz we were a bunch of high school dropouts. Basically told us to kick rocks, because we had the nerve to try and tell 'em they were running things wrong. Didn't stop us. We got our homestead set up and quickly made them sit up and take notice when they realized we had various needs on lock."

Cassie thought she might lose her mind. "What does this have to do with my mum?"

He snorted, spraying spittle at Cassie. "I'm getting there. A few years back, I met this sweet chick named Glenda who ran the Hollywood Climate Camp. She believed in the Guardians' cause and knew we always needed more money, and since the government prints money to dump into those camps, Glenda started funneling some to us. As we got closer, she started telling me about this woman she worked with, called her the mayor of the place. When she said she'd been injured in the big flood and her triplets died in the Collapse, I was like, 'Olivia Clark? No fucking way.' But there she was."

Cassie's stomach somersaulted as she recalled the endless row of buildings and barbed wire, the guards stationed outside with assault weapons. The thought of all those orphaned children, and her mum living with them while she mourned her loss, left Cassie so sad that she had to blink away her tears.

"What kind of injury did she sustain?"

"I dunno. Some type of head wound. I didn't get details. I wanted to talk with Liv myself, but Glenda wouldn't make the intro. Said Liv knew all about me and the Guardians and she thought how we handled our business was shameful."

Cassie bit her tongue, because it *was* shameful. What kind of awful person steals from a bloody orphanage?

"I figured I'd work on Glenda a little, give her the ol' Joey charm, and she'd slip Liv a letter and we could reconnect, but then Glenda got busted for stealing from the camp and found herself locked up."

Cassie experienced a brief flicker of sympathy for poor daft Glenda being swindled by this man, but as Dad always said, *If you mess with a snake, you're bound to get bitten.*

"I need to get to the camp. I need to see her," she said, her head spinning.

"Good fucking luck. That place is armed to the teeth. Without a stage-one security clearance, you're not allowed on the sidewalk."

Cassie didn't care. She'd walk up and tell them her mum worked there and they would...

"They shoot to kill," Joey said as though he were reading her mind.

Okay. That wasn't an option. Mel and Dominic lived in the middle of nowhere and had zero connections. "What do I need to do? To visit the camp? How do I get a clearance?" she asked.

"Ask her brother," Joey said casually.

"Wait a minute. Lucas . . . my uncle Lucas is alive, too?" Cassie asked.

"Oh yeah. I'm not sure what he's been doing all these years, but that dude has made some deep connections. Which was surprising 'cuz I know a lot of folks. But about six months ago, those New Pacific political hacks called us in for a sit-down to discuss business and how we could all work together. Bunch of kumbaya shit. We went to tell 'em that wasn't happening, and that's when I saw him, wearing one of them fancy suits while he took orders from his overlords. I didn't know him well. We met once at your birthday party and he acted like I had dog shit on my shoes. But he's clearly one of us *eat or be eaten* types." He snorted again, proud of himself.

"It's strange, but he doesn't go by Lucas Hays anymore. Calls himself Luke Hays. After the meeting, I asked him about Liv, and again he acts like he don't know who the fuck I am or what I was talking about. When I asked him again if his sister worked at the camp, suddenly security is trying to toss us out on our asses. I say *trying* 'cuz we gave 'em as good as we got."

He puffed out his chest, and Cassie could tell he wanted

to brag about whatever macho thing he'd accomplished, but she was done indulging this arsehole.

"Where can I find Lucas? Or Luke? Or whatever his name is?"

"Downtown. It's where all the politicians live and work. He's not official or anything. From what I hear, he's the guy who knows all the guys."

"Thank you for your time and help," Cassie said as she turned to go.

Joey's hand reached out and gripped her arm, his meaty fingers digging into her flesh. "You're a sweet girl, but you're not as bright as I thought if you really think I told you all that without requiring something in return."

Cassie's heart fluttered, but she wasn't surprised by this turn of events. The world might have changed over the years, but cockroaches would always endure.

"What do you want?" she asked.

"You know we could always use fresh blood here," he said as his hand caressed her arm. Cassie fought the urge to shake him free, aware that rejecting him would only excite him. She allowed herself to stay completely still. Let him think he was in charge.

"You're so darn pretty. It's like your mama came back to life. Such a sweet mouth and that tight little ass."

He pulled her hard against him. Cassie's breath caught at the unexpected move. *Stay calm. Breathe through the fear*, she told herself.

A MOTHER'S GUIDE TO THE APOCALYPSE 313

She could hear Sam's voice in her head. *Because you're a woman, they will always believe you are incapable of taking them down. The element of the surprise is where you have the advantage.*

Joey's hands were all over her body now. She wanted to cry, but Sam had warned that her tears could make things worse. *Breathe through the fear. Swallow your tears. The power is in the control you possess.*

Joey's voice was a whisper. "This will be fun. I promise you."

She smiled and put her hands on his shoulders as though giving in. His grin grew wider, a grotesque expression of joy and domination. He leaned in close, his mouth almost connecting with hers when, with punishing speed and accuracy, she kneed him.

One.

Two.

Three times in the groin.

A Muay Thai side kick is considered a dangerous move, but only if it's done incorrectly. Cassie's sisters hated martial arts, but after fifteen years of training alongside Sam, a man who hoarded self-defense books, Cassie found it easy. She wished Sam could have seen the groan Joey let out as he crumpled to the floor.

"My dad might have buried his head in the sand before the Collapse, but he knew I'd need to know how to handle arseholes like you."

She knelt beside Joey and put one arm around his throat, the other holding him down. His eyes rolled back in his head from the pain, but Cassie focused on what she had to do to be sure he didn't come after her. She put pressure on the side of his neck. All she had to do was compress the arteries and veins that circulated blood to and from Joey's brain, and she would cause him to black out.

She counted softly. "Ten, nine, eight, seven..."

It usually took ten seconds to knock someone out, but Joey was down before she reached five. Probably due to his lack of physical conditioning and limited lung capacity. She left him slumped on the floor and slipped out of the room.

When Cassie stepped outside, it was pitch-black and quiet, but there was no question they would be coming for her. Heart pounding, Cassie began to run. If she were caught, she didn't want to think about what they would do to her. Or Dominic.

Despite her fear, Cassie raced down the hill, unable to stop the giant grin. She had gotten what she came for and was closer than ever to meeting her mum. She simply had to make it out of here alive.

MAMA'S GUIDE TO YOUR BUG-OUT BAG

I'll never forget when your dad and I took y'all on your first walk. Our neighborhood had a cute park about five minutes from our house, and we forgot the diaper bag. It was a short walk, so we figured what could possibly go wrong?

What sweet summer children we were.

Within the first two minutes, Rosie puked up two days' worth of formula, Cassie blew out her diaper, and Bettie got stung by a bee and cried so hard she hyperventilated.

To make matters worse, when your father went to grab Bettie from her stroller, he tripped on his untied shoelace and face-planted into the concrete and smashed his nose. I said later we were lucky we didn't get struck by lightning.

What I'm trying to say is life happens when you least expect it, and you need to be prepared. From that day on, your father and I never left the house without spare diapers, wipes, and a first-aid kit in our stroller.

Think of your bug-out bag as a doomsday prepper's diaper bag.

The bug-out bag is the ultimate "fuck it, I'm out" tool. Packed with enough survival essentials to last you at least seventy-two hours, the bug-out bag allows you to pack up and "bug out" at a moment's notice.

The hallmarks of a good bug-out bag are balance, variety, and an economy of space. Too much of one essential can make it impossible to pack another, so only pack what you need. With some time, effort, and a solid amount of Tetris-ing, you can make a bag that will allow you to set up shelter virtually anywhere.

Note: Y'all should each have your own bug-out bag. Don't cut corners by sharing one.

The Bag

Your bag will probably be between twenty and thirty pounds, so you need to make sure you have a big, durable bag to hold and protect your gear. I suggest a 3L military-type rucksack or camping backpack. Both are designed to take a beating and carry a person's life in them. They also have plenty of pockets and compartments to maximize storage.

Must-Have Items

- Battery-powered or hand-crank radio and NOAA Weather Radio with tone alert
- Flashlight
- First-aid kit
- Extra batteries
- Whistle (to signal for help)

A MOTHER'S GUIDE TO THE APOCALYPSE   317

- Prescription meds
- Eyeglasses and contacts
- Duct tape can save your bacon, so you should always have at least one roll. It will be your best friend in plenty of emergency situations.
  - Emergency patch your tent or tarp.
  - Tape up worn boots or shoes.
  - Make a splint out of sticks and the tape.
  - Make a grip for walking stick or a club.
  - You can also use it to bind a wound if that's all you have.
  - (but if you've read this carefully you know you should have a first-aid kit!)

Identification and Money

I don't know what the value of the dollar will be by the time you read this, but it never hurts to have a couple hundred dollars in small bills in your bug-out bag. You also want to make sure to have several forms of identification (driver's license and passport) so you can convince people you are who you say you are.

Food and Water

Think shelf-stable and long lasting. You're not trying to be listed in the Michelin Guide here, so pack food with expiration dates in the distant future. The last thing you want to do after leaving somewhere dangerous is find out that your food supply has expired. MREs, dehydrated foods, protein and energy bars, and canned goods are all fantastic options. If possible, pack an ultralight camping stove with fuel and a titanium pot. These items will allow you to cook soups and purify water on the go.

Even if you have a titanium pot to boil water, you still need to pack water treatment supplies like iodine or chlorine dioxide pills and a water bottle. If you can fit a LifeStraw, great; if you can find a water bottle with a filtration system built in, even better. Additionally, you'll want at least one liter of drinking water ready at all times.

Sleep and Shelter

At some point, you're going to have to stop running and set up shop for the night. You're going to need all the energy you can muster in these scenarios, so sleep is critical. Pack an emergency sleeping bag that can keep you warm in twenty-degree weather. For shelter, you'll want either a tarp that you can hang above you or a compact hiking tent to protect you from the elements and pests.

Fire

Whether it's to warm you up, signal for help, or boil water, you're going to need fire supplies. Place a bunch of cotton balls covered in Vaseline into a bag and store it in a small tin to use as a tinder kit. Another tinder kit hack is to use dryer lint instead of the Vaseline cotton balls. You'll also

A MOTHER'S GUIDE TO THE APOCALYPSE 319

want strike-anywhere matches, a ferro rod, and a disposable lighter to cover all your ignition bases.

Navigation and Signaling

Since your bug-out bag is based in your home, you should have maps of the immediate and surrounding areas in case you need to navigate through them. You'll also need a compass to find your way from point A to point B. (See my Navigation Guide.)

A GPS device could be lifesaving, assuming the satellite network is still working by the time y'all read this.

In case you need to go somewhere at night or signal to rescuers, pack an LED flashlight with spare batteries. To maximize your daytime visibility, pack a pair of binoculars. Y'all may also want to consider packing a signal mirror in case you're trying to flag someone down during the day.

Hygiene and First Aid

Your first-aid kit should be small yet dense. A small variety of bandages, gauze, antiseptic wipes, spare medication you take, insect repellent, and a tourniquet are all you need.

For your hygiene needs, go with the bare essentials. A bar of soap, wet napkins, two small packets of toilet paper, feminine hygiene products (pack tampons and a menstrual cup), hand sanitizer, and a travel-size toothbrush and toothpaste that will keep you fresh and clean for at least seventy-two hours. You'll also want to pack a small microfiber towel to keep yourself dry.

Clothes

This one's tricky because it depends on where you are and the time of the year. Personally, I believe in packing lightweight items that aren't cotton. You're going to want to have layers just in case, and whatever clothing you have, you'll want it to dry quickly.

Pack light, long-sleeved shirts to protect you from the sun and layer on in case it's cold. You'll also want a windproof and waterproof jacket to protect you from bad weather. I'm weird about underwear (La Perla this is not) and keep five pairs in my bag because that's the one thing I want most of. You'll also want a sun hat, at least two pairs of wool socks, a pair of long pants, sunglasses, sturdy boots, work gloves, and a poncho.

If that sounds like a lot, it isn't. Y'all are going to be exerting yourselves a lot during this time and will need extra clothes. This is why you need a decent-size bag.

Self-Defense

As far as self-defense is concerned, a knife or machete works great, but pepper spray is also a solid non-lethal option. If you do have a gun, make sure you have extra ammunition for it. Lastly, pack bear spray. It can be used on a variety of predators, including big cats, wolves, coyotes, and humans.

A bug-out bag is not something you should pack and unpack. Get it ready, put it in a convenient place to reach, and leave it for when you need it.

Here's hoping you'll never need it, but you'll be glad when you have it.

Love Always,

Mama Bear

ROSIE

The dark motorway stretched on and on, and Rosie's eyes were drooping she was so tired, but she kept moving in her seat and tapping her hands against the wheel to stay awake. They had to be close to the city. It had been over an hour since Bettie had dozed off, and she was grateful for the silence.

It gave her time to think and properly beat herself up for being a bloody idiot and blindly trusting Mel. She could also add *quitter* to her CV now that she was giving up hope on ever uncovering the truth about Mum. But it was pointless. She was dead, and Rosie was a fool to expect anything else to come from this trip.

A loud ringing startled her. She glanced down at the phone, but Bettie was one step ahead of her, bolting upright from her slumber and reaching for the phone.

"Hello," Bettie said. She pressed the SPEAKERPHONE button and Cassie's voice came through, distant and wobbly.

"Bets? It's me, Cassie."

Rosie had never been so relieved to hear her sister's voice. "Are you okay?" Rosie asked.

"I am. I . . . I will be," Cassie said softly.

"Good, because when I see you, I'm going to kill you. What were you thinking?" Rosie shouted.

Bettie glared at her. Rosie shrugged. "I'm sorry, but you won't believe. You can't . . ."

Rosie realized that Cassie was crying. Big gulping sobs.

"What's wrong, Cass?" Bettie asked. "What is it?"

She was still crying. Rosie couldn't take it. "For fuck's sake, Cass, what is it?"

A bigger sob. "Mum is alive. Ro, you were right all this time. She's alive."

Bettie let out a stunned gasp.

"What did she say? Liv? My Liv's alive?" Sam said, his voice a strangled whisper as he sat up in the back seat.

Rosie waved him off. She could barely see the road through her tears. She had to pull over.

"Where is she? Did you meet her? What's she like?" Rosie asked, her words spilling out.

"I don't know yet. All I know is that Lucas is alive, too."

"I don't believe it," Sam whispered. "It's not . . . It can't be."

"Dominic said he's going to take me to Mum, so get your arses here as soon as possible. Ask Mel to arrange it," Cassie ordered.

"We left Mel's. We're driving to LA to find you," Bettie said softly.

"What? What are you talking about? Why would you do that? Where are you?"

"Close to the city limits, I think. Mel's been lying to us about Mum and the interview and who knows what else, and then a few hours ago a Guardian came to the house. Said he was a cop and wanted to take us back to the city—"

Dominic cut in. "What did you say?"

"He said he was with the LA police, but your mum and Eduardo figured out the truth."

"Is Mom okay?" Dominic asked, a hint of panic in his voice.

"She's fine. I'm sure you know she can handle herself. Now can you put Cassie back on the phone?" Rosie said.

There were more raised voices on the other end of the phone.

Dominic's voice grew clearer, his words not meant for Rosie and Bettie. "After your run-in, Joey will be looking to bury you."

Rosie's stomach churned "What run-in, Cass?"

"It doesn't matter," Cassie snapped.

"It fucking matters. Call us when you get to the city limits and we'll give you our location," Dominic said.

"You really think Mum's alive?" Rosie asked.

"We've got no idea. It could be a trap," Dominic said.

The girls weren't stupid. It was a possibility, but there was only one other option.

Cassie spoke. "We can give up now and go home. Forget what Joey said. Or we can keep going. But this time we all have to agree. No more lies and no more secrets."

Rosie looked at Bettie, tears still in her eyes. Sam was too overcome to speak. He reached into the front seat and squeezed both their hands, a signal he trusted them to make the call.

"We keep going. We love you, Cass. We'll see you soon," Rosie said, and hung up.

She took a deep breath, her hands squeezing the steering wheel so tightly, her knuckles had turned white. Her whole body shook from the shock of the news, but this wasn't the time to process her emotions. It was up to Rosie to take charge. "Let's go and get Mum."

MAMA'S GUIDE TO NAVIGATION

There are traits of mine I hope y'all inherited.

My quick wit.

My ability to talk to anyone and everyone about anything and everything.

My hair. It's always been pretty great if I do say so myself.

Then there are traits I hope you didn't inherit, like my navigational abilities. I have the directional sense of a cat trapped in a paper bag. Your father used to joke that I'd need a GPS to get out of it. He wasn't wrong. In fact, I never learned the real layout of the city because it just wasn't necessary. I even had a rule with your father that he could never use cardinal directions when directing me somewhere. None of that "head north" crap. He had to tell me turn right or left, and I could still manage to cock it up. (His words not mine.)

My generation didn't need navigation skills. We had GPS. We had phones that told us exactly where to go. But that's not the future you're going to live in. Which is why y'all have to learn navigation skills. It's one of the most important survival skills, and it will empower you to go virtually anywhere you need. Most important, knowing how to navigate will prevent you from getting lost, which is a _major_ danger when the worst happens. Below are some quick lessons to prime your navigation education.

Finding North Without a Compass

You should always have a proper compass with you, but let's be real, how many times are you gonna carry a compass— or if shit goes south, maybe you won't have time to grab it. So let's say you don't have your compass. You still need to know _where the hell am I?_

Fortunately, Mama Bear is here with the answers. There are some natural signs to look for to orient yourself and find north. For example, moss tends to grow on the north sides of rocks and trees because that is _usually_ where the least amount of sunlight is. I emphasize _usually_ because moss can grow in 360 degrees so you shouldn't stake your life on it.

Conversely, spiderwebs and tree rings tend to favor the south as that's _usually_ where the most sunlight is. The spaces between tree rings tend to be thicker where sunlight hits the tree.

Personally, I like the stick method as it only requires two sticks and two rocks. Place one stick into the ground so it's sticking straight up and mark the end of its shadow with a stone. Wait thirty minutes and then place your second rock

A MOTHER'S GUIDE TO THE APOCALYPSE 329

at the end of the new shadow. Draw a straight line between your two rocks and bam, you've just found the east–west line, and the shadow pointing over this line should be facing north. (It's confusing at first, but if a directionally challenged idiot like me can get it, you can, too.)

If you have an analog wristwatch, hold your wrist out horizontally so the hour hand is pointing at the sun. The north–south line will run halfway between the hour hand and 12.

On a clear night, you can find north by locating the Big Dipper (the constellation that looks like a saucepan). Find the bottom two stars opposite to the handle. Polaris is the bright star at the end of the dipper, which aligns with the North Star. If you use the line made by Polaris and the star beneath it as a measurement, the distance between Polaris and the North Star is around six-ish of those lines.

Note: Don't navigate at night unless it's imperative to your survival. You'll more than likely end up making things worse by getting lost, getting hurt, and/or running into a nocturnal predator.

Make a Compass

I hate this method because it's predicated on you just happening to have a sewing needle or razor blade and magnet on you in the wild, yet you don't have a compass or map. Perhaps you're a tailor who loves magnets. (Please know that I'm writing this after a glass of Cabernet so bear with me!) Anyway, if you have these items, you can make a compass.

Rub the blade or tip of the needle down the magnet about thirty times to magnetize it. Remember, you can only rub the compass needle in one direction. Once you've magnetized your compass needle, place it on a leaf in some stagnant water. The magnetized tip will then orient itself north once the leaf stops spinning.

Have a Proper Compass

Assuming y'all are prepared and have a proper compass on you, here's how to operate one. I should note that a proper compass isn't the one you'll find on the end of a keychain at a gas station. While a gas station compass is better than getting poked in the eye with a sharp stick, a proper compass should have these attributes:

- Transparent baseplate so you can see the part of the map on which you're orienting yourself more accurately. The baseplate should also have a ruler to measure distances on a map.
- A bezel with degree marks to calculate your bearing. Your bearing will be a degree from 0 to 360, and it will inform you the precise direction you will need to go. Your bezel will also have an orienting arrow, which y'all will use to, well, orient yourselves.

A MOTHER'S GUIDE TO THE APOCALYPSE 331

- Sighting mirror to shoot accurate bearings. A sighting mirror allows you to look at the object you're orienting yourself to and the compass simultaneously.
- Clinometer to measure slope angle and to check for avalanche hazards. These are especially helpful if you're on a search and rescue.

Using Your Compass

Understand one thing: This shit ain't easy. Using a compass sounds rudimentary, but it takes math, time, precision, and a lot of practice (none of which I was ever good at), but I learned how to do it, and you can, too.

1. Adjust your compass's declination by moving the orienting arrow however many degrees your area's declination is. Refer to your map for the area's declination so you can adjust your compass to true north.

2. Place your compass on your map. Make sure the map lies on a flat surface with no nearby metal objects. Hopefully, y'all will know where you are on the map; if not, look for nearby landmarks on the map to orient yourselves.

3. Mark your location (A) and where y'all want to go (B). Align your baseplate with A and then rotate the compass so that your baseplate makes a line

from A to B. Your direction-of-travel arrow needs to point toward B.

4. Rotate the bezel so that its orienting lines align with north and south on the map. At this point, look at the top of the bezel for the index line, which should now tell you your bearing. Huzzah! You now know which direction to go.

5. With the direction-of-travel arrow pointing away from you, rotate your body so that the north side of the magnetizing arrow is inside the orienting arrow. This will point in the direction you need to find your destination.

Like Meemaw used to say, "Always remember to follow your heart and trust your gut. It'll never steer you wrong."

Love Always,

Mama Bear

CASSIE

I t's a bad idea," Dominic said. They'd had to haul ass out of Guardian territory, sirens wailing as they sped down the hill.

"They'll be sending all their men to hunt us down," he said as he drove, turning down half a dozen streets and alleys. Thankfully they'd avoided any patrols, but Dominic had driven to an underpass near the freeway and parked. They needed to come up with a plan, which after talking to her sisters had been activated. At least as far as Cassie was concerned.

"You know you've stepped in the biggest fucking hornet's nest," he said.

Cassie understood that. She hadn't stopped trembling since she'd left Joey's. She was well aware that things could have gone a different way. But it was over now. She needed to track down her uncle Lucas and her mum.

"Are you going to drive me downtown? Or do I have to walk?"

"Of course I'll take you. I...Cassie, I can't stay. I have to get home and make sure that my mom is okay."

She wanted to lash out, *So your mum says jump and you say how high*, but Dominic had been good to her. He'd put his own life at risk to help her get answers. It was time to move on.

"Okay, then move your arse," she said.

He burst out laughing, but there was a moment when she thought he might kiss her again. A moment where she wanted to kiss him, too. But that was silly. She climbed back onto the bike and wrapped her arms around him one last time. The motorway was pitch-black until they reached downtown, and then the city lights almost blinded her. There were lights from restaurants and shops, billboards flashing advertisements for concerts and clothing and facial creams. This part of the city looked completely different from the desolate wasteland she'd seen so far. Supercharged and fueled by capitalism.

"I see this is where the action is," Cassie said. It reminded her of pictures she'd seen of Las Vegas—or, as Dad used to call it, Disneyland for old folks.

"It is now. Downtown LA used to be a wasteland. Generally if you worked down here, you were in government, business, or finance, or maybe you lived here because you were an artist who wanted cheap rent. The only downside was you lived side by side with unhoused people suffering from a mental health crisis or someone who couldn't afford the city's rising prices. Thousands of people lived in tents on the streets here before the quake and afterward, but they got rid of them quick. A good deal of skyscrapers were toppled but the overall damage was less severe, not to mention there were a lot less bodies to dispose of, so this was the focus of the rebuilding efforts."

Cassie took in the hundreds of sleek and shiny office buildings and condos and apartments. There was an energy here that the rest of the city lacked. A sense of possibility. She spotted rows and rows of high-end restaurants and shops, and as they continued on she saw streets lined with theaters, designed to look exactly like New York City's Broadway. Or what used to be Broadway before the floods.

Bettie would love this, she thought, and wondered what it would mean for all of them once they found Mum. There was no way they would want to leave her behind, but Dad would never agree to stay here. Maybe Mum would come back to England with them? The uncertainty of it all made Cassie's head ache. She had to stop worrying. She wasn't going to solve all her problems tonight.

"We must be close," she said.

"City hall is up there." Dominic pointed to the gleaming building ahead of them. He sped up and turned into a spot in front of the deserted building. As they removed their helmets, Cassie went to climb off the bike, but Dominic stopped her, his hand lingering on her wrist.

"I'm sorry. For everything that went down. And I'm really glad I got to meet you."

Cassie felt a pull toward Dominic, a sense that he really

336 HOLLIE OVERTON

saw her. Not as one of the triplets, but as someone unique and special all on her own. It was what Max and Bettie had. She got it now.

But it didn't matter. It wasn't like there was a future here. Dominic was Mel's son, and Mel was someone she had no interest in ever seeing again. Cassie shrugged out of his grasp.

"You got me here safe and sound. You should get going. I know your mum will be worried."

The last thing Cassie wanted to do was make their goodbye a big deal. She gave him a quick wave and headed toward the entrance of the sleek new courthouse.

Dominic fell into step beside her. "I'm not leaving until I know that you're safe."

Before today, she might have told him to piss off, but she was happy not to go at this alone. They made their way through large glass doors to find a security guard, a machine gun around his shoulder, stationed at the entrance. "Can I see your IDs?" he barked.

Cassie and Dominic both quickly presented their identification. He studied Cassie for what felt like an eternity. "What can I do for you?"

"We're looking for Luke Hays," Cassie said.

"Mr. Hays and the rest of the delegation are at the New Pacific Festival down the street."

Off their blank looks, he continued. "Weeklong celebration of the ten-year anniversary of the country. Lots of food, music, and booze. You should check it out."

"Right, 'cuz nothing commemorates mass murder like a party," Dominic scoffed.

The guard's eyes narrowed, clearly not pleased with Dominic's assessment of the city's brutal history, which included the murder of over a thousand people during the battle for control of the state now known as New Pacific. The last thing Cassie wanted to do was have an argument over a conflict she had nothing to do with. She turned and took off through the glass doors, racing back down the city streets, Dominic trailing her.

Two blocks later, Cassie heard the music and saw the cheering crowd. There was a Ferris wheel, a giant stage, and a crowd of hundreds, everyone dancing and eating and playing carnival games. This was the New Pacific she'd thought she would find: a city of free spirits, not one with roving bands of thieves and doomsday preppers with messiah complexes.

She pushed through the crowd until she reached the front of the stage and scanned the mostly male faces of the security council. She'd seen Lucas's photos at Mel's, but it had been years since they were taken. Would she recognize him?

A few minutes later, she got her answer when she spotted a man standing off to the side of the stage, smiling and tapping his feet to the music. Some people change drastically as they age, so much so that it's impossible to recognize them. Not Lucas. He was a bit older and stockier than the twenty-something in the Halloween photo, and his blond hair was grayer, but he was still easy to spot. Tall and broad-shouldered, he wore tailored jeans and a white button-down shirt with the sleeves rolled up, a casual look that made him feel approachable. He looked like he might play a doctor or politician in one of Bettie's favorite TV shows. Around his neck was a lanyard that signaled he was someone important—or maybe it was his demeanor that did so: a confident swagger in how he moved and interacted with everyone.

Cassie spotted a group of police stationed at the front of the stage and slowly inched toward them. "I need to speak with the man up there. Lucas...Luke Hays," she said to one of them, a young woman around her age.

"Please step back," the girl shouted above the noise.

"That's my uncle. I need to talk to him," Cassie insisted.

"You heard what I said. Step back." Her voice was louder now. Her hand lingered on her weapon. The other soldiers followed suit. There was an energy shift, all of them waiting for trouble to pop off.

"Cassie, don't be fucking stupid," Dominic said.

She blinked. She had almost forgotten he was there. She turned her attention back to the stage.

"Luke! Luke!" she screamed. "It's Cassie. Uncle Lucas, it's Cassie Clark, your niece."

The band's song ended, the crowd silent as the words "Uncle Lucas" reverberated in the evening air. A scream and a prayer all at once. Lucas saw her. His smile faded. He froze in place.

A MOTHER'S GUIDE TO THE APOCALYPSE 339

Did he recognize her? She couldn't tell. She watched as he quickly moved over to the solider on the stage behind him and whispered in his ear.

The solider beside Cassie grabbed her, arm squeezing tightly. "Come with us."

Another solider took hold of Dominic. They pushed them through the crowd, ignoring their protests. It was hot and sticky, and Cassie's pulse quickened. What if she'd been wrong about Lucas? What if this was Joey's trap? They walked past the stage toward a dressing room; a sign on the door read SECURITY COUNCIL ONLY, KEEP OUT.

Inside the small room were elaborate platters of meats, cheeses, and sushi, as well as a full bar with a bartender serving cocktails, but all Cassie could focus on was Lucas as he hurried toward them. He didn't look threatening. More shell-shocked than anything.

"Is it...I'm sorry, I heard you shouting in the crowd, but it was so loud. I'm Luke Hays. What did you say your name was again?"

She took a deep breath. "Cassandra Clark. Cassie. My mother was Olivia Clark."

She pulled out her passport. Lucas took it and stared down at the photo and back at her again. "I didn't believe it when I heard you. But it's really you, isn't it?"

Cassie couldn't stop her grin. "It is. And you're really my uncle?"

"In the flesh." He paused. "Your sisters? Are they..."

He trailed off. Post-Collapse, you were reluctant to inquire about people because more often than not, the answer wasn't good.

"They're on their way here. We were staying at Mel's house in the mountains."

Lucas shook his head. "I'm sure there's a story there. So that old battle-ax is still kicking?"

Cassie almost snickered. "This is the old battle-ax's son, Dominic."

Lucas had the good sense to look embarrassed. "My apologies."

Dominic shrugged. "She is *still* a battle-ax. It's nice to meet you."

"You too," Lucas said, but he was clearly distracted by Cassie. His expression darkened as he took in her bruises. "What happened there?"

Cassie saw his gaze flicker back to Dominic. "It wasn't him. We went to see Joey."

"The Guardians? Jesus, that was stupid. So Joey did that?"

Cassie shook her head. "One of his followers. I handled things."

A sly smile flashed across Lucas's face. "Another story I want to hear."

"I'm definitely not on his list of favorite people," Cassie said, sounding more flippant than she felt.

"She'll need protection from him. No question,"

A MOTHER'S GUIDE TO THE APOCALYPSE 341

Dominic said. "We've got no idea why but Joey sent men to our home in the mountains, and they weren't coming for tea. You need to notify the authorities."

"I will," Lucas assured him. "Don't worry, Cassandra. You're safe here."

"Please call me Cassie," she said. She could feel the tension leaving her body at the confidence he projected.

"Of course. Cassie, I'm sorry that happened. These militias are like cockroaches. The Guardians are the worst of 'em all. But we've got plenty of security here. No one's going to hurt you." Lucas shook his head again. "Your mom isn't going to believe this. I barely believe it and I'm looking right at you."

"Can I see her? Can we go now?" Cassie asked excitedly. After all they'd been through, could it really be this easy?

"You'll need to get security clearance to visit her at the camp, but I can arrange that. She's going to be...I mean, as you can imagine, losing you girls...well, it was a nightmare. She almost didn't survive the loss and now..."

Cassie had questions, too many, really, but one was weighing on her. "Why didn't you look for us?"

"Who says I didn't? After the Collapse, when internet and telecommunications went offline, no one could get in touch with anyone in the States, much less internationally. It took years for all that to get straightened out, and at that time I had no connections to search abroad. Then there was your mom... Her recovery took a lot of time and patience."

Cassie's eyes widened. *Her recovery?*

"I'll tell you more later, but the headline is that I did try. Once I got connected with the right people, I found... I found British death certificates. For you girls and Sam. It was horrible. I didn't want to believe it, but... there they were."

"Someone wanted you to think we were dead? Why? Who would do that?"

Lucas shrugged. The answer seemed obvious, but he didn't say Sam's name out loud. Instead he changed the subject as though not wanting to upset her. "You said your sisters are coming?"

"They're on their way, but they have a satellite phone," Dominic said.

"Fantastic. We'll call them and tell them where to meet us. I need to let my team know that we're leaving. That's my head of security, Pablo."

Lucas pointed to a hulking man in the corner. He was at least six foot five, with a shaved head and eyes that made it clear he was not your friend. His slight head tilt was the closest she would get to a hello. "He'll be waiting right outside. Let him know when you're ready, and he'll escort you to the car. I'll see you soon."

Lucas shook Dominic's hand and hurried out, leaving them alone in the room. Cassie gave him her most reassuring smile. "See there? You can go. I'm in good hands."

"Are you? You barely know him."

She gestured to Pablo. "I think I'm good. Unless you want to stay. Keep watch over us," she said, a challenge in her voice.

Dominic's face was conflicted. "After what happened at home . . . Mom will be waiting."

She smiled sadly. "Even if you wanted to stay, you can't. You're trapped."

"Says the girl who can't do anything without her sisters."

The gentle tone softened the harshness of his words, but Cassie didn't deny it.

"Did you know your mum was lying to us about all of this?" She wasn't sure why she cared. Now that she'd tracked down her family, they'd never see each other again. But still, she wanted to know.

Dominic shook his head. "Not about everything that went on, but she's never asked my opinion about anything. Mel does what Mel wants. Always has, always will."

"Now I know why you were so hostile when we arrived," she said.

"I find it hard to talk about this, but a few years ago before the others left, there was a girl."

"Isn't there always?" Cassie joked.

He smiled, but she saw real pain in his eyes. She gestured for him to continue.

"We'd met Lindsay and her family in the climate camps, and they came to the mountains to live with us. We got close. Really close. The more rules Mom imposed, the more people resisted. Finally, her family decided to pack up and head north like a lot of resettlers. I decided to go with them. Mom lost it when I told her. Came at me with a god-damn hammer."

He gestured to a scar on his forehead, faded by time. "I had to hospitalize her, but after that I couldn't leave. Couldn't take the chance that she'd fall apart. We got her on meds and she's better, but she's still…well, you saw. When I realized that I couldn't convince her that you and your family shouldn't come, I thought maybe I could convince you to leave."

"Great strategy. It almost worked."

She paused, considering what he'd said. "If you thought your mom was lying about everything, why let me come here and talk to Joey?"

He sighed. "I thought it would be a dead end."

"Plot twist. My mom's alive." Cassie used her best monster voice, which made Dominic smile.

She knew he didn't want her pity, but she understood feeling trapped in your life. "Maybe one day we'll both find the courage to break free," she said wistfully.

Before she could leave, Dominic grabbed her by the hand and slipped a piece of paper in it. "This is my number at home. If you need anything, call me."

He let go of her hand, and Cassie headed toward the door. A part of her wanted to look back and see if he was watching her. She could beg him to come with her and keep her safe, but that was ridiculous.

After a nearly impossible journey to get here, she'd found her mum. In a few short hours, her whole family would be reunited and whatever she had with Dominic would be a distant memory.

r/SoCalValleyPreppers

11,004 Members

PRIVATE CHAT

GoJoe420

Sam came by the job site today, & told me to stay the fuck away from u. It got heated, & my dickhead boss called the cops. Liv, your man is off the fucking rails. Not that I can't handle it, but you good?
Are you okay?
Liv...answer me!

GoJoe420

Liv, can you let me know that you're good?

---

r/SoCalValleyPreppers

GoJoe420

Where is Liv?

Has anyone heard from Liv?

Sweetie24

No, not for a week or so.

VanNuysGuy405

Did you piss her off again?

GoJoe420

Bite me, Van.

Sweetie24

I'll let you know if she messages. I hope she's okay.

PRIVATE CHAT

GoJoe420

I'm starting to worry. Text or call me & let me know all's good.

GoJoe420

Liv, where are u? Sam said u left him. He thought u were with me. What's going on? He said the girls miss u. We all do. Just let us know your okay.

GoJoe420

I know we might never talk again, I love u. I'm not sorry about that kiss. If I'd been married to u, I'd have never let u go. Wherever u are, I hope you know that I'm sorry. I love u.

OLIVIA

It was almost midnight when Olivia slipped into her apartment and switched on the small night-light beside her bed, her loft illuminated by the soft white glow. She was exhausted, but her after-work ritual never wavered. She lit her favorite jasmine-scented candle and began her meditation, a ritual she'd adapted in the years since the Collapse.

Once that was complete, she took out her notebook, which she wrote in every morning and every night without fail. A therapist she met in the climate camp suggested she try writing letters to her girls as part of her healing. In the ensuing eighteen years, this was her greatest comfort.

Despite Olivia's initial reluctance to speak about her daughters, the woman was right. It *did* help. She could write down everything about her life and her memories in her letters and imagine that one day her daughters would read them. She wrote so many that she filled up fifty notebooks. Then a hundred. Eventually she ran out of room to store them and asked her brother, Lucas, to keep them at his home, which was much too big for him and had plenty of storage space. He agreed, but when she arranged to drop them off, he'd been shocked.

"Sis, are you sure about this? You know they'll never read any of this."

He was right, of course. Sam and the girls were dead. That much was certain. Holding on to hope after all these years was wasted energy. But still Olivia wrote.

Today's entry was one that she hoped had a happy ending. A week ago in Hollywood, emergency services brought a newborn baby into the clinic. She'd been abandoned in a drainage ditch and was malnourished and unresponsive. The doctors were upfront that her prognosis didn't look good.

Olivia disagreed. She always recognized the fighters. For five days, she ignored her administrative duties and sat in the dimly lit nursery holding the dark-haired girl they named Nova. She used the same song list she'd used for her girls. Reba, Willie Nelson, and Patsy Cline. Singing to them and playing music. Shortly after midnight on the sixth day, Nova made direct eye contact and took a bottle. The nurses couldn't believe it, but Olivia wasn't surprised. She kept writing, eager to share with her girls how right before she left the nursery, Nova looked up at Olivia and giggled.

A giggle that reminded Liv of her own girls at that age.

A giggle that told her this girl would be one of the lucky ones. That Nova would be okay, and so would Olivia.

A MOTHER'S GUIDE TO THE APOCALYPSE   351

None of these children could fix what was broken in Olivia, but they gave her a purpose—a reason to survive.

That was not to say that her letters sanitized this place. She wanted her daughters to understand that life in the camp was never quiet or relaxing, but that she was used to the chaos. There were so many children here with emotional and behavioral issues to navigate as well as the administrative challenges. That meant there were no days off, and the battle to keep the camps open now that the city had been rebuilt waged on. But babies like Nova showed how desperately the camps were needed.

More than anything, they were a family. They celebrated birthdays together, organized movie nights and field trips to the Laurel Canyon Museum and Climate Tribute Center. They mourned losses and cheered one another's successes. It was chaotic and dysfunctional, but there was so much love. Olivia felt grateful to be the caretaker, but it wasn't part of any plan.

Years ago during her recovery, the director of the camp offered her a job as a nursery worker. She'd been content with volunteering, but the opportunity to live on the property and give Lucas his own space appealed to her, not to mention that if she wasn't traveling back and forth to his home downtown, she could dedicate more hours to working with the babies. In those five years, she spent thousands of hours caring for the tiny preemies and newborns they took in.

As time passed, Olivia acquired more responsibilities,

training new employees and helping with fundraising, but she had no interest in calling the shots. At least not until last year, when they discovered that the current director, Glenda—the woman Olivia adored more than her own mother (who was a narcissistic sociopath)—had been arrested for attempting to funnel money to the Guardians. The Guardians, of all people.

Anyone stealing from children was particularly terrible, but knowing that it was Joey doing all of this was cruel. How Olivia could ever have believed that the man had any intention of doing anything other than lining his pockets was beyond her. She could see her meemaw shaking her head in disappointment. "Livy, how in the blazes are you gonna trust a fella with all them drawings on his body?"

But thinking about Joey and her prepping obsession led Olivia to dark places she preferred not to think about. Besides, he wasn't the only one to blame. The only way she was able to survive was by accepting that.

The biggest surprise came when Caroline, the chairman of the board for the camp, asked Olivia to take over as executive director. Caroline was persuasive, recruiting Lucas and taking them both to dinner. "No one knows the inner workings of the camp better than you. No one has been here longer. You love this place."

She looked to Lucas, who by now was a contractor in charge of the New Pacific rebuilding efforts. "What do you think?"

A MOTHER'S GUIDE TO THE APOCALYPSE 353

He paused. "I want to make sure it's not too much of a burden at your age."

Olivia loved that she'd reached the "your age" stage of life. In her old life as a producer, that was a fate worse than death, but these days it was a privilege to live to your fifties. So many people hadn't.

The truth was, Olivia could make a difference, so she said yes. With one caveat. There would be no publicity. No press releases or dog and pony shows. She would be a figureless figurehead or the answer was no. They agreed.

As the new director, Olivia understood the risks that came with being the boss. The public's hatred for the climate camps endured long after the crisis was mitigated. There were people who still didn't believe climate change existed (Olivia refused to indulge those crackpots); others thought climate refugees were lazy and wasteful and hadn't made the best use of the new world order. But the potential attacks on the facility were real. They'd been firebombed and their buildings had been vandalized, not to mention daily threats to exterminate all the children, whom many claimed were hired to live in the camps and take money from hardworking citizens. This was why they employed full-time military guards, and why a high-level security clearance was needed to visit.

Even with all the vetting, people like Glenda snuck in. For Olivia, her privacy had nothing to do with Joey or any other fringe group. Her biggest fear was that being in the spotlight meant answering personal questions. The last thing she wanted was to discuss her life before the Collapse. No amount of therapy or journaling allowed her to do that without going to some very dark places.

Olivia was proud of the work she'd done. Shortly after accepting the role, she created a proposal that showed how the camp could provide a job training program teaching high schoolers farming and manufacturing—all industries desperate for qualified workers.

Lucas got her proposal into the hands of the money people, and she secured a massive grant that would pay for that program as well as additional funds they needed to modernize the camp's facilities and hire more staff.

But the politicians giving up millions of dollars wanted to meet the person in charge and discuss how they would allocate the funds. Despite Olivia's desire to stay under the radar, she had agreed to attend her first big event, a gala celebrating the tenth anniversary of New Pacific's independence, hosted by her own brother at his estate.

The president of New Pacific and hundreds of other dignitaries were already in town for the weeklong celebration. The gala was the final event of the week, and where they would announce the camp's new funding.

The old Olivia adored putting on her sexiest dress and Louboutins, getting her makeup and hair professionally done, and kissing ass so that the money people would finance her movies. But that life was gone, along with everything else she loved. As the party grew closer, she did her best to get out of going. Yesterday morning when Nova began to show improvement, she phoned Lucas.

"I've got a new infant in ICU, and the preschoolers are performing *Little Mermaid* for their graduation tomorrow. Not to mention there's a leak in the kitchen. And I have nothing to wear."

He groaned, which almost made her laugh, remembering him as a little kid, so deeply annoyed with his big sister and her demands. Now as a grown man in his midforties, the tables had turned.

"C'mon, Liv, these people are writing checks. Big ones. They need to see who runs that place. Show up, smile, and shake hands so you can keep doing the good work you do there."

He knew this would end any further discussion. She would do anything for this place. In some ways, though, it made her deeply sad to think that the majority of the people who caused the Collapse were in charge of rebuilding, but she had learned during her fifty-plus years on this earth that life was not fair.

Thankfully, Lucas played a major role in the city's revitalization. It still amazed her that her little brother, the person who before the Collapse struggled to pay his own cell phone bill, was someone who could oversee the rebuilding of an entire city. She always knew Lucas was capable of great things, but now he was someone everyone admired.

The phone on Olivia's bedside table rang. She frowned. She rarely got calls this late. Not with good news anyway. "Hello?"

"Liv, it's Rory at reception. Lucas is here and needs to see you. He said it's urgent."

Olivia's frown deepened. There was no way Lucas would be here at this time of night with good news. "I'll be right down," she said.

Her head spinning, she immediately jumped to the worst-case scenario. What if they'd changed their mind about the grant?

Or worse, what if they were closing the camp?

Her breath quickened. *Stop it*, she told herself. *Just stop.* She would use all of Lucas's connections to ensure this place stayed open. Hell, she would talk to the press if it came down to it. She wouldn't let it go without a fight.

Olivia threw on a sweater and a pair of sneakers, grabbed her keys, and took the elevator down to the lobby. It would be easy to fall apart or mess this up the way she'd messed up so many other things. But after she'd recovered, she'd sworn that she would never lose control. There were too many people who depended on her.

Seconds later, the elevator doors opened. She spotted Lucas in the sleek gray-and-white lobby, as cool and put together as ever. Unlike Olivia who gave up all forms of vanity years ago, her hair gray and long, her face wrinkled and unadorned with makeup, Lucas looked impossibly polished in his crisp blue polo and khakis, his brown hair with streaks of gray cut short.

She loved to tease him. "You're gettin' more and more fancy in your old age."

He shrugged it off. "Some of us age like fine wine, sis."

He met her eyes and he gave her a nod that said, *I've got you.*

She followed his gaze to a young woman standing beside him. She was in her early twenties with that impossibly dewy skin that can only be attributed to youth. Her strawberry-blond hair was pulled into a ponytail; her eyes were a piercing blue, her face swollen with deep-purple bruises. But she was so familiar.

Olivia's whole body froze. It wasn't possible. Was it? She recognized that face. A face she saw in her dreams, a face that at times haunted and soothed her.

It couldn't be. There was simply no way.

"Olivia," Lucas said gently as they stepped forward. "It's real. She's real."

He knew what she was thinking. She could hear the thick emotion in his voice. Tears streamed down Olivia's face as she looked at this beautiful girl. *Her* beautiful girl.

"Mama, it's me. It's Cassie."

Cass. Her sweet Cass. It was Cassie standing here in the lobby. The calmest, snuggliest baby girl was now a grown woman, and she was here.

A million memories flashed through her head.

Holding Cassie for the first time in the NICU.

Cassie's giggle when her chubby hand waved her tiny blue stuffed turtle over her head, shouting "my tutle" over and over again.

The way she said "hello" with a British accent so that it sounded like "ello."

The tiny hand that gripped Olivia so hard whenever she left to go to work and made her promise to come home.

Her girl.

Olivia flung herself at Cassie, who did the same. It was more collision than hug.

Tears poured down Olivia's face as she clung to her daughter. There were so many questions. How had Cassie found her? Where had she been all this time? Where were her sisters? Where was Sam? Olivia wanted to know everything, but there would be plenty of time for questions. This hug was all she wanted to focus on. The rest of it could wait.

CASSIE

No hug would ever compare to that first one with her mum. It was the hug to end all hugs. The GOAT as they used to say back in her dad's day.

They stood there, arms wrapped around each other. Tears streamed down Cassie's face as Mum, her own tears falling, whispered, "My sassy Cassie."

Those words reverberated in her head as she remembered Mum dancing with her in their sun-kissed kitchen, singing "Sassy Cassie," over and over again. Why was she remembering that now? She wondered what other memories would come flooding back.

Finally, they broke apart. Cassie's mum was in her fifties but looked older, with her graying hair and wrinkles around her eyes and mouth. But it was Mum's eyes that troubled Cassie. They were the saddest eyes she'd ever seen.

Olivia was studying Cassie with equal intensity. "You're a stunner. I mean it, Cass. You're gorgeous...but this..."

She gently touched her bruised face. Cassie glanced at Lucas. Should she mention Joey and the Guardians? He shook his head. *Not now.*

"It's nothing. I'm fine."

"You two already have secrets, huh? I'll get it out of you. First, I need another hug," Mum said.

Olivia's hug was just as crushing the second time, but Cassie welcomed it. The pain made it more real. "My sweet girl, where are your sisters? Are they..." Her voice softened, the unspoken question hanging in the air.

"They're on their way," Cassie and Lucas said in unison.

Like a lot of New Pacific politicians, Lucas owned a cell phone, and he had called Sam and the girls from the car. Olivia's body visibly relaxed, her eyes bright with excitement. "That's... that's wonderful. It's all so much. I can't..."

She was truly at a loss for words.

"Why don't you show Cass your place and I'll wait for the others to arrive?" Lucas prompted gently.

When her sisters arrived, Cassie wouldn't have any more alone time with her mum, so she was eager for all the one-on-one she could get.

"I'd love that. Let's go," she said, linking her arm in her mum's.

"Thank you, Lucas," Olivia said, eyes still wet with tears. She leaned over to hug him. "Who would've thought my baby brother would be the one looking after me?"

He shrugged. "It's a burden for sure, but I carry it well."

"I'm sure you've noticed that he's got jokes, too. You have to indulge him if you want to stay on his good side."

"I'll keep that in mind," Cassie said with a smile as she followed her mum back toward the elevators.

They passed the reception desk, where Olivia stopped to greet a young woman with a short black bob and bright-green eyes. "Rory, this is my..." Olivia's words caught in her throat. She cleared it. "This is my daughter, Cassandra." Rory couldn't hide her shock, which made Cassie wonder what Olivia shared about her family. The young woman quickly recovered. "Cassie, it's a privilege to meet you. Your mom has a lot of fans here."

Olivia laughed. "Better than enemies. My other girls are on their way. Send them up when they get here?"

"Of course, Liv. Congratulations."

The word didn't seem big enough for what just happened, but Olivia smiled back at her in gratitude.

As they stepped onto the elevator, Olivia pressed the button for the top floor and chuckled. "Rory's a doll, but the biggest gossip. Everyone in this place will know about y'all being here in a matter of minutes."

She said it with such pride that Cassie wanted to cry. Everything about her mum, from the way she gripped Cassie's hand to the way she studied her face, made Cassie want to cry. How could someone she hadn't seen in two decades have this effect on her? She understood genetics on a scientific level, but this was something she hadn't expected. Being near her mum made her feel settled and secure and so damn happy, she wanted to burst.

As the elevator doors opened, they stepped into a massive apartment. It must have been at least four thousand square feet, all open space except for a door that led to what Cassie assumed was the bathroom. There were several framed watercolors on the walls, and the room overflowed with candles and plants. It was the kind of place you could curl up and read a nice book.

"This is all yours?" Cassie asked.

"One of the perks of running the place is that I get my own apartment. Not that I spend much time here. There's always so much to do."

Olivia gestured to a small dining table. "How about a cup of tea?"

"You drink tea?" From the movies she'd watched over the years, Cassie had gathered that that was exclusive to the Brits.

Olivia laughed. "I never drank it until I met your father, and he made the best tea. The secret is..."

"Three teaspoons of sugar and a healthy dose of milk," Cassie said at the same time as Olivia. They both laughed.

"He still makes it that way?"

Cassie heard the affection in her mum's voice. "He does. Or he did..." Her voice trailed off. She didn't want to talk about Dad. Olivia busied herself with making the tea, and Cassie got the sense that Mum felt the same.

They were quiet while Olivia finished making the tea.

A MOTHER'S GUIDE TO THE APOCALYPSE 363

She set a cup in front of Cassie and joined her at the table. Mum grasped her own cup, her hands trembling slightly.

Cassie reached out to squeeze them. "It's okay, Mum. You're okay."

Olivia's eyes were wet with tears. "You were always so intuitive. Even as a toddler, you'd notice if I was having a bad day and want to kiss my cheeks to make me feel better. I'm sorry, but I can't seem to find my footing here. I used to have endless dreams about finding you girls. They were so real, I'd wake up and cry for hours. But this is real, isn't it?"

"It is, Mum. It's very real."

Cassie cleared her throat. It wasn't easy figuring out what to say to her mum after all these years, something that wasn't too heavy.

"What do you do here exactly?" Cassie finally settled on.

"The better question is, What don't I do? Everything from managing the budget to staffing. I handle all new placements in the camp as well as coordinating what happens after our kiddos graduate. Some days I'm a plumber. Other days I'm a teacher or a therapist. We have all ages of kids, from newborns to eighteen-year-olds, so the needs are endless. I regret how obsessed I got with the prepping, but the skills I learned have proved quite useful." She paused. "This isn't a job. It's a calling. Or a compulsion if you ask Lucas. But I love it. This place saved me when..."

She didn't need to finish the sentence.

Olivia waved a hand in front of her face. "My girl, I'm sorry. I'm rambling. Tell me about yourself. I want to know it all."

Cassie had just opened her mouth to speak when the phone rang, the noise startling them both. Olivia sprang up from her seat and hurried over to answer. "Send them up, Rory."

Olivia hung up and grabbed Cassie's hand as she headed to the door. Her whole body was trembling now. "Isn't it ridiculous that I'm nervous?"

"No. It's a lot. For all of us. But, Mum, they're going to be so happy to see you. Rosie always believed you were alive. Ever since we were small."

Olivia's eyes filled with tears again. "That doesn't surprise me. She was my fighter."

They stood in silence and waited the endless seconds until the elevator doors finally opened. Rosie's and Bettie's eyes were wide as they took in Mum.

"My girls," Olivia said.

"Mum." Their words were drowned out by the sobs. Four-person hugs are awkward at best, but they didn't care as they clung to her.

"My girls." Olivia sobbed again. "My sweet baby girls."

Their reunion was snotty, their embrace two decades in the making. After a while, Olivia pulled away. "I think I need to sit," she said.

Cassie noticed that her mum was unsteady on her feet

and went to grab a chair, but Rosie beat her to it. She gently eased Mum into it, and they all pulled up seats around her.

Bettie gasped. "Cass, what happened to your face?" she said.

Rosie's smile twisted into a frown. "Who did that? Was it..."

Cassie shook her head. "It's nothing."

"That looks like something all right," Olivia said.

"I promise it's a dull story," Cassie said.

Olivia shook her head disapprovingly. "Even as a toddler, you were a terrible liar."

Bettie burst out laughing. "It's true. Cassie is the absolute worst liar. Rosie could lie without batting an eye. Cassie was decent, but a bit of a tattletale."

All three girls laughed. "Dad never told us this," Rosie said.

Olivia stopped mid-sentence. "Is he... is Sam with you?" she asked.

"He's waiting downstairs. He said the four of us deserved our own reunion. He wasn't even sure you'd want to see him."

Olivia considered this. After all these years, her anger at what happened had faded, but it was still there. The betrayal of the man she loved more than anything was hard to shake, but so much time had passed, she couldn't hold on to it. The hum of the refrigerator was the only sound as the girls waited for her to speak. "He clearly raised you well.

How did you do ... during the Collapse? Were you safe?" Olivia asked.

"Dad and Granny worked hard to protect us. During our rolling blackouts we camped and lived off the land, thanks to Dad's gardening, which was really helpful during the food shortages. During the worst of the heat waves, Dad turned part of the greenhouse he built into a cooling center, and he even built a plunge pool on the property."

Olivia sat up straighter. "Hold up. Your father, Samuel Clark, learned to do all of that, including gardening?"

The girls laughed at Mum's surprise, but Cassie couldn't hide her pride for how hard her father worked.

"You should see the greenhouse on the property. Dad grew enough food to sustain the whole village," Cassie said.

Rosie chimed in. "Cassie oversees it now. They have fifteen employees. It's amazing, Mum. It takes up almost twenty acres."

A blush stained Cassie cheeks. Her sisters weren't usually so effusive about the work it took to keep things up and running. "I can't wait for you to see it," she said, meeting Mum's gaze.

Her smile made Cassie feel warm inside. "I can't wait, either." Then Olivia snorted, which surprised them all. "I'm sorry. I'm trying to process that the man who didn't know a kiwi from a cantaloupe was able to do all of that," she said in disbelief.

The girls broke into another fit of giggles. When they composed themselves, Olivia took them in, one by one, as though memorizing their features. "I owe you all an explanation about what happened when I disappeared. Or at least what I recall..."

Bettie cut in. "It's okay, Mum. We know about Mel and her lies."

At the sound of Mel's name, Mum's eyes widened. "You know? Is she still alive? Is Dominic?"

Rosie sighed. "They are. They live in the mountains near Idyllwild. And yes, Mel's still a liar."

Olivia laughed bitterly. "People always said don't trust anyone in Hollywood, but Mel was the one person I thought I could count on. My first mistake. My second was meeting Joey." She let out a ragged breath. "I'm not sure if you've heard about him."

"We have. It's okay. We don't have to talk about him," Cassie said.

On the drive over, Lucas had suggested they not mention the Guardians or anything that happened when Cassie went to see them. "Talking about Joey and his cult makes her emotional. Let's focus on all the positives," Lucas insisted.

Regret danced across Olivia's face. "Not a day goes by that I don't wish I could have seen Mel and Joey for who they were instead of who I wanted them to be. But I loved your dad. I thought if I could escape all the bad influences in our lives, we could hold on to our family. The night I got hurt, I was at a work dinner. Afterward, I planned to go home and tell your dad that we should go back to England and start fresh. What happened next, I'm not sure. I have flashes of being caught in the rain and being upset, but no memory of anything else. All I know is that I fell during the flood and suffered a traumatic brain injury. I spent months in the hospital in a coma. By the time I woke up, y'all were gone and so was the world as I knew it."

Her voice caught. "None of that was Sam's fault. Or maybe it was both of ours. All I know is that I am glad he gave y'all a wonderful life."

Cassie hesitated. She wanted to ask Mum why Dad told them she was dead or why Uncle Lucas said that he found death certificates in their names, because none of it was adding up. "I'm wondering—"

Rosie cut her off. "Mum, Dad isn't...he's sick. Dementia. Some days are good, but a lot aren't. It's been...hard."

Olivia grew still, a pained expression on her face. "Then we'll have to be grateful for whatever time we all have left together. We can all stay with Lucas. He's got plenty of room, and there's a big party this weekend at his house to celebrate the country's anniversary. He's got his heart set on me being there, and I don't want to let him down. I promise we'll have all the time in the world to catch up and figure out what happens next. Let me pack a few things," Olivia said.

She hurried toward the bathroom and disappeared into the next room.

For the first time in days, Cassie and her sisters were alone together again. They looked at one another, faces giddy. They'd done it. They'd found their mum. Which made Cassie hate what came next. She kept her voice low so that Mum wouldn't hear.

"I asked Uncle Lucas why he didn't look for us. He said he found death certificates in our names," Cassie said.

Bettie shook her head. "That doesn't make sense."

"I know. If that were true, we wouldn't have been able to travel here. Maybe we should call Rita. I know Lucas said he spoke to the British officials, but still..."

"What are you two doing?" Bettie said, her voice sharp. "We found Mum. That's what we wanted. The past is the past. We're all together now. Can we focus on that?"

Rosie shrugged. "You're right, Bets. We should focus on how amazing this is."

They looked at Cassie, willing her to agree. She smiled. "I'm as happy as you are. Let's break out the party hats."

Bettie sagged with relief. Cassie wasn't sure why, but there was a nagging voice inside her head screaming, *Something isn't right.* Still, her sisters had a point. What good would obsessing over the past do? It was time to let go of all of that and focus on Mum and their new future together.

OLIVIA

After her accident, Olivia's doctors were honest about her injuries. The brain trauma she suffered was significant; the fact that she could walk and talk and live a normal life was a miracle. "We've had patients with similar injuries who never recovered, but that doesn't mean there won't be challenges."

That was an understatement. She battled many issues in the ensuing years. Blinding migraines that left her in bed for days. Vomiting and dizziness and sensitivity to light. But the most challenging symptom of recovery and one she couldn't control was the way in which her emotions induced seizures.

It happened on days that were meaningful to her.

Her wedding anniversary.

The girls' birthday.

The last day she saw her family.

She would wake up and those memories would come flooding back; *Sam in his tux on the beach, holding out his hand.*

The operating room filled with fifty nurses and doctors and NICU staff all waiting to help her girls.

The girls' second birthday, a joyous montage of giggles and cake.

On those days, it was as if a switch were flipped. Olivia's whole body trembled and convulsed as she experienced hundreds of mini seizures throughout the day.

No medical interventions worked. No medication could stop it. The only solution was working through her emotions. Intensive therapy and developing self-care tools saved her. Thankfully, she'd been seizure-free for over three years.

But today her body felt wired, as though a seizure were imminent. Finding her daughters created an emotional tsunami inside her. She tried to get ahead of the debilitating headache forming by popping three painkillers, but they did nothing. On a normal evening, when the pain grew unbearable, she would take a sleeping pill and sleep for hours. But that wasn't an option now. She refused to miss a minute with her girls.

Every time she looked at them, she experienced a jolt of surprise at seeing her baby girls all grown up. She understood that most mothers thought their children were beautiful, but the pre-Collapse Olivia, the movie producer who hired actresses all the time, would have cast them as the leading ladies in any of her films. They were so extraordinary.

As far as telling them apart, that was easy, something no amount of time apart would change. Rosie was the firstborn or team leader, Cassie was her troubled sensitive

A MOTHER'S GUIDE TO THE APOCALYPSE 373

soul, and Bettie, even in their brief interactions, was the watchful mediator. Or at least that's what she'd observed so far.

She would have plenty of time to learn more about who they were as individuals. Once Olivia's bags were packed, they climbed back onto the elevator and rode to the lobby in silence. It was close to six in the morning and despite their good spirits, they were all exhausted, battling yawns as the adrenaline of the evening began to wear off.

When the elevator doors opened, the girls kept walking, but Olivia stopped midway to study Sam. He sat on the floral lobby sofa, his gaze vacant. As though he sensed Olivia watching, he turned and stood. He took a step forward and then stopped again. He paused as if to say, *Your move.* He'd always let Olivia call the shots, so she wasn't sure why today would be any different.

"Get your ass over here," she called out.

Sam laughed and so did the girls. He moved toward her. They met in the middle of the lobby, holding hands as they stared at each other.

"You got old," she said as she took in the hunched posture of a man who spent his life golfing and, according to her girls, gardening. He was handsome then, and time hadn't changed that. Even with a face full of wrinkles, she couldn't look away.

Sam chuckled. "I had a dream you said that."

"You mean a premonition?" Olivia teased.

He laughed and gestured to the girls, who were watching their reunion. "They're beautiful, aren't they?" he said to Olivia.

Olivia smiled through her tears. "They're so gorgeous and smart. You did good, Sammy. You did real good."

Sam began to cry. "I'm sorry, Liv. For all of it."

She had no reason to be angry. Sam had done what she wanted most in the world—he had kept her girls safe. She was the one with so many regrets.

"I'm sorry about Joey. About all of it," she said. She loved this man so deeply, and there was so much more she wanted to say.

Lucas stepped in. "I'm sorry to rush you along, but we should get home. Everyone needs to rest."

He looked pointedly at Olivia and then at Sam.

Message received. "Sam, we'll talk later."

Sam was still sniffling as he looked around in confusion. "Where are we going? To the airport? Or back to Mel's? She asked if we'd come back..."

Rosie grimaced. Olivia wasn't sure what that was about, but clearly Mel was still adept at hurting people.

Cassie reached for Dad's arm. "No, Dad, we're not going to Mel's. We're going to stay at Uncle Lucas's house for a few days."

Sam's gaze landed on Lucas. He made a face as though he smelled dead fish and shrugged. Olivia almost laughed, even though it wasn't funny. Sam had never been a fan of

Liv's brother, and with his cognitive difficulties it wasn't surprising that he struggled to fake it.

She looked toward Lucas, who simply smiled with a *What can you do?* shrug.

Cassie reached for her father's arm. "Come on, Dad, I'll sit with you if that's okay."

Sam smiled at her. "That sounds lovely, Cass. You can tell me who the wanker was that did that to your face and where I can find him."

Cassie's expression was part amusement, part grimace as they walked out the double doors and toward the waiting Humvee. Rosie and Bettie walked a few feet ahead of Lucas and Olivia but kept glancing back at her.

"Don't worry, y'all. I'm not going to disappear," Olivia said.

The girls smiled as though she'd read their mind and were grateful for the reassurance. Olivia could feel Lucas eyeing her in that overbearing way of his. "Y'all climb in. I need to have a quick chat with my baby brother."

She closed the door and pulled Lucas aside, her voice low. "Lucas, please don't hover. I'm fine. Better than fine."

"I know, Olivia, and I'm happy for you. But you must be careful. If you aren't..."

Olivia sighed. "I haven't had a seizure in years. I'm okay. But we do need to talk about the party."

"Not this again. You have to be there. Bring the girls. The reunion will make for good press."

Olivia flinched. "The last thing I want is for the girls to be in the spotlight. I don't even want to be in the spotlight."

"Sorry, that's not what I meant. I'm tired, Olivia, and I've worked hard to get this funding. I need you to be there."

She softened. At times like this, Lucas no longer looked like her baby brother, but like a tired man who carried a mountain of responsibility. "I'll talk it over with the girls and Sam and see what they say."

"About Sam...He's not...I mean, Cassie told me."

"I know he's sick," Olivia said.

"Okay, good. This is a lot for anyone to handle, especially someone with his issues, but I want...You should be careful."

Outrage flashed across her face. "Sam would never hurt me," Olivia said.

Lucas shrugged. "He took your kids away and made you think they were dead, didn't he?"

"You don't...You think he faked the death certificates?"

"I want to protect you."

Olivia's head pounded as she took a deep breath. She wouldn't let these emotions consume her. Not now.

As for Sam, she didn't believe it and she'd prove it, but she wanted to make sure Lucas heard her. "I don't know what these girls went through to get to me, but I know what I've been through to find them, so let me enjoy this. Please," she said with a twinge of desperation.

"All right. All right," he said in surrender. "I won't say another word."

With that settled, she climbed into the truck and slammed the door. Lucas got into the front seat beside the driver. Cassie and Sam sat across from Olivia. Beside them Bettie and Rosie. The giant tanklike vehicle roared to life as Lucas's driver pulled out of the wrought-iron gates and onto Hollywood Boulevard.

"And away we go," Olivia said.

Sam chuckled. "That's what your mum always said after we loaded all three of you into the car sweaty and exhausted. Took us about half an hour from start to finish."

Olivia leaned over to squeeze his hand. He squeezed back, and a jolt of memory returned, the image of a hand squeezing her arm tighter and tighter. *"You can't do this to me. We're family. You don't fuck over your family."*

Olivia quickly pulled her hand away and leaned back, doing her best to hide her shock.

"Mum? Are you okay?" Rosie asked.

Her Rosie was so perceptive. She'd have to remember that. Olivia took her daughter's hand in hers. "Baby girl, I have never been better."

ROSIE

Uncle Luke or Uncle Lucas or whatever he called himself didn't like her father, and it appeared that the feeling was mutual. It wasn't anything either of them said or did; it was their body language and lack of direct eye contact.

Rosie considered herself to be a deeply feeling person and often found herself affected by others' emotions, which was why it bothered her. What did Lucas have against her father? And vice versa? Her mum wasn't holding a grudge for anything that happened in the past, so why would Lucas? No one else appeared troubled by it. Sometimes Rosie hated being so intuitive.

They stopped in front of a massive wrought-iron gate. Once it opened, the driver pulled into a massive driveway, revealing a home that resembled a castle.

"This is where you live?" Bettie asked in awe.

"Quite the bachelor pad, isn't it?" Olivia said teasingly.

The home was three levels, with a wraparound balcony. There was a fountain bubbling in the drive and more roses blooming than in their entire English village.

"Liv and I grew up in trailers and dumpy apartments, so

this took some getting used to, but the city council pro-vides housing for all its employees. Your mama used to live here with me till she got the job at the camp."

"Now he's an old man wandering the halls of his haunted castle alone."

Lucas snorted. "Don't mock my man cave," he said.

Rosie laughed, but what a perk. This place had to cost a fortune. Still, Lucas made it clear this wasn't the time for questions and answers.

"Let's head inside, y'all."

After a brief tour, Lucas insisted they go to bed. "If we stay up any longer, we'll sleep the day away."

He led them to the second floor, stopping at the top of the landing. "Your mama's room is at the end. Y'all can each have your own room on this floor, and Sam can take the room upstairs."

Olivia shook her head. "It's hard to believe you girls once fit in the same crib, isn't it?" Her voice trembled as tears threatened to fall.

Lucas held up his hands. "Okay. Okay, let's not let your mama's waterworks get started again. They might never stop, and tomorrow is a big day."

"What's tomorrow?" Rosie asked.

Olivia gave Lucas a warning look. "We'll discuss it after we've rested."

"Liv…"

She shot him a look that said, *Enough*, then turned to

A MOTHER'S GUIDE TO THE APOCALYPSE 381

Dad, her smile wide. "Sam, I'll help you to your room," Olivia said.

He gave her a sweet smile. "I'm carrying my bag. I may be old, but I'm still a gentleman," he insisted.

They both laughed. Rosie wanted to bottle that sound.

Before Mum left, she hugged Rosie and her sisters one by one, holding them tightly.

Once the door closed, Lucas's expression grew serious. "I'm so glad you're here, but I want to remind you to be mindful with what you share with your mom. She's struggled with health issues in the past, and bringing up Joey and the prepping or her accident could trigger a relapse."

"Is she okay? What's wrong?" Bettie asked, her brow furrowing.

"Nothing too serious, but go easy on her," Lucas said.

"I hate to ask this, but what are you going to do about the Guardians? They clearly want something from us or they wouldn't have come to Mel's," Cassie said.

"Or done that," Lucas said as he gestured to the darkening bruises on her face.

Cassie avoided looking at her sisters, not wanting to see their disapproving glares. "I pissed off Joey and his followers. I imagine he's going to be pretty upset."

Rosie shook her head. "Either way, we can't let anything happen to Mum. Not after all this time."

"You're all safe here. We have armed security. There's no way the Guardians are getting close."

Bettie's shoulders slumped with relief. Cassie offered a grateful smile. Only Rosie was uncertain, but Lucas clapped his hands, signaling that the conversation was over. "Y'all get to bed. There's a big party happening later, and you want to be nice and rested."

As he headed off, Rosie turned to her sisters. "He said that Mum is sick? What do you think it is?"

Cassie sighed. "Don't get all Rosie about it."

"I hate it when you say that. He was being vague."

"If it was serious, he would have said. We can ask Mum later. When we've all slept."

Rosie sighed. She was too exhausted to push the issue. She reached out to touch Cassie's bruised face. "Are you sure you're okay?"

"I am now," she said. She gave Bettie and Rosie a quick hug and then disappeared into her chosen room. Rosie slipped into hers, washed her face in the adjoining bathroom, changed into pajamas, and lay on the bed. She tried to get comfortable, tossing and turning in the queen-size bed, but it was useless. A few hours with Mum wasn't enough.

Rosie made her way down the dark hallway and knocked softly on the door. Mum opened it instantly. "I figured you'd be joining us."

Rosie's eyes widened in confusion. Mum opened the door and she saw Cassie and Bettie curled up in the massive California king bed.

A MOTHER'S GUIDE TO THE APOCALYPSE 383

"Are we having a sleepover?" Rosie said with a laugh.

"Looks like it," Olivia said. "I wanted to get you, but Cassie said you're a real cunt if your sleep is disturbed. Her words. Not mine."

Rosie smiled. "I will neither confirm nor deny it."

"I'll confirm it," Bettie said.

Rosie picked up a pillow and threw it at her sister. Mum laughed. Her laugh was better than any song Rosie'd ever heard, a laugh she wanted to hear again and again.

The four of them squeezed into the bed. It was a tight fit, but no one cared. Rosie sank back into the thick white comforter next to Mum. Olivia reached out to stroke her forehead, gently brushing her hair away from her face. She moved on to Bettie and then Cassie. If there was a time in her life that Rosie had felt this content, she could not recall it. Her sisters seemed to feel the same.

Olivia spoke softly. "When I was pregnant, I used to lay my hand on my belly and point here, and here, and here, and I would whisper, 'I am so lucky to be y'all's mom.' I kept waiting to feel you all moving around, waiting to see my belly wiggle, but y'all were so still. I asked my doctor once and he said, 'Maybe they're too busy kicking each other to kick you.'"

Rosie and her sisters laughed. Mum's voice was so soft and familiar.

Olivia continued. "A year after I lost y'all, I met a woman in the climate camp whose son and husband died in the quake, and she said to me that if she could go back and do it all over again, she would've never gotten married or become a mother because she wanted to avoid the hurt. But I never regretted it because I got to love you three... even if it was for the briefest of moments."

Rosie's tears fell. She couldn't help it. She'd held it in, but they kept coming, small sobs turning into big ones. Mum reached out and gently wiped her tears. She leaned over and whispered, "I love you how much?"

A long-forgotten memory, her mum's words came back to them.

Rosie and her sisters replied in unison, "So much."

Everyone grew quiet as the exhaustion and the emotions of the last few days settled in.

As Rosie's eyes flickered closed, she realized how much of her life she'd spent worrying and obsessing about finding Mum. But she'd done it. It was time to enjoy every second they had together.

SAM

It was midday when Sam jolted out of bed. Outside his room, he could hear people bustling around. He was still exhausted, but also desperately in need of something to eat and a cup of tea. He got up, quickly dressed, and headed downstairs before realizing the house was so big, he couldn't find the bloody kitchen.

It was ironic because years ago when Sam and Olivia bought their home, Lucas had acted like a total arse. "It's so big it looks like y'all are gonna start a commune," Lucas said as he counted all the bedrooms.

It wasn't even that big. It had five bedrooms, but they were a family of five. The girls would share a room until they were older, and Olivia had an office.

Sam's mum visited once a year, so they used one room for guests. Back then, Sam always thought Lucas was a wanker, running around LA bartending and sleeping with models, taking money from his sister like she was his own personal ATM. Now he was just a wanker with his own money.

Sam tried to shake off the anxious underwater sensation.

He had so many questions about the past and what had really happened to Liv, but did it matter? They were all together again. No one was looking at him like he'd murdered his wife. Shouldn't he be grateful for that?

After two wrong turns, one into a fitness center and the other into the laundry room, he saw a housekeeper carrying flower arrangements; she directed him to the kitchen. It was a massive room with a white granite island as its central feature.

Lucas stood over the stovetop, intensely focused on preparing an omelet, an impressive array of vegetables sliced and diced on the counter. They had exchanged pleasantries in front of the girls the night before, but Sam had been too tired and emotional for polite conversation. As he watched his brother-in-law move expertly around the kitchen, he thought of how much they'd both learned in the almost two decades since they'd last seen each other.

"Who knew we'd both become domesticated?" he said, determined to make an effort.

Lucas didn't bother to hide his disdain. "I was always quite capable. Olivia underestimated me."

That isn't true at all, Sam thought. No question that Olivia babied her brother at times, but she also encouraged him to dream big and gave him money to pursue any interest that came his way. Painting, sculpture, bodybuilding, real estate. She paid for all the classes and never questioned him when he shrugged and said, "Sorry, sis, it wasn't my vibe."

It wasn't Sam's place to call Lucas out. He didn't really care. "You've done well for yourself. What business are you in?"

"Construction and securities," Lucas said as he carefully plated his omelet. Sam waited for more, but Lucas set his plate down and glared at Sam with dislike...no, it wasn't dislike.

It was something more. Hatred. The intensity forced Sam to take a step back. But Lucas took a step forward.

"Listen, old man, Olivia might be all about forgiveness, but I know what you did and if you stick around, I'm gonna make sure she does, too."

"I don't...What are you talking about?"

"Take your confused fucking geezer routine and go home," he said, getting up in Sam's face.

"Hold up, son. You think I'm scared of a feckin' weasel?" Sam asked. He wasn't going to start a fight, but he would damn well finish one.

He was shocked when Lucas slammed him into the wall. "I'm going to give you one chance to leave. Tell Olivia and the girls you want to go home and get your wrinkled ass back on a plane to England and do not come back here."

Sam's face flushed at the nerve of this kid.

No, Lucas wasn't a kid. He was a grown man, but so was Sam. He still had some fight left in him. He gathered all his strength and grabbed Lucas's shirt collar. "Who do you think you are? What game are you playing?"

Lucas began yelling. "Calm down, Sam. It's okay. Calm down. Please, can someone come help me out here?"

Lucas's voice sounded pleading and desperate, and a second later, Sam felt hands pulling him away. It was the girls. His girls. They were looking at him with that scared, pitying expression he fucking hated. He saw Liv off to the side. He could hear the chorus of "what's wrong" and "what happened" growing louder and louder.

Sam slumped into the kitchen seat. He tried to explain what occurred, but Lucas was talking over him. "He lost it. Went nuts on me. I thought you said he was okay?"

Every time Sam tried to talk, Lucas cut him off. No one was listening. At least not to him. Even Cassie was telling him it would all be okay in that soothing baby voice Sam had once reserved for her. While the girls talked worriedly, Lucas caught his gaze, and Sam saw something in his expression. Something wicked and frightening.

He wanted to shout at his girls to make them listen, but why would they believe a confused old man over their long-lost uncle, especially after he'd lost it on Mel?

Even if he told them what Lucas had said, would they believe him? All Sam knew for certain was that he was tired and homesick and ready to be far away from this place. He didn't want to leave the girls or Liv, but Sam was afraid he was out of fight.

"Please take me home," he pleaded. "We need to go home. All of us as soon as possible."

He heard the panic and urgency in his voice, and the girls heard it, too. He hated to be this vulnerable, hated to scare his girls, but they couldn't stay here.

There was a murmur of surprise, and a furious discussion began. He knew there was an issue with their passports and traveling, but Sam wasn't going to concern himself with logistics. All he cared about was getting out of this bloody country. Because as much as Sam didn't know what was happening, he knew deep in his bones that something terrible was coming.

MAMA'S GUIDE TO PROTECTING YOURSELF

Y'all, I was a lover not a fighter. As a kid, I was short and skinny, with the athletic prowess of a tortoise with asthma, so needless to say, I followed Meemaw's advice to "run away to laugh another day." (Of course, after a few Lone Stars, she'd change her tune, saying things like, "Livy, if a guy gives you any trouble, squeeze his balls till they pop outta his eyes.") You girls would've loved Meemaw.

Anyway, I never really needed to defend myself. Not that the world I grew up in wasn't violent, but there were still rules and boundaries.

One day soon, though, it could be a world in which anything goes, which is why defending yourself may become a necessity. Which means—there are no rules when your life is on the line.

Fighting transcends self-defense. Self-defense, at least the way so many instructors market it to women, is about creating a window of opportunity to run away. For the most part, running away is the best option, regardless of gender. However, there may come a time when running isn't possible, and these tips will help you be prepared.

A Killer Mindset

I've never killed someone before. Thank God. That said, when our house got broken into when y'all were little, I swung your father's golf club at the intruder with the knowledge that I could hurt or even kill her. I hated doing it, but I had to protect you. That was all I cared about.

Most of us aren't born with the killer instinct, but there may come a time when you have no choice. Do what you have to to survive.

Guns

This country's obsession with guns is long and brutal, and too many innocent people have suffered because of it, but the rules are changing, even for those of us who once swore we would never own one. I bought a gun and learned to shoot. Your father was horrified at the time, but I needed to keep us safe.

Which is what I hope you'll do. Guns are a simple and effective means of defending yourself. Point and shoot. If you can get one, stick with rifles and shotguns as they're more reliable and simpler, although a pistol is useful because it's easier to conceal. Use the ammo sparingly, as it will be a luxury in the future.

If you run out of ammo, remember there is still power in an empty gun. People are unlikely to challenge you when you're armed.

If you're held at gunpoint, stay calm.

Make eye contact to humanize yourself and give them whatever money or resources they want. Getting robbed is a lot better than getting killed.

However, if you sense that they may want to assault you or even kill you, fight like hell.

Knives/Machetes

Knives and machetes can be equally effective. They're scary to would-be attackers and cause unfathomable pain and damage when they connect with their target. If you're in a knife fight, stay calm and keep your wits. Only attack when you see an opening, and do your best to keep your enemy at a distance.

If you can't escape, focus on the knife. Circle away from the knife and strike any weak point of your enemy to create an opening and control their knife. You'll do this by grabbing their wrist or trapping their arm, stripping them of their weapon, and stabbing them.

Note: Always have a spare, concealed knife on you. It's insurance, you'd rather have it and not need it than need it and not have it.

Blunt Melee Weapons

There's a reason why Teddy Roosevelt (former US president) said to speak softly and carry a big stick. Blunt weapons like sticks, clubs, bats, crowbars, lead pipes, and staffs are great because they don't require sharpening and

A MOTHER'S GUIDE TO THE APOCALYPSE 393

they create distance. If you're in a fight and have one of these weapons, hitting the side of your opponent's knee can take their legs out, allowing you to escape. Do your best to have at least one of these on you.

How to Fight

I took like two karate and kickboxing classes so please know that I'm no expert. But here are some basic fighting tips you need to keep in mind.

- When you make a fist, never hold your thumb. It'll break once you make contact with your target. Punch through your target. If you stop your strike at contact, you'll lessen the force of your blow.
- The strongest muscles in your body are in your posterior chain: your legs, your butt, your hips, and your back. You should throw your strikes with these muscles while keeping your feet planted to maximize power.
- Don't swing wildly. You'll miss and make yourself tired, which will create an opening for your enemy. Instead, use crisp, straight strikes. A straight strike travels a shorter distance than a haymaker, which means it'll hit your opponent faster.
- Your elbows and knees are the hardest parts of your limbs. Use them like a fist.
- A shot to a soft spot like the eyes, throat, and groin

hurts everyone. A strong liver shot can knock out a person. At the tip of everyone's sternum is a point called the solar plexus. Hit it hard to knock the air out of your enemy.

- If you're being held, buck wild, wiggle, and do everything you can do to get out of the person's grip. Bite them like a dog and don't let go.
- Don't headbutt unless you have to. Headbutts may look cool on TV, but they're also great at knocking you both out.
- Stay calm. Panicking will cause you to lose focus, which is all it takes for your opponent to find an opening and get the jump on you.

Note: While some people are naturally great fighters, the best fighters are the ones who practice. Y'all need to spar at least once a week. Be sure to use sticks to simulate getting out of gunpoint and knifepoint scenarios.

I told your dad to make sure this happens if I'm not there, but I don't know if he will listen. We disagree on such a massive level about all of this that I can't be sure he will even show you this book, but I hope he'll recognize the value in what I've shared.

If I could wrap you three up in plastic and Bubble Wrap and put you in a box for safekeeping, I would. (Silly, I know.) But this is my next best effort. To give you the tools to protect yourself.

Please, my loves, whatever danger you encounter, remember that inner strength that allowed you to survive being born ten weeks early, at just two pounds. Remember the fighting spirit of your mom and your father's passion for life . . . and remember you can battle anything and anyone if you stick together.

Love Always,
Mama Bear

BETTIE

After Dad's outburst, Cassie helped Dad back to bed and returned to the kitchen, demanding they leave immediately. "I'm sorry, Mum, but we can't stay. Dad needs to go home."

Rosie adamantly refused. "We just found Mum. There is no way I'm leaving. Bets?"

Bettie shrugged. "I don't know what to do."

"So you're not going to do or say anything?" Rosie snapped.

Bettie refused to take the bait. Her sisters always wanted her to pick a side, and it never made things better. She didn't love this place, and she was even less sure of Lucas, but how could she leave Mum? She waited for her to weigh in, but Mum hadn't left Lucas's side.

"What happened again?" she asked insistently. "Start from the beginning."

"Olivia, I already told you, one minute Sam was asking when I learned to make an omelet and the next he was coming at me like he'd lost his mind. But it's okay. He's not well. He's been through a lot and simply needs to rest. It's fine. We can all enjoy this wonderful breakfast my chef whipped up."

But it isn't fine, Bettie thought. Dad's history with Mel was troubled, which explained why he might have attacked her in his confused state, but why hurt Lucas? It didn't make sense.

There were dozens of people in the house cleaning and decorating and moving around, but no one paid them any attention. As though there hadn't been a huge outburst a few minutes ago.

"Come on, y'all," Olivia said, taking in the girls' worried faces. "Let's get some food, and we'll talk."

They followed Olivia toward the formal dining area where breakfast was being served.

As they walked through the study to the dining room, Cassie looked at Bettie, her voice low and slightly desperate. "You have to make a decision. As soon as breakfast is over, I'm booking flights. Dad and I are going home."

Bettie didn't know what to say so she kept quiet as they joined Mom and Lucas, unable to believe how much food was spread out on the massive oak dining table. Pancakes, fruit, eggs, and fresh-squeezed orange juice. Dad used to say Americans were gluttonous, and this breakfast definitely proved his point.

In keeping with the opulence of the home, the dining room's ornate bookcases were carved out of white wood and contained hundreds of volumes of books.

A MOTHER'S GUIDE TO THE APOCALYPSE 399

"Are these all yours?" Rosie asked Lucas.

"I'll admit that I wasn't much of a reader before the Collapse. No time to read with Twitter, Snapchat, Instagram, and TikTok."

"He was obsessed. Couldn't even have a conversation, he was so into his phone," her mum added.

Bettie couldn't imagine wasting her time staring at other people's lives, but apparently it was quite popular when she was little. "Once the world went offline, I got bored enough that I found a copy of a book in the hospital library where your mom was rehabbing. It was called *The Winter of Our Discontent*. A little on the nose for my situation, but I read it, and damn, I was hooked. Started collecting books wherever I found them. It's become a bit of a habit."

"He means obsession. But it's one I approve of." Olivia surveyed the shelves curiously. "I meant to ask, where are my letters?"

She smiled at Bettie and her sisters. "I wrote you girls letters every day for the last eighteen years. I wanted you to know who I was before and after I lost you."

A long silence lingered. Olivia looked at Lucas pointedly. "Where are they?"

He shifted in his seat. "There was an issue with the plumbing. I have a few but a lot of them were..."

"They were what?" Olivia snapped.

Bettie was startled by her mum's sharp tone. Lucas relented. "There was a leak in the upstairs bathroom that damaged the library. It ruined a whole shelf of books, including the majority of your journals."

"They're gone?" she said, sucking in air through her teeth. "I can't..." She let out another breath. "Why didn't you tell me?"

"So you could get upset? That's exactly why I didn't," Lucas said, putting down his fork. "With your history..."

"We're not talking about that," Olivia said. "It's got nothing to do with anything."

A heavy tension hung in the air, which Olivia did her best to alleviate. "My brother worries about my health, but I'm fine."

Lucas was annoyed with Mum and vice versa, but that was siblings for you, wasn't it? It wasn't any different from how Rosie and Cass drove her crazy.

He forced a smile and grabbed a bottle of champagne off the table and popped the cork.

"Today calls for a celebration. Our whole family has reunited after all this time, and that is something worth toasting."

She could see from Mum's face that she was still upset about the journals, but she didn't say anything. It felt wrong to be celebrating with Dad lying upstairs, confused and upset, but no one else said anything about that, either, so Bettie kept quiet. She watched as Lucas poured them each a small glass of bubbly. Bettie stared down at hers. She wasn't a fan of champagne before she was pregnant. The

A MOTHER'S GUIDE TO THE APOCALYPSE 401

bubbles always made her head ache. Lucas raised his glass and waited for everyone to drink. He noticed Bettie didn't.

"Come on, Bets, drink up."

Ugh. He called her Bets. Only close family called her that. She also hated being pressured. She was a grown-up, not a teenager at the pub. "No, thank you," she said politely.

"Ah, we found our stick-in-the-mud," Lucas teased. "Come on, it's not every day you reunite with your mom, is it?"

What an arsehole, Bettie thought.

"I really don't think one glass is..."

"She can't drink. She's pregnant," Rosie blurted out.

There was a collective gasp of surprise. "Why didn't you...How could you not tell me?" Cassie said.

"When was I supposed to do that? When you were sneaking off with Dominic?" Bettie asked.

"Fine, okay, but I still can't believe it," Cassie said, eyes lingering on Bettie's belly.

Bettie gave her a weak smile. "I can't, either."

"Congratulations, Bettie," Lucas said, holding up his glass to toast. Was she imagining his insincere tone?

Mum reached over and squeezed Bettie's hand. "Should we say congratulations? Or is this not happy news?" Mum asked softly.

Bettie couldn't believe her mother could read her so clearly, especially since she was still trying to figure it all out. "I learned about the baby when we got here. Dad doesn't know, and neither does my partner, Max. It's a lot," she said.

"It's even more clear that you should be coming home with me and Dad," Cassie replied.

"Don't do that. Don't pressure her to do what you want," Rosie snapped.

"I'm not. I'm telling her what I think. You're not the only one who gets an opinion," Cassie interrupted.

"That's rich coming from someone who thinks her opinion hung the moon and the stars."

A wolf whistle startled them all. They turned to see Olivia grinning. "I guess I'll take these fights over biting and hair pulling like when y'all were little, but let's settle down. I've been thinking a lot about what to do now that we're all together again, and Bettie's news has sealed the deal. I'll need to tie up some things here but I plan on traveling back to the UK to be with Sam and you girls. I'll help him get settled in his new place, and Bettie, we'll figure out the next steps with the baby. We can enjoy life as a family for a while."

"Mum, that's amazing," Cassie said.

"I can't... That sounds wonderful," Bettie said.

Rosie looked down at her plate, and Bettie could see she was struggling not to cry. They all felt that relief that came from knowing they weren't on their own anymore. That Mum was here to help look after them.

"You're leaving?" Lucas said.

A MOTHER'S GUIDE TO THE APOCALYPSE 403

"In a week, once I train my replacement," Olivia said.

"What about the camp and the staff who rely on you?"

"I'm confident Rory can handle it. She knows all the ins and outs. She can run the day-to-day. I'll come back and forth to supervise, but I need to be with my family."

Her mother didn't notice, but Bettie saw her uncle's stricken expression at the word "family."

Lucas put his glass of champagne down. "Thanks for letting me know, sis. Happy travels. Now if y'all will excuse me, I've got to finalize things for tonight." He gave the girls a tight smile. "I'll see you later."

"Lucas, can you come back here? Let's discuss this."

He didn't slow down at all.

"Maybe you should check on him?" Rosie said.

"He'll be okay. He's under a lot of pressure with the party."

Bettie didn't buy that at all. Lucas looked upset, really upset. She wanted to ask more about her uncle, but a young woman appeared. "Hello, everyone, I'm Isabelle, Mr. Hays's personal assistant. I've brought a variety of dresses for you all to choose from for tonight's event."

"Leave it to Lucas to think of everything," Olivia replied. "Thanks, Izzy. Leave them in my room and we'll sort them later."

The girl nodded agreeably and headed off. Olivia studied her daughters. "Tonight is a big celebration. Not just the anniversary of New Pacific, but celebrating my grant for the center. Lucas played a big part in securing it. It's important to him that we attend, but if you aren't up for a party, I'm fine with not going."

Bettie almost shouted that she didn't want to go, but her sisters were enthusiastically agreeing and she didn't want to be outnumbered.

She took another bite of eggs and her stomach turned, a wave of nausea bubbling up. She needed to get away from the smell of food as fast as possible.

"Excuse me, I'll be right back," Bettie said. She hurried down the hall in search of the bathroom. As Bettie made her way down the long corridor, she heard Lucas's voice, sharp and insistent. She inched forward and saw that his office door was open. She knew she should keep walking, but she found herself frozen in place.

"I don't care what you have to do, my sister cannot travel abroad. Pull her passport or put a stop travel alert, but she's not going anywhere. Tell them it's a health issue and she cannot leave. Do you understand me?"

He slammed down the phone. The fury on his face took Bettie's breath away. She stepped back from the door, and her trainer squeaked against the hardwood.

Lucas looked up and smiled. The sudden shift in demeanor set Bettie off balance. "Bettie, come on in," he said.

"I was looking for the toilet," she replied awkwardly.

"Oh, it's right down the hall, but first come in." He

waved her forward, and she couldn't find a polite way to say no. Bettie swallowed hard, not sure why Lucas made her feel so on edge.

He's family. Mum's brother. You're being silly, she thought. *Get it together.*

"I'm afraid I got a bit upset when I heard that your mama was leaving, but it's only because I care about her so much."

"I understand. I feel the same way about my sisters," Bettie said, which was true.

"I'm glad to hear that. I know your mama has big ideas about what she has to do, but I'm not sure the upheaval would be good for her."

"Is she ill?" Bettie asked with concern.

He'd mentioned her health before, but maybe there was something more Mum hadn't told them.

"She's experienced seizures off and on for years. Not to mention debilitating migraines. Stress exacerbates them. Medication doesn't work, so she has to find ways to destress. I don't think going abroad is a good idea."

"Mum seems excited about it," Bettie said. "Maybe this should be a conversation between you and her?"

"I think you and your sisters could be quite persuasive if it came down to it."

"You want us to tell her she can't go?" Bettie asked.

"It's not the right time. You girls can visit, but your mama has a life here. It would be a shame to upend that."

Upend her life? He's talking to her daughters. The children she thought were dead and hadn't seen in over twenty years. What could be more important than that? Bettie's eyes flashed. There was no way she was going to tell her mum anything of the sort.

"I don't think so. We want Mum to come with us. We *need* her."

There was a finality in Bettie's voice that Lucas finally acknowledged. "Okay, Bettie. I hear you loud and clear. I'll see you at the party tonight."

Surprised by the sudden dismissal, Bettie turned to go. "Make sure y'all are careful. You and your sisters and that baby are so innocent. We wouldn't want anything to happen."

The threat landed like an explosive at Bettie's feet. She looked at him to make sure she hadn't imagined it, and saw the challenge in his gaze.

She spun around and raced down the hall to the bathroom. Bettie closed the door and promptly threw up her eggs. Stomach heaving and empty, she sank onto the floor, replaying Lucas's words, her sense of dread growing.

She couldn't ignore her feelings. Yes, Lucas was her uncle, but there was something off about him, and his desire to keep their mum close. As frightened as Bettie was by his threat, she needed to be ready. It was what Dad and Mum had been preparing them for their whole lives. She needed to pull herself together and talk to her sisters. Like Dad always said, they were stronger together, and no one was going to tear them apart.

ROSIE

Sister talk," Bettie said softly to Rosie and Cassie when she returned to the table.

Rosie took in Bettie's red face and tearstained cheeks and knew something was very wrong. She almost wanted to ignore her and pretend things were fine, because they were. Mum was back. But a request for a sister talk was non-negotiable.

Rosie stood. "Mum, is it okay if we rest up before the party?" Guests were due to arrive at eight o'clock, so there was time before they needed to get ready.

Olivia glanced over at the girls. "You three have that same naughty look you'd get when you'd go off to play by yourselves, and I'd find you in your room covered in diaper cream."

Rosie laughed. "We'll do our best to avoid that."

They all stood, prepared to head upstairs, when Bettie flung herself into Olivia's arms.

"We'll see you later?" she asked.

Now Rosie knew something was wrong. Bettie always got clingy when something troubled her.

Mum wasn't as in tune with their emotions, at least not yet. She simply squeezed Bettie in a half hug. "Of course. We'll meet in my room at four o'clock for final touches. I should go upstairs and call the office to make sure there's nothing that needs my attention."

Olivia disappeared into her room as the other girls decamped for Rosie's. They sank onto her bed as Bettie recapped her conversation with Lucas.

"Do you think Mum is sick and Lucas is being overprotective?" Rosie asked.

"Does it matter? He threatened Bettie," Cassie said.

"Maybe he didn't mean it that way," Rosie said.

"He meant it, Ro. I swear if you'd seen the look on his face, you'd know."

They sat in silence for what felt like forever. Rosie broke it. "If Mum is sick and not telling us, we need to know what's wrong. And if she's not sick, we have to find out why Lucas doesn't want her to leave."

"I wouldn't want you to leave me," Cassie said softly. "You daft birds drive me crazy, but I love you. I'd miss you."

They all looked at Cassie, and for the first time since they'd arrived here, it reoriented them. Without saying anything else, they remembered that they were a unit.

This was when they were at their best. Working together, making decisions together. "If we could see Mum's medical records, we'd at least have an idea about what she's dealing with."

A MOTHER'S GUIDE TO THE APOCALYPSE 409

Cassie reached into her bag and pulled out the small cell phone she used with Dominic.

Bettie gasped. "Where did you get that?"

"Allan from uni," Cassie said as she typed slowly on the keypad.

"The skinny lad with the unibrow?"

Cassie laughed. "That's the one."

Bettie looked at Rosie. "It's like I don't even know her."

"Says the sister with the secret pregnancy," Cassie replied flatly.

Bettie raised her eyebrows. *Check and mate.*

"This phone helped me find Mum, didn't it? I'll get rid of it before we go home." Cassie finished typing. A message pinged. "'Give me ten minutes and I'll send,'" she read out loud.

"This is quite illegal, isn't it?" Rosie said.

"No more illegal than stealing a handgun," Bettie replied.

Cassie looked at her sisters in confusion. "What are you two going on about?"

Rosie gave Bettie a pleading *drop it* look, which Bettie understood. Her freak-out about the gun was bad enough. Cassie's would be a level-ten meltdown.

"Nothing. Bettie's being silly," Rosie said.

Cassie looked doubtful.

"We've all got our secrets. Like how you survived almost two days alone with Dominic."

Cassie sighed but knew a losing battle when she saw one.

"When I went to find Joey, he was out doing scouts." She paused. "Don't ask. Anyway, Dominic needed to handle some business with one of Joey's wives…"

"Gross," Bettie said.

"You can't even imagine. Anyway, while I was waiting, I came across these poppies in their compound. They were gorgeous. Absolutely breathtaking. I went to touch one and a petal broke off in my hand and suddenly this girl is slamming a gun in my face."

Bettie and Rosie gasped, but Cassie continued. "After that, Dominic and I were forced to wait in one of their cabins for Joey."

"Where was Dominic when you were getting hit in the face?" Rosie asked, face reddening with outrage.

"Relax, Ro, he tried to stop them. He didn't reach me in time. He's…he's not all bad. I think it's hard for him, dealing with Mel, all the pressure…"

Bettie gasped, hands flying up to her mouth in her typical dramatic manner. "Cass likes him. She's got that same expression on her face as when she went out with that wanker from uni…the one who said that she was prettier than us."

"So what if I do? It doesn't matter. Right now I'm focused on why our uncle is threatening you."

Cassie's warning sobered them. They sat in silence. A few minutes later, they heard a ping from Cassie's phone. "Allan found Mum's medical records."

A MOTHER'S GUIDE TO THE APOCALYPSE   411

Cassie pressed a button and handed the phone to Rosie. "You're the aspiring doctor. What does it say?"

"It says that Mum suffered a brain injury and lists a lot of accompanying symptoms, but there's nothing here about avoiding travel or any reason why she can't travel," Rosie said.

"Then there's only one other possibility," Bettie said.

"Lucas is full of shit," Cassie said.

After another heavy silence, Rosie stood up. "We need to talk to Mum."

Bettie and Cassie moved to follow. Rosie held up her hand. "Wait. If we all go in there and start asking questions, we might upset her. We don't even really know what we're asking," she said.

They didn't, did they? They were reacting off vibes and a threat that could be dismissed as a misunderstanding. What if Mum freaked out? Or what if there was a medical issue and she got upset? "I'll go," Rosie said.

Whenever things were hard, they always fell into their defined roles. Rosie as leader, Bettie and Cassie, her trusted followers.

"We'll start getting dressed and meet you back here in an hour," Bettie said.

Rosie offered them her most confident smile and hurried toward Mum's room. She knocked on the door and found Olivia with her makeup expertly applied, her graying hair cut shorter, hanging in shiny waves down her back.

"Mum, you look beautiful," Rosie said.

"Once upon a time, I did this a lot, but it's nice to know I still clean up well." She gestured for Rosie to come in and frowned when she saw her. "What's wrong?"

Mum knows? How could she possibly know? Rosie struggled to find the right words. Olivia reached out and touched Rosie's cheek. "Even after all these years, I can tell you're troubled. Is it about Bettie and the baby? I imagine it's a shock. It'll change things for sure."

Ah, so she doesn't know about Lucas. Not yet. "No. I'm happy for Bettie. She'll make an amazing mum. I'm actually here because...Are you sick?" she asked tentatively.

Olivia couldn't hide her surprise. "What? No, not at all. I get tired on occasion, but don't we all. I'm sure Lucas mentioned my health issues. Years ago I had seizures, but I haven't had one in years. There's nothing to worry about. I've got plenty of good years left."

Relieved, Rosie let out an exhale. "So there's no reason why you wouldn't be able to travel back to England with us?" she asked.

Olivia tilted her head in confusion. "Of course not. Why all the questions, sweet girl? Did something happen?"

Rosie hesitated. She didn't want to throw Bettie under the bus, but she also didn't want to leave without saying anything. "I heard Uncle Lucas say that he didn't think you should go with us because of your health."

Olivia laughed. "I'm sure that was a mistake. There's

nothing wrong with me. Sometimes Lucas has a bit of an ego, but he's a good man with a good heart. I'm sure it's a miscommunication, but I'll figure it all out."

Rosie swallowed hard. How could she say anything about Lucas now? Mum was ready to nominate him for sainthood.

"I'm glad to hear it. We . . . we can't wait to go home. For all of us to be home."

"I can't wait, either. And, Rosie, I'm so happy to see you're still the team leader."

Rosie looked confused. Olivia laughed. "That's what I called you as a baby. Always leading the charge. Go on and get ready. I can't wait to show off my beautiful girls tonight."

Olivia reached out and hugged Rosie, who hugged her back. She hoped that one day each hug wouldn't feel like their last.

As she left the room, Rosie wanted to believe that Mum was right and Lucas was a good guy who loved his big sister and it was all a misunderstanding. But one thing she'd learned since coming to New Pacific was that you needed to be ready for anything.

Rosie hurried down the hall and back to her room. Her sisters were still getting ready, but she needed reassurance that they would be okay. That she could protect them all. Rosie beelined for the bag beside her bed and opened it up.

She blinked in disbelief, pushing aside the clothes she'd used to hide the gun.

It was gone. The gun was gone.

Rosie lost her breath, and she sank onto the bed.

What if Lucas took it? Was it possible? That meant he'd been in their room. Did he search Cassie's things, too? What if he found Cassie's phone? It was their only lifeline.

Rosie wanted to cry, but what good would that do? Mum said she was going to handle it, and Rosie needed to trust her. They had to get through this party, and then they would get as far away from all of this mess as possible. They just had to survive one more night.

OLIVIA

*D*eep breaths. *Lucas means well,* Olivia told herself as she watched Rosie head out. But sometimes her brother drove her crazy. After her accident, she was no longer the big sister looking out for her baby brother. Their roles reversed; now Olivia was Lucas's project to manage. She kept waiting for him to meet someone, but girlfriends never lasted more than a few months. Which meant she was always the sole focus of his attention.

She was definitely grateful. During the early days of her recovery, Lucas oversaw all of Olivia's medical care, because even the smallest decisions were a struggle. She had so many therapies and medications to manage. When she came home, Lucas made sure she took them all, and he made her healthy meals when, if she'd been left to her own devices, she might have starved, her grief overriding everything.

Lucas was the one who insisted that she volunteer at the climate camp to give her life more structure. She appreciated all of it. It was the only reason she'd made it through.

But the past few years, Olivia started to feel suffocated

by his devotion, which in turn made her feel guilty for all the sacrifices he made. He had such a tight hold on her life. Even now he managed every facet, including her finances. Which worked fine before, but when it came to making decisions about her future with Sam and the girls, she had to draw a line in the sand.

She'd remained calm during her conversation with Rosie. No need to drag her girls into her sibling drama, but she was pissed. Olivia had a second chance at being their mom, and she wasn't going to waste it. She had to talk to him before the party, but first she wanted to check in on Sam.

With her hair and makeup done, Olivia slipped on the long black gown the girls all agreed was their favorite. She paused as she studied her reflection in the mirror. She was...an old lady.

No, that wasn't entirely true. She was an old lady, but the light had come back into her eyes. Her daughters brought it back. Olivia grabbed her bag and headed upstairs to Sam's room. She opened the door to see him lying in bed, his eyes closed, his breathing steady. She stood and watched him.

"Still can't resist me after all these years, can you?" he joked, opening his eyes to regard her. He had such kind eyes. That was the first thing she'd noticed when she had seen him on the golf course. Well, that and his smile. He had the best smile.

"It's true, Sammy. You're still as handsome as ever."

He snorted and gestured for her to join him on the other side of the giant king-size bed.

"Damn, you look good. Still got the best legs I've ever seen."

She smiled, kicked off her shoes, and sat down beside him, their legs touching.

"Not how we imagined spending our golden years, is it?" Sam asked. "We were supposed to have our summer house in Santa Barbara."

"If only Santa Barbara survived the floods," she said wistfully.

Sam sighed. "Ah, yes, I forgot about that. There were so many climate events, and such sporadic reporting. It was all awful, wasn't it?"

"Yes, it was," Olivia agreed. She squeezed his hand, not wanting to catalog all the tragedies they'd survived. They sat together in comfortable silence. They'd been together for seven years before it all went south. Seven lucky years in which they laughed and loved and hurt, and here they were.

"I still can't believe you cook and garden. It simply doesn't compute," Olivia said.

Sam chuckled. "I couldn't believe it, either. But what choice did I have? It was me and Mum. I was flailing, so I took that guide you left us and studied everything in it."

"You did?" she asked. She thought about all the times

he'd made fun of her guidebook. How he'd threatened to throw it in the Pacific Ocean. Instead, he'd used it.

"By the time we left the States, I saw how right you were. I was scared, but I kept studying it. Then I went to the library in Newcastle and got more books about cooking and gardening and self-defense, and I learned what I needed to in order to keep us all alive. But it was all thanks to you, Liv. You saved me. Saved us. All that shite I gave you about the book, and in the end, it's what kept us alive. I'm so sorry. I wish I'd listened."

She did, too. But she hadn't heard him, either. They'd both gotten lost in the shit.

She squeezed his hand again. "Let's focus on the future. We'll have plenty of time to talk when we're back in England."

His eyes widened. "You're coming home with us?"

"If that's okay? I talked to the girls and they want me to, but of course you have a say in the matter. I've missed so much time with them, and with you. I don't want to lose any more time."

"I'd like that," he said softly.

Suddenly, Sam startled. "Hold on. What about Lucas?"

"What about him?"

His eyes narrowed. "He's not who you think he is. Lucas provoked me. I swear, Liv, I'm not making it up. He wanted me to attack him."

Olivia couldn't hide her shock. "I don't think...I mean, why would he?"

A MOTHER'S GUIDE TO THE APOCALYPSE 419

"He's never liked me, but this is different. It's like he's threatened by me...by the girls. You have to believe me," he insisted.

"Okay, Sam. Okay."

"He's hiding something. I'm afraid for you. For us," Sam said softly.

"We're fine, Sammy. I promise. And you...you've been through a lot these past few days."

"It's not about that. It's true that I forget things. I get mixed up, but this...this is real. We can't stay here. We can't. Please, Cassie, please take me home," Sam pleaded.

Olivia blinked away tears. This was Sam's illness talking, and it made her deeply sad.

"We're going home. Real soon," she promised. "Get some rest, okay? It won't be long before you, me, and the girls are on a plane heading back to England."

Her words seemed to comfort him. "You're a good woman. You know that, don't you?"

The words cut her deep. The words he always said. He was a good man. She squeezed his hand and watched as he settled back in bed and his eyes flickered closed. It didn't take long before he was gently snoring.

Olivia did her best to shake off Sam's warning as she hurried downstairs. She found Lucas at his desk, wearing the hell out of his three-piece suit, with a blue silk tie and handkerchief to match. He looked far removed from the little boy she'd cared for and consoled and clashed with. The same little boy she held tight and promised, "We'll always be family," after their mom and Meemaw died. How fast it all went. He was a grown man who didn't want to let her go.

"Can we talk?" Olivia asked.

He looked up from his paperwork and smiled. "You look lovely," he said.

"Thank you. I wanted to look good for your big night."

"*Our* big night. But I know that look. What's wrong? What did I do?" His tone was joking, but she could hear the edge in it.

"You told the girls I wasn't well enough to travel?"

"That's not exactly what I said. I said you've had some health issues in the past, which is true? Isn't it?"

"I'm healthy now and I have been for years. Lucas, the last thing I need is you upsetting the girls. They've been through enough."

"All I said is that I was concerned about the demands of all that travel, but of course you're free to go."

Olivia laughed. "Good to know that I'm not your captive."

Lucas wasn't amused. "Is that how you feel?" he asked.

"Of course not."

Or was it? What Sam said wasn't rational, she understood that, but Olivia had learned that bottling things up only led to more problems. She had to address these things head-on, even if it wasn't pleasant.

"I really wish you'd told me about my journals. You know what they meant to me."

Lucas sighed heavily. "I did. But I didn't want to see that look on your face. It was an accident. Accidents happen. Come on, Liv. Don't make this a thing. Not after all I've done for you."

She hated when he did that. Of course Lucas did a lot for her, but she'd done just as much for him. If she allowed this to continue, they'd be comparing lists until dawn. "Things are changing fast, but we have to adapt as best we can. You must see that."

Lucas smiled, a smile that told her everything was going to be okay. "I do, Liv. I see it all."

Relieved that the matter was settled, she sat down across from him. "Please tell me you have my passport?"

For years, she'd wondered if it was silly to keep renewing it when she had no one to see and no place to go, but she did it without fail. At the time it felt as though she were throwing a penny in a fountain and expecting to win the lottery, but it had all been leading up to this moment.

"It's in the safe upstairs. Can I get it to you after the party?" he asked.

"That's fine. We're booking our flight tomorrow."

He didn't say anything, but his eyes told a different story. "Lucas, I'm not leaving forever. It's a few months, and then I'll be back to see you and make sure the camp is running smoothly," she promised.

"That sounds like a wonderful plan, Olivia. I'm here to help you with whatever you need."

Neither one of them was overly affectionate with the other, but he put his hand over hers and patted it.

Olivia was transported back to a rainy LA evening.

She was at Pace, a popular Italian spot in Laurel Canyon. Rain fell in heavy sheets, but she didn't seem to care. Her face was covered with tears while Lucas's was twisted in fury. His hand gripped her wrist. Hard. She cried out. "Lucas, stop it. Please..."

Startled, Olivia pulled away. She used to have flashes of memory right after the accident. Snippets of the pouring rain, a hand grabbing her, or a scream stuck in her throat, but it hadn't happened in years.

Lucas sensed the sudden shift and moved closer. "Are you okay?"

"I'm fine," she lied. "Excited for tonight. I'll let you finish getting ready before everyone arrives."

Even to Olivia her words sounded flat, but she had to get out of there. She had to get some air. She gave him her best smile and hurried out of the study, desperate to check on the girls. She tried to shake free of the memory. She understood how much tonight meant to Lucas, and she wanted to honor her promise. But afterward, Olivia had no intention of coming back here. She was ready to start this new chapter with her girls and Sam, whether Lucas liked it or not.

CASSIE

There was champagne and waiters in black-and-white tuxedos serving the tiniest, fanciest bite-size appetizers, there were New Pacific celebrities and politicians all clad in designer clothes straight out of one of her mum's Hollywood premieres. There were at least 150 people, drinking and laughing and celebrating the end of a weeklong anniversary. It should have been exhilarating, but Cassie couldn't relax, especially once she learned that Rosie had chickened out.

"You said you were going to talk to Mum about Lucas. That was the whole point of you going."

Rosie winced. "You should have heard her talking about him like he was a bloody saint. I didn't know what to say."

Cassie kept waiting for Bettie, ever the optimist, to weigh in, but Bettie just sipped her club soda in silence. Together the three of them watched Lucas make his way through the crowd, laughing and shaking hands, so charming it was impossible to think they had anything to worry about. They'd done their best to cover up their concerns, and thankfully Mum hadn't noticed—but that was probably because she'd spent half the night by Lucas's side accepting everyone's congratulations. When she was with them, Mum couldn't help but brag. "Have y'all met my babies?" she would say, then launch into the story about their amazing reunion.

Ordinarily Cassie would have been embarrassed by all the attention, but Mum was so happy, she couldn't help but get swept up in the excitement. It wasn't until Mum walked away that Cassie began to worry, unable to let go of a nagging question: What would they do if Lucas wouldn't let them leave?

She'd been surprised when Rosie said she didn't have a plan. The more Cassie thought about it, the more she worried that doing nothing was the wrong choice. She wondered if they should call Rita again, but what would she say? *We've got a bad feeling about our uncle, the New Pacific big shot?* Cassie was about to jump out of her skin. She had to do something. She slipped out of the ballroom and hurried down the hall to the bathroom. She shut the door, pulled out her contraband phone, and dialed. It rang for so long she almost hung up.

"Hello," Dominic said, sounding breathless.

"I think you were right," Cassie said, not bothering to say hello. "About my uncle. Something's off. We're supposed to leave with Mum, but I'm worried that he'll... I don't know if he'll let her leave. Or us." She paused. "Can you come? I need you."

She hated asking for help, especially someone she barely knew.

There was silence on the other end. "Dom?" Cassie asked.

"I came back here to a shitshow, Cassie. I had to bury that Guardian shithead and Mom is pissed that I left with you, and devastated that Sam and you all hate her, and I'm just... I'm not sure what will happen if I leave her."

"You don't think she's safe?" Cassie asked.

"No, it's not that. But she'd never forgive me if I went..."

It was sad. Dominic really was Mel's captive. "So that's a no?" she asked.

"I need... I need a little time."

"If I had more time, you think I'd fucking call you?" she snapped, trying to keep her voice low. It didn't matter, though. She'd made a mistake thinking he was a serious option.

"I guess we're both fucked," Cassie said flatly. "Have a nice life, Dom."

"Cassie, wait," he said.

She hung up. What an idiot she was to think she could trust him because he was a bloody good kisser. She had to get some fresh air and think.

Cassie made her way back through the crowd and stepped outside on the wraparound balcony, breathing in the muggy night air. From her perch, she could see the city lights twinkling. She reached into her bag and lit a cigarette, taking a deep drag.

As she blew out the smoke, she spotted a truck in the distance and sucked in a deep breath: The familiar Guardian flag was blowing in the wind. The windows were tinted so she couldn't see inside, but the hairs on the back of Cassie's neck stood up. Something told her Joey was close by—but that wasn't possible, was it? Why would he be here?

A few seconds later, her question was answered as she saw Pablo, her uncle's head of security, approaching the truck. Two men exited the car and they all shook hands, big smiles on their faces. Pablo led them toward the back of the property. She didn't have to be a genius to know this wasn't good. She quickly hurried back into the ballroom.

Rosie glared at Cassie. "Where were you?"

"What's wrong with you? You can't leave without telling us," Bettie snapped.

Cassie hadn't been gone longer than twenty minutes, but she understood why they were worried. "There are Guardians here. I saw them talking to Lucas's security," she said.

Bettie and Rosie looked panicked as they glanced around the fancy crowd.

"Not in here. Parked outside, but we need to tell Mum and get Dad and leave. As soon as possible," Cassie said.

"Hello, thank you all for coming," Lucas said from the front of the room.

Shit. Even if they'd wanted to leave, it was too late. The dog and pony show, as their mum called it, was about to begin under a bright spotlight, with adoring guests looking on. Cassie and her sisters inched closer. "My name is Luke Hays. I've been part of New Pacific's revitalization project for over a decade, and I am excited to be here tonight to celebrate our rebirth. This city endured a level of tragedy and suffering that cannot be quantified. So many of us have lost family and friends, homes and businesses. So many of us were told that we should give up on a world filled with joy and possibility. That this place would never thrive again. That this city would never rebuild. But we saw a future, and we all came together to make it happen."

He was greeted with thunderous applause. Mum stood beside him, beaming. "What I'm most proud of is watching the people I love overcome incredible challenges and make the best of it. Many of you know that my sister, Olivia, was separated from her triplets, my nieces, Rosie, Bettie, and Cassie, for almost two decades. During that time, Olivia recovered from a traumatic brain injury and went on to successfully run the Hollywood Climate Camp and Refugee Center. Her work at the center has been nothing short of remarkable, and I am thrilled to present this grant for ten million dollars, which will ensure she can continue her wonderful work caring for these children. But, Liv, before I give you the microphone, there are a few people who wanted to be here to cheer you on."

From the back of ballroom, twenty-five young men and women entered, all wearing Hollywood Climate Camp T-shirts and big smiles. Olivia's hand went up to her mouth. Lucas continued. "These are the first group of children Olivia cared for when she began volunteering at the camp. They've all gone on to graduate and get jobs and make a new life for themselves. And they all wanted to be here tonight to thank her for her dedication."

Cassie watched as Mum wiped away tears while the students swarmed her, offering hugs and wiping away tears. Her mum gave Lucas a hug and kissed his cheek as she stepped up to the microphone. It struck Cassie that as much as Lucas wanted everyone to think he was a proud little brother, she could see that he was full of shit. She didn't know how she knew this; she just felt it deep in her bones. The trouble was, she had no idea what to do about it or how to protect her mum from a broken heart. Or something much worse.

OLIVIA

Olivia had to get it together. She hadn't seen these kiddos in years. These were the kids who had given her life a purpose when she wanted to give up. She finished her hugs and handshakes and took a deep breath. She had a speech to give. She cleared her throat. "There was a time in my life when speaking to crowds was commonplace. I talked to studio executives and agents. I gave speeches at awards shows. Y'all, I thought I was a big deal," Olivia said, pausing for laughter.

"But my life took a very different turn, as did so many of ours. I lost my girls, lost what mattered most to me, and in my darkest days, I found a place at the camp, among the most innocent and vulnerable and broken. I am here because the children in our climate camps deserve love and food and education—all of the things we provide for our own children. I am grateful to Lucas and all of you who made this grant possible. I am grateful for the miracles that have happened in my life. My girls came back to me, and I could not have imagined a more magical evening celebrating with the people I love. I promise that no matter what happens, I will never stop working to ensure the camp is a loving home for those who need it."

Olivia smiled down at her daughters. When she turned back, Lucas was waiting to hug her... and it was then that another memory assaulted her. *She was back in Pace's parking lot on Laurel Canyon, two decades earlier, facing off against Lucas in the pouring rain.*

"I have to do this, Lucas. For my marriage. For my family. Don't you see that? I'm losing myself here and I'm going to lose them, too."

"What are you even holding on to? Your best friend fucked your husband and you think those relationships are worth saving?"

He might as well have slapped her. She didn't know what she was thinking, telling him about Sam and Mel. Of course he would use it against her. But it was no surprise. Lucas always aimed for the jugular. Olivia regarded him with sympathy, but her words were firm. "You're an adult. You can stand on your own. Or if you want, come with us to England."

He laughed bitterly. "Thanks for your pity, but I'm not one of your fucking kids."

"Then stop acting like it," she said. She saw the wounded expression. She hated that look, hated when he acted like a child. She'd done her part raising him. She had her own family to focus on. Olivia turned to go.

"You can't do this to me. We're family. You don't fuck over your family." He reached out and grabbed her arm, his fingers squeezing her wrist. She tried to break free from his grasp, but he kept squeezing. She let out a pained cry as he shoved her. Hard.

Seconds later, the wet, muddy ground beneath her gave way. She reached for Lucas, but he stepped back and watched as she tumbled backward.

"Olivia, are you okay?"

She blinked and looked to see Lucas's hand on her arm. She was back in the ballroom, but everything had changed.

The night she fell was the same night as the Laurel Canyon flood. The night her own brother tried to kill her and lied to everyone about it. How easy was it to convince everyone? She was already scheduled to have dinner in that very location. Hundreds of people were injured and killed that night. How easy was it for Lucas to dump her and run?

Olivia could see Lucas watching her with concern. It took everything she had to force a smile. She pointed to the crowd. "Go on. Your adoring fans await."

"I'll see you soon," he said, and she wondered if it was only in her imagination that it sounded threatening.

As Lucas walked away, Olivia stood frozen in place. How could this be happening? Her baby brother. Her best friend for almost two decades was the person responsible for destroying her life?

Olivia's gaze landed on her girls. She remembered how Lucas reacted when she told him: "Whoa, fucking triplets! That's gonna cost you a fortune." Then when she told him the doctor suggested termination because of the risks, he shrugged. "He might be right. It could be a fucking nightmare."

She thought of all the times the girls were sick and she needed extra help, or they'd scheduled family photos and he bailed. Of course he had no trouble asking for money even when they were struggling with NICU bills.

She thought about his insinuations that Sam had hurt her and how he'd told her he found the girls' death certificates. She'd never seen them, never even asked, because why would she? But she knew now that he'd lied.

The thought sickened her, but all she could hear was a steady drumbeat of *why* in her head. Why would Lucas do all of this?

As she watched him move through the crowd, she spotted Rory by his side. Her sweet protégée, the girl she'd hoped would take over running the clinic when she retired, looked up at Lucas with adoring eyes as though he were a rock star and she was his groupie. It was subtle, but she saw his hand graze her back, a tender, intimate gesture. They were sleeping together. It hit Olivia instantly. How had she missed it before? All the times Lucas came by the camp, all the times Rory offered to drop off paperwork at his home, all the times she'd offered to do the bookkeeping so Olivia could go and check on the babies in the nursery or enjoy an early night. She thought of how insistent Lucas was that Olivia stay and run the camp.

Olivia closed her eyes, remembering Sam's voice in her head. *That lad treats you like his own personal ATM.*

Olivia laughed it off, but it was true. Lucas *took, took,*

took from her. But what could she have done back then? He was family. Her only family before Sam and the girls. Hadn't Lucas more than made up for it? Cared for her after the accident? But she'd financed it. Let him sell the house, which was one of the few that remained in the neighborhood. The only way anyone survived the Collapse was if they had money. She'd let him handle all of it, because without Sam and the girls, money had no meaning to her.

All these years, she never questioned how he'd made even more money, because it hadn't really mattered to her. What if all of his wheeling and dealing had nothing to do with the camp and its future? What if it was about padding his pockets?

She had to find out. She had to know. Olivia glanced over and saw the girls sitting at a table, waiting for her. Before she said a word, she saw the terrified looks on their faces. Looks that made her stomach twist. "What is it? What's wrong?"

They glanced at one another. Their silent sister language was beyond her ability to decipher, but she saw Bettie glance toward Lucas, her eyes wide and fearful.

"Please tell me what's going on," Olivia pleaded.

Cassie's voice was so low, Olivia strained to hear it. "Lucas told us not to mention Joey or the Guardians to you. Said it'd make you too upset, but we think he was lying. They're here. Cassie saw them parked outside, laughing and talking with Lucas's security."

Olivia closed her eyes. Joey and Lucas. Was it possible they were working together? She didn't want to believe that, but anything was possible. "What's wrong, Mum? Did Lucas do something?"

They knew. Not the details, but they were smart girls. They saw through her brother in a way Olivia hadn't.

"I can't tell you everything, but go upstairs and pack your bags. I'll be there soon. We have to leave this place as soon as possible."

"Where are you going?" Bettie asked.

Olivia hated the tormented look in her eyes. She squeezed Bettie's arm. "I need to check Lucas's upstairs office. I don't know what he's done, but it's bad, and I'm going to need proof."

"You can't leave. He's been watching you all night," Cassie insisted.

"I have to do this—"

Rosie cut in. "You and Bettie stay here. Cassie and I'll see what we can find. But, Mum, if we don't find anything, we still have to go."

Olivia hesitated. The last thing she wanted to do was put her girls in danger.

"Be quick, and then we'll figure out a way out of here together."

Bettie squeezed her hand as Cassie and Rosie slipped out of the ballroom. Olivia's gaze lingered on Lucas. All these years she had been so proud of what her little brother had accomplished, but now it seemed so stupid. How did she not question all of this? How did she not remember what he'd done sooner? Olivia still couldn't wrap her head around his lies and deceit about her accident, and she probably never would. The only thing she knew for certain was that she needed to know the truth. Then she planned to take her girls as far away from him as possible.

ROSIE

We shouldn't be doing this," Cassie said as she followed Rosie out of the party, jazz music still playing, guests growing more and more tipsy by the minute. Rosie agreed. It was a terrible idea, but she couldn't forget Mum's haunted expression.

"We'll be quick."

They hurried up the stairs. The halls were deserted, and they quickly slipped into Lucas's bedroom. "I'll take the desk. You start with the bookshelves," Rosie said.

They found tax records, bank statements, and business plans, but no smoking gun. Twenty minutes later, they still hadn't located anything useful. Rosie knew if they stayed much longer, there was a good chance they would get caught.

"We should go," Rosie said reluctantly.

But Cassie was studying the room, her gaze focused on a giant cactus in a planter box in the corner. "I've seen these before."

She kicked the planter box, and it echoed. "It's hollow," she said.

Cassie knelt down, lifted the cactus out of the box, and set it on the floor. "It's a safe," Cassie said.

"Great, all we need is a code, which should be no problem at all."

They were both silent. Cassie knelt down beside the lock and tried a series of numbers. Nothing. She looked up at Rosie. "What's Mum's birthday?"

"May seventh. But he wouldn't," Rosie said.

But Rosie underestimated her uncle. Cassie typed in the numbers, and sure enough the lock popped open. Inside were Olivia's passport, a notebook with a list of names and locations, and a large white envelope. Rosie opened it and saw printed pictures of girls ranging from twelve years old to eighteen, with names written on the front in black ink. Names that corresponded with the names in the notebook. Young girls, smiling back with wide, trusting eyes.

"The Guardians traffic girls," Cassie said softly. "I think...I think these are girls from the camp that they plan to sell."

Rosie wasn't naive to the fact that evil existed. What made her sick was knowing that her uncle was the mastermind behind all of this, and that he'd used Mum to make it happen.

Rosie worried that she might be sick. She shoved the photos back in the envelope and gathered everything up. "Now we know who he really is. And Mum will, too," Rosie said.

A MOTHER'S GUIDE TO THE APOCALYPSE 439

Cassie silently reached for Rosie's hand, and they hurried out of his room and back to Rosie's. As she sank down on her bed, she wished again that she had the gun, the only thing that had made her feel safe.

"We should pack like Mum said," Rosie ordered.

Cassie nodded and slipped out of the room. She returned ten minutes later with her luggage and sank down on the bed beside Rosie. The two of them sat in silence as they waited for Mum and Bettie.

And waited and waited.

An hour later, the door flung open. Bettie and Mum entered and looked exhausted.

"We were getting worried," Rosie said.

Mum sighed. "Lucas was holding court. I thought we'd never escape." She glanced at the girls. "Did you find anything?"

Rosie knew that she was about to break her mum's heart, and somehow the words wouldn't come. Instead she handed over what they'd found. Mum stared at the photos and the names. As the reality of what she was seeing set in, her mouth twisted and she began to cry.

"That sonofabitch. He stole you from me and he wants to steal my other girls... All those girls I've promised to keep safe."

Rosie didn't understand what Mum meant about Lucas stealing them, but she hated seeing her like this. All three of them gathered around her and hugged her tight. Rosie wished she could say something that would help, but there were no words for this.

At last, Mum caught her breath. "Thank you for finding this. Thank you for confirming what I already knew."

She stood up. "I'm going to get your father ready to go. Try and close your eyes and rest. We'll leave as soon as the party is over and everyone has gone to bed," Mum said.

Rosie didn't understand how her mum could seem so confident, but before they could ask any questions, she was gone.

Rosie and Cassie were too exhausted to speak. Bettie went to pack her things, and when she came back, they all curled up together in bed like they had as kids. Rosie was certain she wouldn't sleep, but to her surprise her eyes flickered closed.

The next thing she knew, Mum was gently shaking her awake. "Girls, wake up. Come on. Let's go."

Rosie sat up instantly. Bettie and Cassie did the same. Standing beside Mum, Dad looked bleary-eyed.

"Are you okay?" Cassie asked him.

He gave a terse shake of his head. "I will be when we get the hell out of here."

Mum stared at them all, like a general leading troops into battle. "I disabled the security system, but if Lucas is planning something he'll have thought of that. There may still be Guardians stationed outside, but we're not staying here. Follow my lead. I don't think he'll hurt me, but..."

A MOTHER'S GUIDE TO THE APOCALYPSE 441

Rosie turned over those words in her head. Mum didn't *think* he would hurt her.

"Wait," Cassie said suddenly.

They all stared back at her. "What are we waiting for?" Rosie snapped.

"Maybe we can figure out a way to contact Rita."

"I borrowed your phone when you were asleep and tried her earlier. There's no connection," Bettie admitted.

They really were all on their own, Rosie thought.

"Staying here is riskier than leaving. We have to go," Mum insisted, her voice catching. "I need y'all to trust me."

That was all it took. They followed her down the stairs and headed toward the door. It shouldn't have been a shock when Lucas appeared in the foyer to block their path, but Rosie still gasped and reached out to shield Bettie and Cassie. He was still in his dress pants and shirt but no tie. He sipped on a glass of scotch and tried to project an aura of calm, but his wild eyes told a different story. Rosie knew they were in real trouble when Joey stepped into the hall.

"Didn't y'all know it's rude to leave a party early?" Joey said.

Lucas chuckled. Rosie felt Mum's entire body stiffen. Two men she'd loved and trusted. Two men who'd betrayed her.

"Liv, it's been a while," Joey said.

"Not long enough," Mum said, her voice dripping with disdain. "We're leaving, Lucas. It's time to let us go."

"No, I don't think so. Come on, Olivia. Let's have a chat," Lucas said.

Rosie understood that her mum had no power here, but Olivia stood tall and straight. "I'm fine here. I remember what happened the last time I tried to leave to be with my family."

Rosie didn't understand, but Lucas did. "You remembered?"

"All these years, I wondered what happened to me. The doctors said I'd been dumped at the hospital, but by who? What happened to my car? All those therapy sessions trying to piece things together. Months and months of wondering if my own husband tried to kill me."

Sam's eyes snapped to attention. "I would never hurt you."

"I know that, Sammy," Olivia said gently. "But Lucas got into my head. All those years you made me question everything, and it was you...I need to know why."

Lucas looked at Mum, who was now his hostage. "I never wanted to hurt you, Liv. It was an accident. We were arguing and you fell. You have no idea how scared I was. There was so much blood, and you were so still. It was like when Mama died. I knew that I'd messed up, but I didn't want to go to jail. I couldn't...But I took you to the hospital. I made sure you got great care. I took care of you after you woke up."

"You lied to Sam about it. You made my family think I

was fucking dead? And you made me think that my babies were dead!"

Rosie could hardly believe what she was hearing. "Did you know where we were? Did you?" she asked.

Lucas shrugged. "I never looked."

Bettie let out a cry. Cassie put her arm around her sister.

Olivia stood motionless, having already pieced all of this together. "He lied about the death certificates, and I was too trusting to even ask to see them. All those years lost." Mum's voice trembled.

"We were happy, Olivia. We didn't need anyone else."

Mum's face was contorted with rage. "You were always a selfish little shit. Everyone said so. Not me. I made excuses. 'Lucas had a hard life. He lost his mom. He's trying to find his way.' I gave you everything you needed because we were family."

"Fuck that. You made me grovel for every cent. Perfect Olivia and her perfect life."

Olivia looked confused. "Then why not let me die?" she asked.

"I needed you. I thought I'd be able to take your money and property, but to my surprise the government wasn't letting that happen without proper identification. So I needed you, and then..." He paused, as though considering whether to reveal this. "...For the first time in my life, you needed me. It felt good."

Mum's gaze moved over to Joey, equal parts disgusted

and betrayed. "How long have you two been working together?"

Joey grinned. "Ever since poor Glenda got busted. I realized we needed to think bigger. Once I learned that Lucas had some clout, I figured we could help each other out. And here we are."

Rosie's mind was racing as she tried to piece things together. Lucas had orchestrated the interview at the police station and sent that man to Mel's. "You knew Cassie would come here, and that we would follow her?" Rosie said.

Joey winked at her. "Smart girls. They really are like you, Liv."

"So now what?" Olivia asked.

"Well," Lucas said, "you have a nice life and a good job, which I'm happy for you to keep, but I don't think that's going to work, so you'll have a drink with me, take a few pills, and it'll be lights out. The good news is, Rory is ready to take over. She's got your brains, but she won't let her emotions get in the way. She sees our vision on how the business can run."

No one spoke. He was so matter-of-fact about killing his own sister. Lucas shrugged. "As for the rest of you..."

He gestured to Joey, who shook his head. "Cassie's gonna have to come with me. My family is not pleased with her, and she needs to be held accountable. We'll keep the pregnant one, too. She can either raise the baby with me or we'll find it a home. That bun's just started cooking, so she's got time to decide. But I'm not a monster. The old man and that one can go," Joey said, gesturing at Rosie.

Olivia's high-pitched cry didn't sound quite real as she launched herself at Joey. Like a feral cat, she clawed and hit him, but he had fifty pounds on her. He barely batted an eye as he stepped back and watched her tumble onto the floor.

Olivia let out a pained cry and began to weep. "Leave her alone," Sam roared. He went at Lucas, but his movements were slow and clumsy. A quick punch to the abdomen and Lucas had Sam doubled over, groaning in pain. Cassie was by Sam's side while Rosie knelt down to comfort Mum. All the air had been sucked out of the room.

"It's okay, Mum. We'll be okay," she promised. She was so busy comforting Mum that she didn't notice Bettie. Nobody noticed her.

But they all heard the first bullet.

Rosie used to hear people say that things happened in slow motion, but she hadn't thought it was real. And yet that was exactly what happened. She watched as the bullet hovered in midair before it exploded into Lucas's arm. The second bullet hit Joey in the knee. He let out a pained cry and dropped to the ground.

Bettie took the gun? Her Bettie. Was this really happening? Had her sister just shot Joey and Lucas? Joey was writing on the ground while Lucas gritted his teeth and stared at his shoulder, blood seeping from the wound. "You fucking shot me?"

Grimacing, Lucas tried to stand. Bettie aimed the gun right at his heart.

"Don't," she said. There was such power and rage in her voice, it stopped him instantly.

Rosie couldn't believe sweet Bettie, who just wanted to keep the peace, had shot two people. But here they were. For the first time in her life, Rosie had no clue what her sister was going to do.

BETTIE

Taking the gun was the easy part. She'd grabbed it from Rosie's bag when she went to talk with Mum. Finding the courage to use it was another story. It wasn't until she saw and heard what Lucas and Joey were capable of—what both these men would do without a second thought—that she realized she could do this. All her life, Bettie was the obedient sister and daughter. She dated the nice boy. She pursued the career path her father wanted. She listened to her sisters and did what she could to make them happy. But *this . . . this* was too much.

She hadn't aimed to kill. That wasn't her intention. All she wanted to do was to stop them from hurting anyone, but now that she was standing here, thinking about all the people these men hurt, how many people they would continue to hurt, Bettie wanted them gone.

She aimed the gun at Lucas, summoning the resolve.

"Bets, put the gun down. Please . . ." Rosie pleaded.

Bettie looked at Rosie's stricken face but felt nothing. "He lied to Mum for so long. All those years we could have had together," Bettie said, tears streaming down her cheeks.

"Killing him won't change that," Rosie insisted.

"They threatened my baby. What kind of monster threatens a child? Not to mention all those girls..."

Bettie's hand no longer trembled. Cassie joined Rosie, the two of them shoulder-to-shoulder in front of Bettie, a united force.

"Bets, this isn't what anyone wants," Cassie pleaded.

Bettie's gaze zeroed in on Mum and Dad. "Is that true?" Bettie asked. "He ruined your lives. He ruined everything. Do you really care what happens to him?"

She wanted them to tell her she could do this and they would all be okay.

Sam was crying, too. "No, no, no. Don't let her do this. Not my sweet girl," he said, staring at Olivia.

Bettie hated seeing Mum's tears, the sorrow in her eyes. Olivia winced as she climbed to her feet and moved toward Bettie. "My darling girl, we've got a big life waiting for us. So many memories to make. These assholes...they're nothing. Don't let them steal that future," she said.

Lucas laughed through gritted teeth. "You can't escape family," he said.

"Shut up, you sonofabitch," Mum said. "Or I'll shoot you myself."

She gently placed her hand over the top of Bettie's and the gun to prevent her from firing it. She took her other hand and held Bettie's face tenderly, her voice barely a whisper.

"You're going to be a mum. You're already thinking like one. Doing what's necessary to protect your child, but you don't have to do this."

Bettie wasn't sure that was true. Joey said he had men outside waiting. Lucas had all the power. They might still lose here.

But she took in her family: Dad and Mum, Rosie and Cassie. She wanted to hurt Lucas and Joey so badly, but she could see if she did this, her family would suffer. And that was enough for her to hand the gun to Mum.

Mum stared at Lucas with such hatred in her eyes, Bettie briefly wondered if she was going to shoot him herself. But she simply held on to it. "You had so much potential and goodness in you, and you used it to manipulate and scheme and hurt the people you love. Now you'll have to face the consequences," Olivia said.

The pain of his wound left Lucas speechless.

Joey grunted. "You still have to get out of here," he laughed.

Bettie wanted to scream *kill him*. She didn't care how mental it made her seem. But Mum was one step ahead of her. She brought her foot down on Joey's injured leg. He let out a scream so loud, it rattled the pictures hanging on the wall. Then it was drowned out by the sound of police sirens—and all hell broke loose. The front door burst open and police in uniforms stormed inside, guns raised. "Get down on the ground. Get down."

Bettie hurried to lie on her stomach. She looked at the rest of the family, all of them lying down, eyes wide with uncertainty. No one knew what to expect. Were these the good guys? Or was this the beginning of the end?

An outraged Lucas was shouting. "They shot us! We need medical attention. Help us!"

"We're looking for the Clarks. We've been sent by the British consulate to take you home," a man in a dark suit said. She had no clue who he was. Maybe British intelligence.

Bettie could hear Mum's relieved sobs. "They were going to kill us...me and my girls," Mum said, her words catching.

"We'll get into all that," the man said. "Rita has been worried since she couldn't make contact. She's waiting to speak with you. Come on. Let's go."

Rita was behind all of this. Thank goodness. They were safe at last.

At least she hoped so. Bettie imagined there would be questions about the men she'd just shot. As they all stood, Lucas and Joey were still screaming threats, but no one cared.

"How did you know we were here?" Rosie asked.

Bettie almost laughed. Rosie *had* to have all the answers.

"We got a tip that the Guardians had a hit out on you, and you were already flagged in our system by British intelligence. Once Rita heard that, she sent us immediately."

A MOTHER'S GUIDE TO THE APOCALYPSE 451

Cassie couldn't hide her smile. "Dominic came through," she said softly.

Bettie raised her eyebrows in confusion, but she didn't have time to ask what Cassie meant. "We do have questions about what went on here," the officer continued.

"We can answer them all. Just get us out of here," Olivia said.

He gestured for them to head outside. Cassie and Rosie wrapped their arms around Bettie, while Sam and Olivia followed, leaving Lucas and Joey behind for good.

As they headed outside toward a waiting SUV, Olivia put her head on Sam's shoulder. He pulled her in close. It was, Bettie thought, despite all the terrible things they'd been through since arriving here, a core memory.

She had no idea what would happen next—with Max and the baby, with Dad's illness, with her sisters and their futures. But Mum was back. Their whole family was reunited. The rest of it they would figure out together.

EPILOGUE

ONE YEAR LATER

OLIVIA

Olivia heard the baby's soft whimper and hurried toward the nursery before Bettie or Max woke up. Gemma was only five months old and already an early riser like her nana.

Despite the eight-hour time difference, Olivia's routine remained the same. She still woke up before everyone else so that she could journal and meditate, only now her mornings ended with cuddles from her granddaughter and not with the children at the camp.

Olivia opened the door to Gemma's room and slipped inside. She picked up the baby, who gave her a sweet gummy smile. "Good morning, sweet girl. Are you hungry?"

The baby cooed in response and Olivia smiled, gently placing her over her shoulder as she headed into the kitchen humming "This Little Light of Mine."

She heated up a bottle and settled in her favorite armchair in the living room overlooking the garden. She loved this part of the house. Sam did, too. It was the best spot to enjoy the sunset or a late-afternoon rainstorm, Sam and Cassie's beautiful garden on display.

456   HOLLIE OVERTON

Olivia carefully settled Gemma into her arms and tilted the bottle up. The baby drank greedily, making soft humming noises. Olivia would never tire of that sound. Most days she still couldn't believe that she was here, with her family and this miracle baby.

Not that it'd been easy. After they were rescued by British authorities, Olivia and her family were swept up in a bureaucratic nightmare. The New Pacific officials were initially dismissive of the idea that Lucas, their trusted right-hand man, was in bed with the Guardians.

Thankfully the photos the girls had found—not to mention Cassie's smart thinking to record Lucas's and Joey's confessions—made it impossible to deny. A week later, all five of them were on a plane heading home to Newcastle. They were all traumatized by their experiences, but everyone was most concerned with Bettie. Had she been pushed too far? On the flight back, she appeared almost catatonic. Which was why they were all shocked when they landed at the airport and Bettie beelined for Max. She leapt into his arms and hugged him.

"We're having a baby," she shouted, drawing laughter and applause from other travelers. Of course, Olivia understood trauma wasn't something that vanished in an instant.

A few days later, when they had settled in, she cornered Bettie.

"Are you sure having this baby is what you want?"

Olivia asked. "You seemed so uncertain. What made you change your mind?"

Bettie considered this, her big blue eyes filling with tears. "At first I thought, *How can I be someone's mum?* After what I did to Joey and Lucas, knowing what I'm capable of, how could I be a mum? But then I thought about all the girls they hurt, and planned to hurt, and I knew I'd pull that trigger again if it meant protecting the people I love. What you did for us, I'll do for my child. That's what mums do."

Olivia had never been prouder. Thankfully, Bettie's worries about giving up her career were unfounded. Max was unwavering in his support of Bettie. He insisted that he would stay home with the baby so Bettie could finish her studies. Once she was done, Max would get his teaching certificate. They were discussing moving to London when Gemma was a year old, so Bettie could start auditioning. "It's win-win for all of us," Max said lovingly.

Gemma pushed away the bottle, signaling she was full. Olivia put her over her shoulder and burped her and then settled her into her arms, Gemma's eyes already closing.

Olivia wished that she could stay here all day, but in a few short hours, she would be on a plane heading back to New Pacific, where she would face her brother one last time. Lucas had been convicted of embezzlement, conspiracy, kidnapping, and intent to traffic, as well as fraud and attempted murder. The prosecutors said that Olivia's testimony could make the difference between a long sentence and life behind bars, especially because he still had powerful friends.

Olivia contemplated not going, but she knew how charming Lucas could be, and there was no way she wanted him to ever see the outside of a prison cell.

The other bright spot was that, as his next of kin, the courts had awarded Olivia all of Lucas's assets. There was a part of her that didn't want anything from her brother, but that money would allow her to look after Sam and the girls. She planned to tell Lucas all about it when she saw him. She couldn't wait to see the look on his face when he learned all the money he'd schemed and stolen would be hers to do with as she wished.

As for Joey, he finally received his comeuppance. Shortly before his trial while in jail, a man whose daughter had been trafficked by the Guardians stabbed him while he was on the toilet. Olivia loved that he'd gotten exactly what he deserved. She only hoped the rest of the Guardians would face a similar fate, but she wasn't holding her breath.

As much as Olivia didn't want to return to New Pacific, she was relieved that she wasn't going alone. Cassie would be traveling with her—except when Olivia returned home in a week, Cassie would be staying behind.

Without telling anyone in the family, she had applied for and landed a job running the climate camp's Greenhouse Initiative, one of the programs Olivia had conceived to help train farmers and landscapers.

Cassie hadn't been able to hide her nerves when she took Olivia to lunch at her favorite pub to tell her the news.

"Mum, it's wild to even consider, but it's my chance to take everything Dad taught me and everything you've done at the camp, and apply it and give back to these kids. It's a chance..." Cassie paused, looking guilty. "A chance to find my own path without my sisters. Am I the worst?"

Olivia shook her head. "It's okay to want to stand on your own. Yes, it's scary, but it had to happen eventually."

Olivia didn't love that she was about to be thousands of miles away from Cassie after finally getting her back, but she was proud.

"Does taking this job have anything to do with Dominic?" Cassie had been offered a job at Newcastle University after graduation as well as a position at London's School of Botany. Liv also knew that Cassie and Dominic had spent the past year communicating through letters and video chats.

Cassie's smile gave her away. "It's not the only reason, but Dominic is working in the camp's transportation department. We'll be living in the same dorm, so we'll see what happens."

"What about Mel?" Olivia asked. Even though Olivia had done her best to move past all Mel had done, she could never forgive her.

"Dom told her that it's time for him to have his own life. They haven't talked since he moved to LA, but he thinks she'll come around."

Olivia hoped that was true and that Mel wasn't going to risk her relationship with her son because of her ego, but only time would tell.

"All I want for you is to be happy. If Dom and this job are what you want, then you have to do it."

"I am. It's ... I already told Dad and he thinks I should go, but Rosie and Bettie ... will you be there when I tell them?" Cassie asked.

Olivia was surprised by how easily they had fallen into a mother-daughter relationship. Maybe it would have been different if Sam weren't sick, and the girls could rely on him, but she loved being that person. Being their mom. She also understood the codependent bond the girls shared, and that Cassie leaving her sisters would be a hard transition.

So Cassie had organized a "sister talk" and asked Olivia to join them. If Olivia had a crystal ball, she would have predicted that Rosie would lose her shit.

Instead, Rosie let out a sigh of relief. "Thank God. I was waiting for the right time to tell you ... I got into med school."

Everyone let out a squeal of excitement, hugging and congratulating Rosie. She held up her hand to stop them. "Hold on. I haven't decided yet. It's in Scotland. All the schools in England rejected me, but Glasgow has a spot. I'm not sure ..."

Olivia shook her head. "It's not the moon. It's a two-hour train ride."

A MOTHER'S GUIDE TO THE APOCALYPSE   461

Bettie, who at the time had been so pregnant she was about to pop, stared at her sisters in disbelief. "You're both leaving? What about the baby? What about…me?"

She didn't wait for them to respond, bursting into tears as she raced out of the room. Rosie and Cassie wanted to go after her, but Olivia knew pregnancy hormones combined with Bettie's dramatic tendencies were to blame. "Give her a day or two. She'll realize that this is a good thing. That you're all finding your own paths," Olivia insisted.

Sure enough, two days later, Bettie came into the conservatory carrying an armful of clothes. "These don't fit me. You two cows can fight over them," she said.

Her sisters burst out laughing as the three of them descended into a weepy hug.

Olivia hadn't planned on doing so much traveling, but she was ready for it. Whatever it took to see her girls and be part of their adult lives.

"I can take her if you like," Bettie said, interrupting Olivia's musings.

Bettie was already dressed with a full face of makeup, a performer through and through.

"She's got a full belly so hopefully she has a good nap," Olivia said as she gently transferred Gemma into Bettie's arms. Bettie studied her child with that joyful sense of wonder new moms possess.

"You should get going if you want to see Dad before your flight," Bettie said.

Olivia glanced at the clock and saw that it was almost seven in the morning. Her flight didn't leave until later this afternoon, but she'd promised Sam she would drop by for a visit.

Olivia kissed Bettie and the baby one last time and raced out.

For the first few months after they returned from LA, Sam had been fantastic at home. They were all surprised by how few and far between his bad days were. He said Olivia was his cure. They spent hours walking the grounds, working in the greenhouse, talking about everything and nothing at all. They slept in the same room from the minute she got back, and each night when she fell asleep beside him, she felt a sense of completeness that she'd thought was gone forever.

Sam made her feel like she could breathe again. Like things made sense.

Even though the doctors warned them that his illness would progress, when it happened it stunned Olivia. There was the morning he nearly burned the house down when he decided to make eggs and then went to take a nap. More evenings than not, he would be fine one minute and then begging Olivia to take him home the next. No matter how many times she told him they were home, he'd cry himself to sleep begging her to get the car and drive him home.

The night terrors in which Lucas and Joey were coming

A MOTHER'S GUIDE TO THE APOCALYPSE   463

to get them were almost unbearable, Sam desperate to save them and crying when he couldn't. For weeks on end, Olivia didn't sleep, determined to make sure Sam felt safe. It was a struggle, but she promised herself that this time she wouldn't let him down. This time she would stick by him until the very end.

The girls were the ones who made the call. "Mum, you've been fantastic, but it's not fair to you. Or to him. He needs more help than we can all give."

Olivia felt like a failure, but she didn't want Sam to get hurt on her watch. So she agreed. This time, Sam didn't put up a fight. Even he knew that it was time.

Thankfully the care home was only ten minutes away, which meant Olivia could visit every morning and evening. They'd watch TV or read together. If she wasn't having dinner with Rosie and Cassie or Bettie and Max, she was spending time with Sam.

Some days he knew who she was.

Other days he thought she was a kindly nurse. Those days were always the hardest, but it didn't stop her from coming. Nothing would.

Olivia dressed quickly and headed out. She would return home in a few hours, and then Rosie and Bettie would take her and Cassie to the airport.

A week later, Rosie would head to Glasgow to begin her classes.

A new chapter for everyone.

Olivia arrived at the care home, breakfast takeout in hand, and spotted Sam's favorite nurse, Alice. "How is he?" she asked.

"It's a good morning. He was up early. Eager to see you before you go."

Olivia let out a sigh of relief. It was hard enough knowing that she had to leave him. She was hoping for an easy goodbye.

Sam was dressed and sitting in his favorite lounge chair, reading a gardening magazine.

"Good morning," she said, kissing his cheek.

"Today is the day for your grand adventure," he said.

Olivia could already feel tears welling. "Let's not talk about that." She held up the deli bag. "Egg and cheese toasties."

He grinned. "Just one?"

Olivia laughed. "No. I got you two, you greedy bastard."

They ate in comfortable silence. She hadn't even realized she was staring when Sam called her out. "What? Am I drooling? Do I have egg on my face?"

She laughed and took his hand in hers. "I'm so glad we're here. Aren't you?"

"I am." He paused, staring into space. She almost wondered if she'd lost him, which happened more frequently than she liked. But then he turned back to look at her, his eyes as serious as she'd ever seen them. "If you could go back and change what happened, what would you do differently?"

Olivia laughed "Besides kicking Lucas to the curb sooner? Or never meeting Joey?" she asked.

"No, I mean it, Liv. What would you do?"

"We don't have enough time in the world to list all my regrets," she said.

She gave his hand another squeeze. "It used to drive me crazy. I'd play it out over and over again in my head. If I'd done this, if I'd said that, it'd all be different. But I look at our girls and I think about all the things we wanted: for them to be smart and courageous, to be kind and helpful, to find happiness on their own terms. And they did that. No matter what happens to us, they are our legacy."

Olivia leaned in and kissed Sam. There would come a day when she would lose Sam completely. The girls would have their own tragedies, and there was nothing she could do to shield them from that. But Sam was right. They'd given their daughters the skills they needed to survive. All Olivia could do was love them, which required no guidebook at all.

ACKNOWLEDGMENTS

In 2019, I was twenty thousand words into an entirely different novel when the COVID lockdowns began. In the wake of that global trauma, I struggled to focus. The fact that I was newly pregnant with identical triplets didn't help as I tried and failed to find my creative voice. Then in January 2021, I gave birth to three perfect girls, and the next few months were the most intense, and magical of my life.

I'm a writer, so it's no surprise that I'm anxious, but holy hell, triplets amped it up. The whole world looked different. I kept wondering, how can I protect my daughters? How can I prepare them for climate change, wars, and/or political upheaval? What can I do to ensure they're safe if something happens to me? Those questions consumed me and I abandoned that other book, unsure if I could even write a new one. My fears were amplified during the summer of 2022 when there was a blackout. My husband was away for work, and I found myself alone with three toddlers who weren't walking, without a charged cell phone, laptop, or any essential supplies.

It was a terrifying twenty-four hours, but we made it

through. After it was over, I went down my own prepper rabbit hole, and soon I had the idea for my next book. There was one problem. I was afraid to talk about it, much less write it. It felt too scary, too real.

It took a year and some gentle nudging by my longtime and incredibly supportive agent, Eve Atterman at WME, who said, "Do you still plan to write something new?" I gathered up my courage and wrote a one-page synopsis. She wrote back, "I have chills," and asked if she could send it to my publisher.

I'm immensely grateful to Redhook (Hachette Books) and publisher Tim Holman for seeing the potential in this story and allowing me to write the book I wanted to write. I'm also thrilled that my editor, Alyea Canada, new to Redhook, agreed to take me on. Previous editorial letters made me cry (and not always in a good way), but Alyea understood precisely what I was trying to accomplish, and her notes deepened the story and the characters. Also, shout-out to the entire team at Redhook for their continued support. It's not an easy feat to publish four novels with the same publisher, and I am incredibly grateful for their hard work and support.

There's no question that I have the best fellow writers and friends in the business. Without the insights of Kate Smith, one of my favorite writers and best friends, I'm not sure I would have made it to the finish line. Kate read countless drafts and even flew out to LA to write alongside

ACKNOWLEDGMENTS

me. She sat in my office (aka Starbucks) and on the sofa at home while we worked. She allowed limitless interruptions and always had a fix for any story or character problems. And let me tell you, she's a real magician at charming moody three-year-old triplets (baby Poopie FTW).

I also have to thank my guru, Eduardo Santiago, who helped guide me through the first half and trickiest part of the novel. As always, I am thrilled to have him as a creative guide and lifelong friend.

A huge shout-out goes to Adam Santa Maria for taking on the Herculean task of researching and helping me craft Olivia's guidebook. I'm unsure if he's grateful for or terrified by all he learned about doomsday prepping, but he's definitely more prepared.

A special thanks goes to my deep bench of friends and writers who offered emotional support and encouragement: Giselle Jones, Melissa Beyer, Treena Hancock, Michael Robin, Talia Gonzalez, Jeff Thomas, Liza Sandoval, Lindsay Grossman, and Jelena Woehr.

Thanks to my sister, Michelle Clark, who shouts out my accomplishments with unwavering pride. I know that Mom would be thrilled to witness the bond we've formed.

No writer who raises children (much less triplets) does it alone, and I'm grateful to Tanya Quist, our wonderful nanny, who kept the girls happy and entertained during the countless hours it took to finish this novel.

Of course, I couldn't start a book, much less finish one,

without my twin sister, Heather Overton. She's the one who said this book was special, and while I wasn't happy when she read the first chapter and said, "It's not working," she was right, as usual. She read so many drafts no matter how busy her own life was. I'm so proud of the amazing year she's had and can't wait to welcome Vic and Trent to the family. I also know that no matter what comes our way (even if it is the apocalypse), we'll figure it out together.

I am beyond grateful to my husband, David Boyd. We've been together for almost two decades, but this past year truly tested us. When life seemed too hard and I didn't want to write, David promised to hold things down at home... and he did so without complaint. Triplets will definitely push your limits, but we're still here, laughing and making every moment count.

I am grateful to all the mothers in my life: my mom, Betty; my mother-in-law, Linda Boyd, who passed away shortly after I finished this novel; and my sister-in-law, Rachael Hogg. Thanks for being my guiding lights.

I wrote this book because motherhood, and the responsibility of raising three girls in this fractured, fragile world, scared the hell out of me. As fires ravage my city of Los Angeles, I am still scared, but stories offer hope. My wish is that by the time my daughters are old enough to read this book, our darkest days will have given way to light and our world will be safer—and kinder. It sounds impossible to imagine, but I'll never stop writing and willing it into existence.

MEET THE AUTHOR

Heather Overton

HOLLIE OVERTON is a TV writer and producer. Hollie's debut thriller, *Baby Doll*, was an international bestseller and was published in eleven countries. She has written two other thrillers, *The Walls* and *The Runaway*. An identical twin, Hollie grew up in Kingsville, Texas, but now resides in LA with her husband, David, and her four-year-old triplets. Yes, she has her hands full.

if you enjoyed
A MOTHER'S GUIDE TO THE APOCALYPSE

look out for

THE GHOSTS OF BEATRICE BIRD

by

LOUISA MORGAN

Beatrice Bird is haunted by ghosts—a gift she's had since she was a small child. Unfortunately, it's an ability that has now grown more intense, shifting from flashes and feelings to physical manifestations she can't escape.

In a desperate attempt to find relief, Beatrice flees her home, her partner, and her psychology practice in San Francisco for a remote island. There she meets Anne Iredale, a timid

*woman who has lost everything that matters to her.
And for the first time in a long time, Beatrice's gift
will be called on to help someone in need.*

I

Beatrice, The Island, 1977

The seascape beyond the cottage window was beautiful in a monochromatic way. Tarnished silver clouds drifted in a somber sky, and pewter water shivered under restless whitecaps. Sparse evergreens framed the pale scene with their dark, slender trunks.

It was a charming vista, but a painful reminder of how dramatically Beatrice's life had changed. San Francisco was all color, pastel houses marching along the steep hills, scarlet trolleys rattling along their rails, wisps of fog slipping through the vivid orange girders of the Golden Gate Bridge. The island was nothing like San Francisco, and it didn't feel like home. She had to remind herself that she had been here only six weeks. It would take time.

She liked the cottage well enough. She had bought it sight unseen, but it lived up to the real estate agent's description as a "charming woodsy getaway." The door from the wraparound porch opened into a well-appointed kitchen, separated from a dining area by a short bar. A forties-style archway led to a small living room, where wide windows afforded a view of the water. The outside walls were a muted blue-gray, in keeping with the coastal setting. Thick juniper bushes curled along the foundation. The interior walls were cream and rose and butter yellow, warm colors for a cool climate. A short strand of beach, featured prominently in the real estate photographs, ran below the porch, linked to the cottage by a steep stony path.

The photographs and the descriptions had somehow failed to mention one significant detail. Steps from the cottage, a small cow barn nestled among the pines and firs, an unpainted lean-to jutting from one side. Beatrice couldn't decide at first if the omission was an oversight or a deliberate effort by the sellers not to introduce a detraction. She doubted many buyers would see the barn as a bonus, nor would they be happy to learn about its occupants.

In any case, the purchase hadn't disappointed her, even though her ownership felt temporary. It felt pretend, like setting up a dollhouse, or like playing hide-and-seek, which was a better metaphor. The cottage—indeed, the island itself—was Beatrice's hiding place. She was an animal gone to ground, a wounded creature seeking respite, pulling folds of solitude around herself for comfort.

Beatrice was unused to isolation. She had chosen this loneliness, and it brought relief of a sort, but it was the kind of relief that comes from the cessation of pain. She was learning that the absence of pain left space for other

THE GHOSTS OF BEATRICE BIRD 477

discomforts, like the weight of unrelenting silence and the yearning for places and people she loved.

The worst was missing Mitch. At night, in her sleep, she often turned to reach for him. When her groping hand found nothing but a cold pillow, an unused blanket, she woke, and lay aching with loss.

She doubted that Mitch, safe in their blue and yellow house above the bay, felt anything like she did. He had neither written nor telephoned. She could only assume he was still angry.

In fact, the heavy black telephone on the bar had rung only once since she moved in, and that was to remind her that the store at the ferry dock would sell any milk she couldn't use.

Milk, for pity's sake. Who would have thought?

Beatrice moved close to the window to watch a single intrepid boat, bristling with fishing gear, plow its way through the frigid waters of the strait. It was too far away for her to see the people on board, so it didn't trouble her to watch its progress. It trailed an icy wake as it circled the distant silhouette of the big island and disappeared.

Thinking how cold those fishermen must be made Beatrice shiver and turn to the woodstove that dominated her living room. It hummed and crackled, filling the cottage with the spicy fragrance of burning pine. The fire was comforting, but the stove consumed an astonishing amount of wood. The cord stacked against the side of the cottage was shrinking with alarming speed in the face of the cold snap. She really shouldn't put off calling Mr. Thurman to ask him to deliver more, but she dreaded doing it.

Mr. Thurman was a pleasant man. When she called him with her first order, he had rattled and jounced up the dirt road, the bed of his ancient Ford pickup piled high with logs. He had greeted her cheerfully and made quick work of the chore, accepting her payment with a tip of his flat wool cap.

But he hadn't come alone. He would never come alone. Seeing him—them—had ruined what was left of that day. Remembering it, Beatrice pressed a hand to the base of her throat, where the borrowed misery lurked.

Regardless, she would have to order more wood. The radio said tonight would be even colder than the night before, which had glazed the boulders on her bit of beach with ice. She crouched beside the stove to stir up the embers and lift in fresh chunks of pine. She had just closed the glass-fronted door when Alice's commanding call rang out.

Smiling for the first time that day, Beatrice straightened and leaned to one side to look through the archway. Through the window half of the kitchen door, she saw Alice and Dorothy standing below the porch, the two of them gazing expectantly up at the cottage.

Dorothy was tall and rangy, white with splotches of black on her sides and her crooked nose. Alice was tawny and petite, with big dark eyes and long eyelashes. She was considerably smaller than Dorothy, but there was no doubt that she was in charge. At this moment she clearly considered it her duty to inform the new dairy farmer that milking time had arrived.

Beatrice adjusted the stove damper, then crossed into the kitchen to pull on the rubber milking boots left by the previous owners, as well as the secondhand red-and-black Pendleton jacket, her last purchase in San Francisco. She had not expected cows, but she didn't mind them. A woman alone could do worse for company than two easygoing cows.

The elderly couple who sold her the cottage were fortunate in their buyer. Beatrice had grown up in South Dakota. Her father had been a country GP who often helped out the local ranchers when the vet wasn't available. Beatrice had gone with him on house calls from an early age, and sometimes their patients had not been people, but horses, cows, or the occasional pig that had cut itself on barbed wire. She was used to livestock.

She said, "Good evening, ladies," as she stepped down from the porch and crunched across the graveled yard to the little barn. Her voice creaked, reminding her she hadn't spoken aloud all day. As she set Dorothy and Alice to munching hay in their stanchions, she chatted to them, just to hear herself.

She started with Alice, who would stamp and low if she didn't. "You must have been reading Betty Friedan," she said, as she slid the milk bucket beneath the cow's udder and sat down on the three-legged stool. "You're a bossy little bossy, but that's okay. I like that in a cow." Alice gave a small, bovine grunt, and Beatrice took it for agreement.

For all the times she had helped her father treat animals, she had never actually milked a cow, though she had seen it being done. Now she found herself in possession of two of them. No one knew what might have become of the cows if she had refused to keep them, but she hadn't done that. She had figured out how to accomplish the task of milking through trial and error, aided especially by the patient Dorothy. Now the chore went smoothly for the most part. If it didn't, Alice never failed to apprise her of her errors, swishing her tail so it stung Beatrice's cheek, or overturning the bucket with one impatient hind leg.

Beatrice appreciated Dorothy's compliant ways, but she and Alice had more in common.

After the next morning's milking, Beatrice eyed the supply of milk and cream that had accumulated in the refrigerator and made a face. There was no excuse for not taking it down to the store. She had already managed that twice, after feeling guilty for letting a gallon of good milk go sour.

The experience hadn't been too bad. The nun who managed the store and the tiny ferry terminal called herself

Mother Maggie. She had accepted the milk and filled Beatrice's grocery list with a minimum of questions, evidently unbothered by Beatrice's reticence. She was far from young, perhaps too old to be operating a ferry dock, but she had a kind face beneath her short black veil. Even better for Beatrice, Mother Maggie's ghosts were mercifully pale with age. As long as she was the only person in the store, Beatrice wouldn't mind the chore.

She showered and changed. It felt good to put on something besides the wool pants that had gotten too big and the cable-knit sweater she had borrowed from Mitch and neglected to return. She wondered if he knew she had it. If he did, he would understand why she had kept it. It might even make him smile. She missed his smile. She missed his unlikely dimples.

She put on a fresh pair of slacks and a clean sweater, and took up her scissors to hack off a few strands of hair still straggling into her face. She had cut off most of her hair soon after she arrived on the island. The long dark strands lying on the floor around her—to say nothing of the ragged look of what was left—had put a period to what remained of her life. Her hair looked pretty rough, but there was no one to notice. Most of the time she covered it under her knit hat.

One of her patients had made the hat for her from leftover bits of yellow and purple yarn. It was a curious-looking creation, but the knit was smooth and regular, and the hat was warm enough for the damp cold of the island. Every time she wore it she thought of the young people she had worked with in the Haight: homesick kids, stoned kids, frightened kids. She cherished the hat, odd though it was, because it reminded her of them. They were sweet, but so hurt and confused, flower children struggling to accept that the Summer of Love wasn't what they had imagined it would be.

Beatrice pulled on the hat and her secondhand Pendleton, wrinkling her nose at the clash of red plaid wool with yellow and purple knit, deciding it didn't matter. She packed the bottles of milk into a straw-lined basket and set out in the crisp winter air for the hike down the hill.

Mother Maggie was the leader of a handful of nuns who made up a tiny island monastery. She took grocery orders and sometimes delivered them in the nuns' dusty yellow station wagon. The other sisters taught in the little school and took occasional shifts with the ferry ramp. Their brown habits were familiar to everyone on the island, but tourists smiled and pointed at the unusual sight of nuns as ferry operators. They took snapshots with their cameras, as they might with wildlife or historical buildings.

When Beatrice emerged from the quiet of the woods into the clearing around the terminal, she wished for the thousandth time that she had succeeded, in the face of her disability, in developing a strategy for dealing with people. It was what she expected her patients to do, build tools to handle their challenges, but she had failed to do it for herself. She remained raw and vulnerable, and though it hurt her pride, she had fled her problem instead of solving it.

She was glad to see that it was Mother Maggie operating the ferry ramp, which meant she was also working in the store. She wouldn't have to meet someone new. The ferry was churning its way back out into the bay as the nun trudged up from the dock, an orange safety vest zipped over her billowing habit. She caught sight of Beatrice and waved a welcome as she went into the store, leaving the door ajar behind her. By the time Beatrice reached it, Mother Maggie had shed the vest and exchanged her rain boots for Birkenstocks with thick gray socks.

"Good morning, Mother Maggie." Beatrice set the basket on the counter beside the cash register. "Six quarts here."

"Good morning to you, Beatrice," Mother Maggie said with a smile. "We'll be glad to have the milk. Are you settling in all right?"

"Fine, yes."

"The groceries you ordered are in. I'll bag them for you."

"Thank you."

The nun turned to put the milk in the big refrigerator behind her, saying over her shoulder, "Won't you stay for a cup of coffee? I was just about to make some."

Beatrice found, to her surprise, that she liked the idea of sitting down for coffee with Mother Maggie. She hadn't been in company for weeks, and the shades that trailed behind the nun were so faint as to be nearly invisible, their energy almost spent. She could surely ignore them for a little while.

She said, "I'd love some coffee."

"Good. Go grab a chair. I'll just be a few moments."

There were three wooden tables in the back of the room, arranged around a potbellied stove that hummed with warmth. Beatrice pulled a chair close to the stove.

She sat down and started to shrug out of her coat just as the door to the store clicked open with a jangle of its welcome bell. A tall, slender young woman stepped through.

Beatrice froze, one arm still in the sleeve of her jacket.

The woman wore an expensive-looking camel's-hair coat, a creamy cashmere scarf around her throat, and a pair of elegant leather boots. She had fair hair tied back in a low ponytail and a shining leather handbag on a shoulder strap. She was exceptionally beautiful, with long legs and smooth skin, but her slender shoulders hunched as if she were carrying a burden.

As in fact she was. Two burdens. Beatrice saw them distinctly.

One, hovering above her like a storm cloud, was a threatening charcoal gray so dark it seemed lightning might flash through it.

The other clung to her legs, tiny and tragic, the lavender and indigo of confusion and grief. It was accompanied

THE GHOSTS OF BEATRICE BIRD   485

by the faint sound of a child weeping. Beatrice's throat throbbed suddenly, painfully, choking her with anxiety.

Hastily, she thrust her other arm back into her jacket and blundered her way through the tables toward the door. Mother Maggie was saying to the newcomer, "Oh, hello. You just got off the ferry, didn't you?"

Beatrice didn't hear the woman's answer. She was already out the door, abandoning her basket, forgetting her groceries, having not so much as nodded to the woman who had come in, nor said goodbye to Mother Maggie. Her mouth dry and her throat aching, she stumbled toward the forest path that led to her house. She fled.

She was ashamed of it, embarrassed by it, but she was helpless to do anything about it.

Most people saw their ghosts in the dark of night. Beatrice saw them in broad daylight, and it was intolerable.